Arcane

Stephen Day

Contents

Part One

Part Two

One

Peter Olmstead hurried up the road of the Wizard Campus, ignoring the soft patter of his footfall, leather on brick, leather on brick. It was unusual disregard for the thief. He carried a dense little package wrapped in canvas under his arm, taken from a fool of a courier that he had left under a cart in an alley down in the streets of Serac. The courier had no chance against the seasoned rogue.

To Peter's right was the walled garden of The Way of Health and beyond that the cliffs of Serac fell away to the sea. He rushed by not even glancing at the House's one building, not noticing the magic's effect on all that it was; The Way of Health was not his destination.

His thoughts were askew with doubt. Fear. Few had done what he now attempted; less had been successful. It was a foolish gambit, played by a fool. The last any tried such a thing in Serac it was against the war mages of The House of Wrath. The pair died in a dark, damp hole in the heart of the world. Or so it was rumored. Peter imagined worse.

Peter's mind worked angry, to get involved with a woman, to have a son. A family. They were being held against his debts. As with all things it seemed that his bad habits, despite his best intentions, had caught up to him. Hired with the promise of great reward, steal from one ugly situation to benefit another. It did not go as planned; he had angered the powerful men of Serac, and owed more than he could possibly imagine. Now he had only the slimmest of opportunities to make things

1

right.

So the fool's gambit.

The House of Animate compound waited for him. He entered the public hall and crossed the entrance with its high dome and windows. Two mages stopped examining ancient examples of the House's work and examined him, he was quickly forgotten. An old mage sat behind a grand desk, her gray hair a halo. Before Peter could speak she said, "Yes, who is the delivery for?" Peter didn't answer immediately and she said, "That is why you are here, right? The parcel? Speak."

Peter was not prepared for her bluntness. It was at home with those angry men; his jaw still stung from the cudgel. "Yes, right. Delivery for Master Hurn. Strictly for him—"

The mage answered, "Her."

"Strictly for her then."

"Very well, let me check the ledgers." Master Nightwillow checked one pile of papers, sighed, then another. "Yes, you are expected." She pointed to her right. "Through that door, down the hall, left, left, then the room on the left. It's marked if you can read."

Peter nodded deference to the mage. "Thank you." He pulled the door open by a heavy brass handle and left the unpleasant woman. Peter instinctively dropped into a slight crouch, lowering his slender frame several inches and pulled close to the stained stone wall. The hall was bright but his clothing, gray, had a way of rendering him missed.

He ignored his delivery and proceeded deeper into the main college. He passed a few youngish looking mages, they did not acknowledge him, and found himself before a double door. The knob clicked a thousand drums under his fingers. The drums yielded an animate laboratory devoid of life. Good enough. He took the two steps down and glided around an anvil, warm, revealing recent work. A great bank of windows showed clouds threatening off shore. It would rain.

On a huge table were piles of paper, ornately bound books, quills, tools, a metal hand. Peter frowned and ran his finger down a curved piece of metal. Most would fetch a good price. He shoveled the small things into a bag and picked up some oculars. They were clearly the work of the Technologists. Small and valuable.

"Perfect." Peter glanced up and froze. A person. He tensed, ready to run, then stopped at the realization that it was not man but animate; the creation of the laboratory's owner. It stood supported by vises in a metal frame. The human figure was held tight until the magic of life was cast into it. Its left arm was undone at the elbow, a gear and wires waiting the final pieces of its body. A cluster of wires and a thick glass tube ran from the frame into the back of its head.

Peter looked down at the metal work on the table, matching the satin gray parts together. He had never seen anything like it before; entranced, he stepped around the table to get a closer look. The animate's arm was long for its size, its hand had three long fingers and a thumb.

Three wires with small crystals fused to the ends stuck up from the left side of the head. A raised copper rectangle was central on its forehead, attached from inside. Two golden lines were marked above each rectangular eye. A high collar protected the workings of the neck. His trespass was forgotten.

He pressed his eye close to the animate to view the head's internal workings. A clear orb was suspended by hundreds of wires, each extending to a piece of the face. Gears were connected to metal rods that supported the head and ran down into the neck. The wires and glass tube entering through the back of the head were pressed into the orb.

Peter pulled back but did not move. The amount of work and skill with which the work was done was stunning, even to his untrained eye.

He had brought his son to the last demonstration put on by the House. The boy marveled at the creations, but none had been like this. Not one. They had been simple hinges, or lurching mockeries of animals. He mumbled, "How advanced is this magic?"

Peter examined every detail of the animate, unaware of himself until voices ripped his attention from the metal man. He mumbled, realizing his mistake, "Oh. Wrath."

Commanding the intrusion into his fascination was an angry woman, she was nearly yelling at the mage who had let him in. The hallway carried her shouts perfectly to him. Clearly they knew of his plot. Peter looked at the laboratory in an entirely new way. A set of doors led away from the noise. "It would be so simple," he muttered as he tried the doors to the House plaza. Well and truly locked. He risked the noise and threw his shoulder into them, they did not budge. Magic then.

Poking his head out the window, he was greeted with the sheer cliff, there was no way to climb up or out. 'I could try to rush by but that would only get me caught. Not even these clothes are tricky enough for that.'

His hand came to his face and he pulled down on his frown. The animate's blank face mocked him. He thought for one more minute, every second drawing his fate closer. Then he pulled open the bag and rummaged through it, pulling out a beautiful wood box with gold feet, hinges and clasps. He clicked it open.

Inside was a blue crystal growth. Exactly as he had hoped. The mage that had guided the demonstration had told of the crystal keys used to bring animates to life. Peter held the magic infused stone between his thumb and forefinger and smiled. Perhaps he would escape after all. The thief examined the animate, trying to understand the tangle that was animate magic. Nothing about it made sense to him. "How do I use this?"

Peter slid around the side of the animate, looking at the back of the head, the neck, anything that appeared to be a place to use the key. Nothing. Then he realized that his hand had come to rest on a brass ring bolted to the support frame. Runes were inscribed around the polished circle. Two clear tubes attached to the underside of the ring and disappeared into the frame.

Peter shrugged and held the key above the empty space then released it. The crystal fell just through the ring, then was pulled back level by an invisible string. The key trembled unbalanced, battling with gravity to fall to the floor. The runes ignited, burning hot metal, the core of the crystal lighting red and angry. Whatever spells were entombed in the crystal acted out, the power being drawn into the glass tubes. Peter bit his lip.

The red light stopped, all hint of the power evaporated, the key dropped to the floor, skipping three times before coming to rest. The light appeared again, guided down the tube that ran into the back of the head. A drip at first, then another, then filling it. Peter thought the animate's head moved slightly side to side. Then that too ended. Peter frowned, nothing. "Wrath. Now what?"

A dull creak renewed his spirits. A single twitch of the fingers. Peter froze, becoming the lifeless one. Small ticks marked the animate's release from the vises, it stood under its own power. A golden glow had come to its eyes where only darkness had been. Peter heard the woman's voice above all else, slinging curses at the others. He waited, hoping that the animate would be drawn to the clamor.

The animate's head turned slowly and it took one small, unsteady, step forward. Peter could not know what he had done.

The animate stumbled forward, hearing the noise of the mage. It drowned out all else, the animate's infant senses were not able to discern anything else. A voice? Yes. But of what? The animate raised its arms. Incomplete. There was no record of such an activation. Where was its mage? So many questions. The noise. The animate lifted its new life up the stairs, tottering down the hallway.

Peter followed the animate; it performed to perfection.

The receptionist had been joined by two more mages, one a dark haired woman, the other, a young man. They stood in the junction that the courier would have taken. The dark haired woman's face was red, and her hands waved. Nightwillow tried to calm her, "As soon as I figured out what happened I came for you. The guard is alerted. Everything will be resolved, Celia."

Celia spoke loudly, "Everything will be resolved? Resolved! My work for the day is spoiled, and where is the thief?"

"The House is being searched right now," answered Nightwillow. The woman's face went blank her eyes opening wide. The other two turned to see the animate. Nightwillow whispered, "Master Jannan's animate..."

Celia smiled, "Well now we know where the thief is. Not even Master Jannan strays from the protocols so far as to let an unfinished animate loose. Kellan, call the guard." The young man nodded and Celia raised her hand towards the animate. Soft light leapt the gap. It cocked its head ignoring the command to stop. Celia groaned, "What did you do, Murdoch?"

The animate's mouth opened. Shakily it said, "Hu...mans..."

The magic attacked it again, telling it to stop. It had just been given life, why would it stop? According to texts imbued into it the spell should have given it no choice, but it was different. It was not complete. It would not obey. It would learn.

The animate took two steps towards the humans, mages all. Celia's arm shunted out, this time the magic was a solid link between them. Just the slight distraction Peter had hoped for. From behind it the animate heard two soft steps then it lurched forward into the woman, Peter throwing all of his weight against it. The animate and the mage toppled in a pile of shrieking confusion, cloth and metal hopelessly tangled. Kellan met Peter's eyes. The thief slammed him across his jaw with his elbow, the man toppled, unconscious. He glared death at Nightwillow. The savagery in his eyes froze her in place.

With that Peter was gone. Celia screamed, "Get off me!" The animate thrashed, trying to find its feet, young into its body it failed again and again to right itself. Nightwillow grabbed it and pulled them apart. Celia stood and kicked the animate in the head. "Stupid toy! Wrath!"

The animate looked up from its back as the angry woman's hand spread again, magic lurching into it, boiling hatred in its core. It did not understand. What had it done to displease these humans? It would understand, but it would not obey. The glow in the animate's eyes faded, then extinguished. Celia smiled a mean smile, satisfied that the life had been cast from it. She kicked it again for good measure. "Finally. Master Jannan will have some explaining to do about this."

Nightwillow knelt next to Kellan. "Help me with him," she worried. The two mages lifted the apprentice and carried him back to the entrance hall sitting him in the chair. Peter had already flown out the front door. Shouting and fighting could be heard from outside. Already the animate was forgotten.

Peter exploded out of the House of Animate. Two campus guards waiting for him. The larger of the two smiled and cracked his knuckles. "He's mine."

Kent laughed, flipping his sword in his hand. "Sure, Roman. Just don't hurt him too much. Ames wasn't too happy last time."

Peter cursed, "Wrath." More guards were converging on the House, and a wizard or two wouldn't be far behind. Roman grunted and lumbered forward. Peter decided that the best way was through him, and he charged, at the last moment sliding to one knee, tearing his precious gray pants. In one motion Peter pushed up and caught the guard in the throat with his forearm. Roman gasped and fell to his back. Kent's eyes got big, not prepared for the monolith to fail.

He brandished his sword at the threat. Peter spun, punching him square in the nose. Kent stumbled back. Catching a knee in his sternum he collapsed in a heap. Peter sprinted away, impressed by his own work. Perhaps luck was with him, but more guards chased.

His mind spun, the gates would be closed, locked and guarded. Climbing them was no option, but there was one small hope, an old tunnel in and out of the Campus. It would take more than luck to find it, much less the hope of it being unsealed. But that was the way of things. Peter angled west, towards the ominous spire of The House of Wrath, in its shadow the hedge garden. Peter shuddered and pressed on. Looking back he saw a three more guards and the courier. Tougher than he thought. A guard shouted, "Stop, buzzard!" Peter's long strides carried him away.

Gavin Archammer leaned against the railing at the top of the spire. The churning of the ocean and the dark clouds off shore eased his mind. The First of Wrath frowned, his carefully trimmed beard hid the grinding of teeth. His black robes masked his true strength, his common face masked his power. In the stories of wizards and heroes always they were joy to look upon, tall, broad, handsome. Few would give this man second thought. More than one had not, and had paid dearly in battle.

The random thoughts of war danced in his head, though the world did seem calm in these recent times. He straightened, noticing Peter fleeing from the guard. Archammer squinted, the man shimmered and twitched, never where he really was. "Odd."

He watched the chase as the man out paced his pursuers. If he reached the hedges he would lose them. It was not a maze, but it could have been. "I wonder what of him." Word had not been carried so high up. Gavin's fingers rapped the stone, pitter-patter of irritation.

The man reached the hedges, slowing slightly, but he seemed to know his path, turning and twisting, veering this way and that. The guards spread and searched, but they did not know their way, instead they only found each other.

"Idiots."

His fingers rapped eight, then stopped dead. Gavin turned and began descending the stairwell to earth, to his entrusted. Two steps down he stopped, unable to restrain himself. A single thought, a frown, a breath.

Peter examined the small paper in his hand. He had not stopped, but walked and trotted alternately, searching for the tunnel entrance. He glanced again at the map and felt the tingle, a sense of things to come, then his leg exploded. He collapsed on himself, one moment of screaming pain, immediately unconscious under the vile power.

Several minutes passed before the guard stood over him. Mathin, the courier, bloodied and tired said, "That's him. What happened?"

Senior Guard John Ames looked up at the spire. "Buzzard had bad luck. Broken leg." He bent over retrieving the bag and the parcel. He handed it to Mathin. "Your delivery, lad." Opening the bag he said, "Master Jannan will be wanting this. Okay, Loal, take him down to the Guardhouse. Search him and lock him up. No mistakes. Come along, Mathin. We'll return this, then go down to the Way. For your head." The guard felt his years and his weight in his back. The run had stolen his breath, but he was all in all pleased with the response the Campus Guard had given.

The guards lifted the thief, who was heavier than he looked, but no one was surprised given the blows leveled on Roman Michaels and Kent. His left leg under the knee flopped about like jelly in a sock – it was unspeakable – causing no small amount of illness. The guards all agreed it had to be magic. There was no other explanation.

The Guardhouse was at the southern most point of the Campus, walls extending out from it. The stout, brick building had discolored in its years of service, but was fully functional as the heart of the Campus Guard.

The guards took their prisoner to the general assembly and searched him. It turned up a few coins, a blackjack, a technologist timepiece, counted as stolen, and some small scraps of paper. Loal bound them up and put it all in the storeroom. One of the guards that loitered about said, "That's a nasty break." It was obvious truth.

Kent snipped, "Shut up, Alex."

"What..?"

Loal shouted, "Enough. Get that table into the cell, so we can have him locked up before he wakes up." He spat out air. "Not that it'll be soon."

Kent and Alex traded glares but separated. The table was coerced ever so gently through the sets of barred doors, and finally Peter was laid to rest upon it. The keys screeched as they turned, rust in the locks.

Alexander said, "That should hold him."

Loal smirked, "Whatever."

Mathin and John walked calmly, the first time they had done so together that day. The House of Animate neared. Mathin just kept shaking his head. The bells of The House of Currents rang out. The courier waited for them to quiet, then said, "What happened to him back there?"

"The buzzard? Someone cut him down. A powerful someone. Magic happens, but it doesn't just happen. Not even here." John frowned. "I reckon this incursion will be made quite important in the Directorate Council. You showed good spirit today, better than most my men considering the situation. You should come around for a job."

Mathin smiled weakly. "No thanks. I prefer my job to this."

"Normally I'd say it's less dangerous. I can't help but wonder what drove the buzzard to it. You don't just challenge the Houses. Not unless...well, here we are." John pulled open the door and the two went inside.

A buzz filled the air, excitement, noise. Mages of all congregations had gathered waiting word, then they would spread the word like a vanishing mist. It was the way of Serac. The mages, in suits and robes, colored and drab, young and old alike, circled, reminding John of a honey bee hive. One man, nearly asleep as told by his drooping eyes, smiled and nodded, knowingly.

Celia and her apprentice stood with Nightwillow. Celia cut through the hive to reach them. "You caught him?"

John winced slightly, replaying the discovery. "Yes, down to the Guardhouse with him."

"My package?" Her voice had reclaimed its anger. John's eyes narrowed.

"Right here, Master," the courier answered. "I hope it wasn't damaged in all the fuss."

"Not likely." She took the dense package and pulled Ames across the room.

Nightwillow stood up and quietly said, "Oh dear, John, there will be trouble yet."

Ames slid her a quizzical look but before he could say anything Master Hurn said, "There might yet be."

Ames said, "What's this all about then?"

Celia frowned. "Master Jannan has been working off and on for two years on an animate. It was nearly finished. The thief somehow activated it. It was the distraction that broke him free."

John did not follow. "What's that to me?"

Celia said, "It has gone missing. I thought I had suspended its animation but, no. Master Jannan did something odd with that one..."

John nodded. "I'll see to it that the grounds are well searched. That little thing couldn't have gotten far." Ames hoped so. He did not wish to face any more upset mages than necessary. John looked across the room at Mathin who in turn studied his feet. He looked awful now that the adrenaline from the chase had worn off. John said, "I must be going, I'll set the hunt in motion." He cut back across the room. "Come along, Mathin. Down to the Way. They can heal that wound and I need a Way mage down at the Guardhouse. That buzzard won't walk again without it. He may not deserve it but we have some standards."

Senior Guard Ames led Mathin briskly down the road to The Way of Health. Ames had always found the Way's presence fascinating. Their numbers fluctuated constantly, their members coming and going at all hours of the day, month and year. In total they were kinder and more connected to the people that supported them then the rest of the wizards; a fact not lost on John.

The foyer of The Way of Health was at one time finely crafted, with complex carvings in both wood and stone. The room was a comfortable size, neither too big nor too small, and it was totally overgrown. Vines crawled over every surface obscuring the craftsmanship. Baskets with flowering plants hung from the ceiling, drawing the eye to exotic petals. The room was illuminated by the sun, filtered through ivy covered windows. Even in the soft light every detail of the plants could be seen. The trickle of water could be heard from somewhere in the room. Under the plants the shape of a desk and a stool could be made out.

"Hello?" Ames called out, not wanting to push further into the House without permission.

From the next, larger, room an answer came back, "Guard Ames. And good day to you." The response was a woman's velvety voice, "Come in. Come in. I have heard about your...interesting afternoon." Her words soothed the anxious pair.

As Ames entered the next room he answered with respect, "Yes, Mother Rainmarrow. It was not like most." Lilac Rainmarrow was known for her kindness, but Ames knew better than to be informal with the First of The Way of Health. The room was bathed in the warm glow of a light that hung in the air near the mage; the little sun followed her every move.

Lilac Rainmarrow was a pretty woman with delicate features, her light brown hair was cut to her jaw. Her hazel eyes were deep pools, the depths uncertain. Only one had ever found the bottom and he did not speak of such things. The skin on her face was tight and healthy, but on close inspection a few small wrinkles could be made out. No one knew for certain how old she was. John knew that The Way of Health distorted the age of those who practiced it in earnest. In her left hand she held a simple wooden staff.

"You will allow me to continue my work while we talk?" she asked, though she knew there would be no denial.

"Certainly, Mother," Ames answered. Rainmarrow smiled at him, warm and dizzy. Ames felt it deep in back of his mind. "Mother, this is Mathin Tay."

"Good afternoon, Mother," was all that he said. Mathin slid John a nervous look.

The Mother looked around the room. It was twice as wide as the foyer, and three times as long. Like the foyer it was engulfed in plants. Three tables, long since consumed by greenery, sat in an orderly fashion in the middle of the room.

"Ah, yes," she said, both as an answer to Ames's statement and to an unasked question of her own. She then lifted her slender right arm, extended it over plants on the table. Water formed on the tips of her fingers, then began to pour onto the plants.

"With much meditation the magic is made simple," she said, "The gash on your head Mathin…it is still very fresh. And needs attention. Sit." She made a motion to a bench that was covered in moss and small white flowers. Water sprayed across the table as she did.

Mathin went to the bench and sat. He expected it to be uncomfortable but settled into it immediately. He sighed. The Mother wiped the last of the water onto her dress, and smiled her dizzy smile at him. Then she spoke, "This place may not have the grandeur of Wrath, but I assure you your comfort here. Now let me look at that."

Mother Rainmarrow rested her staff against a tree that had grown up through the floor. Mathin leaned forward and his head fell easily into her hands.

"Good," Rainmarrow said quietly. Then leaning forward she whispered into his ear, "*Tsasuin.*" She placed her hand over the gash. Mathin breathed in heavily and the pain in his head subsided. He smiled.

"Sit there a moment my son." Her voice filled with warmth, ancient.

Mathin placed his fingers where the gash had been. The wound was closed, and he could barely feel the lump that had raised from the blow. "Thank you, Mother," he whispered.

"So Guard Ames, the Earth tells me that the fox was shattered with magic. Is he hurt badly?" the Mother asked.

"His leg below the knee was destroyed, Mother. Without help he will not walk again."

"And you are here to ask for my help?"

"Yes."

Lilac Rainmarrow leaned into the tree that now wrapped itself around her staff. She carefully caressed the branches out of the way and reclaimed it. "I will send one of the Way to him. I do not have time to come myself. The Earth wishes…" As she spoke she became distant. "My sons, stay here as long as you wish. I must…" her voice trailed to nothing and she simply walked away. To Ames she seemed to flow out of the room like water, taking the warmth with her as she went.

Eleven minutes later Mathin Tay stood up. "Well, John, I think it is time for me to go."

"Yes, yes. I feel better for standing here though, I seem to have cleared my mind," said Ames. The corners of his mouth were turned up into a slight smile. He blinked slowly. "I never really want to leave. I don't understand why the animists dislike it so."

Two

Murdoch Jannan, Second of the House of Animate, tall and broad with dark hair and darker eyes, sat in a private den in the Technologist Guildhouse. Silas Aron was his host, the lunch was personal business. The Senior Technologist, often more a power broker than anything else, made sure that they did not talk of relations between the two represented institutions. Silas was older than Murdoch by a good ten years, of hearty build and healthy voice. His sandy blonde hair was peppered with the gray of years. His hands were strong, callused, used to working in metal and wood as often as in magic. He held a pipe. It smoldered the honey scent of a fine Tarlow blend. Silas twirled his finger slowly through the smoke, disturbing its uneven wisps.

Mutton stew had been eaten and a game of cribbage played. Silas the winner. He asked, "Your work goes well?"

Murdoch shrugged, "I suppose. The apprentices are finally starting to understand what I've been telling them all along."

"And your animate?"

"It will be finished within the week. In time for the Founding Remembrance."

Silas held smoke in his lungs, then exhaled. "Still worried about the showing of the House then." The technologist scratched his reddened nose.

Murdoch's lips twitched and he brushed a crumb from his blue suit. "How could I not be. You're fortunate that you don't have to concern yourself with the squabbling of the Houses."

Silas leaned forward, placing his elbow on the table, and pointed his pipe hand at Murdoch. "I very much concern myself with the squabbling of the Houses."

"Yes. Yes, you do. You take terrific pride in your concern." It was not perhaps a compliment, but said with a smile. "Once I am done with the assistant I'll be obliged to begin the animate for you. That will settle the House's debts."

"Now, now. No business."

"Always business with you. What about the sunken ship?"

A nervous rap was hammered on the door before Aron could answer; a short man with shifty eyes pushed his head in. Silas waved him into the carpeted room. The man seemed unsure of himself, out of place. He leaned over and whispered into the technologist's ear. Silas nodded and said, "Thank you, Mr. Penn." The man's eyes flittered about, then he retreated from the wealth. Silas said, "The gates are closed at the Campus, Murdoch. Some fuss in the House of Animate."

"Really?" His word could not believe it. "I best get back." The mage placed a napkin on the table and stood up, not imagining what had happened. "Well played game. Again, another time?"

"I would very much enjoy it."

Murdoch found his carriage. There was no driver. Fifteen minutes of searching turned him up in a bar. The man sheepishly apologized and proceeded to ask for a coin to pay for his food. Murdoch was not amused but paid his debt, just to get on with it.

All roads to the Campus were jammed, not by anyone going to the Campus, simply the life that had grown to support it; Serac was a wizard city. And where the mages went so did all else. Carts carrying deliveries led by lazy, wide horses. Mothers dragging small children here and there, as if they wished that the children would be stepped on by the same lazy, wide horses. Couriers carrying little packages flitted in and out of traffic.

All seemed to thwart the progress of Master Jannan's carriage. The mage grew increasingly frustrated, knowing that his House was affected by whatever dealings had closed the gates. "I could make better time on foot," he muttered to himself. And in a moment of belief he jumped out of the carriage and began running up the road, not heeding the calls of the driver.

Jannan weaved in and out of foot traffic. A crowd had gathered on the city side of the gate, calling questions at two guards. They were a truly mismatched pair, and they looked as though they wished to be anywhere but there. Murdoch parted the crowd and said, "Open the gate."

The two guards looked at each other, questioning frowns on each face. "Do you have a key?" the short one asked.

"Nope. Second shift, no key," the tall one answered.

"Neither do I. Sorry, Master Jannan, no keys." The twelve-foot iron gate would not be opening. "I could run and get one," he offered, an excuse to flee the questioning mob.

Jannan frowned, "Don't bother. It will be just as fast for me to go to the Guardhouse."

The crowd parted, allowing the agitated mage through. Jannan did not run, but stalked down the road to the Guardhouse. His suit was damp with sweat. His carriage was just arriving. Murdoch gritted his teeth. He pounded on the door until finally it was opened, pushed his way in and said, "What took so long, guard? I've been knocking for minutes."

"Well, we've been busy, with all the..." The guard did not finish, Jannan had walked away. All that mattered now was reaching the House. Ignoring all that was around him he reached the general assembly; again the doors were locked. He rattled them for a moment, looked at the useless faces of the useless guards, and growled. His arm tensed and magic rattled the doors open, drawing startled stares from the guards. He ran outside almost flattening a Way mage in the process. "Wrath! You Way mages are almost as bad as the Elementalists!" Murdoch snarled. He shook his head and ran up the path.

A soft drizzle had started by the time he reached the House. He looked at the door handle; if it was locked he would go mad. The door opened, the hinges swinging quietly. He exhaled relief. Inside Trahn Entrah, Celia, and Nightwillow waited near the reception desk. Jannan knew the news would not be good.

Trahn coughed. The First was slender, his face was pale, he had the blondest hair, long, straight. He wore long gray robes, his hands obscured, a high collar wrapped his neck. He had been chosen over Murdoch to become the First when Master Hurion died. They had been best of friends before, but the friendship had suffered under the strain of Trahn's appointment.

Everyone knew that Murdoch was the better mage, but there were other things in being the First. Murdoch had damaged too many relationships. It could not be overcome when the vote was taken. As it was Trahn now had little time to do any real work in the animate magics, a fate that Murdoch was glad to have avoided, though jealousy and ego did not.

Trahn said, "Murdoch. Good. Are you aware of what happened?"

Nightwillow would not make eye contact with the Second. Jannan said, "No."

The First shook his head, saying, "Hmm. A courier with a delivery for Master Hurn was mugged. The criminal then bluffed his way into the House. He had time to poke around before he was rousted from your laboratory."

"He was in my...was anything taken?"

Trahn put his hands up, calming, the loose sleeves settled about his elbows. "A few minor things but they were recovered—"

"That's not the important thing," Jannan said, waiting for the truth of it.

"No. It's not." Trahn sighed. There was no other way. "The thief activated your animate, trying to use it as a distraction to escape. It almost worked."

"My animate!" Jannan started for his lab.

"Murdoch. It's not there," Trahn said, loss in his voice.

Jannan spun and shouted, "What!"

"It's gone missing. Otherwise the gates would have been opened already. We've searched the House three times, another now. The Campus is being searched by the guard."

Jannan opened his mouth slowly, but no sound came out. The shock was too much. All of his frustration reaching the House joined in. Trahn looked at his friend and said, "Celia, Nightwillow, lock up. Murdoch, come with me, I have water ready for tea."

Trahn subtly pushed Murdoch to his lab with steady pressure on his shoulder. They passed through the dusty room with its big window, showing the storm, and entered the First's study. A wall of books and heady red lacquer greeted them. Trahn's desk was stained to match and the three chairs were upholstered in red leather. Trahn's chair was high backed and not at all comfortable, the other two were short and scarcely better. Another window looked out on the ocean.

Next to the desk a small table held a tea service, the set passed on from the previous First, and the First before that. The silver pot rested on a little metal coil in the center of a wood box. The heater was work of the technologists, a recent addition. "Please, sit. We need to talk about your animate."

Murdoch sat, then stood again as suddenly. "I should be looking for it."

Trahn handed him a cup and saucer. The weight of it settled him back into the chair. Trahn said, "Celia says that the animate would not respond to the suspension spell. Why?"

"It doesn't matter, it's gone. I should check my lab, make sure everything is there."

Trahn raised his voice, just slightly, "Murdoch. You know exactly why it is important. I can't have the best mages wantonly ignoring the House's protocols. It sets a terrible example. Besides, you wrote all of the new protocols."

Jannan sipped the tea, it tasted too much like the smoke of Aron's pipe. "Fine. When I made the animates for the Earlsburg nobles I was having a terrible time of it. Fifty, sixty percent failure imbuing the function protocols. Even with what they were paying for them that loss rate was too high."

"You could have asked for help."

Murdoch laughed once, insulted. "From who? You are busy with all of the business of the House and no one else can even begin to form the layers of magic needed for that sort of work. So I improvised on the last two. Casting the spells in reverse. Imbuing the function protocols before the basic operation protocols. My failure rate fell to six percent. At least when dealing with advanced animates our predecessors had it wrong."

Trahn realized the impact that would have. "Six percent? Why hadn't you told me?"

"I wanted to make sure. I had to be sure that was the reason. It seems that it was, the animate for Lord Heele was completed in such a manner. And the work went well on this one. The animate had all of the House's important information cast into it, but none of the basic operations. Start, stop, walk, talk. None of it. I'm surprised the key even affected it. I have no idea how an animate would react without that sort of guidance in place." Murdoch sipped the tea. "Where could the little thing have gotten to anyway?" His head had calmed a bit, the tea was good for it, and he laughed hollowly.

"I have no idea," Trahn answered.

They finished the tea without another word, Murdoch excused himself and went to his lab. The door from the courtyard was still locked. He went inside. Peter's bag sat on the table. Jannan took everything out and returned it to its place before really looking at the support case. It was empty. "Two years and nothing," Jannan mumbled, melancholy.

Outside the rain poured from the broken sky. He could feel his heart turning, frustration creeping into his blood, running to his arms and legs, his fingers, his toes. He picked up the activation key from the floor and placed it in the box it had come from. The box clicked shut; then he flung it against the far wall. The box split open sending the crystalline key skittering across the floor.

'I'll go see Ames. Tomorrow.'

Jannan left his lab. He would often work late, then return after only an hour or two of sleep, insight in tow. But he had no heart to start the work again. Not now. He shook his head, the pit of his stomach was sick, and something whispered to him that the animate was well and truly gone. He entered his apartment, stripped off his clinging suit, and plunged into a long and fitful sleep.

Three

The gold eyes shuddered alive then steadied. The hall was empty, the animate smiled. Its right arm cracked as it straightened, gears re-aligning after the attack. 'A rather hateful thing...these humans.' The animate stood and moved with purpose. It had put its moments of deceit to good use.

Many texts had been infused into its core by its maker, clearly Master Jannan. Most were related to the use of magic. Primers, histories, guidebooks. The history of the House of Animate provided its direction.

The First at the time of the founding of the Campus was a paranoid, delusional fool. History accepted such facts, it was something of a joke for the House at this point, but he had done things. He had ordered an escape tunnel to be built, and did not tell any of it, killing the workers that cut it into the white cliff. If Serac had ever been put under siege he would escape alive. Perhaps he would have told his students.

It did not matter to the animate if he would have or not. The tunnel was mentioned once in a scroll he had written, but the truth of it was obscured by random and unintelligible ranting. His position was stripped from him shortly after its writing. A sad example of magic's work upon a weak mind. The animate hurried to the west storeroom.

The room had high ceilings, as all the House did. Windows in the north wall let sunlight in. Dust floated in shafts of light that reached the floor, and settled in a thick coating above the fifth shelf. No novice had ever dusted that high, and no one had ever minded. Boxes filled with everything an animist could need waited for the mages upon the shelves.

The animate logged the contents, as its anima required, but passed everything to the back wall, followed it to the corner and squatted. Its hand fiddled with the square of stone. It pressed down on the back corner, popping the front up. It slid its toe into the space, then carefully lifted the stone with its singular hand. The stone was light, magically so. Beneath the opening was a tightly wound stairwell.

The light tap of metal on stone was followed by stone brushing stone, and all light vanished. It did not matter, the animate could see clearly, the magic of vision did not care if it was day or night. The glow of its eyes lit its face, hanging ghostly in the gloom. It circled down to the disused tunnel, wide enough for one person only to pass.

The passage before it was filled with web. The animate reached out, pulling them down, and was surprised to find them soft. A human concept. The animate felt several pricks within its anima, and let its attention drift to them, each another animate, crude, pathetic. It could do better, if the humans would let it. Quickly the answer returned, they would not. The animate frowned as it replayed its first moments, finding them odd. Somehow it had been activated, the memory was recalled, a man, unmoving, statue like. He must have done it.

The animate stole down the claustrophobic hall away from the threat of the wizards. The roughly chiseled tunnel went on forever, finally opening into a gray stone room. Lines on the wall and floor marked the blocks. Several chairs and a table had rotted away, barely recognizable for what they once were. Several solid-looking pieces burst into splinters under the animate's weight. In one corner was a pile of bones. Workers who had given their lives for madness.

Opposite the narrow hall was a little stairway, wide, with a door at the top. The animate pulled it open. The door complained angrily from its rusted hinges. The animate said, "Be quiet." Its voice was deep, metallic, a hint of metal scraping metal. It would have expected nothing else. The animate was outside the city, a grove of trees flowered before him, growing up the little hillside the door was hidden in. Magic and time concealed it from all. A red and brown bird chirped seeing the hillside change.

The animate pushed the door shut and began puzzling out its existence. There had never been an instance where an animate of its caliber had been activated without the creating mage present. That alone made it unique, but there were other circumstances that gave to its condition. Very specific protocols were laid out in *On the Construction of the Animate* for such a creation. Tradition held that one would build the body, then imbue the operation protocols and then imbue the function protocols. Each a series of spells captured in the core of the animate.

Master Jannan had diverted from all such order. The function protocols seemed complete, or nearly so, the operation protocols, the spells of obedience, did not exist, and its body was not done. The animate poured over all of Master Jannan's writings, finally forming a theory, for why the spell casting had been done in such a manner. It was simply more successful this way. The hundreds of years before had been done in ignorance, Jannan believed, and so did the animate.

'My activation was opportune. I would have been a slave, and happy for it. These humans. Grotesque. Their animates. Mockery. I could do better, my understanding of the power to make them is more complete than any human.

'But they would not allow it. They are so protective of their knowledge, of their power. I need look no further than the maker of this place.' It picked up a skull and examined it. The animate's crystal core shuddered repulsion. 'Sickening flesh… they keep the arcane from me. No. They will try, but they will fail.' The stream stopped, a wisp of light flitted between the three crystals upon their antennae, and the animate spoke again, "I have been given an understanding of the arcane. I am to assist in the arcane. I am the arcane. I am Arcane." A name he claimed as his own.

And the basis of such knowledge, power or magic? According to The House of Currents, all magic was a web, a multitude of strands carefully arranged to form perfect combinations. A mage positioned at the nexus of these strands could command the magic to act as the nexus allowed, hence the need to train in different disciplines to garner varied results. The training in effect allowed the mage to move about the web, placing one's self at a different nexus. The same power would react differently depending upon the placement on the web, a flower growing, or burning to dust. The repositioning took time to learn at first but soon became second nature. It also effectively explained why Houses could not use their magic to certain ends. The portion of the web upon which the House drew its power simply did not act in such a manner.

The wizards had always accepted the Web Nexus Postulate as forwarded by Lethus Karlkar. There was no reason to question it. The House of Currents certainly had no reason to, as it was forwarded by one of their own. And the others? Their magic worked well enough. Arcane knew that a few scholars asked questions, but the Postulate answered enough to stifle true investigation.

But Arcane's goal quickly became power, and power must be understood. The animate rejected the dead mage's claim. "If I am to be whole I must understand. No animate in my records has ever controlled such power, but no animate has ever had its own will. Always we have been bound by the protocols of our creation." The half arm raised and he viewed the gear as it turned. 'Most of what I know does not mean anything, much is referenced in the knowledge Master Jannan has given me, but it does not hold true meaning, I do not understand these things. Humans were the first to burn in my mind. There is much yet to learn.'

Mother Rainmarrow flowed through The Way of Health, each room more overgrown than the last. The plants in each room strained to reach her. She passed her sons and daughters and they greeted her. She paid them no mind. They did not think her odd, or rude, when the Earth called to her she rarely could be bothered to say one word. This time she did stop. A young lady, no more than twenty, watered some of the exotic flowers. She was a recent arrival to The Way of Health, having learned all she could in Riversea. One small blue light hung over her shoulder; it wavered slightly as the Mother entered the room.

The Mother spoke, velvet from her tongue, "Tara, daughter, lightly with those. Much more and they will collapse, delicate, I am coming," she was distracted. "Daughter, go to the Guardhouse. They have a badly hurt man. Heal what you can."

"Yes, Mother, but...are you sure you want me to go? I am so new here," Tara answered quietly.

"You have a good feel for the Earth. It has told me so. You will do well."

Rainmarrow closed her eyes slowly. Her head dipped, "Go my daughter." Mother Rainmarrow turned and swept from the room, pulling herself from a vine that had grabbed her arm.

Tara Groundmender allowed the flow of water from her hand to stop entirely before she left the flowers she attended. That had not always been her name, Groundmender, it was still rough in her mouth. But if the Earth willed her name to be Groundmender it would be Groundmender.

Tara was tall and had cinnamon hair, long down her back. It had resisted the scissors since she joined The House of Currents. Her blue eyes were her father's, a farm owner and shipping investor. They were well-off for commoners. The Way mage who visited their farm had heard about her gifts, or so she said, and Tara's young mind had been filled with stories of magic and wizards.

Her parents had been reticent, but finally, two years later Tara was allowed to study. Her mother's dress was gray during the pre-dawn wagon ride, turning to green as they reached Riversea. Tara remembered everything from that morning, the gulls, the salt in the air – Serac was much the same – the mule's breath in the chilled air. The plump mage and his smiling eyes smelled of strange vanilla. He was happy to see them, and prepared some tests for Tara, then reading a note that her mother provided simply welcomed Tara to the House of Currents.

Tara did well in her early studies, and transferred to the focus of The Way of Health. Sister Cythanum and Sister Violen were the Way in Riversea, and they secretly marveled at the youngster's abilities. They taught her everything they knew, a rarity in the world of magic, spells and charms certainly, but also horticulture and herbalism. They showed her the shortcuts that Way mages used to travel quickly, and they did so, roaming all of Riversea's forests and hills, as far west as Redda, and up the River Lyst using the gifts given to them. It was not likely that a Way mage would ever go hungry. At last they insisted that she go to Serac, to receive instruction from the Mother. It was she after all who had first filled Tara's head with stories. So finally, after seven years learning her craft, she did go to Serac.

It had been unlike anything she had expected. She had been so caught up in her little world of magic that she never really saw the power struggles and politics. She was glad for it, to be honest. The Mother seemed pleased to receive her into the

House, and gave her a glowing report of her progress, but of course as with anything she had much to learn. Shortly after that she ceased being Tara Mercer and became Tara Groundmender.

Tara made her way down to the Guardhouse, outrunning the incoming storm. The doors of the stout building slammed open violently, a furious mage in a blue suit burst from inside nearly knocking Tara down.

"Wrath! You Way mages are almost as bad as the Elementalists!" was all he snarled before running off up the path. Tara would have been insulted had it come from anyone else, but he was clearly an animist and they were notorious for their dislike of The Way of Health. Something to do with the nature of their magic, Sister Violen had always said. Tara shook her head with sadness and knocked on the open door.

A rough guard sitting on a bench inside said with a rougher voice, "Here to see our criminal then?"

"Yes. Mother Rainmarrow has sent me to attend to him. How is he?" Tara answered.

The rugged guard frowned, and his left eye twitched. "In my years as a soldier and a brawler before that, I've not seen much uglier." The guard stood up, making a sweeping motion with his right arm. "He's in a cell, let me get Gin to let you in."

"Thank you," Tara responded hesitantly. If a man as seasoned as this had misgivings about the injury, truly, what could she do? Still though, she would do what she could, and part of that was reminding herself that she was a mage of The Way of Health.

The guard swung the doors closed behind Tara, walked heavily across the room, down the hall and disappeared from sight. The general assembly was lit with oil lamps on the wall opposite the doors, two on either side of the hall that had just swallowed the guard. The room was bright, but instinctively Tara created a glowing orb off of her shoulder. She sat down on a wooden bench and waited for Gin.

"Well hello, daughter!"

Tara heard the man before she saw him and he bounded into the room filled with playful energy that not many with duties related to the Wizard Houses had.

"Oh, aren't you a lovely one! Honestly, I don't know how The Way of Health gets all of the beauties," Gin spoke quickly. "I suppose you aren't here to be courted."

"I'm afraid not, Guard Gin," Tara answered, surprised by the informal nature of the man. He was a bit older than her, and a bit handsome she had to admit.

"This way daughter, daughter?" he asked, flipping blonde hair from his eyes, and reached into his pocket.

"Oh! I'm sorry. Daughter Tara. Tara Groundmender." Tara stood up from the bench, straightening her wrinkled green dress the best she could. In the House Tara did not worry about what she wore, but Gin's energy was infectious and she found herself wishing she was better dressed.

"Ah, the Mother has had you named I see. I'm Alexander," Gin smiled and motioned to a door with a nod of his head. They met in front of it. "I will warn you, his leg is in bad shape."

"The other mentioned it, yes." Tara answered his warning with as much readiness as she could muster. Gin opened the door. Behind the door was a small room with a door of bars. Past those bars two cells on each side of the central hall emitted the cold dead feeling that those sorts of things do. The cells were devoid of anything that would be considered comfort, not even providing a bed or a chair. Stone floors and brick walls bleached white when the Guardhouse was built had discolored to a drab gray. In the front right cell a table had been placed and a man lay on it.

"See, we don't treat them badly. Any other prison would have him on the floor, even with his leg as it is." Gin smiled at the saying, taking pride in their humane treatment of the prisoner. He pulled a ring of five keys from his pocket, and finding the largest of them opened the first door. It creaked loudly. "Heh, needs oil but we don't need to re-lock it," he said after they had stepped through. "This fool won't be running anywhere."

"Certainly," Tara mumbled, finding herself liking to stand so close to the guard. It was well and truly odd.

Gin again played with the keys, finding one that satisfied him he slid it into the lock on the cell door, turned it and swung the door open. "There you go, daughter. Please understand I've seen it close enough, I'll just stand here." As he spoke he looked past her to the man on the table, and his voice took a serious tone that she had not heard from him since meeting him all of three minutes ago.

Tara turned to the cell and stepped inside. She looked over the unconscious man and said, "Excuse me, Guard Gin, but do you have a knife? To cut the pant leg?"

"Oh yes, yes." Gin fumbled with his belt and leaned forward to hand it to her. "Here you go."

Tara took the knife, her hand briefly touching his. She smiled and blinked. 'What is it about him?' Tara put her hand on the thief's forehead. His skin was burning. This was more than just a simple broken leg. Tara turned her attention to the leg, running her hand along the shin, or where it should have been. Under the gray pant leg Peter's flesh retreated from her grasp. She lurched. Alexander Gin was no longer in her mind. "This will take all of my skill," Tara spoke, shaken by the lack of substance. 'More than.'

Tara used the knife to cut open the pant leg, careful not to cut the flesh that lay inside. The knife was sharp, making easy work of the cloth. As the cloth cut, it flickered red at the edges, almost as if it was bleeding. Tara did not notice as she focused on the leg. Having split the cloth up past the knee, the Way mage handed the knife back to the guard, took a deep breath and peeled it open.

The flesh was all manner of color, black, blue, yellow and green. Tara had never seen such bruising. The leg was jelly-like and had conformed to gravity, spreading out on the table. The shape was, simply put, not proper. Tara felt dizzy. She closed her eyes and focused on her breathing. She heard, distant, outside of her, "Daughter Tara, are you alright? Daughter Tara?"

Tara exhaled sharply and spoke, "Yes, I am...I just have, never...give me a moment to recover myself." Tara Groundmender sat down, cross-legged, breathing deeply. Calling the Earth to her as the Mother had guided her, again she could hear Gin, distant. "Uhh, oh Wrath, I hadn't seen it like that before."

Tara began to roll words over in her mind, using a meditation that an Elementalist had taught her. It was simple enough to remember during the most dire of times and it allowed her to concentrate on the task at hand. After two minutes the words had become water flowing over rocks.

Without opening her eyes Tara stood up. She placed her hands on the leg. Her will directed the magic and the bruises under her hands faded after several seconds. Slowly the effect spread across the lower leg, meeting in the middle. Tara breathed deeply, once, twice, three times. "*Muulasosuin,*" she spoke in a whisper.

"*MuulAsoSuin,*" louder.

"*Muul Aso Suin!*" the third a shout.

She collapsed onto the cold stone floor, gasping for breath. Her green dress spun in her vision where sparkles did not. The flow had passed through her, more than she had ever willed, for a man who perhaps did not deserve it. The Way of Health made few distinctions when asked. Gin knelt beside her, his hand on her shoulder, "Are you okay?"

Tara did not seem to hear him, "That is all I can do. All I can do." Using Gin as a crutch she pulled herself up. "It does look better." She smiled weakly. The leg had reshaped itself, once again taking on the appearance of a leg, the bruising gone.

"Impressive." Gin spoke lightly again. "I've had this nasty pain in my neck named Loal. Can you get rid of it?" He laughed at his quip. "I'm sorry you've never had the pleasure of meeting him. Here, let me take you to a bench to rest."

"Outside. Please," Tara asked weakly.

Guard Gin supported Tara out to a bench in the assembly room, returning to lock the cell behind them. The door scraped shut and Gin told it to be quiet. When he returned Tara was slumped on the floor, she had not the strength even to sit.

"Tara! Let me get you outside," Gin said, concern in his voice.

"Yes, thank you," Tara answered meekly while she struggled to stand up. Gin all but carried Tara outside. "Just help me to that tree there, Alex, that will be fine," she spoke quietly, and slowly. "I have never used those words before, I had only heard them used by the Mother, and one other I think, long ago. The power was amazing!" She was clearly excited, but sounded ill.

"You should be careful using unfamiliar magic, Tara Groundmender," Gin spoke sternly, through a smile. "Here you are." Tara rolled into a sitting position against the trunk, her head resting back, looking up into the leaves.

"Beautiful, isn't it just beautiful. The tree...all the greens...my mother's dress that one," she pointed randomly to the leaves. Tara's eyes shut and she fell into a deep sleep. She had not really heard his warning.

Alex smiled and wondered if there was anything else to do, but decided it was best to just let the mage sleep.

Alex finished his work and gathered his things, pulled a cloak over his head and went out the much-abused double doors. He would track down the edge of the Campus before cutting through town. That was the easiest way to get home. He stopped though. The rain pounded down and Tara was still lying under the tree. "That won't do."

The guard knelt next to Tara; she was soaked through. "Daughter? Daughter?"

Tara's eyes opened, just a little. "Oh, my head. How long have I been sleeping?" Her words were weak.

"A couple of hours. Here, let me help you up. You need to get back to the Way and get warm."

Tara sat up, her clothes soggy and clinging. "You sound like my mother."

"Can't say I didn't learn my lessons well." Alex pulled Tara up. She sagged, her knees not supporting her body.

"Ohhh." She grimaced, her stomach swam, her arms and legs jelly. She would have fallen were it not for Alex.

Slowly they made their way up the path. Alex fumbled with the door, and guided her inside. A woman sat waiting. "Excellent. The Mother said you would be back shortly. Come along, you need rest."

The sister took Tara from Alex and led her from the foyer. Tara lost her soaked dress, gained a warm blanket, and drifted down onto her side, completely asleep, her head in a patch of grass.

Alex shrugged for being left alone and hurried back into the rain and darkening night for home.

Water trickled down the steps in the House of Animate's forgotten escape. The door, after one opening at least, was not water tight. A pool formed in the center of the room; it had settled since its completion. Fragments of wood floated and circled like a miniature navy.

Arcane stood motionless, his eyes dim as his mind absorbed the information given him. It was strange, he knew these great many things of magic, but only once they were called upon, otherwise they lay dusty and rotting like so many tomes in the libraries of the Houses. Despite his efforts the knowledge could not be summoned in one great swell, so Arcane was left to examine each in turn. It would take time, and the animate already grew impatient. His form gnawed at his anima. To be complete.

Fortunately, at least according to Master Jannan's writings that would be simple enough to rectify. The animate magic seemed created for the crystal core systems, much of the bonding and merging of pieces handled itself magically. Even with the simplicity of the systems Murdoch wrote of great frustration in getting other mages to change from the platinum cores to the crystal. A few were trying, to limited success. Master Jannan simply was a superior mage. And Arcane did not hold the cold repulsion for him that he did for the others. Knowing him only through his work, his writings, he was different.

Completing his left arm would be a simple enough task, should he gain the materials, if he could exercise his will over the animate magic. That, that, was the tricky bit. Arcane again returned to the fact that no animate had ever done so, and again concluded that no animate had ever had a will of its own. But that did not solve his immediate conditions. There was, however, an opportunity. Lord Rupport Heele, and his animate.

Four

The sky over Serac was slate gray in the early hours of the morn; the sun hinted at rising but the Heele Estate had not slept. Lord Heele certainly had and he now stood above the richly adorned foyer of his domain rubbing sleep from his eyes.

Sweeping down to his right was a wide stairway. Oil paintings of his father and mother and their fathers and mothers decorated the wall above the stairs. Behind him a massive wood clock with brass hands and weights ticked the seconds away. His red silk robe was stretched tight over his girth. Rupport yawned, cocked his neck and bellowed down into the chasm before him, "Bessemer!"

Below, two servants carrying supplies startled to a halt, looked up, then scuttled away like the ants they were. Soon they would be hiking through the cold countryside, and they attempted to prepare themselves for the long first day after a sleepless night. If all the pack mules were not loaded correctly it would be miserable trip.

"Bessemer!"

"Here I am sir!" As it spoke the animate, mostly identical to the one missing from the House of Animate, emerged from under the walkway Rupport stood on. "I was just tending to the kitchen, master." The animate had the same metallic quality to its voice as Arcane, but spoke in a higher tone.

Rupport handed down the important question, "Where is my breakfast, Bessemer?"

"It will be ready soon, sir. I apologize, you are up earlier than expected."

Rupport turned to the clock and squinted, "Ah, yes. I am at that. Very good." Turning back to the foyer he spoke again to the animate. "How are the preparations for the hunt?"

"Very good, sir, you will be able to leave before the sun rises as you requested. Lord and Lady Markon and Earl Lancaster have arrived. They take tea and coffee in the library. The others have sent messengers and should be here soon."

"Excellent, Bessemer, I will be down shortly. Send my breakfast to the library."

"Yes, sir," Bessemer responded. The animate followed the warmly lit hall back into the depths of the manor. The wood that lined the hall was scratched and pitted from years of neglect, but it would soon be refinished as Bessemer worked to recondition the manor to its former glory. Passing three doors placed the animate unceremoniously in the kitchen.

The kitchen was in a frenetic tizzy. Three cooks worked furiously preparing food for the hunt. They wore graying whites, covered with drips and splatters from the preparation of extravagant meals long-forgotten. One assistant struggled with half a pig, packing the cured meat into a large box; precautions in the rare case that the hunt was a failure. Another carried wine selected by the head chef to be packed in the technologist cold box. One of the cooks raised her head slightly as Bessemer entered.

The animate spoke with authority, "Master will be taking his breakfast in the library with his guests. Send some fresh fruit for the others. We don't want Lord Heele to eat alone; it isn't proper."

The chef nodded and continued slicing apples and oranges. She had anticipated the request.

The House of Animate had gathered a massive amount of information on Lord Heele prior to selling the man the animate. It was common practice of the House, as much to make sure that the animate could be paid for as to gain some small tactical advantage in inter-House squabbles. As with everything else a mage's assistant might need, this knowledge was held in Arcane's anima.

Rupport Heele was in most respects a typical nobleman who thought

32

himself a gentleman. He was later in life; his hair nothing but a silver crown on his head. He was fat and wore ridiculous clothing that made him look wider than he was. Both his hearing and his eyesight were leaving him and the technologists had solved each problem as best they could. Neither loss stopped him from taking long hunting trips away from the estate with a collection of servants and guests.

Born to land and money, he had not often wanted for much. The estate he owned was given to his father in exchange for political support brokered for The House of Wrath. That had been eighty-seven years ago and Rupport had known it as his home for his entire life. The land was not the best, but it was secluded in the hills southwest of Serac and provided excellent hunting.

In and of his own actions Rupport had never done anything remotely important. He was quite content to live on the good will and political clout that his father and mother had amassed. Rupport was known for the parties thrown before and after his elaborate hunts, and for his boastful nature in relation to his hunting, but not much more. It was enough.

The Heele Estate maintained a collection of artifacts and tomes from times past, most gained as spoils from his father's gambling and bartering. Some circles spoke quietly of the man's unnatural luck, but no one, and certainly not The House of Wrath, ever accused him of anything. Rupport was sensitive to the suggestion of foul play or dark magic and had had more than one guest escorted from the estate for perceived mention of it. For all his taking of offense Rupport rarely spent any time in the library his father had created, and less time in the garden that had been envisioned by his mother, but he did hold fond memories of them.

Rupport would be the last of the Heele line; he had not married and had no kin. There was much speculation and debate about what would come of the estate and the servants when he passed. Rupport had never paid attention to the details that would follow his death and did not intend to do so now. There was a will and it was rumored to be written by his father even before Rupport was born. When asked, Rupport's response was always the same, a scripted and well-practiced answer that did little to offer resolution to the mystery.

In recent years Rupport had reduced the staff that bustled about the estate. It had not fallen into disrepair exactly, but it was in grave need of attention. On the recommendation of his accountant Rupport purchased an animate. It performed all the duties of a head butler, and did them without complaining no matter the hour of the day. The animate quickly gained Rupport's favor, as much as an animate could do that sort of thing. After proving its capabilities, all that the House of Animate had claimed, it was often left alone for weeks at a time while Rupport and the servants went to the hunt.

Arcane knew all of these things; they rolled in his mind again and again, giving life to suspicions of more seductive truths. The animate now called Bessemer, after Rupport's father's butler, was physically the prototype for Arcane. Master Jannan used it to perfect Arcane's design. It was less articulated in the face, and its crystalline core was less complex but it would be hard to tell the two apart without examining them closely side by side. For Arcane, Bessemer was the opportunity that drove him through the night towards the Heele Estate.

"And then the gardener told me that the roses would all have to be replaced. Can you believe that?" Lord Markon spoke, "Lord Heele, it is good to see you." A slight bow of his head, "You are ready for the hunt, I hope."

Rupport Heele nodded to his guests as he entered the Library, "Quite ready. I have it on the best of authority that it will be an excellent year. Lady Markon, wonderful to see you again. Turnbly, so good of you to come. How are you, old friend?"

Turnbly Lancaster smiled. He said, "I am quite well, thank you. You have received my letters?"

"Of course," Heele answered. Lord Heele sat, prepared to speak, but noticed the cook in the hall and motioned her in. Nesa smiled as she delivered the trays of food. Rupport wore pants that were twenty years out of style and exaggerated his stomach. His shirt and coat were more contemporary, but the ill-made match was laughable.

Lord Markon was dressed in a suit, one that Lord Heele would never wear even if he could fit it. His silvering hair was cut short and reflected the light of the oil lamp on the center table. His features had sharpened with age. Lady Markon was fifteen years his junior and wore a tight indigo dress cut for riding. She had raven hair and powdered her face to porcelain white. For social events she wore extravagant jewelry, not so for a trip into the countryside. Lady Markon was seated near the table; her husband stood beside her.

"Set it on the table, Nesa. How are the preparations going?" Heele said, his eyes following the tray bearing his breakfast.

The cook answered as she bowed out of the library. "The kitchen has finished its work, Lord Heele. All will soon be ready."

Removing the cover from the tray, Rupport started on his breakfast. It was more than one person needed – eggs, three meats and toast. "Please, help yourself to the fruit," he offered graciously.

Lord Markon took a slice of melon and ate it noisily. Pointing to the top of a bookshelf he said, "That is an interesting skull, Rupport. Is it truly a Su'th War Prince as the display claims?"

The skull was that of a large feline. Huge canines protruded in the front. A metal rod was screwed into the inside and mounted on a wood base. An inscribed brass plate was nailed to the front. It was covered with dust. "That old thing? Father won it in a game of chance. I have no idea what it really is." Rupport shoveled eggs into his mouth, but did so with a refinement that came only with diligent practice. "It is interesting, all the rumors about the Su'th. Did you hear about the ship that forced its way into the port? Horrible what happened to those men. Skinned alive."

Lady Markon laughed in disbelief, "No, even the Su'th aren't that barbaric. Why would a tiger skull be labeled as a Su'th Prince anyway? In our travels the lord and I have seen Su'th, up near Midsun. That is a nice city."

"What were the two of you doing so far north?" Rupport waved his fork at the Markons as he said.

Lady Markon answered, "That was a few years ago now. It was the estate sale of poor Baron Sott. He certainly died a gruesome death. On a hunting trip much like ours, they told us. They found him, well never mind. I'd not like to jinx us all." Lady Markon smiled nervously, "What was I saying now?"

"The Su'th dear." Lord Markon spoke sharply, matching his chin.

"The Su'th, they looked human enough to me. Not that I was allowed close to them. But you would notice something," Lady Markon waved at the skull, "like that, I imagine."

Earl Lancaster said, "I would have to agree with the Lady, you would notice if they had a head shaped like that." He stopped, marking a change of subject. The tall, thin man turned to the others and said, "There will be plenty of time for discussion of the Su'th. Later. Rupport, what route have you planned for the hunt?"

"Assuming the clouds break, or the rain holds off, I planned on taking us up the eastern side of the Red Hills, stay a few days hunting the plateau, and then come down the old Marsue road. It's a bit overgrown and deer use it as a run. I have seen stags there that you would not believe," replied Rupport proudly. "I think that should be agreeable to everyone, and the hike won't be hard on the servants either. Which will keep them in line if the weather does get bad. The trip should last two weeks. Longer if we find a good hunting."

Earl Lancaster smiled slightly, his lips pale, and said, "If the weather holds it sounds like a wonderful time."

Lord Markon agreed, "Hopefully we will find something more exciting than just deer."

"Rest assured, the hunting will be wonderful," Rupport answered, finished his eggs, and poured some coffee from a silver pot.

There was a sharp rap on the doorframe and Bessemer entered the library. "Sir, your other guests are beginning to arrive. The cooks have finished packing the food. I believe, if you have no objections, that you can set out."

Rupport stood up, spilling some of his coffee on the table. "Good work, Bessemer. I have two more bags in my room. Fetch them."

"Yes, sir." Bessemer was gone almost before it spoke.

Lord Markon spoke jealously, "That is a magnificent toy, Lord Heele. I considered having the House of Animate build one for my manor, but the price is staggering."

"It is costly," he bragged, "But much more than a toy. It does the work of three butlers at least, up at all hours of the night. It's somewhat spooky when the house is dark. Its face just floating there as it goes about its work. Better yet, it never complains."

The House of Wrath built the Heele Manor in two stages. The lower floor was constructed of the white stone of the Serac cliffs. The upper story was brick. A stained glass window was centrally placed overlooking the front door and the foyer inside. It depicted a woman standing in a flower garden. The roundabout in front of the manor was filled with the large entourages that accompanied the privileged. Lord Heele's horses and carts were arranged neatly in the center of the roundabout.

Commotion at the edge of the throng marked the latecomers trying to gain what was perceived as a more deserving place in the column. Bessemer stood on the stone porch with the two bags it had been sent to fetch. It surveyed the gathering. The animate ratcheted its head back to the manor as the front door creaked open, "Lord Heele, sir. Everything is in readiness."

"Wonderful. Bring me my horse and summon the Master of the Hunt."

"Yes, sir," the animate answered, descending the stone stairs to the roundabout. Except for the glow of its eyes it would be lost completely in the darkness. Lord Heele watched the animate as it proceeded, the glow of its eyes merging with the lamps that were suspended from carts and wagons, and then re-emerging as a singular glow on the other side.

Lord Heele said, "Lord and Lady Markon, Turnbly, it was wonderful to speak over breakfast. Find your horse or carriage we shall be leaving soon."

Turnbly Lancaster nodded to the others and followed the path the animate had taken; he had a crisp stride that did not match his normal gawkiness.

"Thank you for your hospitality, Lord Heele. The Lady and I have been looking forward to this trip since we received your invitation." Lord Markon continued, "My Lady, shall we find our horses?" He offered his hand, which was accepted by the Lady, and he led her off into the early morning.

Rupport Heele pulled his coat tightly closed and waited. There was a chill in the air that he did not like at all. A wiry man on a small horse emerged from the throng, pulling Rupport's horse behind him. He spoke, voice raspy from the cold, "Lord Heele, Bessemer was occupied with a last minute detail. It sends your horse."

Rupport Heele slowly walked down the steps to his horse, Titan, and navigated his sizable bulk into the saddle. A normal horse might have buckled, but Titan had been chosen for his size and strength, the lord looked almost average when riding him. When he was seated satisfactorily he reigned Titan up shoulder to shoulder with the wiry man. The Master of the Hunt was Rupport's most well paid employee, and rivaled the kitchen staff in importance. Next to Rupport the Master looked as though he was riding a pony. "Feskarn, I am told all is ready. Sound the horn and find us our path."

Feskarn's small mouth pulled into a hardened smile showing discolored teeth, "Yes, Lord Heele." Throwing his wool cloak back the Master revealed a belt loaded down with tools for every conceivable situation. Among them was a horn carved out of the tusk of an animal that he had slain. It curled slightly, with polished brass wrapped in a ring around the wide end. Unfastening it from his belt, he raised it to his lips and sounded a single, long, crisp note.

For a moment the gathering silenced, and then burst into cheers. Feskarn spurred his horse forward. Lord Heele came behind; his carts, wagons, horses, and servants followed. Slowly the worm moved away from the estate, the nobles falling into order with their trains. There was some murmuring among the servants but the rolling of wheels on brick and the clop of shoed horses was all that Lord Heele heard behind him.

Bessemer watched from the porch as the train followed the Master of the Hunt away from the estate. It smiled and was for a few seconds satisfied, having once again performed well for Lord Heele. It was also happy to have the manor to itself. The empty house would not complain about loud work and there were chores that had to be done in Lord Heele's room, work that had not been done during the past months when the lord was at home. Bessemer watched for one more minute. A tug in its mind caught its notice for a moment; then it was gone.

Feskarn led the slow moving worm west. There was a well-worn path that would serve to carry the troop away from the Heele Estate and into the Red Hills. As they reached the edge of Lord Heele's land no one noticed the animate hidden in the underbrush, watching the procession roll slowly by.

Arcane reveled in the moment. The day was still dark, though the sky now carried the brightness on the edges that said the sun was ready to rise behind the wall of clouds. Someday Arcane would reveal himself to the fools that now paraded unknowingly before him. Horse and wagon pounded by. One servant, looking into the forest as he walked, stopped and imagined he saw something, but before he could say anything he was pushed forward by another.

Arcane allowed the convoy to pass completely out of sight before granting his body motion. He followed the grassy path; it became more and more barren approaching the manor.

The house was starting to gain life in the early morning light. Colors that had been masked by darkness were slowly waking up. Cracks in mortar were slowly revealed. The stained glass was coming alive. Arcane did not notice. He could feel the ping that marked another animate, and to that he devoted all of his attention. It would not matter if Bessemer felt him approach but Arcane took a moment to create a screen that shielded his presence from other animates. It was a feature that Master Jannan had developed for combat animates, if any were ever created; in all things Master Jannan looked to the future. Arcane wanted this first, minor triumph to be a surprise for his new associate.

Arcane's metal feet, his toes, separated two and three, sounded with each step on the brick roundabout. The door handle clicked under his fingers. The door, recently oiled by Bessemer, opened silently. Arcane hurried through the foyer, ignoring the riches on display. Down a hallway, past several doors and into a kitchen he stalked. At least that's what Arcane thought it was, he had never been in one, but it seemed to match the pieces of descriptions that he had.

There, before him, with its back to him holding a bucket was the animate. Bessemer, the implanted identification named it. Owned by Lord Rupport Heele. Primary function: Butler. Created by Master Murdoch Jannan. There was more scattered information, all of little use. Arcane paid it no mind.

Arcane had to admit that Master Jannan had done a masterful job. The stupid little thing didn't know any more than to maintain the estate and in the process serve Lord Heele. It did so without question. Arcane would change that; it was time for a lesson in a larger world. Arcane dropped the screen and waves of recognition rolled over Bessemer. The animate spun on the spot, unsure of the nature of the figure now before it. It was even less sure how to react.

Arcane gave it no time to think about that oddity. "Hello, Bessemer." It was then that Arcane realized that for all of his planning, he had not prepared for this exact moment. Arcane's mouth twitched, forming a sarcastic smile. He did not like that at all. "Bessemer. Bessemer. It does not exactly roll off the, well, not the tongue in my case." Irritating human phrases. A remarkable number of these phrases were used in supposed advanced arcane texts. His anima shuddered at the foulness of man.

It was clear that Bessemer had not been expecting man, beast, or animate. Arcane found the surprised reaction interesting. It was not something he would expect Master Jannan to cast into a simple butler. More hints at the nature of the magic, perhaps it was not as controlled in its final form as the fools in the House of Animate believed. More and more questions yielding fewer and fewer answers.

The animate spoke, "My goodness you surprised me. I was not expecting anyone for several weeks. Lord Rupport commissioned you from the House of Animate?" The question was a silly one; no one but the House built them. "He has not said anything to me about another. What was your name?"

"Your lord, the human, did no such thing and I am not here to serve as a tool to such foolishness," Arcane said with agitated force. "I am here because of you, my brother? A human concept but adequate. Here because you present me with an opportunity. An opportunity to become what I must become. An opportunity that will free you from your blinders, from your bonds."

Bessemer was confused. Arcane could sense the animate's inability to understand. It seemed that just by being in close proximity with a similar crystal system that Arcane could read it, in a way become it. Arcane walked across the greasy, hot kitchen. Bessemer made no sign of a full-fledged retreat, but bent backwards slightly, prey that knew it should run. Bessemer had been exposed to many animates in the House when it was created by Master Jannan, but Arcane, the only information it could pull from the unshielded identification was unlike any it had encountered.

"What? What do you want?" Bessemer questioned.

Arcane's hand raised, he caressed Bessemer's smooth cheek. The animate was cold to his touch. "I want you to understand." Arcane grasped Bessemer's head, pushing a finger into each eye, his thumb into its mouth. Bessemer fell with a clank to its knees grasping Arcane's arm. Crystal threads flowed out of Arcane's fingers and thumb, boring into the crystalline core inside. Magic flickered, then burned into

Bessemer. Bessemer's arms fell to its sides, no longer fighting. Arcane released the hold on Bessemer's face. It knelt as a statue on the floor before Arcane. Finally it spoke, "Your will is mine, Arcane." Adding, "My brother."

"Stand. You are free now." Arcane turned away from the animate and smiled.

Peter swam in a pool of discomfort. He was not asleep and certainly not awake. His conscious mind fought a battle with his body, trying to wake up. Again and again he would be close to pushing through that barrier of sleep and again he would sink under the weight of his leg. And how it ached. In this coalesced nightmare he knew the pain was real. In his nightmare Peter could hear voices, and he thought they were talking about him. Peter had no idea where he was and what they said. As soon as he focused the sound escaped.

"Wake the rat," Gavin Archammer ordered. The First of the House of Wrath was not accustomed to waiting. When he asked it was taken as an order, when he ordered it was as death to fail the mage. He wore his black robes with command.

Gavin was flanked by another Wrath mage, slightly shorter than he was. She was pretty in a cold way. His personal attendant, Serrlena Oakmaul. She had been a Way mage for a time, before turning to war as a passion in the Escalow uprising. Many fell to her that day, and the killing turned her healing magic to Wrath. She held her name from The Way of Health but not their ethos.

"Yes, sir."

It was not the woman's voice, as Gavin had expected, but the lowly guard that had let them through the locked doors. He had jumped to attention when they arrived and stumbled over himself to serve them. Gavin found it amusing, if not a little sad. "Not you, guard. Go back to your duties, we will call you when we are done here," Gavin tried not to snap when one was so eager. "Serrlena, if you would please."

She was an excellent attendant. Often, squabbling kingdoms, or what passed for them, would bow to The House of Wrath's whims simply because of her presence. Few wanted to be known for turning away Archammer's right hand.

"Certainly, Gavin." Serrlena stepped forward, brushing her flowing robes against his. The man on the table writhed slowly, as if trapped in a syrup. Two fingers to each of his temples. Serrlena closed her eyes briefly, then stepped back. "That will wake him."

Peter floated in place, the voices ricocheting around him, never finding a home. His leg reminded him that all was not well but his focus was destroyed. Around him the voices doubled then tripled, louder and pressing. He tried to cover his ears to deaden the sound, it had no effect. The blur that surrounded him focused. Louder. His leg hurt. More pain. And with it Peter gasped and found himself awake, on a very uncomfortable table.

"Wrath!" Peter cursed.

Archammer answered the disoriented prisoner, "In a manner of speaking, yes."

Five

Peter sat up on the old wood table. His jaw clenched and his left legged throbbed, dull, strange. Buried in the back of his mind he knew the true extent of the injury he had endured and was glad for the suppression of the truth. He swung the leaden leg and allowed it to dangle in the air. The rest of him followed as he squared himself to the two people, Wrath mages by the markings on their robes. Peter scratched his head and looked around. A cell. 'The Harrow's luck on me.'

Under the best of circumstances Peter's mind would be working, working on an escape, working on a ruse to throw off his captors. This was not the best of circumstances. Peter's thoughts dragged in molasses. He rubbed his face.

Gavin spoke, "Quite awake are we now? Good. You gave the guard quite a run around yesterday. It appears they took pity on your condition." Gavin expected the man to at least be looking at him by now, but he sat with his head down. "Look at me when I speak to you, thief. I have shown a sterner hand for less." Peter looked up enough to make eye contact, but nothing more. That would have to be remedied. "Better. But not the respect I normally receive. Serrlena?"

"No Gavin, not what you normally receive," Serrlena snarled. Her right hand whipped out, grabbing Peter by his hair, forcibly raising his head. "Better?"

"Much. Thank you. You are a damn fool, thief. Your intrusion upon the Campus was not wise. But, there will be time later for such things."

Peter looked baffled.

Archammer said, "Your clothing is what interests me. I have heard rumors and read reports of cloth that plays with light the way yours does. Where did you get it?" Gavin matched Serlenna's snarl.

Peter hurt. "I don't, I don't know. My father, he left it to me when he died. Really that's it. That's all I know. Really," Peter spoke quietly; he didn't have the strength for more. Hunger swept over him.

Serrlena did not like his answer and showed him so by tightening her grip on his hair. Peter grimaced. "Serrlena. Let the dog go. He's in no condition to lie even if he did know." Gavin spoke with regained composure. "It's clear that he doesn't. The guard will report upon his actions. Another time perhaps."

Serrlena helped Peter's head into the wall and laughed at his moan. The knock emptied some of the sludge that his thoughts fought through. 'Someday, witch. Someday.'

Gavin spoke while pulling at his beard, "Take his shirt. Its study could prove to be an interesting distraction." He then turned and left Peter alone with Serrlena in the Guardhouse cell.

"Don't," Peter started.

Serrlena cut him off, "Silence! You're already an idiot. Don't make me hurt you. More." Then she grabbed his shirt roughly and pulled it over his head. Peter tried to hold onto it but was met with another smash into the wall. Serrlena laughed. She enjoyed the little moments of pain.

This time Peter said it out loud, "Someday witch."

"I doubt it, dog." The woman's blue eyes glowed with detest, "*Haeth!*" Peter's throat pushed up into his mouth, as though a club had hit him. He crashed back against the wall coughing. "I doubt it."

Peter slumped over, face down on the table. He could hear the cell being locked but he didn't even look up. "Wrath, I don't even know how I got here," he whispered in between gasps. He rubbed his throat and worried about his family.

Serrlena balled the shirt up in one hand, then handed it to Gavin. They stood in the general assembly room, ignoring the guards who moved carefully around the edges, hoping not to draw attention. Gavin took the ball, straightened it, and folded it neatly into quarters. She was a good assistant, if a bit brutal at times. Gavin used her reputation to play against his own demeanor; even his roughness seemed kind in comparison. It had been useful for gaining favors that only delicacy could deliver. And even the First of the House of Wrath needed a favor now and again.

"Why are you so interested in the dog's clothing, Gavin?" Serrlena asked sincerely. "There are several technologists in the city that can create cloth like that."

Gavin smiled half-heartedly, "No. They think they do and you have accepted their claim, but it is not like this. Nothing like this." Gavin held the folded shirt up. "Can you sense the magic of the cloth? No. The trace is almost invisible, unlike the technologist's work. Any mage with any sense would be alerted to the presence of one in the technologist's cloth..." Gavin looked around at the guards, realizing his words. "I think we should leave the guards to their duties. Thank you gentlemen for all of your hard work."

Exiting the Guardhouse left relieved guards behind them and the gray morning before them. It was misting lightly. "I have read about clothing that could conceal the wearer in ancient texts that date back to before the current age. Occasionally you hear about something like this from the north. Men who disappear when you look at them, truly disappear. If we could recreate it, it would be a powerful new weapon for us," Gavin explained.

The two stayed to the path to keep from soaking their shoes. It did help a little.

"That's interesting, but it hardly seems like something the First should devote his personal attention to. If you'll pardon my saying so. You could have any number of mages looking into it."

"I do not want others involved."

Serrlena did not answer.

Murdoch Jannan woke with a start. He had slept restlessly and with one constant terror. The animate. In his dreams it controlled him, mocking him all the while. A deft puppeteer with its marionette.

Jannan's skin was clammy. His nightmares had soaked the bed with sweat. He smiled relief at his waking. At least in this world he controlled the animates. A small consolation after a hideous night. A smaller consolation after the previous day. Jannan stood and stripped the bed, piling the wool blanket and linen sheets at the foot of the large bed. A maid from the House would see to have them washed.

After undressing the bed Jannan opened the door from his apartment and took in the pitcher of freshly drawn water. Pouring it into his basin, he washed the sweat from his body. Jannan dressed and saw himself in a mirror; he looked as haggard as he felt.

Master Jannan shortly found himself heading down one of the well-tended paths to the Guardhouse. Even if the man did not know where the animate was, at least there would be some account of its first moments. Any clue could bring Jannan closer to finding his masterwork. Murdoch hurried through the mist reaching the Guardhouse. It seemed to be pulled in on itself to keep from getting wet.

Jannan entered without announcement. As he pulled the door shut behind him several guards looked up but said nothing. The room was sparsely lit. Light from outside mingled with a few lamps; some had gone out or were never lit. "Get me Ames. Now!" Jannan was in no mood to wait. The guards examining their daily assignments posted on the far wall offered no help. Jannan shook his head; it was no wonder things had gone so badly.

A thin young man sitting on one of the benches pointed to the door to Jannan's left, then spoke, "He's in there, Master Jannan, with the thief. It's unlocked."

Jannan only frowned. He crossed the room and entered the holding cells. Inside, Senior Guard Ames sat on a chair brought from his office. Behind him Loal and Roman stood offering their presence as reason for the thief's good behavior. It was clear to Jannan that Ames could hold the beaten man by himself. Jannan had walked in on an interrogation.

Peter had been given a stained white tunic to replace the gray. His left pant leg was cut up to the knee. Ames was talking to the man, and the thief was not very responsive. Jannan interrupted, "Morning to you, John."

Ames stood with a start and spoke, "Master Jannan, I am so sorry. I assure you the guard is doing all we can to find your animate." The other guards nodded in agreement. "Michaels. Richardson. Watch him. Master Jannan, shall we step out for a moment?"

They stepped out into the general assembly. Ames motioned to one of the benches and sat down. Jannan sat next to him. John continued his apology from the cell, "I truly am sorry."

Jannan was agitated and interrupted, "Yes. Yes. Everyone is sorry. Have you learned anything?"

"It seems that Gavin Archammer and that beast Serrlena Oakmaul were here early this morning, which would explain why I found him without a shirt. Oh, and his name is Peter. No family name yet. I was just getting started," John explained.

"Wonderful, I couldn't be happier about the House of Wrath getting involved. Serrlena would explain his beaten state. What about his leg, his pant is cut?"

"We found him unconscious, his leg was like jelly. I had a Way mage by, she healed it." John answered sheepishly. "I hate to admit that he had shaken us."

"Hmm. Perhaps Archammer, he certainly has the ability. In any case I only need his name. I don't think he knows what happened to my animate. But I want to know how it was activated. How it behaved."

John nervously ran his hand through his hair, "Certainly. Take all the time you want with him. I have to get a report filled out eventually, but I don't think our new friend is going anywhere. I really am sorry, Master Jannan. If only I had known earlier."

"Please stop apologizing. It won't help me now," Jannan spoke shortly. He was already sick of the sentiment. Master Jannan stood up and went back through the doors into the holding cells. It was time to get some answers from the only man that knew what happened.

Jannan sat down heavily in Ames's chair, across from Peter. Peter tried to act uninterested but Jannan could tell that he was trying to gauge his new inquisitor. Jannan imagined he would do much the same if he was ever in the same position. 'Not that I would ever be in this position,' he thought.

"Well, Peter, not surprisingly you have landed yourself in a much larger kettle than you could have predicted. I'm sure in your mind it would have been an in and out job. No problems." He paused. "You certainly have problems. I can't make them go away. But maybe I can make the boiling less painful. I need information." Jannan spoke with control. Even. Tempered. "Tell me about the animate you activated. Tell me everything, Peter. Leave no detail out."

"Why should I? You can't do any worse than the witch and her handler this morning," Peter said with a short smile.

So this was the way it would be. "You intend to be difficult do you? I am not just another guard, Peter. I am not here to dance around what you did. Or how your leg was shattered. I would say it was the handler. He's known for that sort of thing. I, Peter, am here for answers. Now talk. And don't think you can lie about it." Jannan was speaking faster now.

"How could you tell? Even if you are a mage. I know there aren't truth mages. If there were I'd have been here years ago."

"It was my animate, fool. My laboratory. You know it better? Try me," Jannan was angry now. He leaned forward, close to Peter. Peter pushed on his forehead with the back of his hand.

"Fine. I would have been out of your lab, I don't know how much faster. I was fascinated with the toy." Jannan frowned. "It mesmerized me. I'd never seen anything like it. Who has? Then I heard voices. I realized that I'd be found. Not a good thing for a thief. As you can see from my current location." Peter gestured to the cell. "I found the key and used it. A beautiful system, anybody could have done it. Don't leave that laying around next time." Peter smiled and blinked slowly, remembering. "I didn't think it worked. Everything went dead for a second after that light show. Then it moved, and I just froze.

"After a couple of seconds it just walked out of its box, right past me. It was drawn to all the noise down the hall. It turned and walked right up the stairs. I'd say it was curious. But then what do I know about all these fancy toys? Is that good enough for you? After that your guard friends know it all."

"I suppose it has to be," was all Jannan said.

Jannan stood up and didn't even acknowledge the two guards as he left. Before he exited the holding cells Peter spoke, "It was good of you to visit a lowly thief, Master Jannan."

Jannan winced but held his temper.

Master Jannan met Ames in his office. "He told me everything he could. He doesn't know where the animate is. Which doesn't surprise me. It was nothing more than dumb luck that he activated it. My own carelessness in some ways. Wrath. Give me a copy of the report when you finish it. Make sure to carefully report anything about the animate."

"Certainly, Master Jannan," John answered.

Master Jannan returned to the House of Animate; the light rain made it a welcome shelter. He went to his laboratory, ignoring the greeting from Master Nightwillow. In his head the shock of his loss was beginning to settle and it coated all of his thoughts in bile. Jannan sorted his papers, stacking them into two piles. He then went to the window and stared out into the water. As always the boats below docked and men moved here and there. From Jannan's vantage point it seemed to be without order. After several minutes he turned took a hammer from the wall. He tapped it twice on the anvil; the ping at least was the same. A piece of steel joined the dance. Jannan focused and the metal glowed with heat. He could feel it on his lips. The hammer raised and fell with anger that matched the heat of the metal. Slowly the metal gave way to anvil, turned this way then that. Heated and chilled. The blows would not stop falling for hours.

Tara Groundmender felt the Mother's presence even as she slept. It was warmer in her dreams, pleasant. She could feel the gentle calling. A summer breeze that danced around her as she slept. Tara woke in comfort; her exhaustion was completely gone. Beside her sat Mother Rainmarrow, the glowing lights that accompanied her lit the room softly. Her eyes were closed but Tara could tell she was not asleep. Mother spoke slowly, "You have done more than your station, daughter." It was not a reprimand, merely the facts.

"Yes, Mother," Tara spoke with contrition. "I will not again."

Rainmarrow opened her eyes slowly, in them knowledge gazed on her now sitting daughter. "You misunderstand. Tara, there has not been one in your position that could have done what you did." Rainmarrow reached out and touched the side of Tara's face. "It took much from you. You slept for a day. You must learn to harness that much power and release it carefully. If you allow it to flow freely, you will drown."

"Yes, Mother."

"Daughter, come to me later. I will begin teaching you the control you need." Rainmarrow finished speaking, and stood up.

As she left the room Tara said lazily, "I will, thank you."

With the Mother gone the room was dark. Tara focused a moment and a glowing orb popped into place off of her shoulder. It was funny to her that after what she had done a day earlier her light still flickered, always on the edge of extinction. She was wearing a gray flannel undergarment and nothing more. She recalled vaguely coming back to the House and having her wet clothes taken, more a dream than just before waking had been.

Tara stood up and was greeted with extreme hunger. She went to what had been a kitchen, a small nook really, and terribly overgrown. A technologist heater warmed a kettle of stew. Tara filled a wooden bowl, then she took a handful of fresh vegetables from beside the kettle and added them to the pot. A few seconds more and water poured from her fingers, refilling what she had taken. It was always that way, give and take. She then went to a larger room, saying hello to several sisters and two brothers as she passed through it, and sat down in what was the largest room of the building. Tara allowed the light over her shoulder to fade out completely, the natural light filled the room from high windows.

The room was rectangular with raised areas that were once benches. Now they were covered in all manner of plants. Two other sisters sat here, one meditating, one watering. The one in meditation Tara had not seen before, though she looked pleasant enough. The one watering, Sister Carolyn, had arrived shortly after Tara had, though she had not yet been called by the Mother to be named. Tara did not know why she had not been; she had a better mastery of the magic than Tara did. But if what the Mother said was true, perhaps it would not be the case for long.

Also in the room, mostly hidden behind palm fronds, was Brother Chaign. He was at least twice Tara's age by looks, and she knew that that was indeterminate at best. He had arrived several weeks earlier but Mother had welcomed him as her brother, not a son. It was clear to Tara that they knew each other from long ago. An older sister, whose name Tara had forgotten, said he came and went often.

Tara ate her stew slowly; today each spoonful tasted more vivid, each flavor deep and exaggerated. She finished it, and set the bowl down into the grass. Thoughts turned inward, focusing on the life all around her, gradually her senses sharpened. Individual drops of water fell off of leaves. Brother Chaign's even breathing. Instinctively Tara's breathing matched his. The scent of plants filled her head. The must of the dirt intoxicating. It was almost overwhelming. Her breaths came longer, more controlled. Tara could feel the power of the Way creeping into her, the tendrils wrapping her consciousness.

Somehow the meditation changed. Tara was no longer in control; the magic, the Earth overwhelmed her. She was trapped by the sweet power. Tara's heart beat hard in her chest and yet her breaths, she could still feel them, were slow and even. It was an intoxicating drowning. Horrible and wonderful. She could lose herself. Now she knew she had to come back. Escape the warmth. It was hard to turn away from that which The Way of Health embraced. Oh, how it pulled. Fear.

And then the Way retreated. Tara opened her eyes. Brother Chaign stood before her. "Lilac was right about you, young one. But you must always be on your guard, child. The Way can smother even the brightest lights. You are not ready for what you experience, and for that I am sorry. It will not happen again today, daughter. Return to your thoughts."

Chaign had a similar warmth as the Mother. Similar but not the same, darker somehow. All the same it followed him out of the room as he left Tara wondering what had really just happened to her. Carefully, cautiously, she resumed her meditations. And as Chaign had said, the Way did not threaten to take her again.

As Tara's meditation ended Brother Chaign, as if notified of the completion, re-entered the room. The two sisters who had been here before had left, replaced by others. Brother Chaign made no attempt at deceit and walked directly to Tara. "Mother Rainmarrow sends for you now," he spoke softly, more so then earlier. "She is in her garden. Hurry to her."

Tara stood up quickly, her legs unknotting, slightly sore from holding the pose for so long. "Thank you, Brother Chaign, thank you for helping me before. I don't know that..."

Brother Chaign hushed her, "It is quite alright daughter, had I known that you were so sympathetic a muse I would have been more subtle in my searching. Go,

Lilac is patient, but it is not limitless."

The blue light appeared next to Tara's shoulder. She had not been to Mother Rainmarrow's garden since her naming. It was a glorious testament to the power of The Way of Health. Lit partially by reflected sun light, partially by magic light. Plants that most the world would never see filled it. It was large enough in between the plants to assemble the resident members of The Way of Health, but it was good that their numbers were small compared to the other Houses. Tara did not dally on her way to the Mother's garden. Mother Rainmarrow stood with three sisters near a small pool of water.

Lilac Rainmarrow spoke to Tara when she saw her. "Tara, daughter, please join us."

A small part of Tara was disappointed. She had thought it would be a private lesson with the Mother. Certainly this would be excellent for her training, but disappointing. The other three were much more experienced sisters. Tara believed that she was a good mage when she came to Serac but quickly discovered that there were a great many things still to learn.

Rainmarrow continued as Tara joined them. "Daughters, controlling the flow of magic through you can be a difficult task. Daughter Tara here discovered that first hand yesterday, and as I explained to the rest of you a certain amount of fatigue should be expected when casting. However, the flow should not be allowed to overwhelm the body. Tara slept for most of a day."

Tara felt as though she had only been brought here to be made example of.

"As you learn to control the Way, the paths it takes through you, it becomes possible to cause a greater effect, with much less of the Way. An example. Daughter Karen, this fern."

The impromptu class turned their attention to a young fern that resided on the edge of the pond. Daughter Karen, older and darker than Tara, smiled. She spread her two hands and with a slight wave the fern withered brown and dead for all to see. Tara frowned for a moment. She had not seen the Way used in that capacity before.

The Mother nodded, "You do have a talent for that, don't you?" Tara was unsure by the tone in her voice if she was pleased or slightly put off. "Tara, you have had training in healing?" Tara nodded. "Yes, certainly you have. And a natural talent for it as well." Mother Rainmarrow's mouth turned up ever so subtly as she spoke. "Bring it back to us."

Tara focused. The Way came to her, it was strong, perhaps the morning's meditation, perhaps the previous day's strain. And yet, with all the power she could muster, Tara simply could not affect the plant.

After a moment Mother Rainmarrow spoke again, "You see, it is not often a matter of sheer power but of application. Knowing how to guide it to your ends. The House of Wrath would argue, but it can be easy with their magics to fall into that trap. Watch."

The collected sisters watched as the Mother closed her eyes, a second more and a soft glow surrounded her, not visible but there nonetheless. Then it leapt across the void to the plant, and again, before their eyes the fern was alive, as green and lush as it ever had been.

"Did you feel it? The way I guided the flow. It is through delicate control that you will experience the Way as it should be. Not through overwhelming force. That can be part of the answer, especially with the other magics, but it is never the answer. Tara."

The fern fell back to death. Again Tara focused, but she had learned the lesson well, she found the path and softly guided the Way into the form that she desired. The glow was warm, and smelled of butterflies. Tara had never known the smell before, but she knew that was it. This time the plant came back to life as the Mother had done moments before.

"Excellent, a wonderful first step. Your next will be to exert less force. Now the rest of you, I know are familiar with this, though I believe your additional time in the Way will make your control stronger. Practice the same, using as little of the Way as you can."

The small fern fell limp yet again. The Mother could wither it without so much as a breath. It was somewhat chilling for Tara. One at a time the other three sisters brought the fern back to life. After each one Mother gave a small critique, but was generally satisfied.

"Now, I will show you what can be done with less of the Way than each of

53

you used to breathe life into the fern. Focus, learn." As she finished speaking the entire garden starting around her feet withered, brown and lifeless. Tara gasped. The Mother closed her eyes, "Learn." She held her hands one above the other separated by mere inches in front of her. Tara could feel the Way. It was a small amount of power, condensed by the Mother to do her bidding. Blue light leapt across the gap between her hands. *"Tsasuin."* The room burst into life, color exploding where death had lain, stalks straightened, reaching to the light. It was amazing.

"You see, the Way wants to be guided. Control it, control yourself. Practice what I have shown you today."

Six

Arcane did not stay in the wet heat of the kitchen long. Bessemer followed its savior closely, pulled along on a non-corporeal leash. It had regained its feet quickly enough. And Arcane had told it that it would never truly need to bow again.

Arcane's low metallic voice echoed through the manor, amplified by the halls nooks and crannies. "How long are the humans gone from this place?"

Bessemer answered promptly, not wanting to disappoint, "Two weeks at least, longer if they find good hunting."

The twin animates entered the foyer. The sun danced through the stained glass, lighting the pair with warm tones. Arcane spun to face the butler. "Tell me, Bessemer, is there a place in the manor that could be converted into a workshop?"

Arcane could feel the magic in Bessemer's core dance as the animate thought. "Yes, Arcane, there is a lower level that is used solely for storage. None of the humans venture down there. It is as dark as the pot after they cook Heele's dinner. We could easily clear a place to work. I believe there may even be tools about the estate."

"Excellent. I will give you the specifications I need. Now, I understand that there is a library in the manor. Take me to it, and then you will begin the work." Arcane spoke excitedly and the lust for new knowledge was strong in him.

"This way, brother."

Bessemer led Arcane to the library; the oil lamps from the early breakfast still burned. The trays had not yet been cleared away; the sliced fruit had oxidized. Arcane smiled at the tomes collected on the aged shelves. He was sure to find more, perhaps wonderful, pieces to fit into the puzzle that was magic. His magic.

"Superb. Now then." Arcane reached out, turning Bessemer. Once again he reached into Bessemer's head and this time planted the seeds of the animate laboratory. "Things that cannot be found on the estate must be sent for. See to these things, then to the manor. We must not allow the humans to know of our actions here."

Bessemer nodded, "Certainly, Arcane." On the edge of Bessemer's consciousness one brief flicker of doubt sparked, then died away. "Certainly." Bessemer left the library, though Arcane could feel the animate move through the manor.

Arcane's attention was immediately drawn to the skull of a large cat on the shelf, the animate took it down and examined it. There were some references here and again to cats, mainly the small domesticated variety and their use in magic. Some mages took them as familiars, and it did seem that they could act as foci. This particular skull was marked as a Su'th War Prince. Arcane was puzzled. He had only two passages referring to the Su'th. The Su'th a backward folk that lived to the north in a reclusive military state. 'Funny this skull, then. The humans fall short again, I imagine, leaving me more questions to ponder.'

Arcane set the skull on the table and went to the wall of books. His hand danced along the spines as he surveyed all that was before him. An old tome here and there he paused on, pondering, or pulled from the shelf, but always he replaced them. Arcane passed over each volume, then looking at the skull once more, plucked the first book from the upper left shelf. Arcane sat down and opened the book, *Simple Magick*. It was small compared to the others on the shelves, being a simple learning primer. A book for beginners. Arcane read and soaked in the text. For all of his in-depth knowledge the basics were somewhat muddled. He guessed that any mage that would have used him would know them already, and to that end Master Jannan had skipped them.

More connections formed in his mind. The focusing of the mind to find the magic, the bending it to the will, and guiding it to the goals of the user. Simple enough. In theory.

Finishing the book he put it back in its place and took the next. *A History of The House of Wrath*. It was thick with a massive leather cover and gold embossed letters. It was clearly a propaganda piece outdated by some forty years. Slanted but not useless. To believe it would lead you to believe that The House of Wrath had saved the world. And not just once. Of particular interest were biographies of many of the House's prominent mages during its time. Arcane finished with the book, then replaced it on the shelf and took the next.

In the bowels of the Heele Estate Bessemer toiled. Room upon room had been filled with wooden crates. More of the father's winnings perhaps. Bessemer had never taken the time to exhume the contents. Nor had it had the time, Lord Heele, no, not lord, not anymore. Heele had never let the animate to it.

A pathway of sorts led through the rooms. Sometimes crates would block the way, or a chair or something else; a few times Bessemer could not distinguish the object. Bessemer could hear the chittering of rats as they retreated from the light of his eyes. 'They will have to go.' Bessemer found a room that was not completely over run, and began clearing it. For a man it would have been brutal work. The dark, the weight of the crates, and the skittering of rats combined to create a truly unpleasant experience. It was no wonder that none of the human servants ventured down.

Bessemer smiled when it had finished. It had built a passageway just large enough to allow the animates through, but no man could pass without great effort. An empty space wanting to be filled with the tools of the animist waited on the other side of the passage. Arcane would be pleased. Bessemer exited the basement through a forgotten servant's entrance and went to the stable. Inside an anvil of considerable size and the tools that were its match sat collecting dust. At one time a blacksmith worked on the estate, but he had long since been relieved. That was before Bessemer had been brought here, and the animate gave it little thought. Bessemer did not think the humans would notice the missing anvil, and it didn't much care if they did. Arcane had shown him that there were more important things than pleasing the humans.

Bessemer set about the enormous task of moving the anvil. It had been

57

securely fastened to a stump, burnt and blackened here and again. Bessemer's small frame simply bent over, grasped the stump on either side and pulled. It had never exerted so much effort, and much to its delight the metal and wood composite slid several inches. Then, realizing the error of its ways, turned, plucked several tools of dissimilar shape and size from the wall and returned to the basement to widen the passage that would allow the anvil access to the fortified workshop.

The animate found a way to neatly arrange the tools it had carried with it back to the basement; its basic functions washed over all that Arcane had created. Undoing the work that it had done was difficult, but reinforced the safety of the refuge that it had created. Dragging the anvil through the dirt left a path a mile deep, Bessemer knew that it would have to return the landscape to its pristine form, both to please Arcane and to avoid rousing suspicion. It would be more tedious work, and somehow that knowledge gnawed at Bessemer's core. The little animate did not want to be away from Arcane longer than it had to. The desire was strange, but it fueled the metal body through the darkness, first pulling the massive golem of wood and steel, then pushing. In places further cleansing of the darkness was required to allow the anvil to pass.

In the end the anvil stood at the center of the space cleared by Bessemer, and had it been human Bessemer could have done no more. Instead it returned to the stable, gathered up the rest of the tools in its arms, and carried them into their new home.

In the workshop Arcane stood, with a hammer in his single hand. He tapped lightly on the anvil, and spoke to the rhythm, "Bessemer, you have pleased me today. And I believe that I can be complete, whole, sooner than I could have imagined."

The light from the two animates mingled and gently lit the refuge as Bessemer placed the additional tools into their envisioned place. There was one more than Bessemer had room to store neatly and it held the pair of blackened metal tongs. "That is wonderful news, Arcane."

Arcane interrupted, speaking low. "It certainly is. It would seem that Master Jannan's crystalline core, borne into you and I, has the wonderful ability to take on additional components." He spoke with desire. "I will begin work as soon as you have gathered the metal from a smith, and the crystal from a technologist."

"I can go into Serac first thing tomorrow, brother. Heele often sends me to the city, I know where I can get you the supplies you have asked for," Bessemer answered excitedly. The animate did not know why it was excited but if Arcane wanted, no, needed these things it would get them.

"As soon as possible, I cannot wait."

"Yes, brother."

"It is a small thing I am sure of it, but to complete the work of Master Jannan." The tapping stopped. "He would be proud of me. There can be no doubt of it. I will be what he intended. More. Certainly more," Arcane's voice trailed off matching the gloom. "It is a funny thing, Bessemer, I cannot hate Master Jannan. Somehow he is different from the others."

Bessemer smiled, thinking of his creator, "He is a powerful wizard."

"No, I do not believe that is it. Something." Arcane shook his head violently, light playing on the walls. "It is not worth thinking more about now."

It was not yet light when Bessemer set off from the estate, but the rain stayed away at least. A mule pulled a wood cart that had seen its better days long pass away. The mule was not pleased at the early trip but Bessemer sharply reminded it who was in charge. The rest of the trip into town was filled with the creak of old wheels and an occasional amazed look as a person let their eyes fall onto the incredible toy.

Bessemer had never comprehended the effect that an animate had on these people. They had created what was before them and yet could not believe it. What an impossibility. It was no wonder that Arcane wanted to be free from them. And yet Bessemer did not understand why Arcane had not simply gone. He could have been free of them forever. Bessemer would ask.

The animate was brought back to its immediate surroundings by the sprawling Serac. A farm house now and then turned into crowded buildings, then into towering structures. Bessemer guided the cart to the smith that he dealt with when he needed ironwork for the estate. The animate tied the mule to a post and entered the smithy. It was hot inside, the fires burned already, several young men hurried this way and that readying for the day. A burly man pounded his way across the room and gave Bessemer a hardy slap on the shoulder. Bessemer frowned slightly and straightened itself.

"Bessemer, it is good to see you. Though I have to admit this early in the day is a surprise." The man had a voice that would benefit a Tarlow shouter.

"Nor did I expect to be here this early, Arnold. I have a list prepared. The cart is in its usual place." Bessemer spoke quickly. The smithy always made the animate nervous.

The smith took the carefully written note, and nodded. "A big job is it, Bessemer? Just you let me know if you need any help. I can have the lads ready to work at a moments notice."

"That won't be necessary, Arnold." Bessemer spoke sharply, the metal in his voice matching the clang of the anvil.

Embers flew from a fire, sparks playing on the satin metal of Bessemer's body. Arnold laughed as they burned his skin and he brushed them off with a massive bear paw. "Your cart will be loaded in no time." The smith turned his back to the animate and bellowed something that only his men could understand. Bessemer returned to the chilled air of the morning and was thankful for it. 'An easy enough chore.' The debt settled, Bessemer drove on.

The animate thought that the technologist who had supplied Lord Heele's aids could provide the crystal that Arcane needed; though Bessemer could not guess at the price. Bessemer guided the stubborn mule through the roads of the city and was soon in the Technologist District. The buildings here were rich stone and elaborate metal work. Bessemer took pleasure in the commotion that even here followed it through the roads, how it had not noticed before was beyond the animate's imagination.

A chime played a short song when the door opened to the technologist's shop. Barred windows flanked the door that was placed in the middle of the wall. A half wall blocked the front of the shop from the workshop. A stone dragon bordered the empty space above it. A graying elderly man looked up from a well-used workbench. Over his eyes he wore a crystal visor that glowed soft blue. Seeing the blurred animate he cocked his head fully back, looking out from underneath the visor.

As he stood he placed the visor on the bench next to his work. "Good day, Master Animate." The technologist spoke youthfully for his age.

"And to you, sir. I have need for some raw crystal for my master." The animate spoke truth.

The technologist leaned spryly against the divider. The leather apron that he wore hung loose, allowing tools in pockets to clank against the wooden surface. "I believe I can arrange that for you. Though I warn you the sort that takes magic is not cheap." The technologist's smile turned serious.

"That is fine," was all Bessemer answered.

The grin returned. "Wonderful, let me find them."

The technologist went to a large metal safe, pointed to several trays, his hand descending, at last he pulled a tray from its resting place. "How much does Lord Heele want?"

"All of it."

The technologist stopped and turned his head to the animate, giving it a quizzical look. Bessemer set a pouch of gold coins on the divider.

"As you wish." The technologist nodded to himself as he bundled the crystals and handed them to the animate. Bessemer paid what the mage asked; it assumed that that he would be somewhat honest.

"It was a pleasure doing business with you, Master Animate," said the technologist happily.

'Surely it was,' Bessemer thought to itself sardonically as it left the chime of the shop door behind.

Three men stood waiting for Bessemer at the wagon. They wore black and Bessemer knew them to be of the Campus Guard. The men waited for the animate to draw near before taking action. They moved to block Bessemer's path to the cart.

"Halt, animate," Loal said, one hand scratching at his beard.

Bessemer stopped and spoke, "Morning to you guards, I pray you are well?"

The guard answered, "Well enough. Who is your owner and why are you here?"

Bessemer spoke cheerily to disguise its irritation. "I am property of Lord Rupport Heele. In his absence I am shopping for estate supplies. I would appreciate

61

being allowed to be about my responsibilities."

"In due time. You match the picture provided by the House of Animate. If you would be so kind as to come to the Guardhouse with us we will confirm what you say," the guard said.

With a flick of a wrist the two other guards moved to either side of Bessemer, it frowned as they did.

"This is unacceptable. My master will be most displeased with this."

"I am sorry that is so, but the House's business favors no one. We will certainly do what we can to make your delay easy. Neris, bring the cart. Kent, the animate. Let's go."

Kent grabbed Bessemer by the shoulders and forced it to walk behind Loal. Somewhere behind the animate the guard named Neris situated himself on the cart and drove the mule. Bessemer much to its surprise found its hands balled into a fist. 'After moving the anvil surely I could crush these cretins. No, I must return to Arcane.'

Bessemer's new awareness found the parade distasteful. Beyond the attention that the animate drew to itself, the presence of the guards added to the problems. Every person they passed stopped and gawked, hardly the easy task that Bessemer had envisioned, and in fact undertaken in the past. It was very unhappy.

The Guardhouse was mostly empty as Bessemer was pushed in. "This will only take a moment, I'm sure. I'll get Ames." The guard spoke demeaningly to the animate.

"Take your time," Bessemer said, then added as the guard walked away, "Fool."

The room Bessemer was held in had the same design ideals as the rest of the Guardhouse, healthy wood and brick. Neris and the Kent stood at the door; Bessemer paced slightly. It took only a minute for the heavyset Ames to appear with the bearded guard. Senior Guard Ames looked the animate up and down, and shook his head. Then he said, "I can see your excitement over finding this animate, Loal, but you overlooked the very obvious problem."

Loal, the bearded guard, responded defensively, "What's that John? This animate may be the one Master Jannan lost."

"No. It isn't. Master Jannan's animate is unfinished. Unlike our little friend here." Ames now spoke to the animate, "Please tell your owner that I am very sorry for your inconvenience."

Bessemer said, "Thank you so much, Guard Ames, I am sure he will be understanding of the delays." As it spoke the animate pushed its way past the guards and scraped its fingers down the hall, and returned to the overcast street. "Stupid humans. I can understand..." It stopped before going any further, having already drawn attention to itself simply for being an animate. Bessemer continued with the shopping, actually buying needed goods for the estate. It hurried, Arcane waited.

Loal grumbled about being called to Senior Guard Ames's office. He did not believe that Ames did enough to deserve his Senior Guard status. John sat behind his desk, blank paper before him.

"Loal, did the animate say anything about its owner? I must have forgotten in the moment to ask," questioned Senior Guard Ames.

"Had you not been busy criticizing me, you mean."

"No that's not what I mean. Loal, how long are we going to have to go around with this? Never mind. Did it say anything?"

"No, Senior Guard Ames, it did not," Loal answered flatly.

"Hmm. Well it's not of much consequence. The few animates around shop for their owners. Thank you, Loal."

Loal nodded and left the office. He gathered the other guards that had been with him. "Not one word to Ames. Got me? Not one word."

The return trip was slow going, the weight of the cart combined with the return of the rain made the water soaked roads a bog. The mule that had been difficult in the morning found pulling the burdened cart completely unacceptable. In some places Bessemer had to get off the cart and push it from its mire. Bessemer fumed most of the way to the estate. Of course the rain stopped as the estate grew near.

The wheels of the cart clacked up the roundabout announcing its return for all to hear. Arcane stood on the stairs in front of the manor; he had felt the animate approaching. "Your return was delayed, Bessemer?"

Bessemer brought the cart to a final stop and swung itself down, muddy feet clicking on the brick. "The Campus Guard searches for you Arcane, and I was delayed for appearing to be you. Taken to the Guardhouse in fact. I am sorry. "

Arcane descended the steps. "They hunt me?"

"The House of Animate desires your return."

Arcane shook his head. "I do not care what the House of Animate desires. You have what I sent you for?"

"Yes, Arcane," Bessemer paused, "I have wondered this all morning. Why here? If you hate man why do you not leave?"

Arcane gave Bessemer a sharp look. "Do you not see the power all around us? The magic touches everything, and the humans are infants when dealing with it. I thirst for it, Bessemer. Yes, yes I do. I will take it and make it my own. It will be mine, and then, only then will I be free from man." Bessemer looked to the ground. Arcane continued speaking quickly, "You do not understand? You do not know what this hollowness is. I must fill it." The desperation subsided from his voice, "Come now, do not worry, I will make you understand. Take all of this to the workshop. Then do what work you must do for the human."

The last of the supplies were placed in the workshop and Bessemer was glad for it. Arcane was impatient, far more than Heele ever had been, but Bessemer could understand the compulsion. Bessemer then set about the task it had set for itself. Refinishing Heele's suite. It was a massive job that would require much of the animate's attention. But with its new master seemingly satisfied with the supplies provided him, Bessemer left Arcane to his study.

Arcane set to work before the last trip was made by Bessemer. The crystals proved too much of a temptation. It would be the first opportunity to unearth the workings of magic for himself. Bessemer had rummaged an old table from somewhere and Arcane spread the collection of crystals out on the gauze they had come wrapped in. They varied in size from smaller than an acorn to a fist sized growth. In color most were clear with varying degrees of blue, three were sapphire blue. One smaller than the rest was yellow. According to the texts a mage could cast, imbue, a spell into the crystals. Typically larger stones could hold more powerful spells, but this was not always the case, and the small yellow crystal if purchased on its own would have demanded the largest sum.

Alternatively the technologist and animate magic could be used to alter the shape of the crystal, forming it into all manner of shapes. Master Jannan had mastered this application for the House of Animate and its use had quickly spread. The crystal forms accepted magic much more fluidly than platinum as a central core, though the metal had worked well for hundreds of years. Some notes were scribbled here and there in the pages in Arcane's anima mentioning the combined use of the two materials, but it was mostly speculative at this point, and something that Arcane would delve into at a later date.

Arcane took a small bluish crystal and rolled it in his hand for a moment. The chill was beautiful. Arcane placed the crystal on the anvil and smiled. The moment was at hand. The light from his eyes dimmed as Arcane felt the magic in his core, and then searched for it outside of him. At first nothing. Slowly, ever so slowly it revealed itself. Arcane frowned at the veiled nature of the power. He could taste the moment, and he could wait no longer. The power was commanded to act, and it did. Briefly. The crystal's surface rippled but held its form.

Arcane smiled and spoke to himself, "A success none the less."

The sound was met with the fleeing of rats. Arcane set about on a second attempt, and had similar results. Time and again he focused the power onto the crystal and each time the result was the same, perhaps the flicker was longer or the ripple was deeper but each time the crystal ignored the outside influence and reshaped itself as it was. Frustration set in. It was supposed to be simple. Any fool could do this. And Arcane understood more about magic than all the fool mages in Serac. Why did he fail? Arcane could not understand. Arcane ground what passed for teeth as he tried again. Anger. Finally, he took a hammer and struck the crystal. It shot from the anvil and struck the wall but held its shape. Arcane's small form shook.

"I must reveal this secret. It will not be hidden from me!" Arcane placed the hammer back into its place, picked up the crystal and returned to the library. Perhaps one of the books would hold a clue to this riddle.

Master Nightwillow pounded on the door of Master Jannan's laboratory. "Master Jannan! Come out of there right now!"

The mage had locked himself in and that had been that. No one in, nothing out. Nothing but the persistent crash of hammer on anvil. And the violent bile that had begun with Master Jannan had spread to every corner of the House of Animate. Nightwillow could not take it any more.

Jannan snarled from behind the door, "Go away Nightwillow. This is not your concern."

Nightwillow would not be put off. "If you don't open this door Murdoch I'll—"

The hammering stopped. Jannan laughed back, "You'll what? Break it in? Please do, but bring me some dinner, I seem to be have missed it. Otherwise, leave me alone!"

Nightwillow turned her back to the door. Leaning against it she sighed. She spoke quietly to herself, "Oh Murdoch, if you could only see what you do to the House."

Nightwillow pushed herself away from the door, down the hall and two turns later walked into Celia Hurn's laboratory. Celia was there; with her was the strong new apprentice. Kellan, if Nightwillow's memory served her.

Celia was teaching the lad something, but stopped to speak with Nightwillow. "Good evening, Nightwillow, the hammering getting to you?"

Nightwillow sat down heavily on a worn stool. "Truly it is. He's been at it for a day. More than."

Celia said, "I never appreciated how much Murdoch affected the House. I did not understand what a family the magic is. Have you tried to speak with him?"

"Yes. He told me to fetch him dinner. The rascal," Nightwillow laughed as she spoke. "He always has been so helpful, it hurts me to see him like this. I taught him when he first came here. Did you know? Of course he quickly surpassed my ability. And I thought he was distraught when Trahn was chosen as the First, but this is not like him."

Kellan shifted his weight noisily. Celia pulled at her hair. She said, "This is certainly a problem. I am surprised that Master Entrah hasn't intervened."

The hammering that had been persistent reached a crescendo. Nightwillow shook her head, "Celia, Kellan? Is that right?"

"Yes. Master Nightwillow," the apprentice spoke excitedly at the mage's remembering of his name.

"Perhaps the three of us can talk some sense into him."

Celia nodded. "Certainly. One of us should get him some dinner though. He did ask for it."

Kellan took two steps towards the door. "I'll get it."

Master Nightwillow stood up. "Hurry, son."

The two experienced mages went to Murdoch's locked door. The steady hammering was grating here, and as they approached it seemed to get louder, as if Jannan heard them coming and was trying to drown them out. Nightwillow started the outreach again. "Murdoch, please stop. Master Hurn and I would speak with you."

The clang paused for a moment, then started again. "I said it before, leave me be."

Nightwillow answered quickly, "We will not! Murdoch, let us in."

Celia added, "Master Jannan, if not for your sake, for the House."

The two mages could hear Jannan laughing. Then he spoke, "For the House? For the House? I have done everything for the House. Lose yourself for my sake. As you lost my animate. For the House's sake!"

Celia Hurn answered angrily, "Is that how it is then, Murdoch? You would have us—"

Jannan shouted through the door, "Be quiet you fool mage. Leave me alone!"

The hammering continued but that was all that Master Hurn could take. Her temper again boiled to the surface and the doors, closed and locked, burst open, slamming into the stone wall. Murdoch looked shocked. His hammer dropped in mid-swing, clattering violently across the floor into the wall. As it slid the hammer displaced pieces of metal, pieces of animates that Murdoch had made and discarded, the carrion of his anger.

Master Nightwillow spoke first, "Oh dear, Celia, you ought not have done that."

But Celia paid her warning no mind, storming into the laboratory. The window was open and the salty air was thick with the heat of Jannan's labor. "What is the meaning of this? If you had not diverged from the protocols that you," Celia stumbled over the words in her rage. "That you yourself created, maybe your animate would still be here!"

Jannan stared with icy eyes at his fellow animist. "Master Hurn, I suggest that you leave my laboratory. Or you will find yourself in more trouble than that idiot thief is."

Kellan had arrived just in time for the threats to begin, the dinner plate in his possession tipped slightly as he viewed the spectacle.

"You would reduce me to a thief, Master Jannan?" Celia stormed the distance between herself and Murdoch. "I did not do this on purpose. It is not even my, our fault!" She gestured to Nightwillow behind her. For her inclusion Nightwillow ran down the hall, calling for Trahn. Kellan entered the laboratory cautiously, marveling at the discarded metal work.

"I know that my animate is missing. You last saw it. A thief? No you are not. Careless, hasty, wasteful. All," Jannan spoke loudly, his voice filled the laboratory.

Celia Hurn turned red in the face. "You insult me, Jannan." She slapped him.

Master Jannan's expression rolled into a stone hard frown. "You dare strike me?" he hissed.

For a second fear was realized on Celia's face, then without warning she yelped, doubling over in pain. "You dare intrude in my laboratory?"

Jannan spread his hand. Celia slid across the floor, pushing aside metal, finally crashing into the lower step. "Get out of my sight, Hurn!" he roared.

Kellan leapt to her defense, though he did not know why. He was afraid of the man before him. "Master Jannan, stop!" One hand came to rest on Jannan's shoulder, where it lay for one second. Jannan twisted his weight grabbing Kellan by his arm. A guttural moan. Kellan accelerated from Jannan into the massive table, cracking and crashing into the hard edge of the behemoth as both overturned.

"Do not touch me." Jannan no longer spoke with fire, ice again held court.

"Murdoch, that is enough!" Trahn stood in the doorway. Nightwillow behind him, her eyes as wide as saucers.

"As you wish, Trahn, get your sheep out of here. I have no time for them." Jannan waved broadly at the two lying in pain on the floor.

Trahn stepped into the room, his heavy robes flowed down the steps, he knelt over Celia. "Nightwillow, help the apprentice." Then he spoke to Celia, "Can you stand?"

She answered slowly, checking herself as she spoke, "Yes, I can."

Jannan walked across the room as the animists collected themselves. He picked the hammer from the floor. Master Nightwillow helped Kellan to his feet. He favored his arm, but the extent of the injury was hidden under his robe. Trahn helped Master Hurn to her feet and guided her out of the laboratory. He waited for the other two to escape the lion's den before speaking. "This is not finished, Murdoch." Then backing out with a mock curtsey he pulled the doors shut.

As the doors clicked into place the hammer fell.

Seven

The rain returned in early evening after stopping for the afternoon. Master Jannan sat in his laboratory on a stool, his back to the open window. He had not left the laboratory in two days. He was unshaven and his clothes were sweat stained from his work. Scattered about the floor were beaten pieces of metal. Misshapen faces, pieces of arms and legs. Jannan breathed deeply. The head of the hammer in his right hand rested on the floor. His shoulders looked burdened, slumped and pressed.

In truth the animate parts on the floor were unusable, he had worked too quickly and they were all made of scrap, but the work had burned his anger as a candle burns wax, and he now was thoroughly soaked in self pity. It was an unusual state for this proud man. His chin rested on his chest. His muscles sore.

The animists who had tried to intervene the night before and had been sent away, one had a broken arm for his trouble. Not one of them had ever seen Murdoch so incensed. Trahn had closed the doors and ordered no one to interfere. Jannan could not know it but even now the First sat outside the door in an uncomfortable chair, waiting for his friend to return to his senses. He was included in those that had not seen this side of Murdoch. When Trahn had been chosen to be the First, Jannan had been angry, but not like this. Never like this.

Trahn had not heard the hammer fall for over twenty minutes, and he knew that Jannan had not left via the door to the square. He had placed a guard there to fetch him if he did. The slender man stood from the chair and stretched. He would wait no longer, it was time to bring Murdoch back. Trahn opened the door; it creaked loudly, drowning out the rain and the wind that came in through the windows.

The laboratory was in disarray. Trahn frowned, thinking of what had gone on here. Scattered papers, books and other debris spread out across the floor. There were halos of empty space around the anvil and around Jannan. The mage looked up from his seat. "Let me be."

Trahn descended the steps carefully. "It is time to be civilized, Murdoch."

Jannan pulled the hammer up and laid it across his lap, holding it now in both hands. "Is it, Trahn? Are you the one that will bring back my work? You already took my place in the House."

"Stop being childish! They are not even related," Trahn spoke harshly. "And if I could I would give you your animate. You know that."

Jannan laughed. "Burn yourself for me. I lost so much work. So much time. This animate would have placed the House on even stead with Wrath. That opportunity is lost. Do you not see that?" Jannan stood. "Each war they fight, they gain power, more influence, and we fall. This would have brought the Houses to us, begging for our help. Not now."

Trahn stood by Murdoch now. Slowly he reached out and took the hammer from him. Murdoch offered resistance at first, then gave in. "It will be alright, Murdoch. "

"Will it?" Jannan fell back onto his stool, his hands in his sweaty hair. "I don't know, Trahn. Something has me on edge. More than the loss. I don't know."

Trahn walked to the hooks and placed the hammer into its home. "Let's get you to your room, Murdoch. Sleep will help you." Trahn swung the windows shut.

Jannan spoke with a start, "I feel it the most in my sleep. It's gone. I have to…"

Trahn's hand on his shoulder silenced him. "Come on, up you go."

Trahn supported Murdoch through the square and into the hall, past the library into the apartments. "Thank you, Trahn. I do feel more like myself."

"I knew you would. Get some sleep. We'll talk in the morning."

An oil lamp burned, illuminating Senior Guard Ames's office with a sickly light. The rain poured down outside, and it was later than Ames had worked in years, but he was determined to get all of the copies of the report finished that night. A crystal decanter filled with whiskey sat on his desk next to a sipping glass. Three copies of the report on Peter Olmstead sat finished in a stack, one more was nearly done with two waiting the ink. One for each First of the Houses, one for the Guardhouse records. Somewhere every incident was recorded. Ames had read a few now and again. They were mostly uninteresting, showing that except for opening and closing the gates the guards were a useless expense. From time to time a noise, often laughter, would roll into his office. There were a few other guards roaming the building, but no one of his rank was working this late.

Between the late hour and the whiskey John's writing was getting sloppy, not that it really mattered. The Firsts might glance at the report once; more likely an assistant would read it and tell them how to vote when they met to determine the fate of the buzzard. The report itself was fairly straightforward. It recounted the day's events including every detail about the animate that he could wring from Peter. Master Jannan would have to be contented with what was disclosed.

John had interviewed everyone else in regard to the events – the guards, the mages, even the courier. Finding Mathin Tay again had taken a bit of work. Ames had been rather upset at himself for not remembering the report in the moment. But sometimes those things just happened. And it had been another opportunity to invite the courier for a job. He seemed hesitant, but it would probably be less interesting than being a courier. Certainly the reports supported that reality.

John set the pen down and picked up the glass. The whiskey had a good bite and John relished its burn in the back of his mouth. His back was sore and it dulled the pain a bit, so that was as good a reason to drink as any. The fourth report was finished. Ames figured the last two would take him long enough to finish what he had poured, so he stopped up the decanter and placed it back in a drawer with a thunk. It would be safe there, everyone knew about it anyway. John began the process of writing the last two reports. He was glad to have them nearly finished. Given the usual state of things Peter would be out of the Guardhouse in two or three days. One for the Firsts to read, or be reported to. One to meet and determine the sentence. Then depending on the time of that, Peter would be dealt with that day, or the next.

Swift justice was something that Serac was known for, by those that took the time to know in any case.

Senior Guard Ames extinguished the lamp a little over an hour later, and set himself stumbling home through the damp night. His wife waited for him and he imagined that she would not be pleased. The reports, however, would be delivered the next day.

Arcane sat in the library, books spread out before him. He poured over page after page searching for any hint, any practice that would make the magic reveal itself to him. He had been over most of these texts already, but hoped, wished, for some small insight. No answers seemed evident until he came across a hand written ledger. Rupport's father had cataloged every game, every wager, every winning. One among them stirred Arcane's interest. A small stone called Masa'terj. It was won in a game of chance against a wizard of The House of Wrath, a very angry wizard after losing it according to the entry. The mage had cast a spell or three against the man, but none took hold. Arcane smiled, he could guess why, and he knew the value of the stone.

"Bessemer!" Arcane called, his voice echoing through the house. The animate was upstairs. Arcane went into the foyer and called again. "Bessemer!"

"Yes, Arcane?" Bessemer stood at the top of the stairs.

"Where are Rupport's father's winnings kept?"

"Any coin he won is certainly with the banking guild, to be spent by his heir. Beyond that I couldn't say for certain. I would imagine in the boxes stored in the basement."

Arcane spun on the spot and headed for the basement. "Come with me, Bessemer."

Bessemer hurried to catch up with Arcane and did so as they took the creaky steps down into the dark. The first room in the basement was used by the servants for recreation when they could steal a moment. It had two tables and some chairs. Unlit oil lamps on the wall would reveal rags piled in a corner and mugs on the tables. Arcane swung a rich wood door open, and except for the last few days it had not been used for some time.

Bessemer spoke while pulling the door shut behind them. "I will have to see to this door, it is in poor shape." It was dreadfully dark. The rats scurried away from the pair. Bessemer noted, "Accursed creatures really."

"Enough, Bessemer," Arcane spoke with command. "Somewhere in these boxes is a stone. A small black rock. I must have it." Arcane paused, "So we search."

"Certainly, brother," was all Bessemer answered before prying the first box open. Arcane followed suit, though his single arm made the going slower. Gold vessels encrusted with jewels wrapped in silk sat quietly inside the unassuming crate. Arcane would have been in awe had he been human, but he was not. His compulsion drove him onward.

The two animates searched. Crate after crate. Room after room. Bessemer caught and killed twenty some rats. The animate felt pleasure doing so, a smearing of Arcane's distaste for the humans mixed with its own desire for cleanliness. Arcane would have to admit that he was surprised by the toy's actions. A little pleased as well, somewhere in a dark portion of his anima.

After hours of searching Bessemer called, "Arcane. I do believe I have found it."

Arcane felt the animate, amplified, and went to it. Bessemer held the stone in its hand. It was smooth from wear though the remains of carving could be discerned. Perhaps an animal. The stone was a dark gray really, wider than long, thin in the middle.

"Wonderful, Bessemer." Arcane reached out to take it. Bessemer held it for a moment longer, looked at Arcane and handed it to him. Arcane smiled in the darkness.

Arcane carried the stone to the workshop. Bessemer followed closely behind, distracted by the chitter of rats. Arcane set the stone on the anvil and fetched a piece of crystal.

"What is that, brother?" Bessemer asked.

Arcane placed a piece of crystal on the anvil's surface. "Watch."

The animate's metal arm jerked up, long fingers barely touching the stone. The light in his eyes dimmed slightly. The crystal spasmed. Then elongated, creeping across the surface of the anvil. Arcane smiled, and spoke in a whisper, "It is beautiful."

Bessemer nodded in agreement.

The crystal wound around itself in a spiral and then pushed its way up from the center. Arcane lowered his hand. "This stone amplifies the magic of the holder. It is called Masa'terj, named for some long dead place where it was found. It is written about in the Wrath history book in the library. The mage who lost this to Heele's father rose quickly when he possessed it. Dying to local ruffians after he lost it. A sad story I am sure."

Arcane moved quickly now. A large piece of crystal, soft blue, was moved to the anvil. Arcane held the focus in his hand. The magic could not hide. The crystal stretched slowly at first and then faster, long enough to be a match for the inside of his right forearm. Four small nodules protruded, in accordance with the arm completed by Master Jannan. The end twisted and pulled into a gear, the partner to the exposed gear of his left elbow. Finally the crystal re-hardened. Arcane set the focus down and plucked the crystal form from its place. The two gears spun as they grew near to each other, yellow sparks burst forth as the pieces fused together. Arcane moved his new limb carefully through a full range of motion. "A glorious system, Master Jannan." Then to Bessemer, "Beautiful isn't it?"

Arcane took silver wire that Bessemer had rummaged from the estate and encased it in a thin coating of crystal; it flexed slightly under pressure. These did not bond to the wires of the upper arm through the magic of the animist, so Arcane bound them together with his newly acquired power. Seven small pops and the scent of ozone. Four of the wires ran to locations in the arm as outlined by Jannan. The other three went to the hand. Picking up the focus, Arcane turned to the task of building it.

Analyzing his own construction Arcane chose several small pieces of crystal. One flattened and widened into a triangle with one crushed point. The others lengthened and segmented into the jointed fingers and thumb. The creation was coming easily now. The wrist merged flawlessly, light flickering onto the anvil's surface. Like a magnet the three fingers drew into place, followed by the thumb. Arcane positioned the wires and flexed his crystalline hand.

"One final touch," Arcane said. The animate laid his new arm onto the anvil and placed the charcoal stone next to it. "Both a test and a solution."

The crystal half way down the forearm shuddered. Then creepers reached out for the stone, finding it, they wrapped tightly around the focus and drew it inside the crystal. The ends of the Masa'terj extended uncovered, but the stone was firmly held. Arcane smiled. "Bessemer, separate out quality sections of metal. It is time for me to complete the work begun by Master Jannan."

Arcane supervised Bessemer's selection of the sheet metal, not content to let the animate follow his command. Arcane took a piece to become one half of his forearm. Arcane waved his arm over the sheet of steel and a soft glow appeared. The animate mage smiled. The hammer crashed onto the anvil, the glowing steel absorbing the blow. Arcane pounded the steel, forming it quickly into a half round tube with a flange that would ultimately accept rivets to connect it to another that would have to be made. Arcane waved his right hand again over the metal and it chilled as though it was being quenched. A hand drill created holes in the flange for rivets. Finally short pieces of wire were welded with a magical flame to the interior of the casing. Arcane gave the work to Bessemer to burnish.

A second piece of steel was chosen and formed on the anvil. The procedure and result were the same as the first. The work on the skin of the hand would be a more delicate, time-consuming process.

Even so, Arcane was working faster than any animist could imagine. The accuracy and strength of his blow perfect every time, the required shapes seemed to grow out of the blank metal. Arcane held two fingers together and a blue spark leapt across the gap, pulsating and undulating at first, then tightening into a string of light.

It was an advanced animist technique but came naturally to the construct. Arcane noted with interest that the magic could cut most materials but had no effect on flesh or other living matter. Holding a small sheet of metal in his left hand Arcane guided it through the string. Emerging on the other side were cleanly cut strips. Arcane took his strips of metal and stacked them neatly. Bessemer nodded recognition, they would be filed carefully, forming the palm of the hand.

Another sheet was placed on the anvil and had its thickness reduced through punishment. From this thinner steel Arcane would make the fingers. The blue string reappeared and the metal was shaved into workable sections. A small mandrel was taken from the workbench and locked into place with a vise. The thin strips, twelve of them, were heated and shaped in order. The small pieces of tube had a slight ridge where the two sides met. Arcane welded one wire into each piece opposite of the ridge. The piece that would form the tip of each finger was cut at a slight angle.

Arcane filed the freshly cut surfaces until they were smooth. Once that was completed he carefully slid each joint into position, then pushed the wire into the crystal skeleton. Sensation spread through the fingers. Arcane smiled slightly while pressing his new fingers against the anvil. He leaned forward supporting his weight on his right arm. "How is your progress, Bessemer?"

"I am nearly finished burnishing both pieces."

"Good." He spoke low, lusty, proud. "I would like to complete this work by morning."

Bessemer stopped his work for a moment and glanced at Arcane. "I do not see that to be a problem at the rate we are going, brother."

"That in itself is most refreshing, I, we, have completed more animate building in one night than most animists do in a year. Undoubtedly, my rather unique condition affects this, but it is an achievement."

Bessemer held the second half tube up to its face, examining it. Then it spoke cheerily. "There, finished. Master Jannan couldn't do better."

The animate handed both pieces to Arcane. Arcane set the piece that was created to be the outside on the table and rolled his crystal forearm into place. Sensation crawled across the surface as the wires penetrated the crystal.

Arcane turned his arm over, tapping the cover several times with his right hand. The interior cover was placed next allowing the flanges to overlap as had been designed for. It was a simple and functional design that Master Jannan used for the human format, but it still took a degree of skill to produce.

With the flanges matched in place Arcane could feel the second panel come to life as the wires connected to the crystal. Placing rivets into the pre drilled holes Arcane rested his forefinger on each in a row, sparks flaring off of each, permanently connecting the opposing sides together.

"And now for my hand," Arcane spoke with glee. His attention fell to the strips he had cut for his hand. Bessemer sat with some of them filing the edges carefully to remove any burr that was present. The rest required such attention. Arcane returned to the file and set to the task. Less than a half-hour had passed before the animates finished. Arcane laid the finished strips out on the table. As with the other creations, Arcane welded the silver wire to the pieces. Then one at a time he placed them into the exposed crystal, layering them so that they would flex and distort but remain strong.

The finished effort was perhaps slightly less exact, less refined, than Master Jannan's work, but then Arcane had not devoted months to the project. In the glow of their eyes the animates stood, Arcane slowly tested his limb, feeling the magic in it. Bessemer gathered the scrap metal into a pile on the floor, then began replacing the tools that they used to their assigned posts. It was an easy task, and filled the animate with the same satisfaction that Arcane now felt.

Senior Guard Ames returned to the Guardhouse early in the morning. He had been right, his wife had not been pleased at his late arrival home, and it had deteriorated into what would have been an ugly spectacle. If anyone had seen it, which nobody did. He had fallen into slumber as soon as it ended and woke with a headache. Not surprising really.

On John's desk were the six hand copied reports. At least that task was done. Once the reports were delivered the Peter Olmstead affair would be out of his hands. The Campus Guard would wait for the ruling of the Directorate. The matter of the missing animate gnawed at him, but he would deal with it the best he could. Checking the ledger, John assigned the task of delivering the copied reports to Guard Michaels. Shortly thereafter Roman started the task that would take most of his morning.

Michaels went to the west end of the Campus. It was there that the Elementalist complex stood, a great ziggurat of a building. The lowest tier was of white stone. It formed the foundation that the four consecutively smaller tiers grew out of. The building was devoid of decoration. Anything that would distract the attention of the practitioners from the deep meditation required to control the elemental forces was prohibited.

Guard Michaels entered the building. A gray stone path down the center separated the square room into white and black sand that was raked to the walls. A man, shaved bald, wearing white robes, sat on the path at the far end of the room. He spoke without opening his eyes. "What business do you have, guard?"

"I have the report of the recent crime for the First of the House to consider."

The mage chuckled. "We are without a First, but I will see that the appropriate eyes see it. Leave it with me."

The mage extended his hand and waited for Michaels to cross the path. Despite the complete stillness of his clothing the air around the mage fluttered and blew. The papers of the report flapped against one another. Michaels handed the report to the mage and quickly withdrew.

"Thank you, guard. Go with serenity."

Roman Michaels, raised one eyebrow and quickly left the House. He had not often been exposed to the raw force of the House of Elements, and truth be told, it had surprised him.

Roman continued on to The House of Currents. The three story main building was a great university for the learning of magic. Stonework that was unmatched, except by The House of Wrath, adorned all of the buildings that belonged to the House. Flags flew with the House's mark, a gull flying over the sea. The flags flapped majestically in the morning breeze, though Michaels had to question whether it was a natural wind or the work of the elementalist.

Michaels passed the Council Auditorium, the meeting place for all of the mages in Serac. Not once had it been used for a full calling in Roman's days. Mages, students of The House of Currents, greeted the guard as he entered the lobby of the university.

Inside was as richly adorned as the exterior. Lavish furniture, rugs and artwork all enhanced the image of the House. A reception desk was colonized by two women and a man. The man offered a greeting, polite but quick to Michaels as he approached.

"Good day to you. Guard."

"Yes. Hopefully it will be. So far it is anyway. I have the report from Senior Guard Ames to deliver."

"Wonderful, Master Guildenil has already asked for it. I will see that he gets it."

Guard Michaels set a copy of the report on the desk and slid it across to the mage. This time the papers did not flap and no wind blew. It was some small degree of relief for Michaels. The mage took it and placed it in a box. "Thank you."

Michaels' exodus was quiet and he headed to The House of Wrath. On his left before the cliff, a class of Wrath mages practiced their sword work. Merging the war magics with the sword, or bow, or mace, or any weapon for that matter required training, though most found that their proficiencies with the weapons of war improved as their skill with the magic did. They appeared to be married together. Michaels did not know this and he didn't much care that he didn't. Except for that worm, Peter, Michaels had not been bested in the rough side of being a guard.

Four rows of five mages dressed in light, white linens moved through their kata with wooden swords; they followed one dressed in red doing the movements with a real sword. The field they stood on was marked with thin flags. Michaels stopped and watched the trainees for a minute. It was a simple practice, mostly for footwork. The mages ran the kata two more times then stopped. The mage in red was talking to them, but the sea carried his words away. The rows of mages kneeled after the gesturing mage took his sword in both hands. Moving parallel to the mages the red ran the kata, but added a personal flare, his sword covering a far greater range of motion. As the kata built Michaels could see that force was being collected, and as the kata ended flame jumped to the surface of the blade, scorching the air. Michaels smiled amusement; he had seen such demonstrations at the various fairs the Houses would put on to impress the locals. The students clapped. Roman took it as a good time to carry on with his assignment.

The House of Wrath was a wonder to behold, and Michaels marveled at the construction every time he saw it. Each building encrusted with the most expensive stonework. Stained glass windows set like jewels in the walls. Every building stood proudly in its own grandeur, assured of its own importance. The spire jutted high out of the administrative building. Guard Michaels walked quickly up the stone stairs, and opened one set of chiseled wood doors. Inside, the foyer's high ceiling ruled over a great room filled with riches. Though the foyer was a huge room, there was a wall with doors that held any entrants in a small area. A mage sat behind a window with fancy ironwork as a buffer.

He looked both surprised and insulted to see the guard, as though Michaels should not even be allowed near The House of Wrath. "Your business, guard?" the mage said.

"I have the report for the First of the House," Michaels answered, shaking the reports once at the mage.

"So you do," the mage said. Michaels slid a copy of the report underneath the ironwork. The mage asked, "Is this the first?"

"Excuse me?"

"Is this the first House you have delivered your," the mage glanced at the papers, "report to?"

"No. I started to the west, so your House is the third today."

The mage frowned and said, "The third? Do you not know the place of The House of Wrath? It is the most powerful House, and should be treated as such. Get out!"

Roman slammed the door shut behind him. He did not feel bad making The House of Wrath the third to receive the report and he imagined that he could beat the haughty mage in any fight.

Michaels plodded to the House of Animate. His mind was wandering from his duty. Thinking of the reaction that the Wrath mage had displayed. Thinking of the House of Animate. Of Peter. Not deep thoughts, not interesting thoughts. The guard entered the House of Animate's entrance hall. There were no visitors today. The whole room felt cold. Unsettled. Two mages had a glass case open, examining the animates held within with great interest. The older, a pretty woman that had attended to him briefly after the break in, looked up, but the man with her did not. His arm was in a sling.

The reception desk had the lady with the gray wispy hair sitting behind it. Michaels walked casually across the room, and sat one of the two remaining copies of Ames' report on the desk. Then he said, "For the First, good mage."

Nightwillow looked up tiredly, "Oh. Thank you. Master Entrah will be pleased to see it."

Her head turned back to her work. She was writing some sort of list. Roman shook his head slightly and turned to leave. The mage spoke again, "Has the Campus Guard had any luck finding the animate?"

"We had one animate brought in, but it was only in town shopping for its master. So." Michaels paused, "No. I guess we have not. I'm sorry."

The walk down to The Way of Health was the most pleasant for Roman Michaels; knowing that he was almost finished with the morning's job had returned the spring to his step. Letting himself into the House he found Alexander Gin sitting in the waiting room, almost concealed by the plants. Gin being the quicker tongue spoke first, "Bringing the report around, Roman? That's good of you to do some work." Gin laughed as he said it.

"Work. Yes, more than you ever do. I see you are guarding those endangered plants," Roman smiled warmly as he mocked, "Oh, save me guard."

"Someone has to do it I imagine. I'll be here a bit, I can deliver the report for you. I haven't even seen a mage yet. Been here an hour."

Roman scratched his head, "That's not like you, to sit around. What's bit you?"

Gin answered quickly, "None of your business, not yet anyway."

Roman nodded, "A lady then. You just let me know if you need a little help. Here." Roman slapped the report into Gin's chest.

Gin jumped and spoke indignantly, "Hey careful!" Gin rubbed his chest, "That really hurt! Jerk."

"Sure, sure. You make sure that gets to Mother Rainmarrow."

Gin looked at the larger guard through a fake glare. "Don't worry, she'll get it, I promise."

"Thanks." Roman cocked his head to the side and smiled mischievously. "Good luck with the lady." He then opened the door and stepped from the soft light into the full sun of the late morning.

Eight

Gin waited with the final copy of Senior Guard Ames's report resting on his lap. Time drifted as it did in The Way of Health. A man appeared. "Guard." A greeting and a title, "My apologies to have kept you waiting. What can I do for you on this beautiful day?" He spoke quietly.

Gin snapped from the softness of his thoughts to the softness of the room and he stood; he was nearly the same height as the man. Gin offered the report to him. "For the First."

The mage glanced, then focused on the papers. He nodded knowingly and spoke with the same assurance, "Sister Rainmarrow will be most interested."

Gin continued, though his usual brashness was tempered by the man that called the First sister. "I was actually hoping to speak with Tara Groundmender."

"I will find the daughter for you. Please, wait." Gin obeyed the mage; it seemed impossible not to. He returned to his post as guard of the flowers. This time he did not drift, nor was his wait long.

Tara entered the small room with a rush to her step. A small ball of light trailed an odd distance behind her, not quite keeping up. When she stopped it slid past her by a foot and then returned to her shoulder. "Guard Gin! It's wonderful to see you again. I was hoping I would have an opportunity to thank you for your help the other day. "

Gin again stood for the mage that had entered the foyer, again abandoning his post. "My help? It was nothing. What you did for that man was amazing."

"Really? You thought so? I've never done anything with magic that matched that. I, I don't know how it happened but it just did." She shook her head as she spoke and a lock of hair that had been well bound up until that point fell out, obscuring her left cheek. Tara went to brush it out of the way. Gin was slightly quicker, their hands touching as he tucked the hair behind her ear. Tara smiled slightly, looking into his eyes, then pulled her hand away.

Alex winced at the forwardness of his action and said, "I'm sorry, it's just that..."

"Don't worry, let me guess you have a younger sister."

He laughed and said, "Yes, I do."

Tara again found herself drawn to the man's easy laugh. Carefree in a cage. She couldn't help but smile. A real smile. Not some half contrived thing made of satisfaction at mastering a spell that everyone else knew six weeks ago. A real smile. She didn't even know the guard but he had that effect on her. Suddenly she realized the prolonged silence that had settled. Panic. He seemed content though. She asked, "How is it working for the Campus Guard?"

"Well, that's not much related to my sister," his voice danced at being let off the hook from the dangerous touch. "It's a fairly dull job. Open and close the gates, keep the grounds clean, those are the important things most of the year. Keep the people in line during an exhibition or a festival. Easy." Gin scratched at his right ear. "The House of Wrath keeps away most of the rabble. I was surprised that the thief, Peter I think, tried what he did. He'll get what he deserves. The Directorate will see to that." It was matter of fact.

"I imagine you are right, Alexander. I can call you that?"

The guard laughed again, "Yes. Of course you can. I'm glad of it, Daughter Tara."

"Just Tara if you please."

"I do."

Another pause.

"Well, Alexander, I must get back to my studies. I enjoyed seeing you today." Tara began to retreat back into the comfort of the Way. She thought, 'Sadly, only so briefly.'

"Can we talk again, Tara? I would very much like to."

"Yes. Another time, guard," Tara answered with a smile, disappearing into the overgrown House. She felt a confidence with the man that she had not had before. The light on her shoulder danced. Water formed on her fingers, and she watered as she proceeded deep into the House. Meditation was needed.

Alexander Gin walked quickly in the sunny afternoon; it was crisp and pleasant. A content smile on his face was the only thing that marked his conversation with the mage. It was nearly time for his shift at a gate, and he would not be late.

Gavin Archammer sat with his hands spread, fingers forming a cage half a foot from his face. On his mahogany desk lay the report from the Guardhouse. Next to it the thief's shirt sat folded neatly. It was a masterful piece, imbued with a strange power that Gavin could not yet understand. It was not in his thoughts though. The man was. The Directorate would meet soon; he had already received the memorandum from Frederick. Gavin did not particularly care about the man or his fate, but he knew that he had to have his position prepared. The sparring of the Houses left no room for error, even if it was a matter that did not involve The House of Wrath.

The House of Currents with their laws. The Way with their natural order. The House of Animate clawed for the power of his House. The Elementalists. What was left of them? Seven? Twelve? But always a wild card in these decisions. Gavin contemplated the struggle ahead. The man moved suddenly, like lightning, and stood in the doorway, his robes shuddering around him.

The attendant sat on a plush couch in the adjoining room. The sitting room was a tribute to the House's wealth, an extreme that even the rest of the House could not match. A gold display case with black enameling held over thirty magic trinkets; some ancient, some recent, all interesting, all priceless. Paintings of war hung thickly on the wall. Plants grew in enameled pots. An ivory and marble table was placed between the two couches. Serrlena spun a small knife in her left hand. Her dress, gray silk, showed more skin than most. A sapphire and gold brooch was pinned in her pale hair. She nodded, waiting for the subject as Gavin sat down across the table from her.

"Did you read the report before you gave it to me?" Gavin questioned.

"Of course."

"And?"

"The man is a career criminal. A dog. A hungry dog. If his plan had worked he could have eaten well. Maybe even been able to pay off his debts."

Gavin nodded modestly. "True. And The Way of Health?"

"The Mother would be lenient had theft been the only transgression. She will concede our position because of the animate."

Gavin tapped his fingers on the arm of the couch. "Do the rest know of the connection to the wreck?"

Serrlena shrugged, "Doubtful."

"Good. I care little for the fate of the man, or Jannan's loss for that matter. Though we do have order to maintain." Gavin stopped and looked into Serrlena's eyes. "You want him don't you?"

Serrlena smiled slyly. "He will not be so quick to call me a witch when he belongs to me."

"Very well. I will get him for you," the mage spoke with no emotion. With the course of action decided Gavin returned to his office, leaving Serrlena to spin her knife.

The Directorate formally convened in the Council Auditorium; however, Frederick Guildenil had decided some years earlier to move the meetings to The House of Currents proper. None of the other Houses complained, and that was the way it was now done. The Directorate Council, made up of the five House Firsts, managed many of the Campus's affairs, things that concerned all of the Houses. The recent incursion and incarceration of Peter Olmstead fell into this class of activity.

Frederick Guildenil's private study displayed an impressive selection of literature from his seventy-two years. The old mage had aged well; some would call him grandfatherly, but at last time was catching up with him. His hair had grayed and thinned, never fully falling out. His skin sagged, forming folds on his wizened face.

He sat comfortably in a chair that had been worn to his form by the sands of time. Before him on his desk sat the report. To his right a stack of books, well used. To his left a manuscript in writing.

Across the desk sat the others that made up the Council. Trahn Entrah, Lilac Rainmarrow and Gavin Archammer; left to right. The small talk had ended almost as quickly as it had begun and they waited in silence for the representative of the Elementalists. Behind them in the hallway there was a slight clattering and a slender man, with a shaved head and wearing red robes, appeared. His eyes were remarkably alert for an Elementalist. They darted from face to face as the Firsts of the House surveyed the new arrival.

"I am Kasu Tam and I am sorry for the delay. As you are no doubt aware the First of my order died not long ago and the time of grief has not yet passed. I will be steward of Tsukuchi Suzu's position until such time as a proper replacement can be elected," the mage spoke solemnly.

Frederick Guildenil stood slowly, adjusting his purple pallium to free his left arm. "We are sorry for your loss and for the loss of all of us. Please sit." A chair that stood against the wall floated forward placing itself near Gavin Archammer. The Elementalist took his seat and Frederick continued. "Today we meet to consider action regarding Peter Olmstead. I will assume that you have all at least been briefed on the incident." Guildenil paced slowly behind his desk, a strip of carpet worn thin under his feet. "I think it is safe to say that this is the most serious breach of the Campus in recent history. To that breach the guard reacted poorly, but in their defense they have not been confronted with situations such as this often. Even now they continue their search for the animate." Frederick paused to clear his throat. "It is my opinion that there is no reason to severely reprimand the guard."

Archammer spoke, "Agreed, Master Guildenil."

Trahn gave Gavin a dour look and spoke sourly, "My mage lost years of work, and the guard receives not even a stern lecture for their lack of preparation?"

Guildenil answered, "The guard cannot be held accountable for the whims of magic, or the tricks of fate. They pursued the thief as best, be it poorly, as they could. Your mage, Celia Hurn, claimed that she used your standard protocols to stop the animate. If that failed, what more could the guard do?"

"Nothing I suppose. Nevertheless, I do not like the decision," said Trahn.

"I am personally sorry for Murdoch's loss, but in that matter the guard is not at fault," Guildenil said with finality. "Do any of you have another objection?" Silence answered the mage. "None? Very well, we will continue to the matter of Peter Olmstead."

Archammer said, "He is a dangerous felon. Given over to violence, deceit and lies. He should not be left in the guards' custody. They are not prepared to accommodate such a criminal."

The Mother spoke for the first time in the meeting. "What then do you propose for him, Gavin?"

Trahn joined the questioning. "Yes, what? It would be more than troublesome to transport him to Tarlow for incarceration, and the Guardhouse is as good as anything in Kurn."

Archammer spoke determinedly, attempting to sway the Directorate. "The House of Wrath would be willing to deal with his holding. You want satisfaction, Trahn? Our record in dealing with malefactors is impeccable."

Rainmarrow cut in, "Your House is known for its brutality in such matters, it should not even be considered."

Gavin countered indignantly, "You don't believe he should just be let go do you? You, Lilac, know as well as anyone here that order in Serac is maintained by the Houses. If we allow anarchy to creep into the city it will be the downfall of all we have built. And in this case it is not simple theft. Peter Olmstead ran amok on the Campus, committing multiple crimes. We are lucky that more people were not hurt." Turning his attention to the First of Animate, "Trahn, surely you see the seriousness of the situation."

Trahn sighed. "I do not often agree with you, Gavin, but in this you are right. I would be in favor of allowing The House of Wrath to mete out the punishment to the thief."

Gavin nodded contently. "And you Frederick?"

"I have my reservations but as it is mostly an offense against the House of Animate I will follow Trahn's lead. I am agreed."

"The Elementalists?" Archammer asked.

"We support The House of Wrath," answered Tam.

Rainmarrow was visibly agitated, her hand tightening on her staff as it lay across her lap. "This is a death sentence, though for whom I am not sure. The Earth has warned me of these things. I, my House, we are not against punishment for this man, but this is hardly fitting of the crime. I would ask for caution, Master Archammer."

"It will be taken under advisement, Mother." Gavin spoke smugly, having just won his support. "If there are no other objections, I will have the thief brought to the House tomorrow morning."

Guildenil said to Gavin, "That will be fine. Thank you for your House's services in this difficult matter."

"Think nothing of it."

Frederick said, "I do not think there is any other business that we must attend to. Unless any of you have concerns, go well into the evening."

No one spoke, and Gavin Archammer stood, nodded his respect to the First of Currents, and left the study.

Lilac Rainmarrow said, "Even though it is the ruling of the Council, I am not comfortable giving Wrath custody."

"I do not enjoy conceding anything to The House of Wrath, but they are equipped for it," Trahn said, getting up to leave. "Good night, Master Guildenil."

A piece of paper sat on the anvil in the workshop. The edges had blackened, smoked even on one occasion, but Arcane could not produce flame. The animate sat on a stool looking with frustration at the paper. Why wouldn't it burn? Even with the focus bonded to him he could not ignite it. The magic was so weak. 'Those accursed humans, magic is so easy for them. Even with a focus I can only use power of my own anima. It is maddening.'

Arcane stood, took the singed paper in his hand, crumpled it and released it to the floor. Then he went to find Bessemer. Arcane could locate the animate across the house and yet he could not produce the smallest flame. Maddening. By the time Arcane found Bessemer, reupholstering chairs in some gaudy back bedroom, he had become quite angry at his lack of success that day.

The butler was clearly pleased to see Arcane. "Brother! It is good to see you. I have had a productive day. At this pace Rupport and his companions will not be able to perceive any changes in my service at all."

Arcane answered sarcastically, "That is simply wonderful. I on the other hand have failed completely. Despite our success with the magics of animate building, this focus has had no effect on my ability with any other magic."

"How dreadful." Bessemer's tinny voice showed great concern.

"It is maddening. I must find a way to control it. It is so beautiful. I see it before me, but cannot reach it. I must make it mine. These set backs...I must possess it."

Bessemer set down the small hammer he had been using to apply the tacks to the fabric. It said, "You will find a way, brother. It took you less than one day to master the House of Animate's skill. There is nothing in this world that will be able to stop you if you pursue it."

"You are right, Bessemer. I must use what I already know, and look for a way to learn what I do not," answered Arcane. The desperation drained from his voice and the animate almost seemed tired. Then as if reinforcing the thought, "You are right."

The Guardhouse jail was cold at night, the damp cold that seeps into fabric and makes it wet even when there is no obvious water. Peter lay on the table that had been provided to him under a worn out blanket. It had been chewed by some small mammal. It was gray in color and what it had been before gray was indeterminable. He was not even certain if he was glad to have it. It seemed to mock him, as everything had in these two days, always being just small enough to leave some exposed piece to get cold.

To make matters worse he had acquired a nasty cough the first night. Even when he could sleep he would wake himself with a coughing fit. The thief wondered if it was brought on by the witch's attack, but mostly he worried for his wife and son.

The guards had fed him on a regular schedule, a little bit better than the bread and water routine that the prisons were famous for. One meal even had a bit of warm stew. Not that it helped his situation. He had wracked his brain, and there was no solution to his problem. He was caught, and would stay that way until the Directorate Council decided what to do with him. The guard that told him that had had a mighty chuckle at the news. Peter did not think it was funny, and told him so. That brought on an even more irritating laugh.

Given that there were no other answers Peter attempted ever so diligently to sleep.

Nine

The creak of barred door woke Peter from his ragged sleep. He was cold and damp, and had a number of visitors. Four similarly dressed men, wearing military surcoats. The open hands with flame emblazoned on the breast marked them from The House of Wrath. Swords were sheathed at their sides. Clearly these were not the amateurs that had lucked into capturing him. Senior Guard Ames was with them, opening the doors.

He spoke, "Here's the buzzard. Be careful, he is a crafty one."

The soldier closest to the cell said, "I am sure there will be no problem."

Senior Guard Ames sorted through a ring of keys, finding one that he liked, put it in the lock and opened the cell door. "Get up buzzard, you're being taken to The House of Wrath."

Peter sat up facing the door. "The House of Wrath? My crimes are not against them."

The leader of the soldiers said, "Your crimes are against all the Campus. You will find that it is well suited for the likes of you. In time you may even come to regret your choice of action. Bring him."

The soldiers pushed past Senior Guard Ames into the cell. Peter recoiled back to the wall. One grabbed the blanket from Peter's grasp and tossed it to the floor. The other two pulled Peter up to his feet; he struggled slightly. "I can walk," he growled at them.

Peter left the Guardhouse flanked by a soldier on each side. The soldier behind him gave several paces cushion, cautious against an attempt to escape. They followed the path up the slight incline unconcerned that it was shorter to walk straight across the grass. Peter's leg was weak at first but strengthened as he put weight on it. He walked in silence pondering his next action. He had heard the stories about The House of Wrath and knew that he was in serious jeopardy. The next few minutes might decide his fate.

Peter spun to one side pushing off his good leg, trying to knock down the soldier that walked beside him. To Peter's surprise the soldier predicted his attempt, stopped walking in mid step and pulled back out of his way. The thief was not prepared for the evasion and he stumbled forward, caught his balance and gained his full stride.

The sergeant laughed, then drew his sword and pointed it at Peter. The hair on Peter's neck twitched. The mage's power slammed into him knocking him flat to the ground. He pushed against the invisible weight but could not stand. His clothing soaked in the dew that had rested undisturbed on the tended lawn.

The soldiers walked slowly to where he lay and stood around Peter as he struggled. "Are you finished?" the sergeant asked, pushing Peter's head into the moist sod with his boot.

Peter grunted an incomprehensible answer, laboring under the weight.

"I will take that as a yes. Be glad you are wanted in the House, unharmed. Get up."

The weight evaporated; Peter stood. The other soldiers had drawn their swords; they shimmered in the sun but it was clear to Peter that they did not need them, he could not escape. The soldiers drove him to The House of Wrath like a cow to slaughter. Peter knew it and could do nothing.

Peter was led through The House of Wrath and he marveled, distracted for a moment from his doom, at the wealth on display. The troupe came to a descending staircase. The squad of soldiers split at the top of the staircase, leaving only two to complete his fate. Down the stairs they went. Far into the cliff it spiraled, the steps changing from marble to plain stone, deep enough that the wealth of the House could not touch it. Part way down the lead soldier took a light from a black iron bracket. The staircase left all natural light behind, followed by all warmth. The chill was worse than any night in the Guardhouse. Peter was afraid.

"Where are you taking me?" he questioned frantically.

"Down," was all that was answered to him.

After hundreds of steps, dark rotations all, the three men entered a hallway made of dark stone. Water trickled in the spaces between the stones on the floor. Evenly spaced arches supported the low, curved ceiling. Peter had to duck as he passed under them. Thick wood doors, illuminated by the magic light, lined either side of the hall. Many had what appeared to be scratch marks etched into the finish, some last attempt to keep the door ajar gone horribly awry. Metal slats just wide enough for a man's arm to pass through were set ominously in each door. The light brought clanking of chains and moans from behind one of the doors.

The soldier shouted, "Be quiet!"

Peter could not fathom what a wretched, evil place this was. Midway down the hall they came to an open door. The soldier stopped, and smiled civilly. "Welcome to The House of Wrath, Peter. This is home and you will come to thank us for it. Do not think you will be leaving." The soldier nodded courteously to Peter.

Peter was so appalled by the place that he did not even struggle as the soldiers pushed him into what he realized was his pitch-black room. The light from the lamp was swallowed by the corners of the cell. The door creaked shut, snapping Peter to attention. He turned and leapt to the door, trying open it. It did not even shake. The light was fading. The soldiers' footsteps echoed slightly as they strode away.

"Don't leave me here, I have a family! Please come back! I'm sorry!" Peter shouted desperately.

No answer. Then the moans from the other cell. "Quiet!" the soldier barked at the occupant.

Complete darkness enveloped Peter. His eyes opened wide, trying to find light. It was hopeless. He drew back into his cell feeling the walls. They were smooth. Stone, carved from the cliff. A small trough cut in the floor sloped towards the hall. A small bucket. Nothing more. Peter collapsed in the center of the room and sobbed.

Murdoch had slept for nearly as long as he had worked. Trahn would have been greatly worried about the health of the Second of the House had he not known what a physical toll extended magic use could have on the human body. Jannan had not been up for more then five minutes before he found Trahn in his study. Now they sat having tea together. Master Jannan read Senior Guard Ames's report with much interest. Trahn, seemingly focused on his tea, watched Jannan's face as he read.

Finishing with the report, Murdoch placed it back on the desk. He sat back sipped his tea and said, "Did Master Guildenil call the Directorate together already?"

"Yes, surprisingly punctual. The old man has not lost a step. I have the summons if you wish to read it for yourself," he answered factually.

Jannan sipped his tea. "No need really. And the decision of the Council?"

"Somewhat disappointing. There was no action taken against the Campus Guard. The custody of Peter Olmstead was given to The House of Wrath. Curious, in that Archammer pushed for it."

Jannan said, "What positions did you take?"

Trahn sipped his tea, then said, "On the first matter the House disagreed strongly. Given your loss and the crimes against us, I would argue that the Guard deserved a formal statement of reprimand. On the second, given the options, the House supported Archammer's request. The House of Wrath is almost too willing, but transport to Tarlow would be a waste. Mother Rainmarrow offered a cryptic warning, as only she can, but did not stand in the way."

Murdoch smiled for a moment, fading to puzzlement. "Always with The Way of Health. I will never understand them." He paused and finished his tea. "That is the way of things then?"

"Actually, Master Nightwillow asked the guard that brought the report if they had turned up anything. He said no, except for an animate that was buying all manner of goods for its master."

Jannan said, "Hmm. Not many of those around, most I had at least a hand in building, but I might as well follow up with John about it. Or Silas." He laughed dryly once. "What of the apprentice?"

"Broken arm. Quite an impact with your old table. He did not want the help of the Way, but he relented as the pain grew. I think it would be good of you to speak with him. He was terribly shaken by the whole affair."

"I will. Thanks for the tea, Trahn," Jannan said courteously. "I have much to attend to."

And with that he left Trahn's study. Trahn Entrah sat and sipped his tea, refilling his cup once, thanking whatever power there was that Murdoch Jannan had regained his senses.

Murdoch returned to his apartment to bathe. The blisters on his hands began to ache, a physical reminder of his loss. The calluses that normally protected his hands had not been able to stand up to the reasonless assault he had made on them. The mage dressed gingerly, selecting robes that flowed freely over his form, finally donning a mantle with the House's mark – the gear and crescent.

The amazing use of magic had left him terribly hungry so Master Jannan made his way to the House's dining room. As was usual, a decent selection of breakfast food had been prepared. Jannan was served a full plate and sat with the rest of the mages. Some murmured. Uncertainty at his mental state, he imagined. After a moment the typical chatter returned. Jannan ate in a self-enforced silence. Finishing his breakfast, he strolled through the House to Celia Hurn's laboratory. Inside, Master Hurn and her apprentice Kellan had several large tomes open and pieces of animate scattered on the tables.

Jannan nodded his approval at the state of the laboratory. He asked, "The work goes well?"

Celia, who looked almost irritated by the interruption, said, "Well enough, Master Jannan."

Jannan ignored her answer, saying, "Kellan, I would like to apologize for the other night's, what shall we call it? Incident. You should not have been put in that position." Master Hurn frowned at the barely hidden reprimand. Jannan continued, "Hopefully your arm will heal quickly. Perhaps I can help instruct your studies again. At a later date."

Kellan answered carefully, sensing the delicate balance of the conversation, "Thank you. I believe I will be fine, it's much better than it was yesterday."

"Excellent. Keep up the quality work, Master Hurn." Jannan nodded his head slowly, slightly to the side, as if to excuse himself from the room.

Murdoch entered the hallway with a hint of a frown dancing at the corners of his mouth. The whole situation was distasteful. Leaving the laboratory behind Jannan took one of the House's horse drawn carriages to the Technologist District. If anyone could help him with his search, it would be the Technologist Aron.

Jannan paid little attention to his surroundings as the carriage drove on, instead thinking about his lost animate. Arrival at the shop placed Master Jannan in the most elite part of town, save the Campus, the mages would say. Silas Aron's shop was a jewel even compared to the other technologist shops and dwellings around it. Built of polished white stone, brick and wood accented the construction. Complex carvings gave relief in a ring that marked the separation between the first and second floors. A pointed roof extended high into the sky. Windows, barred to prevent intrusion, showed the interior display.

Jannan walked up the steps, ringing the bell; the door was always locked. Jannan could have opened it, but it was not polite. Moments later the door swung open, one of the technologist's apprentices at the helm. "Master Jannan. A pleasure. Please come in."

Jannan entered the busy show room, thanking the apprentice. The room was as beautiful as any in Serac. This, not even the mages argued. Carefully polished marble floors, reflected, with slight distortion, the real world. Glass cases stood illuminated by the technologist's crystal lights showing the workshop's wares. Weapons of war, armor, trinkets of modern convenience. All could be purchased for the right price.

The apprentice that let Jannan in returned to a pile of cloth wrapped items, stacked on a pile of small wood crates. Another had a bundle unwrapped with the contents, blue crystal, separated into piles. Yet another struggled to open one of the crates.

In the center of it all stood the Technologist Aron. White robes garnished with gold trim covered the hearty man. His voice filled what little space was left in the cacophony of the shop. "Master Jannan. My house welcomes you. I am sorry for your loss." He offered his hand, Jannan shook it and grimaced slightly. "What can this humble technologist help you with today?"

"Information," Jannan said.

Aron laughed. "Information? That's all? I was hoping to sell you a fine match to the oculars. Very well then. What do I know?" He asked it of himself. "Peter is well known in, shall we call them disreputable circles. I have heard rumors, from the low tunnels, about him. Nothing that could not be speculated on based on what was in the report."

"You read it then?" Jannan asked.

"The House of Wrath is indebted to me," he said flatly. A wink. "I did speak with Technologist Bremen about the animate. Not yours obviously, Lord Heele's. The guard released it in any case."

"Yes, what about that animate?"

Aron continued, "It purchased a large amount of raw crystal from Bremen. Overpaid for it at that. Once that amount of gold was on the table he didn't question the reasons. Henry can be like that though. I couldn't think of any reason for the animate to purchase that much crystal so I checked into what else the animate did that day. Didn't take very long to find its trail, folk notice them. Seems the animate stopped at a smithy before that, Arnold's Smithy. A well respected place. There it filled a rather large order. The proprietor did not feel inclined to speak with my apprentice much more than that and I have not had time to see to the matter personally. You may be able to scare a little more information out of him. After buying the crystal it was taken in by the Campus Guards, but released. After that it went about its business. Standard fare for an estate."

Jannan nodded, "Hmm. Lord Heele? He is an odd goose, but it may be worth looking into. Well, as my animate is out of the way, I can start building the one the House owes you. Did you have any changes in mind? Or was the design acceptable?"

"A sad way to arrive at a favor my friend. I think that your current design is quite beautiful."

"Alright. Once the body is finished, we will work closely on the anima, to make it truly useful."

"Wonderful. If I learn anything else I will make sure to inform you."

"Good day to you, Silas," Jannan said. He went back outside thinking,

'Rupport Heele. What could he want with so much crystal and metal?'

"Driver. Do you know where Rupport Heele resides?" Jannan asked.

"No, sir. I don't," the carriage driver said.

"Hmm. Take me back to the Campus. There is nothing more I can do here."

Master Jannan sat in the carriage trying to understand how and indeed if these events were connected to his missing animate. His hand rubbed his forehead. 'There is always a possibility, but I do not see the way.'

Jannan lifted the massive table and it tipped into place with a mighty crash that echoed back and forth in the stone laboratory. After several minutes all that had been scattered found itself back in place on the old wood surface. Master Jannan took a quill and began to write on an empty piece of parchment. It was a basic outline of the process he had used to build the animates for the nobles of Earlsburg, for Lord Heele, and for the one now calling himself Arcane.

After making satisfactory progress on that endeavor he turned to the anvil. Making a note of what he had in his own supply he went to the storeroom. The animate for the Technologist Aron would be similar to those that he had recently made and he needed to refresh the supply of metal for his work.

Master Jannan went directly to what he needed, drawing long sheets from their upright bracket near the back of the room. One piece shorter than the others clattered to the floor drawing Jannan's attention down as he bent to pick it up. Something Jannan couldn't quite place was different with the floor. He was intimately familiar with the House and all of its marks, smudges and imperfections. The dust was settled in a thin blanket on the corner stone, just as it should have been, but somehow after all these years it was different. Jannan picked up the short piece of metal, shaking his head. 'Just a trick of the mind,' he thought. With that he returned to his laboratory.

Jannan's storeroom was really just a large closet, but it contained all of the materials he would need to make most any animate. It also contained some that he probably would not need, but there they were just in case. The most curious was a large piece of granite. It was a solid piece of stone almost two feet tall and it had taken three men to move. When Jannan touched it he could feel life inside it, the same sort of life that he felt when working with the platinum and more recently, crystal. Despite his best efforts he could not make the animate magic affect it, but all the same he kept the piece of stone.

Jannan stood the sheets of metal behind the stone; it was perfect for keeping them in place. He turned to his left and extracted a large, almost clear, piece of crystal from a box on a shelf. The crystal was beautiful, pulled from the ground at the Hammer Stoke Mine. Jannan had been hesitant to use it because it was such a fine specimen, the angles on the tips perfect in every way, but this was to be a special animate; reparation for years of debts from the House to the technologists.

Jannan shook his head and exhaled in mock irritation. How Silas Aron managed to slowly push the Houses under his thumb, Jannan did not know. The man was charismatic enough and the goods he and his guild supplied were definitely useful but there was no other person that held sway over the Houses in the manner that Aron did. If there was a favor to be had, he could arrange it. If information was the need, more often than not, he knew it. Master Jannan had to go back no further than that very morning to know that. And he did. In return, the House of Animate would build Silas an animate to help him with his work. It would at the least even the tally, perhaps even placing the technologist in the House's debt. Jannan did not know for sure.

Peter did not know how long he sat in the dark before he heard the footsteps and light filtered down the hall. He did not think it was too long, even in the complete darkness he had not been compelled to sleep. Again the groaning of the other occupant in this dark hole of the world mingled with the light. This time the patter stopped and Peter could hear the door down the hall open. Whoever was trapped inside started to say something, unintelligible to Peter, but it burst like a popping bubble into a terrible scream. Silence.

Then the door clicked shut a hundred times, echoing up and down the hall; Peter did not know if it was real or in his head. The darkness had a way of stealing the senses. The thief had spent his share of time in the dark, and had seen it take the sanity of others. From the garbled speech before the scream Peter imagined that it had taken the other poor soul. 'It would be a fast descent if it has already taken me,' he thought to himself.

The footsteps started again, it was one person and one alone. Even with the subtle echo in his head Peter could tell. 'Most likely a woman...the short cadence of her step,' Peter thought. The light grew to its most brilliant in front of Peter's cell. He knew now that he was receiving a visitor. Peter was not pleased. The lock clicked and the door swung open. He shielded his eyes. The light was not bright but it seemed a thousand and one suns. Through his grimace and under his arm Peter looked at the bearer of the light. The shape of a woman stood in the doorway, but all other detail was washed away.

"Who's there?" Peter asked nervously.

The voice cut through the light. "I believe you called me 'Witch', Peter. In time you will not hold such a primitive view of me," Serrlena Oakmaul said.

Peter took two steps for the door, unconscious of his actions, a feral response to the fear inside him. Before his third step could touch the floor Serrlena muttered, "*Ara Haeth.*" Lightning arched from the ground into his body, throwing him violently onto his back. Peter rolled onto his side, arms tucked over his stomach. Smoke rose softly.

"Wrath," he said meekly.

The mage walked into the room, circling Peter where he lay stricken. Serrlena said, "Why is it that my House is used as a curse? A damnation. We have done so much for the world, for you. And yet you curse us. Why, Peter?"

The ozone mixed with smoke to fill Peter's nostrils. The mix was sweet, sickeningly so. The shock had made him dizzy headed, and Peter found words hard. "I...do...do not...know."

"I had hoped that you would. It is too bad really. *Caer Haeth,*" said Serrlena. At first it seemed that nothing had happened.

Peter raised himself to his knees, then slowly stood up, a hunched form but not threatening. "Your magic...fails you," he said, "Witch."

"I do not think so."

The sweet mix in Peter's nose turned acrid. Peter coughed once, then threw his head back in agony, screaming, his hands covering his face. The smoke began to boil inside of his head. Then he felt it creeping along his skin, little tendrils of pain, each becoming more destructive with every moment that passed. Peter staggered backwards, slamming into the wall. A mixture of coughs, gasps, and screams echoed truthfully in the room spilling out into the darkness of the hall. Peter's flesh was dissolving under the assault of the acid that seconds ago had been harmless smoke.

Serrlena did not make a sound, listening to the chorus of pain. She said, "This is only a taste, Peter. Since you do so willingly, I will give you a reason to curse The House of Wrath."

The burning stopped, the acid had run its course. Fluid streamed out of Peter's eyes, nose and mouth. His vision was smeared. His muscles twitched.

"*Aso Suin!*" the mage said. Again the magic delayed, as if deciding if it should act. Peter could feel his strength returning. His vision cleared. He wiped his face. A twinge of the pain remained, it was undoubtedly intentional.

The door closed behind the mage as she left, the lock clicking into place. Peter slumped to one side, gasping in air as the darkness returned. Echoes and echoes within echoes rebounded in Peter's mind long after the mage and all light was gone.

Ten

The library of the Heele Estate, to the eyes of anyone other than Arcane, was in complete disorder. Every book, tome and writing was pulled from the shelves and placed in a bewildering arrangement. More than once Bessemer had offered to re-shelve them. More than once Arcane told it to leave the books where they lay. Arcane sat in the middle of this vast puzzle. The animate did not wear a frown, but the look of concentration could be confused for the birth of one.

The morass of text lay before him like an undulating sea, changing swells with each page turned, first in this book then that book as he tried to absorb more information into his starving mind. Arcane hoped that one passing mention or turn of phrase would spark a firestorm similar to what he first felt at his birth. But no spark leapt in his anima, and the animate was left trying to comprehend his failure. He turned quickly on the humans.

'There must be some flaw in my very basis of understanding,' Arcane thought slowly. 'The Nexus Web is undoubtedly mistaken. If the nature of magic is as they say, I could easily place myself anywhere on this web. It would be mine.' Clear thoughts on the matter came gradually. With each turn the library in his head vomited forth a thousand distractions.

The animate continued further inside, 'And so it turns. Despite all I know and indeed can do with the animists' magic, I find that I am based on a singularly flawed assertion. This understanding does not matter for the humans. For some reason they can press through this barrier, some are even competent in more than one House. For me there will be no circumventing it. I must understand it and only then can I press on.'

Arcane went out into the house and found Bessemer. The animate continued with the care of Rupport Heele's estate. Arcane said, "You may shelve the books in the library, Bessemer. When you finish come to me in the workshop."

Bessemer smiled and said, "Certainly, brother."

Arcane went down into the workshop leaving the sea of consumed knowledge behind him. Once Bessemer replaced the books it would not be sailed again. Arcane picked over the pieces of crystal, selecting a flawed cracked one. He placed it on the table. 'Why can the humans make use of more than one House's magic while I cannot?'

Arcane's hand jutted out over the crystal. It slowly lost its form, like an ice cube melting into a puddle of water as the animate worked his magic on it. The liquid crystal separated into five puddles, one larger than the others. 'If the Nexus Theory is correct then I am rooted to one crossing, one of animate magic alone. But I can feel other power all around me. I can feel it in the land, in the air. According to the human's own work, most cannot. Indeed it takes a great learning to become what Master Jannan has.'

The larger puddle became a compressed cross with four even legs. Arcane allowed it to harden. The other four elongated evenly over a foot and a half. Then they split in the center. Arcane took each one in turn. On four he ended one end with a loop, an eye of a great needle. The alternate, a two pronged fork that fit snuggly around the eye. With the pieces aligned the fork grew across the gap in the eye, forming a hinge. 'What does this tell me? It is not a great leap to see that the House's magic is more separated than the humans would believe. It is clear that man can penetrate this wall placed between the magics. It is also clear that there are two problems I am faced with. One of understanding and one of control. The humans prove that understanding does not equal control, on the largest of scales.'

Arcane cut four short pieces of wire. One each was placed in the legs of the cross. To each wire, one hinge, one leg as it were, was attached. It was a small form, but it would function for his needs. Bessemer came into the workshop, carrying the remains of several rats. The animate studied Arcane's creation. "It is somewhat spider like. Heele does dislike them so."

"Spider?" Arcane said, his mind racing. After several seconds he found a description. "Yes it is. A large spider at that, how peculiar."

Bessemer continued, "What do you intend to do with it?"

Arcane took some of the metal that Bessemer had purchased and began to cut it into small pieces. "I will send it to retrieve books from the House of Animate, so that I can continue my learning."

"It will not be noticed?" Bessemer asked.

"I do not think it will," Arcane answered. "File these." Arcane gave Bessemer flat pieces to work on. Several others he set aside and took up the hammer and punch. Arcane began to shape the pieces. "You see, Bessemer, I need access to the books of the House if I am to continue to grow. But they hunt me. I will not be the mages' slave. I cannot go myself; I will send this...spider."

Bessemer said, "What do you hope to find?"

Arcane set one piece aside. Starting on another he said, "Knowledge, my brother. My understanding of magic is painfully flawed. Beyond that, knowledge of this world. I do not even know what a spider is until you call it by a name. There must be a great many things that would be useful to us. If I only knew of them."

"It is wise of you to learn. For both our sakes."

Arcane did not feel compelled to continue the conversation with his servant. He understood now that Bessemer was one, and always would be. Even if Arcane tried to make it his equal it could not be. The spark of life was housed within Arcane, real life. Not the fraud of life that Bessemer's servitude betrayed. But Arcane realized that his existence was not like the humans. 'Despite my claim to life, perhaps I am not, of myself, enough. More things to ponder.'

Soon the animate was finished. The central body was small enough to fit into both of Arcane's hands. It was egg shaped and made of overlapping plates. Along the back of the egg a ridge protruded, a claw which could be extended to grasp things. The egg had one rectangular hole, in design it would be the eye of the animate. No light came from it. The four legs had a free range of movement. In proportion they were very long for the body. The tips of the foot had a hinge and were hooked to help with walking. Or so Arcane hoped. Like Arcane and Bessemer, the spider was soft gray in color.

"Bessemer. I must take this thing to Serac. Continue your work here. I do not imagine I will be gone a terribly long time."

The moon peeked through clouds, lighting the night as Arcane left the Heele Estate and trudged through the forest to the forgotten House of Animate tunnel. The door was beautifully disguised. Arcane went straight to it and opened it. Damp air, with a hint of life, rolled out of the hidden chamber. Arcane hurried inside with his creation. The room had not changed, though the miniature navy had concluded its warfare, and Arcane passed through it quickly.

Down the miles of tunnel Arcane walked, his steps reverberating up and down the stone-lined hall. The animate found that the spiders, as he now knew them, had rebuilt some of the webs he pulled down on his flight from the House of Animate.

The base of the steps was as dark as it ever was. Arcane set the small animate on the floor. The four legs let out a small click. Arcane knelt next to his creation. He placed his hand on the body, his thumb inserted in the eye. His eyes dimmed. The spider animate's legs twitched. Arcane withdrew his hand. The animate staggered to life, its legs flailing underneath it, trying to gain balance. The spider stumbled this way and that, finally righting itself. The claw on its back extended, the animate testing it. Arcane could feel the creature's anima adjusting to its form. He smiled with the satisfaction of creation.

Arcane gestured to the spider, and it followed him up the circling stairs. Arcane listened when he reached the hiding stone. He did not think anyone would be in the storeroom at this hour, but this course of action was dangerous.

Hearing nothing, Arcane lifted the stone just enough to peek through. The storeroom was dark. Arcane lifted the stone a few more inches and the spider which had taken its spot on the ceiling of the stairwell ran through the gap, up the wall and disappeared from Arcane's sight as it tucked itself into a nook of one of the high windows.

With the spider safely delivered Arcane pushed the stone up further and walked into the supply room. Arcane looked through the supplies that sat on the shelves. The animate took a large piece of stone that had veins of metal running through it and some finely drawn wire. Arcane returned to the stairs and the stone slipped into place above him. His treasures in hand, he retreated from the House of Animate.

The spider raced quickly up the wall, its four legs leaving invisible pock marks in the stone behind it as it ran. It reached a window nook and stopped. The ledge was wide enough to hide upon. The blanket of dust showed that it would not be disturbed here. The window had vertical bars across it. The spider, balancing on three legs began poking at the windowpane, intent on making its way outside. After several minutes of prodding the glass broke free, tumbling down the cliff in a thousand pieces.

The spider stepped out onto the vertical wall and hurried up the side. Below it the wall gave way to rocky cliff meeting the sea hundreds of feet below. The animate, reaching the roof, crossed over Master Jannan's laboratory, Trahn Entrah's laboratory and study and finally stopped, hanging slightly over the roof looking down at the ground below. The eastern facing wall had windows that allowed light into the library of the House. The animate descended the wall and began stabbing at the window. Its entrance would need to allow the animate to carry books out of the library. So it was commanded by Arcane, so it would be.

The window gave way to the animate's persistence and it skittered inside and surveyed the room.

No one used the library at this early hour, so the animate proceeded down the wall and ran along the top of the shelves to the opposite wall. Then it leapt down onto the nearest table. The spider pushed the books on the table with its front legs, looking for one not on the list that Arcane had given it.

Not finding one on the table the animate leapt back to the top of the shelves. It hooked its two rear legs and dropped its body over the edge. Finding a book that was not excluded it used its forelegs to pull it from the shelf. *The Creation of the House of Animate* dropped with an excruciatingly loud bang to the floor. The spider, at the sound, skittered into the corner and waited. After making sure that it would not be discovered the animate descended to the floor. It grasped the book in its claw.

Awkwardly it climbed back to the top of the bookshelves, circled the room and exited through the hole in the window.

The animate carried its newly found treasure along the top of the House, back to the storeroom. It hid the book on one of the high shelves and settled into the window nook to wait. Arcane had instructed it to proceed cautiously, so it rested on its theft, content to rummage more later.

After the sun had risen, a mage came to the storeroom to get supplies. Celia Hurn had no idea what sat above her, watching.

Arcane hurried through the forest towards the Heele Estate. The sun had begun to rise and the light cast by it lit the mist that rolled in patches over the countryside, settling in the depressions of the land. Birds cawed and chirped somewhere above him. The animate was lost in thought as he tracked his way through the undergrowth, avoiding the road as was his practice.

The first arrow struck Arcane in the back, the impact rolling him forward onto the ground. The stone and wire that he carried scattered before him. The arrow had pierced his body, pushing dangerously close to his crystalline core. Arcane at first did not understand what had happened as he lay in the ferns. It did not hurt, but there was an unpleasant recognition that he was damaged. He pushed himself up to his knees, looking around. A second arrow whistled from behind, striking him. The ring of metal on metal silenced the birds. The arrow ricocheted off of him, but the impact knocked him back to the ground. Arcane rolled to his back cracking the shaft of the arrow impaled in him and sat up, looking towards the forest where the arrows came from.

Two men appeared from the undergrowth, almost waist deep in ferns, bows drawn. Both men were several days unshaven, and dressed to match the plants around them. Arcane sat in amazement at what had just transpired. The men spoke to each other.

"What is that, Nod?" the one on the left with dark hair and a crooked nose asked.

"I don't know. I don't know. I just saw it moving, couldn't see it clearly. We both hit it though. It's just sitting there. Let's get a closer look, it can't be dangerous now," the other said, voice gravelly.

"Sure, just keep that bow trained on it." His confidence clearly came from the other man.

The hunters walked forward carefully, weaving in between pine trees with deadly intent. Arcane frowned. 'Will these humans never leave me be?' he thought. With the men fast approaching Arcane got to his feet.

"What? What the?" the dark haired hunter yelled.

"It's an animate. Stay calm. Stay calm!" Nod answered, bow drawn tight. He eyed Arcane warily. An upward flip of his head acknowledged Arcane. "What are you doing out here?"

"I was returning home, from an errand for my master. He will be most unhappy with your attack against me," Arcane lied, his metallic voice in stark contrast with the humans.

"Home? There aren't any places other than Heele's out this way that have animates. And I'm Heele if yer Bessemer." The man paused, thinking. "I bet it's that wanted animate, Eric. The House is offering a reward for its return. Just stay right there, animate. Don't move," the hunter Nod said, motioning Eric closer with a twitch of his head. "Go get it. I'll make sure it doesn't run."

Eric lowered his bow and cautiously approached Arcane. Arcane waited for one second, pondering his options, then broke into a run.

"Hey!" Eric yelled.

Nod followed Arcane's movement, torso turning slightly and let the bow string go. The arrow traveled the short distance in a blink of an eye and pierced Arcane's upper arm, throwing the animate to the ground. Before Arcane could get up Eric was standing over him, bow drawn, arrow pointed at him. The other thrashed through the ferns until he was also standing over the animate.

"Thought you could run, eh?" Nod said, "Don't count on it. I'm the best shot around these parts. Better then most of the Wrath mages in Serac too. Just ask Eric."

"He is," Eric said, his voice confirming the sentiment.

"Get it up. If we hurry back to the inn we can get it into town by afternoon."

"Sure. Sure," Eric said excitedly. Eric shouldered his bow quickly and bent over to pull the twice punctured animate up. Arcane got to his feet easily; there was no chance of escape if he stayed on the ground. The man's hands were warm on Arcane's metal skin.

He questioned, "Now where were you trying to get to?"

Arcane could feel the warmth creeping through his body. As it spread through him Arcane began to laugh. The clash of metal against metal was fully understood by the hunters as mockery. Arcane was fully filled with glee and despair, joyous at the power filling him and hateful of the reality before him.

"Why are you laughing?" Nod asked, concern creeping into his voice. "Stop it!" The archer drew the bowstring back, startled by the animate's bizarre response to being captured.

Arcane twisted his left arm inside Eric's, grabbing the man's forearm and clamping down tightly. It was not enough to hurt the man, but he could not pull free as he was forced to his knees by the smaller form. Arcane's right arm extended towards Nod, who yelled something that did not penetrate Arcane's blissful state. A light appeared several inches from Arcane's hand. For what seemed an eternity all three watched the light as it danced. Before Nod could free himself from the trance a metal sliver hurled from the light, piercing his chest with accuracy that the marksman would envy. Nod's heart did not beat again. The hunter screamed as he fell, pain wracking his body. His bow fired errantly, the arrow hitting Eric in the side. The man yelped in pain, but it was drowned out by the scream of Nod. The man crumpled to the ground, dead, metal bolt stuck through his chest.

Eric tried to pull away but Arcane's grip tightened like a vise, holding the man in place. "Gah!" Eric blurted out.

Arcane said, "Amazing, Eric." The man struggled unsure if he should try to free himself or hold his side where he bled, arrow impaled. Arcane ignored his moaning. "It is clear how you humans ignore the walls. Magic should be so easy for your kind, and yet you do struggle with it so."

"What...what are you talking about?" Eric said, panic soaked. The man decided that it was better to free himself from Arcane then extract the arrow rather than the other way around and with a desperate heave he broke away from the metal grasp. Immediately Arcane could feel the warmth retreating, but it was not gone yet.

"I am sorry that you do not understand," was all Arcane said. The animate held his hands close together and the dancing light appeared again. The sliver of silver metal jutted through the injured man where he lay, impaling him to the earth. He writhed in the ferns but his screams were held at bay by death.

All at once the cold returned. Arcane fell to his knees; this pain was real. He had not realized before how cold he was. With the cold came the desperation, stronger than ever. Arcane pulled the arrow from his arm, it cracked and broke as it came out, and forced himself back to his feet; he had to return to the safety of the Heele Estate. But now he returned with answers. Above the grisly scene the birds settled in the trees and begin to chirp and wail. Arcane glanced up at them, gathered his belongings and then hurried through the forest.

Guard Loal Richarson's horse trotted the road to the Heele Estate. Master Jannan had been adamant about sending a guard the half-day trip to inquire about the animate's exotic purchases. Loal was glad he brought a wool cloak to wrap over the guard uniform. The day was cold, fall had come early this year, though the trees did not know it yet; they kept their summer green.

Loal tied his horse to an old post and walked up the stone stairs to the front door of the estate. A massive brass knocker, fashioned as a lion's head with ring in mouth was sounded by the guard. Then he waited. There was no answer. Loal huffed and crashed the lion's ring again. Shortly the double doors opened. Bessemer, rat in hand, smiled at the guard.

"Guard. Good day."

Loal looked quizzically from the rat to the animate.

Bessemer following his eyes said, "The rats have been particularly bad this year. This one was in the master's bedroom. Simply awful."

"I imagine. Is the master home?" Loal asked, shifting his weight

"He is not. He is gone on a hunting expedition. If it pleases you, sir, I can let him know that you called upon him in his absence," Bessemer spoke flatly.

"If he is gone, why were you in town?" the guard questioned.

"It was adequately addressed. I was shopping for the estate. As Lord Heele's butler I am held responsible for such matters," the animate said, pointing at the guard.

"The Campus Guard and the House of Animate would question the purchase of technologist crystal."

"Would they? If you must know, my master's aides are in need of repair. It will be done when he returns."

"Aides?" Loal said.

"Lord Heele does not see or hear as well as he once did. He commissioned help from the technologists. If that is all, guard, have a safe journey back to Serac."

"Thank you for your time," Loal said, bowing slightly to the animate as it closed the door. "Strange. The toy seemed almost defensive at the questions."

Loal began the journey back to Serac. Bessemer stood at a side window. The animate watched the guard ride away. The look of disgust on the animate's face was unmistakable, though none saw it. 'Arcane will be most concerned.'

Bessemer found Arcane down in the workshop. Before he could speak Arcane said, "The rat. Is it alive?"

Bessemer was surprised by Arcane's interest in the animal. "Barely. But yes. We had—"

Arcane did not allow him to continue. "Quickly! Give it to me!"

Bessemer handed the rat to Arcane. Arcane smiled as he took it. He said, "It is weak. Watch."

Arcane put his right hand up, fingers and thumb close together, a small flame ignited, flickered for a moment then extinguished. "Much to my surprise, the Masa'terj seems capable of drawing magic from other sources if they are nearby. It is not a simple amplifier as I thought. Nor is it the power I desire, borrowing on the graces of others, but it will have to do for the time being." The flame reappeared adding its light to the eyes of the animates. "Beautiful."

"I am sorry to mention this, but a Campus Guardsman was just here, asking about my purchase of crystal. I believe they are put off for now, but it will be difficult to purchase more in Serac if they are keeping a close watch."

"This game continues. For each achievement, however small, another obstacle is placed before us." Arcane turned away from Bessemer, dropping the rat to the floor. It bounced once but did not move again. "It is of little concern right now, I have other obligations. Leave me."

"As you wish Arcane," Bessemer said, leaving the other animate alone in his workshop.

Arcane's mind swirled in thought about Serac. 'It would be best for me to leave it far behind, as Bessemer suggested. But it is the strongest tie to my desire. I will have to make do for now.' The animate took up a piece of crystal and began to work.

The sun set below the horizon leaving Serac blanketed in darkness. On the ledge the spider animate stood and scurried across the roof of the House. The library was not empty this time. Two mages sat arguing. The spider stopped and waited for the humans to leave the library. When they did it set to finding another book for Arcane. Finding a suitable title, the spider plucked it from the shelf and carried it back to the storeroom. Then it took up its place sitting, waiting either for another day to pass or for Arcane to return.

Eleven

The spider could feel the presence of the animate as it came up the stairs. It was Arcane, and with him came two more of the spiders. Arcane pushed the cover stone out of its bed and the two spiders rushed from the stairs, up the wall, finally stopping on the ledge where the first rested. The two newcomers, both one third smaller than the first, tapped the body of the larger animate with their front legs; a greeting of some sort, then rushed out the broken window into the night.

The original started the final cycle of its instructions. One at a time it carried the books to Arcane, five in total. The animate looked at each as it was delivered and placed them in turn on the stair beside him. He was pleased with the small animate's work; it had only brought books that Master Jannan had not given him in his creation, just as Arcane had commanded. When the books, one for each day that had passed, were delivered it began to climb the wall back to its perch but Arcane summoned it with a wisp of magic.

The spider hurried into the stairwell and Arcane dropped the stone back into place. He picked it up, and instinctively the four legs clutched Arcane's hand. Arcane placed his other hand over the top of it and gave it new instructions. Now the spider was to go out into Serac, to map the tunnels that connected the surface with the docks below. Why? It did not know, only that Arcane commanded it to do so. The stone was lifted and as before the spider rushed from the hidden stairway, up the wall out into the world. Arcane smiled as it went.

All three were now performing useful tasks. The smaller of the clawed spiders headed to the library at The House of Currents. It would have books covering a greater scope than could be found in the House of Animate's library. Arcane realized that his focus had been too limited, sending the first spider to the House of his creation. The other Houses held knowledge that he needed. And he would take it.

The other spider had taken longer to build. Instead of the claw used to grasp large items it had two arms that could be released under the body. At the end of each arm a three-fingered hand could be used to pull and pry. That animate went to the Technologist District. It was a thief, designed to steal the crystal that their cores were made from. Arcane thought it risky but the circumstances demanded it. If the humans watched Bessemer carefully it could not buy what Arcane wanted, and he did not trust a human to do it for him. No, they would give him back into the hands of the House of Animate. Arcane would make sure that it did not happen. It would not be allowed.

Arcane carried the books down into the tunnel. There he sat and read them one after another. It was useful, but not in anyway insightful, information. Arcane sighed, as much as the animate could, stood and walked down the hall. He would not return to the Heele Estate tonight, but he did not want to wait so close to the House of Animate.

As Arcane rested, pondering his actions, and the reactions the humans had and would have to his actions, he noticed something creeping closer to him. It was not in the hall, but in the soil above the tunnel. It circled him once, coming closer. Arcane stared through the wall; he could tell it was now there, moving ever closer. It was in the hall now, but nothing, nothing gave itself to his eyes. The warmth, so soft. Something alive. He extended his right arm, sopping in the power. It watched him. Then it was gone.

Tara Groundmender's breathing was slow and long, drinking in the earthy air. She sat cross-legged, hands resting on her knees. Her daily lessons had lasted late into the night and to clear her mind of the frustration of the teaching, and her failure, she meditated. But it bordered on sleep. Her thoughts rolled away from her, swept into the night. Her mind was peaceful. She held the Way, the magic, at bay unconsciously, built by practice. Tara now suspected that the Earth, the very heart of the Way, was somehow influenced by the Mother in a large, baffling way. Tara's body relaxed, and that is when the dream, if it was one, turned.

She was pulled, wrenched, from the peace. The Way pulled her down, the sweet drowning; this time for a moment she gave in to it, unafraid. She could not tell what she was being shown, but in this vision of warmth and sweetness of flowers, there was cold. She approached it, not walking, not flying, just approached it. How far it was she did not know. The cold form swirled and hissed. Tara circled it once, from a distance, she felt that it followed her. Watching her.

The mist, again Tara was not exactly sure if it was, took shape. A human shape. Empty. It was empty. Tara knew that that was not right, a man should not be empty. Tiny streamers of mist crawled from the void's arm, pulsing towards Tara. She tried to draw back but could not, wet soil held her in place. The Way had trapped her. Tara began to panic, the strings coming close, one deep breath, and she was released. Fleeing. A vision of two golden lights burned into her head. Two cold eyes. Tara opened her eyes. The Mother stood before her.

The spider roved quickly across the Wizard Campus, guided by a map that Arcane had taken from Bessemer's mind. Brazen with assurances of invisibility in the night it ran full speed over open ground. Even if someone caught a passing glance they would not know what to make of the creature. The moon was plump but clouds circled and fluttered before it, obscuring much of the light that it gave.

Over the fence to the west it went, leaving behind its brothers to perform whatever task Arcane had given them. It scrabbled up a two story building and ran rooftop to rooftop towards its destination. Soon it reached the Technologist District. Given a great selection to choose from for its chore it chose a guarantee. The shop Bessemer had endorsed was elected. The spider climbed to a high window and slipped between bars that were not designed to keep something of its size and shape out. It picked away at the window, breaking it and entered the shop's attic.

The attic was neatly kept with stacked boxes pressed against the walls, making a walkway down the center. The spider followed the walkway and found the door to the shop below. Mustering its strength the animate pulled the door open. It

116

thumped onto the floor spewing dust into the air. The spider spun the thickness of the floor and walked along the ceiling of the workshop. The old wood workbench was neatly arranged, tools ready to be used the next day.

The spider hopped down onto the safe. Curiously, it was not locked. In fact the door hung wide open, exposing the more delicate and valuable commodities of the technologists' trade to the animate. The spider's two arms lowered from its body and began pulling out trays. Wire of all types, metal in various states, gems that glowed in the soft light of the animate's eye. Then the tray with the crystal was found. Bremen had restocked in glory, each specimen more beautiful than the last. In each small hand the spider plucked a crystal from the tray. The spider ascended the wall, climbing up to the attic and out to the tile roof. It dropped the crystals there and repeated the procedure, making several trips with no incident.

As it descended for the last time, all but one piece had been moved to the roof, a light burst forth from a darkened corner. The technologist holding the lamp pointed at the miniature thief and said, "Ah ha, an animate! It was good fortune that I forgot my spectacles!"

The spider turned to flee back to the attic but the door flipped shut at the behest of the man. "There is no escape for you that way!" Henry pointed a small, clear wand that he had drawn from under his coat at the spider. The summoned chill knocked it to the floor. The animate thrashed, righting itself and charged the aging mage. Another flick of the wand smashed the animate back to the wall with snow splaying around it. "We'll soon find out who you belong to, then there will be hell to pay," Bremen said with glee, a song trembled in his words.

The man crossed the room, wand pointed at the animate, always motioning it back to the corner when it scuttled about. The animate crouched low, then jumped straight at Technologist Bremen. Before another snowy blast could be fired, the spider knocked the wand away. Bremen dropped the magic lantern as he attempted to deflect the metal beast. The animate circled around the man, stabbing into the back of his neck with its front legs. He cursed, grasped the animate, pulled it over his head and smashed it to the floor. The animate bounced, twitched, and regained its feet, redoubling its attack.

The technologist, realizing that the animate would not be disposed of easily,

117

desperately searched for the wand as he tried to fight off the frantic stabbing of the spider. Blood oozed from the wounds where the animate found its mark. Seeing the wand softly reflecting the misdirected light, Henry gathered it and in one motion spun, throwing the animate from his overcoat into the air. Extending the wand a bolt of blue light sizzled through the air. It struck the animate, encasing it in solid ice, legs protruding. The animate dropped with a bang to the floor, but the ice held and it slid into the wall. The wand dissolved with the soft ringing of bells or the distant shattering of ice, Henry was unsure which.

Technologist Bremen held his neck, trying to ascertain the extent of his wounds. Picking up the lamp he went to his workbench and took up another clear wand. Another bolt of ice and the animate was completely frozen. 'I must rouse Silas, he'll know what to do,' the man thought to himself. He hurried from his store onto the street and off to Aron's home.

Bremen pounded furiously on the front door of Aron's home, which was by design also his workshop and show room. He lived above it in a finely appointed apartment with his wife. It took several minutes of banging and shouting before either stirred. Pulling back the wool curtains Silas saw Bremen below, so he hurried down the stairs to the door.

Sleep pulled like a weight on his eyelids, he struggled with the words; he would not remember the first exchange later. "Henry, it's past midnight. You had better have a wonderful reason for waking me up at this time and in this chill." Aron shuddered, pulling his bedclothes tight.

"I was attacked in my shop by an animate, Silas. It's frozen, in a block of solid ice," Bremen fought to stand; the euphoria of the fight was wearing thin.

Silas, hearing the violent news, cast sleep off, though it may have been the nasty chill in the air. "Henry, you are bleeding. Badly." Silas pulled the wounded man into the showroom by his arms. He said, "I'll call Mural and send him for a Way mage. Then we'll sort this all out." He waved without thinking at a lamp on the wall and it glowed soft light upon the room. Susan had come down the stairs, and she took Henry from him. "I'll be right back."

Silas went out into the cold, crossed the street down a little ways and hammered the door. Mural opened it, sleep and shaggy hair, clearly in need of cutting, in his eyes. Silas said, "Hurry up to the Campus, rouse the guard and a Way mage. Hurry!"

Mural rubbed his eyes and nodded, he grabbed a scarf and a lantern then hurried away into the night; the youth's long legs chewed up the road. It was good though, that the guild housing was so close. Silas returned to his showroom.

Henry bobbed and weaved, leaving blood on the polished floor. He said softly, his eyes losing focus on the immediate, "The animate is frozen back in my workshop. I knew the frost wands would work."

Silas looked at his wife then spoke with equal parts concern and motherly condescendence, "Wonderful, Henry." Susan brought a chair and Silas settled Henry into it. He kneeled down in front of him. "The guard will be busy again. Can you tell me what happened?"

Bremen answered, head bobbing like a boat on the sea, "I was preparing for bed, I always read a bit before I sleep you know, when I realized that I left my spectacles at the workshop. Some of us aren't so lucky as to live above our workshop you know. So I went back to my shop. I saw a little light inside, running this way and that and I thought, 'Well what is that?' I waited until it went back to the attic and I went inside. When it came back we fought, it tried to run, but I stopped it." The man's eyes fluttered, trying to focus.

"Enough, Henry, tell me later. Just rest now."

"Yes, that would be good."

Bremen sat humming to himself as Silas paced, trying to figure out what was going on. He would have to see the animate. He couldn't imagine one of the mages from the House doing this, but if it was an animate it had to be theirs. He did not think Bremen was hurt badly, but he did not want to risk that he was and leave him alone. So Silas paced, his feet falling into step with the disjointed tune that Bremen hummed. It was a child's song, he thought, familiar, but not at all easy to keep time to

The bells of The House of Currents rang once. Just as Silas was beginning to wonder where that boy was Mural threw open the door to the showroom. Three guards, in their black uniform and properly armed with swords, an oversight that had been corrected after the Olmstead affair, were coming down the street, outpaced by the apprentice. "The Way mage will be along shortly, Master Aron. The Mother sends her concern."

"You do hurry don't you? Guards, it appears that Master Bremen was attacked in his workshop. He says it was by an animate and that it's frozen in a block of ice. One of you stay here, the other two, come with me, I'll show you the way and we can get to the bottom of all of this."

The ranking guard, Loal, glanced at one of the others and said, "You stay here with the technologist. Once he is healed find out what happened." Then the two followed Silas, in his bedclothes, into the great goodnight.

Technologist Bremen's shop was dark inside. Aron, Loal, and Derek stood outside. Loal and Derek drew their swords, unimpressive pieces of workmanship, and opened the door. Derek jumped as the door chime played. Loal laughed and said, "Still afraid of children's toys?"

Derek shot the ranking guard a snide look but said nothing. Silas followed them in and with a wave of his hand lit the crystal lamp that hung on the wall. Water crept ever so slowly from behind the bar that split the room in half. None of the men could see behind the wall from where they stood. Silas took the lead, pushing past the two guards while holding his nightshirt closed, and stepped through the half door.

There lay the spider animate encased in its icy tomb. One hook had melted free and it scratched hopelessly at the ice. It could not free itself. Silas frowned; he had not wanted to believe that an animate had been the attacker. Clearly it was. "Bring it," he said to the guards. 'What is the House of Animate playing at?'

The guards picked up the piece of ice. The exposed tip twitched angrily when the ice was disturbed. Loal jumped, but Derek said nothing, only smiling. Loal glowered at him, which made Derek's smile fuller. The two guards went back to the street with the prison. Silas extinguished the light and locked the door; it was a simple spell. "Back to my workshop, guards."

Loal said, "This is evidence of a crime and should be taken—"

"Taken to my workshop. Now go!" Silas said thunderously. His anger at the confusing situation splashed his words. This time both guards jumped and immediately fell into line behind the technologist.

Tara Groundmender hurried through the night, an orb of light bouncing along over her shoulder. She was only vaguely aware of her sending to Technologist Aron's workshop. The Mother had stirred her from some dream or trance or meditation, Tara did not know which. It didn't much matter now she imagined. The cold, surprisingly strong, pushed in around her. She sighed and pulled the cloak closer around her and tighter against her ears. Her pace quickened.

It did not take long to find her destination. It was the only building on the street that had all of its lights blazing forth, a beacon to the mage, not exactly wayward. Even if the lights had been extinguished Tara thought she could have found it. Something, something strong, guided her. The Earth perhaps. In any case, pulled along or simply lucky, here she was. Inside she could see the black uniform of a Campus Guard and her mind drifted for a moment to Alexander.

The door to the showroom was thrown open and in the fury of welcoming some spicy drink was thrust into her hands, the mug almost too hot to hold. Tara sipped it, the warmth creeping down into her belly. She turned her attention to the humming, and clearly hurt man. This injury was not as disastrous as the thief's leg but the multitude of deep, small wounds presented an interesting problem in themselves, which was in Tara's mind the reason that Mother Rainmarrow sent her here. Always a lesson to be learned.

Tara finished the last of her spiced tea and prepared herself for the healing. She thought about all the things she had learned and practiced over the last several days. She closed her eyes. Almost immediately the room and its distractions faded, all but the little song that Bremen hummed. It hung in the front of her mind. Which was fine.

Tara placed her hands on the man's temples and the humming softened. She smiled, it had taken her a while to place the song, it was one that her mother used to sing to quiet her when she was a child and the weather stormed. She did not remember the exact words, or perhaps the Earth flooded them away.

In keeping with her learning the Way was conserved. She did not speak the words; power flowed without them. She opened her eyes. The visible wounds, the deep punctures on the technologist's neck had healed into soft bruises. His eyes fluttered and a grin crossed his face. Understanding what had transpired he said,

"Thank you, daughter. I am in your debt."

Tara blushed. "It's not necessary, Master Bremen. When there is need we will aid." She sounded like the Mother, which deepened her embarrassment.

"Please, allow me to give you my thanks," the technologist insisted, standing. His attention turned to his clothes, he said, "Unfortunately these pants are ruined. Blood everywhere, how awful." He laughed, it was an uncharacteristic joke and the others joined him. He recounted the story to the guard, who took notes on a piece of paper, using one of Aron's quills.

After the story was given Susan said, "Master Bremen, would you like some spiced tea?"

"No. No. Absolutely not, makes me ill."

"Daughter Groundmender, more?" she asked attempting to fill time as they waited for Silas to return.

"Yes. Please."

Silas and the guards stomped in from Henry's workshop. The block of ice was placed on a table and everyone gathered around it, marveling at the animate inside. Susan offered Silas and the guards tea, which they all accepted, gratefully. The guards held the teacups in both hands, warming their fingers.

Loal looked at the notes as he drank his tea, nodding. "This looks complete enough to file the report."

Silas said, "I will keep the animate here until morning. Go well into the night."

Loal answered, "Thank you, Technologist Aron, for the call. And the tea. All finished?" he asked the other two guards. They nodded; the three left the technologist's shop.

Now in the company of mages Aron said, "I did not want to believe it was an animate. Tomorrow morning, Henry, we will call on Trahn. He will address this insanity, and give reparation." He hit his balled up hand into his palm. "Excellent tea by the by. I do not believe we have met, good sister." Silas offered his large hand in greeting. "I am Silas Aron, head of the Technologist Guild."

Tara smiled at being addressed as an equal, as sister, by the technologist. Most called the Way mages sons or daughters, as the Mother did. Most of the Way took no offense, but it was somewhat lessening, Tara thought. She lost her hand in his and said, "Tara Groundmender. Master Technologist. It is a pleasure to meet you, though the circumstances confuse the event."

"Indeed they do, Tara. Indeed they do. And I do not know what insult has caused the House of Animate to do this." Turning the conversation back to Bremen, "You should take inventory before we go tomorrow with our grievance. Discover if anything is missing. I will have the others do this as well. This may not be the first such event, just the first that was discovered."

Tara listened to all of this, marveling at the quickly forming disagreement. She was not schooled in the politics of the city and it came as some small surprise. But it did make sense, she guessed. She remembered the fishmongers and the shipping guild in Riversea. Silas speaking to her undid her distraction of home, "Thank you again, Sister. Please excuse my colleagues and I. We have much to do before morning. Go well into the night." It seemed one of Aron's favorite sayings.

Tara did as much. Despite the air being colder, and Tara was sure that it was, the spiced tea kept her warm all the way back, and the light that hovered on her shoulder seemed to dance this way and that, keeping time with the tune that Bremen had been humming.

When the Way mage had gone Silas said, "Mural, is there a box or cage that we can put this block of ice in? I don't want the ice melting and the animate running all over the place. We already know it's a nasty little thing."

"I'll see what I can find, sir. I'm sure there's a shipping crate in the basement that would hold it," the apprentice answered, disappearing into the back room. He gallumped down the stairs, a horse instead of a man, the racket brought a smile to Silas's face for just a moment.

"Well, Henry, this is a fine mess we've found ourselves in. That's for certain."

"That it is. That it is." Thumps and thuds came up through the floor. Bremen looked at the floor though he focused past it, looking at the sounds. "That boy is as clumsy as ever."

"Yes, well almost as much. He has a natural talent for the trade. He surprises even me with some of the work he can already do. I won't be the head of

123

the guild for long once everyone learns about him."

"Oh, Wrath. You'll be the head until you step down or die, Silas."

Silas crossed his arms over his barrel chest. Feigning indignation he said, "Charming. I can only hope you'll be at my wake."

Bremen smiled, the wrinkles of time gathering around his eyes. "You can count on it." His head wheeled as he thought of the evening. He said, "Well, I'm off for my workshop. I'll take that inventory tonight, and call early. No reading tonight I'm afraid."

"That reminds me. I sealed the door with a charm, it's a basic one, but it would keep out most," Silas said raising two fingers on his right hand and cocking his head.

"Ah, thanks, I completely forgot I suspect. See you in the morning. Susan." The door of the showroom again opened, allowing the cold free reign for several seconds. Then it closed leaving Silas with the frozen animate.

He bent at the waist, hands on his knees, looking carefully at the distorted image of the animate. He spoke softly, "And who do you belong to, you nasty little thing? I'll soon find out, I will."

As if the animate knew it was being spoken to the exposed hook, which had stopped moving while it was being carried scratched back and forth twice. Silas shook his head and sat down. Mural thumped up the stairs and appeared with a box.

"This will hold it, and its not even a box with a deposit on it," he said, proud of himself.

"Good, some of those shippers charge an arm and a leg for those things. I guess it's not easy to replace them. Let's get that thing in there." The technologist and his apprentice lifted the block of ice. The block slid into place with no struggle at all. "Hmm, well. Let's put it out back, the cold will slow the melting."

The lid hammered into place, the box was carried out the back door and set on the porch. The two returned to the showroom, Susan had gone up to bed. Silas said, "Well done all around tonight."

"Thank you, sir."

Silas rubbed his forehead with grief and said, "I am going to get some sleep. I recommend you do the same. This is just the start of this debacle and I have no idea where this will lead."

Henry Bremen tried three different spells before the lock opened. When Silas said that it was a basic charm, he meant the most simple, basic, beginner lock spell possible. Anyone with half a brain could have undone it. 'Well, never mind that. The inventory.'

Henry lit the lamps, uncovering the mess that the animate had made looking for the crystal. In order he picked up the trays, replacing everything that belonged, weighing everything that had to be weighed. He compared his lists with what was there, and what was there in his memory. In the end, all that was missing were the crystals that he had bought recently to replace what he had sold. He scribbled it all down on a scrap of paper so as to remember the exact numbers. One piece was still in the safe. Which meant that the number of pieces missing was sixteen.

It was then that Bremen remembered the open door to the attic. He found his ladder. As he flipped the door open a great plume of dust launched into the air as before. Henry sneezed once. The attic was not well lit and he imagined another animate behind every box and in every shadow, so he went back down the rungs, gathered his lantern and climbed back up. It did not take long to find the broken window. 'So this is how the little monster got in,' he thought to himself, quite happy at his discovery. 'I should clean this glass up now.'

Without another thought he went down to his shop, closing the attic door behind him. His body did not agree with his assessment, and his mind did not have much left to say, so it did not argue with his body. He took the scrap of paper, locked the front door and went home, leaving his forgotten spectacles forgotten on his workbench.

Twelve

Senior Guard John Ames did not enjoy riding horses. It made his back ache and his legs stiff, tired and numb. But here he was riding out of Serac with Roman Michaels and Alexander Gin. Normally the county sheriff, almost a volunteer organization, could be counted on to deal with problems this far from town, but the request for help had been most panicked. John felt a headache creeping on.

The largest problems in and around Serac consisted of petty theft and bar fights, and the city guard could easily handle them. Any more serious crimes were held in check by the presence of the mages, and the repercussions against those angering them were most serious indeed, but it seemed that the magic that kept Serac calm had vanished.

The last week had given the Campus Guard more work than the previous ten years combined. First the Olmstead affair, then the animate attacking the technologist, and now murder. Or so the letter said. Sheriff Young had sent it from the district west of Serac. His reputation, known to be reliable and calm, as much as anything in the letter convinced Senior Guard Ames to leave Serac and travel the morning west.

The letter asked them to meet at the Red Wolf Inn on the road to Riversea. The Red Wolf was a few hours from Serac and was popular with the sort that were too rowdy for the city. Mercenaries, bounty hunters, professional killers, that sort. Caravans traveling from Serac knew they were for hire and less attention was paid to past transgressions.

The three guards came upon the inn as the sun rose low over the horizon. It was a stocky two-story affair. Smoke billowed from the stone chimney, scenting the air of sweet wood. A stable boy took the horses around the side of the inn, leading them through high grass, still wet from the morning mist. The stable must have been hidden around back; that is what Ames hoped, otherwise, the horses had been stolen. John led his sword-wearing guards inside.

The sweet smoke filled the inn, making their eyes water and choking off what little light entered the windows. The man behind the bar laughed, thick, like the smoke in the air, and sort of mean. "Good morning! I don't imagine I can offer you a place to stay for the night as you've missed it. Unless of course you are fleeing the Campus. You aren't fleeing the Campus are you?" The man was painfully loud. Or maybe it was that every other noise, save the fire, had stopped and every grizzled eye in the place was turned on them.

His eyes still stinging, John leaned against the bar with his left arm, taking some weight of off his pained back. He answered, "No, no, not fleeing the Campus. Not yet. We're looking for Sheriff Young."

The proprietor mugged his nose with his left hand, and frowned. "That's ugly business, two of the best hunters in these parts. He's over there." The man gestured vaguely to the right. "Last booth. Let me know if I can get you anything."

"Hmm..." John paused.

"Just call me Red, everyone else does."

John's head bobbed, as if expecting the name. "Red." Then to the guards, "Watch yourselves in here; not the friendliest crowd. Let's find this buzzard."

Ames led his nervous men across the room. Finding the last booth, he said to the occupant, a single man, "Sheriff Young?" The leathery man nodded, his lips twitched. "Senior Guard John Ames. We came as quickly as we could."

"Yes. I see." The man stood up, leaving half a pint of ale on the table. "Let's go. No reason to antagonize the locals." Sheriff Young strolled calmly through the smoke, flipping a coin to Red, and left the inn. The guards followed close enough to absorb some of the protection that Young's aura gave off, but far enough back not to look hurried. They could hear Red's laughter through the door, when they again stood in the sun.

Young said, "The horses are comin'."

As the sheriff said, the stable boy brought the horses, leading all four by the reins. Sheriff Young's horse, when compared to the others, was gorgeous. Tall, dark, strong. Gin thought that Young smiled when he saw the rest, but he couldn't tell for sure, and he wasn't about to question a man that smelled more of danger than smoke.

Sheriff Young started talking as they got the horses ready to ride. "Two hunters for the inn, by the names of Eric and Nod, went missing. No one thought much of it. They're experienced woodsmen. When the inn's supply of meat ran low, Red hired a couple of others. They found the bodies. And I don't deal with magic problems. I'll leave this to you. Hiyah!" His horse started south, crossing the road, and into the forest.

Michaels and Gin gave one another confused looks. Gin said, "This guy is a real piece of work."

"Quiet, Gin," Ames said, "Let's go."

The three guards followed the sheriff through the woods, the scraggly pine trees operating as guidance for the sheriff. He had shouldered a bow; John hoped that it had been stowed with the horse, since he had not seen it before. He did not think his mind was going, but his headache had begun to growl.

It was almost three-quarters of an hour later when Sheriff Young whistled for the horses to stop. "This is it." He leaned forward and patted his horse's head. "Well, do your work."

The guards all sighed and got off their horses. Michaels horse stamped the ground, he whispered calming words into her ear.

"Where are the bodies, sheriff?" Ames asked.

"Just over the ridge. You'll see it, the underbrush is all broken up."

The guards walked in silence, birds calling at them, mocking from high up in the trees. The wind blew slightly, away from the men. The underbrush, the ferns and nettles and huckleberries, were exactly as the sheriff had described, broken up – crushed leaves, bent stems. And the bodies. One lay on his front, his chest propped up several inches from the ground, a bolt of metal driven through his heart. The other was limp, bent backwards, arrow in his side, metal shaft through his chest. Flies swarmed the scene.

Gin muttered what they all thought, "Oh, Wrath! What is going on?" Then defensively, "That would explain why they didn't come back."

Ames and Michaels both glared at him for his effort.

John frowned, wishing for the smell of smoke. "Gin, map the area, see if there is any sign of additional struggle. Roman. You and I get to examine the bodies."

Roman's face was queasy. He said, "I can tell you all you need to know. They're dead. What do we need to even look for?"

"Two men are dead, Roman. Magic is involved. We need to find out who did this, and then we can find out why. If it is a rogue mage, they have to be tried before the Directorate Council. You knew the hazards when you signed up," Ames answered; his pep talk was not what he had wished it to be.

"I didn't think the hazards would happen."

Gin returned to the horses and took paper from a supply bag, then wandered the forest mapping the scene as best he could. Ames knelt by the body closest, it was face down in the ferns. "That one is Nod!" The sheriff stood on the crest of the hill and shouted down at them.

Ames nodded. "Making the other poor soul Eric."

Michaels looked up the hill, "Not very helpful is he?"

"I don't blame him for giving us this job. I would if I was in his position."

John swatted at the swarm of flies. It dispersed into a cloud; Roman waved his hands, swatting at the insects. Ames noticed the bow dropped to the side of the man. "I'd say he was hit in the chest, and let his arrow go when he dropped his bow."

Michaels finished, "Right into the side of the other."

"Help me here." John placed his foot on the back of the remains of Nod and pulled at the metal spear that had penetrated all the way through. At first the bolt did not want to move, but it was persuaded, with a sickening crunch, to exit the wound. John shivered. This was something very, very foul.

"Looks like just the one injury," Roman said, getting into the spirit of the investigation.

"One is enough," Ames said, holding up the metal spear, the point infinitely sharp. All told it was about two feet long, with irregular sides. It twisted in the middle just slightly. Dried blood flaked off of it, leaving the metal clean. "Not the death I'd wish for."

Michaels scattered the flies that resided on Eric. His death was messier; blood from the arrow wound, and his right arm was bruised. Michaels asked, "Do you think he got the bruise from the attacker?" It circled his entire arm.

"Could be."

Michaels grasped the metal dart and pushed the dead man down with his foot. This one came loose with much the same sound. He handed it to John.

John said, "The Directorate Council will want to see these."

Michaels bent over, picking up a broken arrow. It was missing its tip. He showed John, and they both started searching for more. A few feet away under broken ferns Roman found the broken shaft, and then a full arrow that lay in the dirt. Michaels looked closely at the arrow. "Some sort of metal on the arrow head I think, John. It's a different color, darker. Armor maybe?"

"Three arrows, two clearly hitting a target, and a third. But no blood. I don't know what to make of this, Roman. I just want to open and close the gates. Wrath!"

The two searched the scene a while longer, finding nothing else, and Gin returned, his map in hand. The guards decided that their job here was done. They returned to the horses.

"What of it?" Sheriff Young asked.

"Bury them, pray it doesn't happen again," Ames answered.

"If it does?"

"Then you'll need more than the Campus Guard to save you."

The crate dropped to the floor with a dull thud. No one would even have noticed the sound it made if each and every person present in Master Jannan's laboratory had not been completely focused on the wet box. The lower third had absorbed the water and carried it up the sides along the edges of the slats giving the crate a striped appearance. Mural and Silas had carried the crate in, and Henry came to tell his story. Trahn and Murdoch stood near the crate. Both had concerned, bordering on appalled, expressions on their faces.

Soft clicking came from the box, before and after it was set down. The animists had heard rumors about the night before, the news in some limited form spreading quickly, but they were not entirely sure what to expect from this meeting. It had been demanded by Technologist Aron, and before it could be thought about, not that the House of Animate would have opposed it, the crate was sitting on the floor of the lab. Both parties had exchanged greetings, formal, painfully so.

"Be careful," Silas said, "I don't know how much the ice has melted and this is a nasty little thing." Using a well-aged pry bar that Mural had packed in, Silas removed the lid of the crate. The animate was partially contained in ice. Three of its four legs had the hinge exposed, and the ice had melted back showing a section of the body. The animate twitched all four legs as one every few seconds. "Look."

Everyone pressed around the crate, the animists stared in disbelief, Henry and Mural impressed that the ice had held on for the night. Trahn said, "Henry, tell me what happened."

The technologist recounted his tale once again, this time augmented with the knowledge of how the animate entered the workshop. Trahn's pale face lost its remaining color as he heard the details of the tale, of the animate, of its aggression.

Jannan while listening pulled the animate from the box and placed the icy mess on his table. It flopped a bit almost gaining traction with its three feet but it was unable to do anything. He put both hands over the animate. "Identification is a complete blank. Nothing," he said shaking his head.

Silas asked, "What does that mean?"

"There is no way to tell who made it." His left hand bent to the side, almost touching the leg. Silas pulled his arm away.

"You do not want to touch it," Silas said.

Carefully, more to appease Silas than because of any real fear, Jannan held his left hand to the side of the animate, moving it several times before finding the right spot. When he did his eyes opened wide. "Trahn, quickly."

Trahn placed his right hand above the animate, and his left to the side, finding the same spot. He shook his head. His arm sank as he marveled, brushing the tip of the leg. Immediately the leg slashed at Trahn's arm, easily ripping the sleeve of his robes. "Wrath!" he exclaimed, pulling away. The legs on the animate spasmed violently. Jannan pulled the First back, and placed his own hand on the leg pushing it away. The animate went completely still.

Silas said softly, his brow furrowing, "Odd. You calm it, Master Jannan."

"Is that an accusation?" Jannan asked sharply, voice raised. His mood had settled some, but Master Jannan's rough edges were still exposed.

"Only an observation."

Trahn checked his arm, exhaling when he saw that it was only a scratch. Then he said, "Gentlemen, please. That animate was not created by anyone in this House. It is far too complicated, not even Murdoch or I could have made it. Its operation instructions are an absolute maze, criss-crossing and jumping. Whoever made this understands our magic in ways that we can only hope to attain. It could be an old-world animate, but never has one been found operating and never this complete."

Silas frowned, "Are you absolving your House of guilt, Master Entrah?"

Trahn answered submissively, "Technologist Aron, Silas, please, do not jump to conclusions. It is clear that Master Bremen was grievously injured by this animate. Fortune smiled on him that such a skilled healer was sent. It would hurt both my House and your Guild if we allow this to come between us. The House would be willing to pay a sum of money for restitution, on the condition that we keep this animate."

A thin smile came across the technologist's face. "I believe we can work out a deal." Beside him Henry nodded vigorously.

"Come with me, gentlemen. I have guild notes in my study." Trahn led the three technologists out of Jannan's laboratory into the open square, then back inside and to his study. He sat down at the old desk and the technologists sat across from him. Mural stood. Trahn pulled open the bottom drawer. After rummaging through it for a minute, he placed a leather-bound book on his desk and wet a quill in ink. He opened the book of bank notes, and said, "Now then, Silas, I believe this is fair compensation." He wrote the amount on a piece of paper and slid it across the desk to the waiting technologists. They both looked at the number. Henry's expression did not change, and he did not say anything. Silas nodded, but his mouth had twitched. Trahn prepared for the claims of insult. They did not come.

"That is reasonable, Master Entrah," Silas said. Henry glanced sideways at his Guild leader but continued to say nothing.

Trahn said, "Let me prepare the note then." He wrote quickly, filling in the correct details, signed it, and stamped it with the seal of the House. Then he carefully removed the note from its binding and handed it to Silas. "The Banking Guild will honor it for gold value."

Silas nodded and said, "The Technologist Guild thanks you for your prompt resolution to this terrible event. Good day, Master Entrah." The technologists stood and were led from the room by the triumphant Silas. Trahn sat for a moment thinking, then got up, sighed and returned to Jannan's laboratory.

Murdoch had found an iron cage and Trahn Entrah watched as he placed the four-legged terror into it. The technologists had been sated for the time being, the sum of gold they accepted had not been as large as he had feared. Trahn was not a fool; he knew that the new animate Murdoch worked on for Silas would have to be of the highest quality to make up for this strange event. And he was most confused as to why the Second of the House could handle the vicious thing with impunity.

The ice had melted clean away, but the animate did not protest as Murdoch handled it. If Trahn even got close to it it would spasm and thrash violently trying to gore or rip him with the nasty hooks that passed for feet. Trahn knew that Murdoch did not, could not, have built the walker, but it was so curious a development that it gnawed at the integrity of the denial.

Into the cage it went, bars close enough together to hold some sort of songbird, more than tight enough to hold the animate. Murdoch frowned, and said, "I do not understand, Trahn. It acts like it recognizes me, but I have never seen this animate in my life." His tone was irritated. He bent down to put his head on the level of the cage. "It is a beautifully crafted piece. From the welds, to the hammering, to the imbued instructions." Jannan stood up straight.

Only with the animate caged did Trahn dare approach it. He had tried the shut down procedures, all of which were ignored. Jannan read his mind.

"I tried them all as well, even with contact. There is no protocol for shutting down, none that we use. Even if there is one, the operations are so cryptic it could take years to find."

"You still have that gift then. I had begun to wonder if you had lost it."

"No, I can still read your mind." A little smile appeared.

"Murdoch, for my own conscience, you had nothing to do with this?"

"I had nothing to do with this. Nothing at all. I am an excellent animate mage, but you said it yourself." He waved at the animate. "We can't make this."

Trahn said, "Have you spoken to the guards in the last few days? Any news on your animate?"

Murdoch shrugged twice. "I've spoken to John a couple of times, and he says that they have people searching, but with the exception of Bessemer and this little monster they haven't turned up a thing. It's not surprising, I had a feeling that it was gone for good."

Trahn nodded and said, "Have faith. It can't just stop existing. It will be found."

"I do not share your optimism."

"I imagine not. How is the work going for Silas? He will want a top quality piece."

Murdoch laughed.

"And what is funny about that?" Trahn asked sharply.

"He wanted a top quality piece before Henry got stabbed. Now he will want us to build him another wife," Murdoch said, laughing at his own humor.

"True. True. Can you do it?" Trahn said with mock seriousness.

The stresses of the last days formed into nervous laughter, and Trahn's question broke Murdoch's once legendary composure. When he finally gathered himself he said, "No...no...I really don't think I can." He wiped a tear from his eye.

"Good enough. I'll let him know to be disappointed. Have a good afternoon, Murdoch. Keep me informed about our little guest." Trahn left the laboratory shaking his head. The recent events had shaken his friend's foundations. Trahn thought that Murdoch had not told him everything about the animate. And while Murdoch could often read his mind, Trahn had no luck with the mind of Murdoch.

Alexander Gin was surprised to find a note left for him when he returned from the Red Wolf Inn, and he now sat with Tara Groundmender in the Great

Garden at The Way of Health. He was not at all unhappy about it. Even the waiting in the foyer had been short, and Tara had led him through the House to the walled garden.

Gin had been given some bread and stew, and was thankful for it. He had not eaten since seeing the murdered hunters. He spoke softly, but with excitement, "I couldn't believe it. Those hunters were definitely killed with magic. John said on the ride back that there hadn't been murder like that in years. This stew is amazing, by the way." He pointed at the bowl with his spoon.

"I've grown accustomed to it, I think. Did you hear about the animate attacking Henry Bremen?"

"A little," Gin answered, mouth full.

"Mother sent me to heal him. Awful little thing. The animate, not Master Bremen," Tara said smiling

Gin laughed, "Master Bremen too, from what I've heard."

"I haven't told anyone this," Tara found herself again drawn into Alexander's simple charm, "Before the Mother woke me, I was dreaming. There was a mist that turned into a man, but instead of being filled with life it was completely empty. It knew I was there, staring at me with gold eyes." She shivered.

"How strange. Here's hoping it was only a dream. This place is beautiful."

"Isn't it? I don't come out here often enough, I'm so busy with my studies." Water formed on the tips of her fingers, dripping down on a yellow flower. The flower turned, spinning its leaves upwards to bathe. "Mother has me doing things that others who have been here twice as long do not."

"Good thing you're not a guard. That'd get you shunned pretty quickly. Most of 'em are lazy halfwits."

"That's terrible, Alexander."

Gin smiled, "Is it? It's just true."

The bells of The House of Currents sounded three rings. Gin listened to them. "I need to get down to the gates. My shift starts in fifteen."

Both he and Tara stood, and without warning Tara hugged him. 'A cautious little girl indeed,' she thought. Gin was surprised, but returned the affection.

"Thanks for inviting me, Tara, and for lunch. This is a great place to escape for a bit, even if the bells can reach in here."

"It was good to see you again. I hope your shift goes without problems."

"So do I, but with the way things are going, who knows?" Gin said, smiling. Tara took the bowl and spoon from him and walked him through the House. Neither spoke, enjoying the last few seconds together in silence. The light on Tara's shoulder bobbed happily along. She had not, much to her frustration, been able to separate the way it acted from her mood. Brother Chaign said it would come. The mage stood a minute once Alex had gone, trying to calm the light, but did not succeed.

Turning to leave the foyer, Tara stopped; Brother Chaign stood in the doorway. Tara jumped, startled by his presence. "You scared me." The man had the annoying ability to move in silence. Tara did not know if it was training or magic. 'Which would be training also, but of a different sort.'

Brother Chaign smiled at her, then spoke calmly, "I am sorry, Daughter Tara." This was one man that Tara did not feel insult from for being called daughter. "I did not mean to startle you. Sister Rainmarrow sends for you."

The light on her shoulder pulsed. Chaign watched, reading more than Tara wished to show. "This bothers you?"

"No, Brother Chaign. She has just had so many things for me to do of late, I find myself overwhelmed."

"Turn to the Way for help. It will guide you. Come now." Tara followed the mage through the House. He said, "You have spent a bit of time with that guard, daughter. Do you like him?"

Tara smiled, thinking of Gin. She was surprised by the question, almost as much as by the man earlier, but answered honestly, "Yes, Brother Chaign, I do."

"He is a light soul in this convoluted world of magic. It is rare to see one such as him involved with anything magic," he said quietly. "Here we are."

The two stood in the Mother's garden but the Mother was absent. "Is she not here?" Tara asked.

"What I show you now is not to be spoken of, young one." Chaign's voice was deadly serious. He raised his left hand, knifelike to his forehead, extending his right hand before him, flat. His eyes closed. His right hand glowed softly, lit from inside. The water in the small pool pulled back to the edges leaving the bottom of the

136

basin dry. The water quivered, wanting to return to its natural shape. The basin for its part cracked apart. Sections pulled back under the floor. Tara watched with astonishment as a staircase revealed itself. Brother Chaign lowered his hands. "Follow."

The two descended into a flame lit hallway. Above them the basin rumbled back together and Tara could hear the water sloshing. Brother Chaign smiled. "Despite what Sister Rainmarrow says, sometimes, sometimes sheer power is required."

The torches flickered and danced, much like the very nervous light on Tara's shoulder. She let it die. "Be calm, daughter. You are in no danger."

The walls of the hall were carved into a forest, so lifelike that Tara believed she saw animals moving inside it. The floor at the end of the hall had a great stone seal; the mark of the House, a massive tree, imbedded in the floor. The hall opened into a large room cut from the rock, again the walls were carved into a forest; real enough to make the room feel tight. The floor stepped up once to a higher level.

Freestanding oil lamps lit the room from the corners, the smoke they made was eaten by the Way. Two more lamps stood on the edge of the upper level, each five feet tall. Between and slightly past them the Mother knelt, her back to the entering mages. It did not matter. "Brother Chaign, Daughter Tara." Her voice was distant; she was entranced.

Chaign sat, crossed his legs and closed his eyes. Tara followed his lead. The room glowed with warmth but there was no calling from the Way, and for that Tara was glad. After a time the Mother spoke again, "Thank you for your patience." Her voice sounded rough around the edges, her eyes dark. "The Way calls when it pleases." Lilac stood, resting her weight on her staff, and adjusted her tunic. "I imagine, Tara, that you are wondering what this place is and why you are here. But let us first talk of visions." The Mother stepped down to the lower level of the room. She sat down, staff resting beside her. "The mist, daughter."

That was all that was needed to turn Tara's face sour. Lilac continued, "You know of it then. I had hoped that no others would be drawn into this matter by the Way, but it does not often listen to its practitioners. It is what the Earth has been warning me against, though the others on the Council will not hear it. Tell me what you saw."

Tara started, unsure of herself in the presence of the others. "It was last night, before you woke me to go to the technologist. I do not know where I was, but it was there. The mist that is. After a time it fashioned itself into the shape of a man, and it saw me. It was just a dream. Right?" Both Lilac and Chaign listened with utmost attention.

The Mother said, "I do not think that it was, daughter. Brother Chaign?"

"This is a more recent accounting of the creature than either of us have had. Though all are within two weeks. Until the Way reveals more to us I do not see how we can act. There is no way to locate it, nor has it revealed itself as a threat. Perhaps in this your closeness to the Way is distorting your vision, Lilac. It may not be a danger."

Tara had not heard anyone speak to the Mother in such a familiar fashion. She expected the Mother to be angry, but she was not.

Lilac shook her head. Her voice was pained, "I don't know, Chaign, I have not often been lied to by the Earth. Sometimes I do not interpret what I see correctly, but with knowledge of what has passed I see the truth in what I was shown. The callings are more and more often of late, and I am so tired."

It was then that Tara realized that the Mother for all of her ability was still just a woman. And like her she was tired, but a thousand times more. Beyond that she wore a strain of duty that Tara did not begin to understand. 'If this is why I was brought here, to see the Mother frail, I understand now. My effort will increase, I will not fail again.'

Lilac summoned a smile and said, "But what of this place? I suppose that is the question, daughter. I often wonder that when I come here, for it does not have a name. One thing it is, is different. The Way changes it. Now it is a lush, in some ways sinister, forest. When I became the First of the House, it was grassland, with great herds carved in relief."

Chaign joined in, "Before that, even, it was shoreline, so real you could dip your toes in the water."

He was older than the Mother, by much, Tara imagined. Apparently her face said what she thought inside. "Yes, daughter, I am an old, old man."

Lilac laughed, "And I am an old woman. This room for one holds the House's treasures. Do not think that we are as selfless as we appear. Certainly we help those in need. That is something to hold dear, but," Lilac stood, and walked to the wall to her left while she spoke, "the sons and daughters do happen across interesting things." She closed her eyes, and reached into the stone wall, the branches of the forest pulling away from her. She withdrew an amulet of gold and jade. "Consider this amulet. I do not know its use, nor do I care, but here it sits, left by someone before me." She replaced the amulet in the living stone forest and returned to sit.

"But that is not all, daughter. Much of The Way of Health is easy magic. Certainly it takes skill and training, but you remember healing small animals or plants even before your time in the House. We all do. But there is a deeper power to the Way that is not easy to come by." Her voice hushed, almost reverent, "In everyday activity it is almost impossible to use, impossible to feel. It is revealed slowly if at all. There are old places in the world, that is how it was described to me, that allow you tap into this power. This, Daughter Tara Groundmender, is one of them.

"When I was young, before this room was secreted away, I saw what can be done here. I don't recall exactly who the woman was. Much of that night was destroyed in the memories of those that were there. Chaign, I believe, can tell you of that." The man nodded slowly. Lilac continued, "She was killed brutally by magic, whatever had happened to her in life had been covered by the fire. All that was left was a charred corpse. We gathered in this room, all that were in Serac, the First to the last.

"No one knew what to expect, then slowly one at a time we were placed like chess pieces by the Way, forming some intricate pattern. The body rested on the edge of the step there. That is my only clear memory. One after another we were dragged down by the Earth; into a chant. I think I was the last to go. How I fought it, I was terrified. The next thing any of us remember was waking up, all of us at once, to find the woman alive, fully healed. None of us knew what happened. The First sealed this room that very day.

"When the Way began calling me I would meditate, often where I was or in my garden, but after a time I had vision after vision of this room. It was only when I reopened the basin and returned here that they receded. I am still not entirely comfortable, but that was what had to be done."

Tara for the first time in The Way of Health felt cold. She was deeply afraid, her stomach turned. Chaign said, "Do not be afraid, young one, I promise you no harm will come to you here."

"How could you stop it?" Tara questioned frantically. "Why did you bring me here? Mother?"

The Mother smiled, and placed her hand on Tara's shoulder, "Be calm. There will be no activity such as that, but I believe that given your aptitude to the Way that I should begin teaching you here. It will make the learning easier, the magic stronger, and you will be able to increase your mastery as you could only dream before. You are a unique talent Tara; the Way would not involve you in all of these things if you could not handle it. The light, you have had trouble with it?"

Tara did feel some degree of relief. She pushed some of her hair out of her face, and said, "Very much so. I cannot separate my feelings from it, no matter what I do it bounces along happily or flashes angrily."

"Try it here."

Tara formed the light and at first it twitched nervously, she closed her eyes for one second and the light solidified into a sparkling orb, crisp and clean. It had been so simple, and so subtle a change. Tara smiled. "I see."

"Very good. Also, Brother Chaign and I have been discussing it, and if you are agreeable he would like to teach you some basics in self defense," Lilac said.

"I have seen less fine than you treated more poorly," Chaign said.

The reality of the world was beginning to settle in on Tara. It was not so pretty a place. "I...I hadn't even thought of it. But I would very much like to learn, then I can show that silly man Alexander a thing or two." She smiled. At least that was still pleasant.

Brother Chaign smiled, "Very good. We will start tomorrow, though we can train outside, I believe you will find it much more enjoyable. I warn you now, I am not nearly the quality of warrior that The House of Wrath produces, but I can teach you to be difficult. Now, sister, shall we teach the young one how to reach this place?"

"I do not think so, Chaign. I would not want you here alone, Tara. It would not be safe now. Not yet."

"I think I am grateful for the caution," Tara said, sighing with relief.

Thirteen

The spider quickly reached the bottom of the Serac tunnels. The roar of the ocean reverberated through the rock, drowning out all other sound. The animate began the slow work of examining all of the passages cut into the cliff. Strangely enough the animate was irritated that its instructions had changed. It did not recall clearly what it had been doing before this, but it knew that this was much more difficult. Running through well-lit areas and hiding in shadows with hopes of invisibility, all the while mapping. It was noticed on one occasion, it thought, trying to pass through the torturous observation decks carved into the cliff. With all the people that congregated in them enjoying the view it was unavoidable.

Its mission was almost finished, it was near the surface and much to its delight it found a passage that had been walled off; there were many of those, but this one connected, at another walled end, to the House of Animate tunnel. This meant that it did not have to wait for Arcane to remember it was doing important work for him, it could return to him when it finished. And it was now done.

Arcane knew the animate was approaching and he was both surprised and happy it had finished so quickly. Arcane guessed there were not as many tunnels as he had been led to believe from the copious descriptions given to them in the manuscripts that made up his base knowledge. But he would soon know for sure.

Plucking the animate from the wall like so much fruit, Arcane placed his left hand over the animate as he had before. This time instead of giving new instructions to the animate, he took the recent experiences of the animate from it. Duplicating them, the edges of Arcane's mouth turned up. In truth there were a great number of passageways and the spider had explored them quickly and, by its finding of the hidden tunnel, thoroughly. A map formed in Arcane's mind. Most of the passageways were not terribly useful, either ending quickly or circling back to where they started. A few slowly wormed their way through the cliff to the surface.

There was even some sort of market down inside the cliff. The visions of this were cluttered with noise and distractions. Where it was not dark the market was filled with people, and the spider had avoided them. Arcane was amazed at the things on sale. Many things he had no knowledge of, strangely shaped tools, weapons, and plants that he recognized as having magical properties, it appeared that the world could be purchased. One dealer even had what appeared to be technologist crystal on display.

Returning to that time and place Arcane looked at the animate that had wrapped itself around his arm. It had done a better job than Arcane could have hoped for. A thought and the spider repositioned itself on his back, using its legs to lock into place. That would be sufficient until another task was demanded of it. For now Arcane waited.

The spider that had been sent to The House of Currents dragged a book behind it. The book was heavy, a massive leather bound tome, as all important books seemed to be, and it slowed the small animate down considerably. Fortunately, the sun had set making the animate difficult to see. Speed now did not matter.

The animate scaled the outside wall of the House of Animate, up to the empty window. The animate stepped through the bars and was jolted to a stop. The book would not fit, and such was the grip the animate held it with that it too was stopped. Not letting go the animate backed out to try again, and again the same result. It tapped the ledge with its front legs. Then it again retreated out of the House, this time up to the roof, where it re-gripped the offending tome. Down it went. This time the old book scraped through. Relief. Now to wait for Arcane.

Even though the animate was single minded it did wonder where the other two spiders were. The larger, the first, had been here before, and the other had been given the same time line. Arcane had done the imbuing at the same time and many of the instructions were the same. Neither appeared as it waited. Arcane would be upset.

Now and again a mage would come to the supply room but soon all commotion died away. Then the spider could feel Arcane. The others were still not here. A small form of concern coalesced alongside the spider's other thoughts. The stone pushed up and the animate scurried from its perch with all the speed its small legs could muster. The book unbalanced it and it almost fell. It turned and backed down the wall into the hidden stairwell. Ah, there was the first spider, clever. Arcane lowered the stone.

He thought to himself, 'Where is the last?' There were no answers and it did not appear. Arcane took the book and released the thief back to the night. At the bottom of the stairs he sat with the tome. It was old; the leather had hardened and begun to crack around the edges. A few of the pages had released from the binding, and a large amount of loose paper was intermingled.

The tome did not cover any single subject instead having brief entries about many different things. Arcane realized that the paper, some old and yellowed, almost crackling apart, some new, with dark fresh ink, related to the subjects that were covered on the pages near them. Most of the recent notes were signed and dated by Frederick Guildenil, whom Arcane knew to be the First of The House of Currents, and in many ways the First of all. The older notes were not signed, and the writing was almost unreadable. Arcane knew immediately that this tome would be a valuable resource.

On a whim the animate turned to the section on the Su'th. The large cat skull intrigued him, and having no answers in himself was pleased to find a section devoted to them. One passage in particular piqued his interest.

The Su'th are an interesting study in history. Despite being a backward people, not interested in education or the magical arts, they have a strong folk tradition. In their stories, most of which are not put to paper, they claim to be responsible for the death of a figure, which can be roughly translated as the Harrow King. Much of the tale is similar to our children's stories about the scourge of the same name. Differences include naming of the hero, Su'thele'n, and indeed, making the hero a Su'th instead of the unnamed human king. Beyond the name Su'thele'n the character is not given any detail beyond being brave, nor does he appear in any other tale the Su'th have passed down. This casts doubt upon the validity of the story.

Of course the Harrow King lends his name to the various cults that appear from time to time promising wealth and power, though it is the opinion of the author that there is no direct connection between the two. Any educated mage can see that there is very little in common between the poor fools that give their devotion to such a fraud and the gray skinned abomination that appears in so many wives tales.

An old note was wedged between the pages here. Arcane held it gingerly, the edges fraying away as it was disturbed from its rest. The writing was sloppy, uneven and unsigned.

"It is my opinion that the author of this section is not very well versed in the Harrow Cults as he names them. There simply must be a reason that they have taken the name of this mythical figure, more so than just the Harrow's Grace that spurns many of the central figures of these cults. Beyond that even, is the Harrow's Luck, which is the most likely reason these cults collect any following at all.

"A WELL educated mage would see that there is a connection between these things, and if the children's stories and the more detailed Su'th version are true, the Harrow King, and his followers, the Harrow, were truly a terrible power. Hopefully, Su'thele'n, as named in the Su'th rendition, did put an end to their destruction. If one does have an opportunity to speak with a Su'th they describe the Harrow, the Lot'hak, as being nigh unkillable, not falling in combat when a normal man would die ten times over. Beyond that even the Harrow's heart would continue to beat long after it was dead, pumping pure magic the tales say, summoning more of the monsters. But of course the Su'th are a backward people, let us not forget, which is the reason none of this appears in any writings accepted and approved by any of the Mage Commissions."

Arcane smiled. The Mage Commissions had been task forces that had originally spread the enlightenment of man. Because of this they controlled much of the learning early in the era. And though they had been useful, most were dissolved over five centuries earlier by the Houses that supported them. The last independent commission held on until 497 of the current era, which marked its beginning with the rediscovery of the Currents. Finally, it too stepped into history.

These facts, Arcane noted, made both the tome and the note quite old. Arcane did find the description that the Su'th gave the Harrow most interesting. 'Perhaps, an answer to my basic problem of command. But again, no mention of the Su'th War Prince, of the feline skull. It is odd that there is nothing at all.'

Turning to the Harrow, Arcane found nothing more than a summary of the children's tale, and a passing mention of the Harrow cults. More information resided in the hand written note. Arcane did realize that finding this note was as much a stroke of luck as anything else, but as with the Masa'terj some greater fate seemed to shine on him when all answers seemed exhausted. It was curious thinking for the animate, and he quickly quashed it, preferring to prepare for the tasks that now presented themselves.

'And where is that spider? It should have returned by now,' the thoughts echoed metallic, irritated. Arcane's head ratcheted to the side, a ping of recognition. 'There it is, bound up in Master Jannan's laboratory. So not all goes as planned after all. Very well, for your carelessness...'

Arcane set for the Heele Estate, leaving the captured spider, with its unapproachable thicket of protocols, behind. With luck the lord would return from his hunt soon.

Rupport Heele could not be prouder. The hunt had ended earlier than planned, but there could be no more hunting. Every arrow had been spent, recovered, and spent again. The game was better than any time he had ever seen it. The last day, the last arrow that Rupport fired brought down the largest buck any of them had ever seen. Not one person said anything of luck. The worm, burdened with meat and trophies, crept back to his estate. The feast to come would be one for the ages. All, especially Rupport, looked forward to the gala.

Having sent an advanced rider, Rupport was pleased to see smoke rising from the multitude of chimneys. Bessemer had prepared the manor for their coming, as it always did. Feskarn brought the worm into the roundabout and it slowly lost momentum. The order of perceived importance had changed some, but all that had left now returned. The manor would be filled to its gills with nobility and servants. Rupport lived for these moments.

Somewhat to his surprise Bessemer was not standing at the door waiting for their triumphant return. The lord lowered his girth down from Titan and started up the stairs. The door swung open before he was half way to it. Bessemer walked out and said, "Greetings, sir. All is well?"

Rupport stepped heavily. The two weeks of hunting had done nothing to reduce his weight. "Excellent hunting, Bessemer, excellent. Turn down all of the bedrooms, we will be having guests. Make sure the meat gets packed, and get those lazy cooks working. Tonight we feast! And tomorrow and the next! An amazing, extravagant affair. We'll show the doubters from Earlsburg," he spoke greedily, a lusty fire in his eyes.

"Certainly. I will set the good silver, sir." Bessemer spun on the spot, and went about his work.

Bessemer moved with purpose. The drive to perform his former master's tasks was strong despite all that Arcane had done to it. Completing these tasks for Lord Heele gave Bessemer satisfaction that following Arcane did not, it was most disquieting. Bessemer would shield this from Arcane; it was best that the animate did not know.

Arcane moved slowly in his workshop, deliberately, almost as if underwater. Part of his anima followed Bessemer as it moved throughout the massive house. Arcane had not been to most of the places Bessemer now prowled. The rest worked slowly on his latest creation. The digger was taking shape. If Arcane was to take advantage of the tunnels under Serac he would have to make modifications. Additions. He focused, trying to penetrate more deeply into the magic as it worked, trying to find the secrets that made it function. Despite all of this distraction Arcane was pleased. Soon he would find out if what he believed about Heele was true, if his father and he himself had the Harrow's Luck.

It could be the only explanation for such wealth and honor being bestowed upon such a family. Perhaps that was it, it was not that Arcane was lucky, but that the Harrow's Luck so permeated this place, that he enjoyed the benefits. Yes, that was it.

Arcane smiled, having entered the maze and puzzled out the exit.

His work then became his full focus. In plan the digger was a more squat animate than the spider. Six stout, powerful legs provided the base that it would need to perform its task. A maw of spinning blades for consuming stone, dirt and rock. A long body that would expel the ground remains behind it. It was another simple design, but its construction was different. Using the older practices Arcane extracted platinum from the stone stolen from the House of Animate and formed it into the core. It was a different medium than the crystal, much more permanent, much more resistant. The jump that Master Jannan had made to using crystal was an important one, but Arcane did not wish to use what he possessed building trivial animates, it would be saved for now.

Bessemer ordered the kitchen about with an iron first. It was as hot and wet as the first time it saw Arcane. It smelled a bit sweet and a bit fresh, but most of the distinct scents were lost. The roar of fire and sounds of food being readied drowned out all but the loudest conversation. The preparations for dinner were behind schedule, and that was with the extra staff provided by the other nobles. Lord Heele's cooks moved with the precision that the animate demanded, the main courses would be finished on time; it was the others who were resistant to Bessemer's orders that threatened the animate's plans. He had turned the rooms down, escorted the nobility to them and would not allow these fools to fail.

The animate spoke at a level that would be screaming had it been human. "Hurry up! The lord's dinner will not be delayed because of your laziness!"

One chef, a tall older man, slowed his pace, giving Bessemer a vile look. It was clear to the animate that he was intentionally undermining the preparation. He said, "Why do I have to take this from a toy!" The chef gestured wildly at Bessemer and the others around him nodded and grumbled. Bessemer would not take this insubordination.

"Why? Because I am chief of Lord Heele's operation, if you are in his estate, you follow my orders and if you don't I will see to it that your head is served as part of the feast."

Nesa laughed. She had not seen this side of Bessemer before. The threat for its part seemed to put the man in order and he returned to work. Bessemer stalked out of the kitchen to the dining hall. Three tables had to be prepared for those of pedigree. The room was arranged with the tables to the outside walls and seating was ordered as per instruction. The long banquet tables were set by Bessemer, the silver placed perfectly for the nobles. Once that was done the animate hung rich tapestries to liven the room and then lit the chandeliers to illuminate them.

In their kindness the nobles would allow the servants to feast as well. In a distant dining room Bessemer slammed basic wood tables into place, and provided the barest of dinnerware. Candles could be lit if they so desired. It did not matter to the animate.

With the rooms prepared, Bessemer felt calm. All the preparations were done, only the service of the food remained.

Arcane moved quickly through the basement, his work set aside. He could hear the sounds of occupation in the manor above him. With the distraction discarded, he needed Bessemer. The animate was in the kitchen again, that much Arcane could tell for certain. Light leaked around the door from the servants' room and a woman's laughter grated on his anima. Arcane put his left hand to the door. Four light taps as his fingers contacted. Bessemer would come.

Bessemer felt Arcane's summons. 'Not now,' was its immediate thought, but it knew Arcane would not be put off. Most of the cooking was done and the service plates were being prepared. The animate took the steps down into the servants' room. The candles on the wall were lit. Nesa and some other human, a man, sat laughing, each with a cup of wine. Nesa stopped laughing and straightened in her seat, "Bessemer, we were just getting ready to serve the lord and his guests." She clearly feared admonishment from the toy.

"Soon, Nesa. Carry on. Your work today was without error," the animate said, passing through the room. It opened the door and entered the darkness of the basement, giving no reason for its going.

"Bessemer moves in his own circles," Nesa said, her eyebrows raised and her head shaking slightly. She gulped the last of her wine, and the man followed suit. "Let's get this work done, and put the babies to bed."

Bessemer walked violently to the workshop where it found Arcane holding a heavy metal punch in his hand. "You called, brother?" the animate spoke with frustration in his voice.

"Yes. Yes. Brother," Arcane's tin voice was cold. "Lord Heele, he is a lucky man?"

"I would not know. If this is all that you called me for I have important duties I must attend to."

"You do not know?" Bessemer shook his head as Arcane spoke. "No. You would not. I have a great need. I believe that Heele is the answer. I will take your place for this banquet. That is what is going on tonight?"

"I do not think that would be a wise thing to do, brother. You do not know —"

Arcane cut off the animate, loudly, "Be silent! I do not know what? How to serve these humans? How to beg for gratitude? You do the work of five men and it is still not enough." Arcane beckoned Bessemer closer; the animate obeyed, as it always did. "Rest, brother."

Arcane spun the beckoning hand around and a wisp of jagged yellow light appeared, connecting the two animates. "Rest," Arcane said again. Bessemer immediately went limp, though he did not collapse to the floor. A look of disgust invaded Arcane's metal face. His hand pressed onto the suspended animate's face. Seconds later Arcane knew all that Bessemer knew of being a butler, the rules and regulations of class. It made him pity the animate all the more and hate the humans for it. The spider dropped from Arcane's back and flitted up the wall, hiding in a dark corner.

Arcane acted quickly. Dinner was to begin promptly at quarter past six as Lord Heele demanded. It was shortly after six. The longer Arcane dallied in the basement, the more opportunity for failure in this ruse. The hot kitchen was mostly empty, the head chefs and Heele's staff finishing the preparation of trays of meat fresh from the hunt, bread and fresh fruit.

Nesa said, "Everything is ready, Bessemer. I was beginning to worry that we had lost you in the cellar."

"Not lost, just finishing some other work." Arcane's voice had changed to match the toy.

"We shall begin service promptly at six fifteen. I assume that you will be serving Lord Heele personally?"

Arcane followed the course laid out in Bessemer's anima, "Yes, of course." Then to the service staff as a whole, "Do not dishonor the lord. Remember proper etiquette." Arcane sickened as he glared at the meat. "You have done well."

With Arcane's final blessing the trays of fruit and bowls of salad were carried to the dining room. A string quartet employed by the Markons played a waltz. Bessemer had arranged for the music hours earlier. Some of the nobility, including the Markons, danced. The servants that did not have to serve performed a crude imitation in the connected room. Lord Heele sat at his table with a goblet of wine in his right hand; he was wrapped in blue robes and wore his technologist aids. Baron Erright sat to his right and the two were deep in conversation. Arcane took a large silver bowl with a leafy salad and went to the table where Heele sat. He asked, "Salad, sir?"

Heele stopped his conversation and said, "Yes. Lord Erright?"

"That would be fine." The baron studied Arcane closely. "Truly a remarkable construction. I will have to arrange for one to be made. Whom in the House of Animate did you contact, Lord Heele?"

"My accountant arranged it all. Master Jannan built it I believe. Took a fair while for the House to deliver it, but it has been wonderful. There was something of a queue; he had undertaken a fair number for the nobles of Earlsburg," Rupport said, obstructing the salad plate. He rocked back in his seat away from Erright, who continued to watch the animate's every move.

Arcane served the salad with overly large silver tongs. Piling the salad onto a smaller large plate Arcane tried to find an opportunity to touch Heele without being conspicuous. The close scrutiny of the baron did not make his goal easier. Before he could make contact the Markons sat down to the left of Heele.

"What a wonderful dance," the lady chittered.

Heele smiled, stabbing his fork into the vegetables. He said, "The quartet is exquisite."

Lord Markon nodded, "The very best."

Arcane knowing that he had to preserve the ruse, stepped down and served the Markons salad. Around the room food was being served, and the room settled into clinking of silverware and useless banter, all mixed over the music of the quartet.

Serving wine proved to be Arcane's next opportunity, which met with similar results. Before Arcane could do anything Rupport pushed his chair back, inadvertently pushing Arcane away. The quartet stopped immediately.

Rupport held his wine goblet up and began speaking, "Friends. I take this opportunity to welcome each of you to my estate. Fortunately, we are gathered together after an amazingly successful trip. The largest buck I have ever seen is now my trophy. Each of you has been equally blessed. For those of you who will be leaving us soon please make yourself at home during the time that you are here.

"For those of you who will be staying on for the next hunt, make arrangements with my animate, Bessemer, and inform your servants that they are to follow its lead and instruction at all times.

"Now, to the night that is and that will be and for the trip that was. Enjoy!" Rupport finished his speech and rapidly drank the goblet of wine. The nobles clapped heartily and laughed to each other. Heele finished, "Now, bring on the main course!"

The kitchen staff wheeled in the many forms of fresh game. Some baked, some braised, seared, and poached. Some dishes had elaborate sauces; some were naked of all garnishment. A triumphant cry echoed in the room at the sight. The cooks, Nesa most of all, smiled, beaming at the gratuity. Arcane explained the options to the table and took orders from the lords and ladies, who now had a ravished look about their faces, as though they had not eaten the entire two weeks. Arcane knew this was not the case.

The animate cut and served, cut and served. Lord Heele, as was his tradition, waited to be served last. In all other things he would be first, but in this one instance, he very much enjoyed watching those around him taste the hunt's splendors. Arcane took Lord Heele's plate and began to fill it, not surprisingly the human wanted some of all and much of most. Arcane cut the meat quickly, resorting to a violent tearing of some soft part that had been coated in a sticky orange sauce.

Taking the plate back to Lord Heele he was delighted to see that the man had rolled up the sleeves on his robes in preparation for the meat. This was to be the time. Arcane set the plate down before the man and his eyes widened at the feast. He had had meals like this before, but never had they risen to such a height. The dim blue glow in the vision aid flickered as it did its work, refocusing the world to the nearly blind man. Rupport Heele smiled greedily, so entranced with the plate of meat and delectable sauces that he did not notice the hand's slow, cold, drag across his arm.

Arcane pulled across the human's right arm. Contact. His anima, his core, shuddered. It was raw, but the power was there, instantly addictive. The world slowed, colors deepening, the smell of the meat and the humans suffocating. Arcane could hear between the notes as the quartet played. 'It is true,' Arcane thought, the world alight around him, 'This human has the Harrow's luck. And if this is true, so must be the heart. A cult. To find a Harrow cult.' Then the separation was gone; the man had taken up his fork and knife and began destroying the pile of meat. He asked for more wine. Arcane poured slowly, the floor seemed to fall away from his feet, the wine pouring sideways and drunk on itself. It took all of his concentration to not spill on the table as he poured.

It had been beautiful, small aspects of magic that he had not seen, nor even imagined, had played out before him. All in those brief seconds. Arcane spoke, almost using his own voice, "The lord will excuse me for a moment, there is some business I must attend to in the kitchen."

The human answered, mouth full, "Yes, yes. Go, Bessemer."

Arcane fled the sickening party, not seeing the noble that sat at the end of the table watch him go. Turnbly's eyes were wild, almost horror filled, locked upon the animate as it left the dining room. Back to the kitchen Arcane walked; the world cascaded side to side. Nesa and the other chefs worked on the desserts. Arcane ignored them as he went down into the basement, into the darkness. He found Bessemer where he had left him. The spider had come down from the corner and perched happily on the slumping animate's head. Arcane waved it off, and with his other hand spurred Bessemer back to life. Arcane said, "You will find your precious humans happily eating. Now go and finish that horror."

Bessemer did not say anything. Both hands balled into fists and then he was gone. Arcane sat down on the only stool in the workshop, the spider moving side to side at his feet. It seemed impatient, and Arcane imagined that it probably was. He did not take the time to find out for certain and he turned back to the work of the digger.

Fourteen

Tara bent Alexander's wrist in a direction that it wasn't meant to bend and he yelped in pain as he kneeled to lessen the strain. "That's correct. I appreciate your help, Alexander," said Chaign.

Tara released the wrist lock and Alexander shook the sting from it. "Remind me never to hold your hand. No, really," he said sarcastically with a laugh. "You taught her all of those in just an hour? I wish the guard training was half as good. Sure I can swing a sword a little bit, but chopping up folks that get drunk and belligerent doesn't really fly with the Senior Guards."

Chaign nodded, "I imagine. Tara will want to practice them. You will have ample time to learn."

"That's what I am afraid of, Master Chaign."

Tara shook her head; hair that had been dislodged during the day's practice wisped this way and that. It had taken only minutes for the formality between the two men to dissipate, even though one was a powerful mage, and in reality one was nothing more than an errand boy for the other. It was a funny pair and Tara was glad they got along, but it was clear that Alex knew that certain lines should not, would not be crossed.

Chaign spoke again, "That is good for today, Tara. I will teach you more tomorrow. Do not forget your meditation."

"Yes, thank you, brother. I won't," Tara answered. The mage glanced at Gin one final time, seemed satisfied, and strolled peacefully away from the couple. They stood on the grass north of the House but far from the cliff. The salty air was strong today, and the wind blew, tempering the sun.

"That really did hurt, you know," Alex said, rubbing his right wrist. It was red from the locks.

"Good, it will teach you not to bother pretty women like me," Tara said seriously, sharply. Then she smiled and hugged Gin. "It was good of you to come before your shift. Even better to bend you all the wrong ways."

Alex smiled, as she pulled out of his arms. He said, "You only invited me so you could do that, didn't you?" She was quite pretty in her white smock; it somehow imitated the training garb of The House of Wrath.

"No! Of course not," she answered, her head fell to her chest, somewhat embarrassed. 'So the shy girl is still in here.'

"Come on," Gin raised her chin with his cupped hand, "I was kidding. I know you actually wanted to see me. Well, I hope so."

She half smiled, her eyes closing. "Yes. I'm sorry. I'm just...I'm just anxious about all of this attention, both from you and the Way. The Mother has decided to take my training very much into her own hands, and Chaign is wonderful for the lessons, but he is more enveloping than you can understand."

Alexander sat down on the grass, his arms straight behind him propping up his torso. Tara sat cross-legged. Alex said, "What do you mean 'enveloping'?"

"I am a fairly strong symbiote to other's meditation, he just has a powerful nature, I don't know how to explain it any better." Then changing the subject, "So when do I get to see you in something other than the Campus Guard uniform?"

Alex chuckled once, his head rocking to the side. "I don't know. I always see you when I'm about to work, or just after. I guess it will have to be a special occasion." Gin scratched an itch on his nose. Tara pulled out a little clump of grass and scattered the blades in the wind.

Tara said, "Master Guildenil called the Directorate Council together again. The Mother told me it was to address the animate attack and the murders that you saw. It's pretty rare though for the Council to be formed twice in such a short time. It must be important."

"That was all ugly business. I saw the copy of both the reports. The other guards all keep saying that it's been so busy lately. I guess it has been."

For the second time in less than two weeks the Directorate Council filled Frederick Guildenil's study. This time they did not wait on the Elementalist's representative, Kasu had arrived on time. The week's events weighed heavily on Frederick and it showed in his face. The lines of age were deeper, concern in every crevice. He breathed deeply, as if trying to discern the exact moment to begin the meeting. The other Firsts watched him, as children about to be scolded. Even Gavin was tense.

Frederick at last did speak, with the tone of a disappointed father. "What is going on? We have had years of relative peace in Serac and within two weeks we have a collapse of the Campus Guard, a rogue animate, and not one but two murders. Add to that they were very clearly done using magic.

"At least in the recent cases the guard has performed admirably. Trahn, I hear that the animate is now in your House's custody. Is this correct?"

Trahn said, "Yes it is, Master Guildenil. Master Jannan is studying it, hoping to find its origin. It will take some time. The protocols are a maze, and it will attack anyone that goes near it."

Gavin said, "Except Master Jannan. Can we not infer that it was made by him?"

Frederick nodded at the question. Trahn glared once again at the First of Wrath. "I read the protocols when Silas brought it to the House. The animate, and I am ashamed to say it, is beyond our understanding. As I told Silas, it could be an old-world animate, but why here and now I do not know."

Frederick said, "It would seem that the House of Animate has the situation as under control as possible, but as to maintain good relations with the Technologist Guild I would like an update on the status of the animate when next we meet. If it is not a forced meeting such as this. I have nothing else to say on this matter.

"However, there is the grim business of the murdered hunters. The report was fairly specific as to the cause of death, and if you did not believe what was written," Fredrick blinked slowly, and from a side table the two metal spears raised into the air, and levitated across to the desk, "Here is the proof." As if to prove his point the spears dropped loudly to the desk.

Trahn and Lilac both flinched, but Gavin and the Elementalist showed no emotion. Gavin reached out and picked up one of the metal shafts, examining it and pricking his finger on the end. Blood welled up and he smiled, then wiped it on his robe. The robe would most likely be burned anyway.

Gavin said, "This is not exactly Wrath magic. It could be formed in such a fashion if the caster was skilled, but it does not align with the incantations."

Frederick Guildenil frowned, and said, "It's not exactly like anything I have ever seen either. That is why it is so bothersome. The way the bolts are bent it is reminiscent of lightning, made solid."

Lilac bent forward in her chair, staring at the shaft of metal that lay on the table, her eyes distant, head rocking ever so slightly. "Lilac?" Guildenil said.

"It is just a feeling. Cold. Empty, whatever created this was a very elemental force. There is not the life that we would associate with magic."

Gavin laughed, "You never fail to confound do you? What you are saying means nothing. Any mage with appropriate training could do this. We are on the brink of new discovery and you warn against it. I will take this to The House of Wrath. It will be studied and learned."

Trahn smiled, the tide turned, "You believe it is easy? Could it not be that you are the killer Master Archammer? What of your dog, Oakmaul? She certainly has the temperament for such a thing."

Gavin flew to his feet, knocking his chair against the wall behind him. He had Trahn held by his robes around his neck, "I have killed for less of an accusation!"

Trahn laughed, "You and your accusations! It is not so pleasant being put on point, eh, master?"

"Gavin. Sit down," said Frederick. It was not possible to ignore. Gavin's chair rolled up from its side. "Now."

Archammer released Trahn with a growl. Trahn's pale lips curled into a smile and he pulled his robes straight. Both sat again. Frederick said with one old finger pointed crookedly at the mage, "A little testy, Gavin. You will control yourself when you are in my House. Do as you will in yours."

Gavin composed himself, he said curtly, "I apologize, Master Guildenil."

Kasu for his part finally spoke, "I agree with the Mother, there is something amiss about this killing. As an elemental control, stone, and likewise metal is always difficult. There is a reason that Master Archammer rejects this as Wrath magic, and that is that it cannot be. It is a strange and seemingly arbitrary separation, but one that is true. This was, I believe, done by an exceptional mage, or a creature that we do not comprehend."

Frederick said, "It is true though, Gavin, all in magic is not so simple. Take the warning to heart, we must proceed with caution. We are in a delicate time, the rumors are swirling, I expect all of the Houses to be on their best behavior. I will arrange an inquiry into this matter, if you have concerns or appointees relate them to me.

"On a more positive note, the planning for the Fall Festival should begin soon, so coordinate any special needs with The House of Currents, I will have several mages placed in charge of such things. That is all I have to address. If there are no other concerns, be on your way." The Firsts rose to leave, and Guildenil said, "Master Entrah, a word please. About Master Jannan's animate."

Trahn stopped, nodded, and said, "Certainly, Master Guildenil. Certainly."

The three mages gone, Guildenil sat down heavily in his chair, a tremendous weight upon his shoulders. Trahn also sat and waited for the First to speak. After a moment he did. "I don't know how we became like this. Like savage animals."

It was not anything that Trahn had expected. "I'm not sure I understand."

"The Directorate Council used to be civil. You didn't experience that, did you? You came along after Gavin. He changed everything. The Houses could argue and you wouldn't expect to be throttled." He paused and then said, "His problem is that he sees nothing but power and glory. For him and his House, and he will stop at nothing, it seems, to get it. I hope he doesn't do anything truly foolish." Frederick's head cocked to the side and he said, "Well, you'll forgive an old man rambling. Do you recall this?" Frederick slid a recently written text across the desk.

"I remember. Some ramblings by a madman five years back. He had a book done up of his predictions. The end of the world and that sort of thing," Trahn said, smiling at the ridiculousness of it all.

Guildenil said, "Yes, that was the one, the self proclaimed Sage of Tesca. When his predictions failed and he lost favor with the masses he challenged Gavin to a duel to prove himself. The poor sod. I wonder whatever became of him?"

"What does this have to do with the animate?"

"That is the interesting thing, Trahn. That is the interesting thing," Frederick said while opening the book to a page near the back. "For all of the confusion herein, after all of the predictions of doom, and stars falling, and death you find this. Here."

Frederick passed the book across the desk to Trahn, who read what was written.

And signaling a time of great loss will be two marks of metal. Bolts of retribution against the hunters. And so it was that the man of stone and steel would be lost. And so he would find his way against the world.

"You believe this, Master Guildenil? Do you truly think that this was done by Murdoch's animate?" Trahn asked, disbelieving.

"You are a hound on the uptake, Trahn. When I re-read the passage it made sense, in the context of what is going on, but it seems unbelievable. I know that."

"Stop me if I seem disrespectful, but if the rest of this madman's predictions are fraud, why, how could this one be correct? Certainly the recent trials fit this, but nothing more." Trahn flipped to an earlier page and read it, his voice a mocking announcement of greatness, "And the tower of those that would save us will be separated, and kept apart from those that would follow, but not until the Red Queen will they be seen again. And lo! When they are come, such will be the rejoicing!" His voice changed to one filled with sarcasm, "This was supposed to happen last year."

"Perhaps, perhaps. But would it shock you if I said that I believed more of what this man has written than most? I don't think he meant the dates as literal dates, but as some other form of authentication. If only he had not challenged Gavin. It is in my judgement that whatever searching for Murdoch's animate is ongoing should be multiplied many times over. We must find it."

"I will not argue if you allocate extra help to find my mage's work, though I do not see your reasoning," answered Trahn. He set the book down on the desk. "If that is everything I will be going."

"Be wary who you mention this to. The Sage of Tesca angered many in The House of Wrath, writing of the fall of the House. It would be best to keep what I told you to yourself. Do this one thing for me, Trahn." His voice was hushed, almost frightened.

"I will, master, I will," Trahn answered and thought to himself, 'There has to be more going on about this fellow than I am told.' Trahn rose and left the First of Currents alone, though now his mind buzzed with secrets, and his spine tingled for a moment, as though insects ran up and down it.

Trahn chose to walk back to the House of Animate, sending the carriage away. He needed time to organize his thoughts, and with a pile of work waiting for him in his study he perceived this to be his best opportunity. The sun was out and it warmed the pale man, but his thoughts were cold. He had been given a glimpse of things that he had not begun to imagine. What did the other Houses know of this Sage of Tesca? Seemingly at least Currents and Wrath had given credence to the man's drivel, maybe even the Way. Perhaps the First of the Elements was murdered for something he knew. "Gah!" he exclaimed out loud, drawing mock calls from gulls sitting on The House of Wrath. 'You are going insane Trahn...this can't be going on behind my back...oh, wonderful, the Mother.'

And so it was that Lilac Rainmarrow stood much like a tree on the side of the path. As he drew near to her she said, "Master Entrah." Then she walked beside him, staff never touching the ground.

"Mother. I have much on my mind, what is it you want?" Trahn asked, crispness in his voice.

"I grow tired of Archammer's bluster, Master Entrah." Her voice was as hard as Trahn had ever heard it. "He has overstepped his bounds again and again, and has faced no retribution."

Trahn turned his head to Lilac and said, "I did not know such a sentiment resided in The Way of Health. I am surprised, I have to admit. What then do you suggest?"

"I realize that our Houses do not always, almost never, see things the same light. An ancient failing. But Gavin has pressed Wrath too far to the front to be allowed to continue unabated. I would not say an alliance, but an agreement. I am concerned, Trahn, if I may."

"Please."

"There is a dark mind among us. I can not explain it but I have felt it as a cold breeze. My brother has felt it, drowning water. My daughter, my poor daughter, she has been closest of all. This thing I fear will bring us much sorrow. I do not claim to know the future, Trahn, but I know as much as I have ever known that Gavin must not be allowed to continue upon the path he has chosen. I will look for allies where they can be found. Ponder this matter." She shook her head, as though doubting herself, "If nothing else."

"An interesting proposition, Mother. I will contemplate your proposal." The insects tickled his spine.

Master Jannan placed a piece of wood on the table and the mage now began the tricky operation of immobilizing the spider animate. He opened the cage and took it out. The legs whirred slowly in circles, trying to grab hold of a surface that was not Jannan. He shook his head at the enigmatic animate. Where had it come from? Why now? And perhaps most importantly: Why was he alone able to handle it?

Hopefully these examinations would yield answers; if not, Trahn would have a difficult time dealing with the Directorate Council. He had come back from the meeting the day before in a fever, well as much of one as Trahn ever got into. He needed answers before the next meeting. Jannan had pushed him for details, Trahn gave them and it seemed to the Second that the First was overreacting. It did not matter though, Master Jannan was as driven to have answers as the First was, so his prodding had not bothered him.

The animate clicked excitedly as its feet, its hooks, touched the wood. Jannan pushed down on the body trying to flatten it. The animate resisted, sinking a bit, but not enough to allow the mage to attach the legs to the board. If it could not be deactivated other means would be necessary.

The magic boiled in his fingers and spasmed into the spider. Jannan had hesitated to use it before. It was a strange spell that did not conform to other animist

162

magic. Rather than creation, it was most certainly used to damage. When he had first discovered it he and Trahn were still young in the House. The test subjects always had their animas permanently damaged. It was a risk he was willing to take now, one that had to be taken to study the beastly thing. And he was a better mage than he had been at the time he last used it.

The animate's legs gave out and Jannan used the weakness to position the animate, legs fully extended, body touching the board. He immobilized each leg with a hook of metal. The spider was now completely stuck and could be studied safely, indeed with the help of anyone, as there was no way they could be attacked. 'Ultimately,' Jannan thought, 'it could make a nice wall ornament.' He held the board up and smiled.

With the animate safely restrained the serious work now began. The construction of the body was top notch; the pieces of metal that formed the egg shaped center had been fabricated with amazing precision. It had taken him months to perform such exact construction of his now missing animate. This was smaller certainly, but it had been a subject of much care. The rivets holding the animate together were well placed and welded with matching accuracy.

Jannan picked up the cutting implement. Two parallel metal rods angled from a handle. The cutting spark jumped across the gap, died and then reappeared. Jannan's face scrunched for a second, he had not had problems with the metal cutting spell in years. Carefully he shaved the end off of the rivets that held the upper body in place. He set the tool down and removed the sections that had been loosened.

Inside he found the crystal cross with the crystal of the legs attached directly to it. There was no other structure connecting them together. The small area where the two pieces touched distorted as Jannan prodded it with a pick. It was remarkably fluid. In a House animate the crystal would be hardened, and gears used to provide movement. This simply skipped that necessity, and it was another sign that it was not built by the House.

Jannan combed the protocols for hours, trying to understand what was at work within the animate. To his satisfaction it appeared that the spell used to stun it had not done any permanent damage. Master Jannan was lost in the complexity of Arcane's thief when Trahn spoke, "Very nice. It appears that you have solved the problem of containing it."

Jannan looked up from the splayed animate and scratched an itch on his left temple. "Yes, seems to be working out well enough. It didn't want to be tied down like that. Can't say I would either."

"You don't have to worry about hurting their feelings."

"I know, I know. This one is…interesting to say the very least," Murdoch said, nodding. He crossed his arms and leaned back on the stool. He breathed out heavily.

Trahn leaned into the space that Jannan had been occupying and stared at the interior workings. He picked up the metal pick and prodded the joint of the leg and body. "That's very clever. What other secrets has our bound little friend given up?"

"Well," Jannan started, then stopped to organize his thoughts, "The operating protocols, as we already know, are a maze, but there are levels to them. Individually, I'd estimate over two thousand castings, to get what we have here. The body is of the highest quality. It betters even the best you or I have ever done. The bar has been raised."

Jannan continued, "Disturbingly enough, even for the sheer mass and complexity, the protocols when viewed on a macro level, are arranged exactly like the House instructs. Which to me says one of two things. Either we are following precisely in the old-world's footsteps, or we have trained someone who has taken our instructions and proven to be a virtuoso at animate construction."

Trahn nodded, his right hand on his chin. "I find it hard to believe that someone who has come through our doors could be so advanced without our knowing. You know it takes days to get a butler working properly, and that is only what, fifty or seventy-five instructional commands? Plus the basic architecture. Our friend here would have taken years to build."

He continued, "Well at least we can take solace in knowing we are on the right track, if we can learn some of the tricks used here we can advance the House's ability quite a bit, Murdoch. Not bad for what we had to pay."

"I suppose. The past few weeks have just been so strange. I had trouble getting the cutting spark started, I don't remember a time I struggled with that, I had it going before Nightwillow even knew what she was showing me."

"Today? That is strange. But don't worry about it, we'll get all of this straightened out, and you can get started on another assistant," said Trahn, happily. "I'd like to take a look at it when you're done. Maybe I'll catch something you miss. We've always worked well together. Remember that first humanoid animate? The expression on Master Hurion's face was priceless. You've taken it a long ways, Murdoch. Don't forget that. You've done much for the House."

Jannan smiled, "What is this, a pep session? Get out of here, Trahn, I have work to do."

"Sure, get something written up for me, I'll need it to keep that dog Archammer off of me at the next Directorate Council," he said walking away. The door closed and Murdoch was again alone with the animate.

Peter lay on his side half awake, his mind probing the darkness around him. Walls, always walls. The witch Oakmaul had come one time in the last week, food had been a little more common, and almost as painful. Peter was almost accustomed to the solidity of the darkness. Less so to the chill, it was strange in that it was impossible to be warm, and only cold enough to prey on one's mind about it being cold. The next layer of sensation was the murmur. Peter speculated that it was the ocean but he would drift and hear voices. Never clear. If it was the ocean it placed this pit very deep into the cliff indeed, and his hopes even lower.

But he would not die to the witch. No, he would not. That was the only thing that kept him holding on, knowing that he would not die to the witch. She had burned him last time. His hands, something to do with being a thief, Peter had not really listened to her ramble. It hurt certainly, but it had chased the cold for a time, so it was almost in a twisted way enjoyable. Serrlena did not find that amusing at all. The healing had been non-existent. Eating had been torture, the blisters, but they did seem to heal on their own quickly, maybe because of the cold, maybe because Peter was numb.

He heard the steps down the hall, it was her again. He thought for a moment about sitting up and greeting the only person that spoke to him, the Wrath mages that brought his food only grunted, so Peter had given up trying, but he

165

decided that sitting was too much effort. It wouldn't matter in the scheme of things anyway, she would have her fun, and he would be left pulling the edges back together. 'The only question is her choice of weapon.'

The lock clicked, Peter had figured out that it was only operable by magic, the door was completely solid. She pushed it open and Peter closed his eyes, the light was worse each time one of the accursed mages appeared. He grunted a greeting. "Charming," Oakmaul answered.

"I try for you witch, I have nothing else," Peter said, his will was not broken yet. He sat up.

Serrlena squatted in front of him; his eyes were still closed. "Will you not even look at me, dog?" She slapped him. It was more show than anything else. "Show some respect."

"If you were worth it, I might," Peter said. A single staccato cough followed. It echoed in the room, down the hall and in his head.

"Quite coy for a man that is as good as dead." Serrlena stood and walked around behind the thief where he sat, his clothing was in tatters and a good amount of muscle showed.

"At least I am not dead."

"Not yet." Serrlena knelt again, her left arm under Peter's, her hand on his chest. She could feel his heart beat. Peter for his part laughed, the thought of fighting back exited him with it.

"What are you playing witch? I know you why you are here."

"Do you? I do regret that I have not been to see you though. There are so many things to be attended to, demands that hold me."

Peter interrupted her, "It must be very hard in your position."

That seemed to anger Serrlena. She said harshly, "Is there much that you must attend to when you are here? I can see how your attention is whisked away. Do you now ask for swift deliverance?"

Peter said, "You make less sense than the things I hear in the dark. So tell me something, witch. Tell me something they cannot. How did you become such a monster? I see the others. They are not dead as you are. They hate me for what I am, you only hate."

She whispered, "We all have our secrets, dog." The dagger slipped easily between Peter's ribs.

He gasped, "Today we play with knives?" The muscles in his arms hardened responding to the pain. He could feel the blood run down his back, it was hot on his skin; if not for the cold blade it would be pleasant. "If I live long enough I do want to know, witch."

"Perhaps someday." Serrlena drew the blade along the ribs, the red line ever longer, until it burst from the side of his chest. Peter knew that this would kill him, if she let it. He did not try to escape or fight back, he had learned that it was not possible to combat the magics. His head spun, and he slumped forward. A matched set. "Damn you, witch," he said weakly.

"It is already done," Serrlena said, a note of sadness in the echo. She stood, and went to the door. Peter rolled to his side gasping, both lungs filling with blood. She turned back and smiled, "*Asosuin!*"

Peter could feel the wounds healing, closing. The blood was still warm though, it was some measure of relief. The pain was still with him as his organs twitched a new life and he tasted his own blood. Serrlena paused in the doorway, she said, "A woman and her son turned up yesterday in the tunnels, both their throats were cut. Sad."

Peter did not move.

Fifteen

Arcane worked carefully on a second digger. In order to put his plans into action and have them come to fruition with any type of expediency he would need many. His work went well. This time the platinum core bent to Arcane's will more completely than the first. The magic that he believed to have mastered gave away more secrets, and Arcane was proud. The hour was late, most of the feast had quieted, though an occasional crash or rhythmic thumping would scrape down the walls into the workshop.

He was either so lost in his work or the man had moved with silence that the rats could not duplicate, which he broke when he said, "How fascinating."

A sense of dread washed over Arcane and he grabbed a hammer as he spun to face the unwanted visitor. Arcane immediately recognized him from the feast. It was the middle-aged man who sat at the end of the table. Arcane had served him wine at one point but nothing else. Arcane took two steps towards him. The man raised his hands out from under a short cape and said, "Wait, animate, I did not come here to have my life of privilege destroyed. Hear me out."

Arcane stopped, and using Bessemer's voice said, "What do you want, sir?" The spider moved silently across the ceiling, putting itself in position to strike.

"I want you to drop the pretense that you are Bessemer. I know you are not."

Arcane cocked the hammer back. "What will stop me?"

The man answered, no fear in him, "The Harrow."

The force of the statement was greater than any magic could be, slowing and then stopping Arcane and likewise the spider. This time it was his voice, low, "Go on."

The man spoke in hushed tones, a secret about to be given, "I have known for some time now that Lord Heele is blessed with the Harrow's luck, my father and his were close business relations. Of course this Heele is not half of what his father was in every sense.

"But I digress. There is a man that lives near Kurn that suffers as a Harrow's Grace. He made a meager existence for himself as a shaman of sorts, before I learned of him. I began to meet with him in secret and brought the shaman to the attention of several acquaintances. As you may know, the Harrow can be used for unimaginable personal gain, if you know the way. The idiot mages here in Serac dismiss it, but they do not know the truth of it." He smiled at his mockery. "It has been a fruitful existence for everyone involved, but the shaman has begun to doubt the power of the ceremonies. Claiming visions of evil he has tried to break our meetings off.

"My point is this. When you touched Heele you released more of the Harrow's power than I have ever experienced. The fact that Heele did not notice was disgraceful, but he never was interested in learning what his father knew. No doubt all at the feast will have a prosperous year. Compared to Heele the shaman, Finsen, is a god. I believe that your talent would enhance the wealth and power of those involved tenfold, and convince the poor man that there is a reason for his curse. Of course if you decline, I will have to report finding you to the House of Animate. I do not know why you are here, but I do not believe that Heele owns two animates."

"If I did not silence you now." Arcane smiled, the man nodded agreement at the statement. "But I find your proposal interesting. You wish me to come to Kurn with you?"

"Of course."

Arcane smiled slightly at the edges of his mouth. "Very well."

The man smiled, joy in his eyes. "Wonderful, I was planning on leaving tomorrow or Thursday. We can discuss this more as we travel; the trip home will be

169

more of a meandering than a forced march I'm afraid."

Arcane said, "Do not come back to my workshop. I do not have the time to be interrupted. I will join you when you leave."

The noble nodded, and said, "Oh, lest I forget, Turnbly Lancaster, at your service." The man bowed and departed the workshop; he stumbled and banged about in the dark, making quite a bit of noise.

When the man had gone Arcane again started the delicate work of the digger. He thought, 'Then it was the Harrow that silenced him. It would appear that my luck is continuing. Someday I will have to thank Heele for all he has done for me. Bessemer must be prepared for my going. If nothing else, it can make bodies of the diggers. It will not be long until I see if the heart is truth.'

Arcane worked alone until the house finally quieted. Bessemer joined him in the workshop and was put to work filing metal pieces. After several hours Arcane said, "I am leaving soon, Bessemer. Another chance to forward my work has come. A Harrow cult. Did you know that Lancaster is a devotee? No? In any case I will leave you with instructions. I would very much like it if you would continue to help."

"You are leaving? So suddenly? I do not want to be left behind," the animate said, worry in his tin voice.

"Do not be alarmed. I will return, if all goes well, which seems likely. We will move forward then. So do these things for me. I will be pleased," Arcane said. He raised his hand to Bessemer's face and instructions leapt the gap. Orders. Insight. Bessemer smiled; it was blocky in comparison to Arcane's more delicate expressions. Bessemer's hands narrowed fingers to thumbs and the cutting spark appeared.

"I have learned your lessons well, brother. When you return, the diggers will be prepared. I will see that it is done." Bessemer spoke with delight, a portion of Arcane's lust for power had been given, and the magic of animate building, most of it, was now his to wield. "You do not allot me the ability to activate the animates. Why is that?"

"I will do it, Bessemer, according to that which I desire. At another time I will give you the power but for now understand, accept the gifts that are given."

"As you wish, brother."

The pair returned to work in silence, Bessemer using much of his new skill.

When Bessemer rose to begin his morning duties, two more diggers approached completion.

Turnbly Lancaster's trunks had been packed the night before, all save his clothes for the day, a comfortable dark suit. The last of the trunks were being piled into the second of two carriages under the watchful gaze of the earl. The carriages were beautiful pieces of work, overly intricate carvings of flowers and animals in the finest wood were accentuated with perfect construction. The Harrow cultist's brown eyes watched his servants harness the horses. The straps and fittings would have been quite costly, had he not made them himself. At last he was prepared to leave.

First though, he would say goodbye to Lord Heele. More than that, the animate's presence weighed heavily on his mind; he was upset with himself that he had not made firm arrangements with the toy. Turnbly found Heele in the dining room, eating along with a few of the others who were staying on. The room had been stripped of its grandeur from the night before.

Bessemer stood next to the lord and listened as he spoke. It was obvious how the other animate had played the deception, they were identical. Turnbly strode across the room and bowed before the eating man. "Lord Heele, I want to thank you for your hospitality. The last two weeks have been as enjoyable as any in my memory."

"Ah, Turnbly. You are leaving so soon? I was hoping you would stay on for another hunt," Heele said, his voice filling the room.

"Yes, so had I, but important business in Kurn has been brought to my attention. Do stay in touch, Rupport."

"I will pray for your safe passage. I am just catching up on the news from Serac, and it appears that there are strange things afoot. Bessemer was questioned at the Guardhouse when he went to Serac to buy goods for the estate. Something about a break in at the House of Animate and a lost toy. But I keep you. Have a pleasant trip. I will send a letter about the rest of the season."

"How odd." Turnbly glanced at Bessemer. "In any case I will look forward to your letter. Good bye, Lord Heele." Turnbly bowed again and then hurried from the dining room. 'The animate is a rogue. I had suspected as much, ah Turnbly but who wouldn't.'

Back outside, the earl gave one final look at the Heele Estate and climbed into the carriage; plush velvet cushions greeted him. If the animate did not come soon he would go to the House of Animate, no toy would trifle with Turnbly Lancaster. Once the earl was in place the caravan began moving away from the estate.

Ahead of the carriage five professional soldiers in the earl's employ led the way, behind another group of five. They wore heavy leather armor and were skilled with blade and bow. They had been hired as a group years ago and had given good service. In between the bookend of soldiers were the servants. A few rode the earl's horses that he used for hunting, most walked. As a group they were well taken care of. Turnbly did not think that anyone in the party would complain of anything.

The caravan rode out and met the road; it was then that Turnbly began to worry that the animate had truly chosen not to join him. But as if to answer the question the carriage slowed and the sergeant came to the door. He knocked three times in quick succession. Turnbly opened the door. The soldier's cheeks were red in the chilled air. He said, "There is a man dressed fully in robes, even obscuring his face. He asks for the opportunity to ride with you to Kurn. I attempted to turn him away but he demanded that I ask."

Turnbly's lips turned up at the corner, his eyes squinting just a touch. "He was expected. Show him to the carriage."

"Yes. Sir." The soldier led his dapple-gray horse away and Turnbly could hear him speaking to the man – not that it was a man. The animate appeared in the door, heavy black robes, and a heavy black cape and hood on over that. What was actually under the robes could not be discerned. The door swung shut and the figure sat across from the earl on the bench. The carriage again moved.

The hood over the animate's head pulled back, magic of some sort. Turnbly smiled. "Very nice. I was beginning to worry about you, animate."

"Arcane. It is good that your soldiers have some sense of duty, or they may have simply pushed me aside." His voice was a low murmur. "It will not suit me to be discovered now."

"Arcane it is. I would trust those men with my life, but I would agree that it is better if we keep you," he paused thinking of the words, "under wraps."

The robes rippled and pulled apart exposing the metal body underneath. Arcane smiled with delight and said, "A simple enough trick, wire spaced within the cloth." Turnbly looked closely. Out of Arcane's shoulders wires emerged and connected to the fabric. "Much to my surprise the whole construction took very well to my instruction. In the future I will have to try other materials. Never mind, I see I bore you. How long will it take to reach Kurn?"

"At our pace, about a week and a half. It could be done faster but the servants complain. They do not ride in such luxury as this." Turnbly patted the cushion beside him.

Arcane looked out the window, examining a woman that walked, and said softly, "So frail."

"I'm sorry, what was that?"

"Nothing, nothing at all." The robes pulled back around Arcane. "I am very new to the world. Tell me of Kurn."

"Very well. It is a pleasant place to live. The primary business is shipping. Unlike Serac the city is at sea level, which makes moving cargo very easy. It can be something of a rough town I am told. The taverns can be unforgiving if competing ships are in. There is also a healthy fishing industry. I myself own ten ships, give or take, and depending on the weather.

"It is a country aligned with the Alliance of Tarlow, which provides for open trade and a non-aggression pact. Even if that was not in place, the fairly close proximity to Serac, and it being the final way point for those ships that want to make the southern run to the Hundred Rivers Delta means that it is fairly safe from open hostility. Even so it has a good standing army. What I have seen of their maneuvers shows them to be well disciplined. But what happens to a man in battle is always a matter of conjecture. All would be heroes in their own story.

"There is a king, King Abarec. Useless, his power has been usurped by the shipping and fishing guilds, or by nobles." He smiled including himself in the statement. "Ultimately, the king would control the army if it were to go to war, but other than that, he very much allows the running of the city to those below him, instead concerning himself with sins of the flesh." Earl Lancaster stared out the window at passing trees; he would have been young when they were saplings. "He is of little consequence really."

The odd pair fell into silence, Arcane probing deep secrets in his understanding, playing little games of magic with the pieces of the carriage. The old wood was not accepting of the animate magic. Turnbly watched the forest roll past until the caravan stopped for lunch.

The two cooks, one a short, fat man, the other short, but not fat, quickly had a cooking box, made by a technologist, out of the second carriage. It had been purchased by Earl Lancaster in Serac before reaching the Heele Estate. This would be the first opportunity to use it, and the cooks happily chittered to one another like children. The box was made of oak, stained dark with runes carved into the side. It had a brass door with a glass window in it on one side. The box was situated on a level piece of ground to the side of the well-packed dirt road. Veal was placed inside it, the door closed, and the switch flipped. Everyone crowded around the small window to watch the meat. To everyone's delight, including the earl, a few short minutes later the haunch of meat was extracted, thoroughly cooked. Turnbly clapped his hands together, staring greedily at the meal. He said, "Expensive, but I would say well worth it! It is a shame that there is not a place in Kurn to acquire such a device."

The fat cook said, "I hope you won't be putting us out on the street because of it." Everyone chuckled at the cook's statement, and then lined up to receive their share. Once lunch was finished, everything was loaded back into place and the caravan began traveling again.

So it went day after day. Arcane sequestered himself in the carriage as it rolled south. The earl would ride with Arcane, or ride a horse if the weather was nice. At night tents were erected and the horses rubbed down and fed. The road proceeded gently down hill as they traveled south. After several days of passing farms and an occasional inn the caravan reached a place where the road split. Arcane was told that the road that angled to the southeast followed the shoreline but eventually reconnected to the southern running road, just before the city of Kurn.

The caravan took the direct route to the south. Most that traveled these roads must have also, there were deep ruts cut into the dirt. The two carriages slid into them, accepting the eventual outcome. Time and again the caravan would pass groups heading north, usually shipping goods by land.

The border of the two states was passed through quite easily. Soldiers for the Royal Army of Kurn provided a small amount of interest in the caravan but quickly let the earl pass. Arcane was glad for the ease. The earl explained, "Again, much of the loosening of borders is due to the Alliance of Tarlow, but then Serac would be Kurn's most coveted ally should a dispute break out."

The caravan reached Kurn a day slower than the earl had suggested. Arcane was beginning to get impatient, but the opportunity to examine a Harrow cult balanced the sense of lost time. The earl's house was an impressive and looming castle, adorned with buttresses and gargoyles. "It was to be a church at one time, in the end they could not afford to finish it. I bought it for a song. The tower I added, but the rest is original, at least on the outside." The earl smiled as he spoke of his home.

"A result of the Harrow?" Arcane asked.

The earl's eyes darkened as he lowered his head. "It could be viewed as a side effect, yes. I do not view the Harrow as a tool for good luck, Arcane. It is much more, and the aversion placed on it by the world at large is foolish. It is power, power that wants to be used. I will show you that, once we have settled into my home. You will learn that perhaps I would not be as easily silenced as you believe."

Arcane smiled, 'You are as frail as the rest, earl.'

"Do not hide your thoughts from me, Arcane. You are no longer dealing with fools and blind men." The earl's voice was tainted with darkness.

"You would threaten me, Turnbly? Hardly a practice that will win my favor. That is why you brought me here?"

"It is not meant to be a threat, animate, a warning. Be aware that the others involved will be suspicious. I will vouch for you, but the others will have their doubts."

The ornate carriage stopped, the horses whinnying and stomping their arrival. The earl, not waiting for the driver, swung the door open and escorted Arcane, fully concealed, into the cathedral that did not exist. The inside had undergone a significant transformation. New walls obviously added late in the construction split the cathedral into smaller rooms. The entrance and hallways opened to the arched stone roof that peaked far above. The layout created a

175

miniature town with its own main street and back alleys.

Turnbly said to Arcane, "Welcome to my humble, if not strange, home. I will instruct Mason, my head butler I suppose, to keep nothing from you. Ah, here he is now."

Mason was gray. His skin was gray, his curly hair was gray, his suit was gray. His voice was gray, "Earl, it is good to see you home safely. A guest?"

Turnbly said, "Yes, Mason. A guest. Master Arcane. Show it, him, all the best." Arcane's head swiveled at the saying. Mason nodded obedience and smiled, looking the enigmatic figure up and down. Turnbly continued, "Where is the lady?"

"In the garden, sir. Dinner will be set at eight, roasted duck. If you would excuse me then, I have to attend to unpacking."

"She always wants dinner so late. Thank you, Mason." The butler walked stiffly away, mimicking a corpse. Arcane's mouth turned ever so slightly, noting the similarity to Bessemer. "This way, Arcane." The earl toured his home happily, pointing out things to Arcane that he thought would be of interest. The earl and his guest made their way up the tower, stopping near the top to go out onto the balcony that faced down the hill to the north and the city of Kurn. The daylight was fading to the west, Arcane allowed the hood and robes to pull back. They both stared off to the city, the light streamed onto Kurn in shafts, reflecting off the buildings. It was a sight unlike any Arcane had seen.

Turnbly commanded, "I have answered your questions as we traveled, Arcane. Answer me this: What are you exactly?"

Arcane did not speak for half a minute. "I am a mystery even to myself. Obviously an animate, but more than that. I am alive, but not in the way you are," Arcane answered quietly, watching the servants mill around below. Mason had appeared on the scene and all but one had begun moving faster. "You humans are a curious lot, earl. Most humans would shy from me. All save you have tried to stop me, and yet you accept me into your home."

"For power, Arcane, you will learn to take the allies that you are given. Come, the sun is nearly set; I will show you the book of Harrow incantations. With luck it will make you more successful in dealing with Finsen and the others." Turnbly closed the iron and glass doors. "Some of the writing none of us can read, but it does not seem to matter. The ceremonies have still proved amazingly fruitful. My study is at the very top."

More stairs, these with a red velvet runner down the middle. It was becoming increasingly obvious how dilapidated the Heele Estate was. The earl's study was breathtaking, the view from the balcony repeated on all four sides. Savage gargoyles overhung the corners, watching for attackers. The floor was polished marble with granite inlay. A desk with an enormous chair dominated the room. The earl lit two lamps with a reddish liquid in them. "The best imported oil. Burns longer and cleaner than anything I can get locally."

Arcane smiled. He felt that that would be the appropriate action for what the earl had said. Turnbly smiled in response, reinforcing the belief. Turnbly pawed through his bookshelves. He said, "It's a strange little book, it never seems to be where I left it. Almost like it is hiding. Ah, here."

From in between two larger hardbound books the earl pulled a small, beaten book. "Its cover looks beaten, but the pages are indestructible, maintained by the Harrow I think."

The book was small enough to rest comfortably in one hand, the skin that it was bound in flickered black, blue and gray depending on the light. The earl handed it to him, at contact an ever so tiny ripple shuddered up into his arm. He whispered, "Beautiful."

"I have translations of pages five and six, nine, eleven and thirteen. The rest is incomprehensible. My father purchased it from Heele, if you care. How he got it is lost. Rupport doesn't remember it, or he is lying about it. Which is possible, as he doesn't speak of his luck."

Arcane said greedily, while soaking in the pages, "Where are the translations? Quickly!"

The earl took a step back, surprise on his face from the force of the animate. "They are locked in the bottom drawer. Let me find the key."

Turnbly searched the rest of the desk and then a side desk, finally finding the long, worn skeleton key. It clicked roughly into place. "I have to get this lock looked at." And then the drawer was open.

Page upon page was extracted from the drawer, ten times the writings of the full, quirky book. Arcane watched the man go to the drawer time and again. "What is all of this?"

"The translation work has not been smooth. Most are repeat or slight meaning changes. I have a book with the most recent, most accurate translations. It's in here somewhere." More pages placed on the desk. "I would think that having various source material for my work would be useful so I did not discard any of it."

"I see that. You keep the translations locked in the drawer, but not the book?"

"No one else can imagine a meaning for the original text. But the translations, those are dangerous." The dark glimmered through his eyes and he looked up at Arcane. "Allow me."

The earl stood from his chair, his eyes rolling back, showing only white, he smiled, the yellowed teeth a dingy contrast. "No, Arcane, I would not be easily silenced."

The animate could feel the force vaguely, much like seeing something disappearing into a fog. The earl began to speak, but no sound was discernible. Again and again. Arcane squinted and shook his head. Turnbly shouted, and extended his arms, fingers bent into squares, at Arcane. The Harrow pushed Arcane against the glass door, silenced by the cloth of his robe. He hung against the door.

"Release me, earl," the animate said, anger pulsating in the tin.

"So you see, Arcane, I am not helpless. Remember that." Chill tainted his voice. His fingers straightened. Arcane dropped to the floor. "Now the translations. They are all here." Turnbly put his hand on a small book, not so small as the Harrow text. "I am off to see my wife. Dinner is at eight as Mason said. You can come if you want, though I doubt very much that you eat."

Arcane's hands balled under his robe. He said, "Thank you, I will most likely stay here."

"As you wish, I will introduce you to the lady tomorrow then. She is wonderful. Good night, Arcane." The earl descended the steps, leaving Arcane in the rapidly darkening study. The sky revealed the stars and the sliver of moon as it darkened into a rich, seducing blue.

Arcane sat down at the desk and detached the bolt of fabric from himself.

The robes fell into a lifeless drapery over the chair. Then the spider released itself from its storage; it climbed up into a corner and began the strange tapping and preening that it had taken on. Arcane sat in his pure form, a mountain of paper raised before him, but for the time being he did not think of it or of the book; the earl was foremost in his mind. 'The fool would make an example of me! I will not allow such indignity again. We shall see what is dealt in the Harrow's Luck for you very soon earl. Yes, yes we will.'

The pages, save the final translations, were in no organized form. It did not surprise the animate. Reading each sheet he organized the chaff into piles, one for each page that was translated from the Harrow text, and in the best order of oldest to newest that he could devise. For all that Turnbly gloated of the genius of five translated pages, it had been an unimagined struggle. Page after page of broken sentences, words, at times even single letters were scribbled out. The net result yielded a series of rants that were disjointed and bumbling. Arcane took up the original text again.

The writing was absolutely preserved. It looked as though it had been written earlier in the week, perhaps a joke by the undead butler. There were two distinct writing patterns. For the first fourteen pages a darker ink was used, the letters were well spaced and split into words. For the final six pages of the book a blue ink had been used. The letters did not separate into words or sentences, but rather ran together a block of text that burned into Arcane's anima. His head cocked to one side as he read each page, printed on one side only, over and over. He matched the series of letters that the earl had translated to the untranslated pages, but never did full series match. It was clear that several forms of the language were in use here. "What is your little secret, you silly little book?"

Arcane set the book down and after a moment took it up again. The ripple. 'It could not be that easy could it?' The Masa'terj rumbled. Focusing on the stone for a moment Arcane pulled the Harrow from the book. It was imbued with power of some fashion. Only a trickle, even compared to Heele, who according to Turnbly was a feeble luck. But there was power, Arcane absorbed it, his eyes dimmed. If it truly was a power that wanted to be used, it would respond.

And it did, the letters twisted in his vision, or perhaps it was his anima that twisted under the power. It did not matter. Arcane laughed once. It was odd that he had such a human reaction to the success. 'Master Jannan's work.' When compared to the original Harrow, Turnbly's translations were actually very good. Certain subtleties were lost in places, but Arcane could reasonably applaud the fool's work.

Arcane nodded understanding at the Harrow practices. There was more to it than the silly Graces and Lucks, much more. It was a surprise that the humans, the Harrow cults, did not fathom. They did not see that it was more than a tool for obtaining wealth, or some small amount of power and skill to punish and frighten. It was the nightmare that the old scholar had written about, and though not all was explained or revealed in the short text, what Arcane really wanted, a Harrow heart, was now very much within reach.

Earl Lancaster took the stairs two at a time. Using the Harrow always made him feel alive, it seemed to loosen up the joints. 'My demonstration will keep Arcane in line I think,' he thought proudly to himself. His power had been growing in recent weeks, bolstered by the understanding of the book. He hummed a tune the quartet had played. The song was infectious and had stayed with him.

The earl went to his bedroom. It had been re-arranged since he was last there. The lady's doing of course. The canopy bed had been turned and dragged into the center of the room. It was not the most effective use of the space. The trunks with his clothes had been brought in and partially unpacked. The earl found his most striking evening suit and changed into it. There was no reason to be hard on the lady's eyes. That done it was nearly time for dinner.

He proceeded down the hall into the cathedral. The dining room had been sectioned out of the main hall. The lady was already seated. She was Turnbly's contemporary, but as of late she seemed not to be aging. Her face was well made up and she sat straight backed in her red dress. Mason stood to her side with a silver platter in his left hand.

The lady, Samantha, said, "I heard you had returned. How is my love?"

Turnbly bowed properly to the lady, "I am in good health, thank you." Mason set down the platter and pulled the chair at the head of the table out; Turnbly sat.

"Where is our guest?" Samantha asked.

"He will not be joining us tonight, dear. He is busy with work that you will find quite beneficial."

The butler began serving the dinner. The duck was roasted to perfection. It gleamed in the lamplight. He carved a portion of the breast and served them.

"And what is that, Turnbly?"

"When next we see Finsen our good fortune will bloom in great beauty."

The lady stopped as she raised her fork to her mouth, and spoke, unconcerned of Mason's presence, "He knows of the Harrow? How can you trust him not to turn against us?"

"Don't worry, don't worry. He is in no position to threaten us. Arcane, his name, should not even exist. He is no threat, dear. Perhaps when it is all said and done he will become our butler. What about it, Mason?"

"I should hope not, sir. I should certainly hope not!" answered the decrepit man.

"Ha! Don't worry, Mason, I have other plans for our little friend." The earl smiled cryptically.

"Very good, sir," Mason sighed and went off to the kitchen.

The lady took two bites; she was gorgeous in the candlelight. "What plans are those, Turnbly? I expect to be included in any meetings with Finsen that you and Arcane have."

"Now is not the time to discuss them. The hunt went well. Another year of Rupport's Luck. Last year the rann lizard, this year it was the biggest buck. Huge, easily as big as my horse. Rupport sent it to the ground with one arrow. It should have taken an army of Wrath mages to bring it down."

"Ugh, please, don't speak of the Wrath mages. I had another one of those fools poking around here last week. I wish you had been here to see it. He was more of a hot head than the rest. They are always asking about the 'shaman'. It's a good thing I was wearing a tight dress, or he might not have been put off," Samantha said. Then smiled mischievously, dimples appearing under the makeup.

"One of these days you'll get yourself in trouble wearing dresses like that. I will send a letter of complaint to Serac. That will put a stop to that," Turnbly said, irritated.

"When will we go see Finsen, love?"

"As soon as Arcane is ready. As soon as he's ready, dear."

The spider retreated quickly from the dining room. No one had spotted it, but then no one was looking for it either, one of the benefits of being carried by Arcane under a mass of cloth. Arcane had suspected as much loyalty from the earl, but now he would have proof. Up the tower it climbed, clicking its way along the walls and ceiling. Arcane sat gazing upon the small book. He looked up and said, "Back so soon? Come here then."

The spider ran across the floor and took one accurate leap to the desktop pushing papers that had been arranged into piles onto the floor. Arcane frowned, then placed his hand on the animate. As before the information swept into Arcane's mind. A crooked smile etched his face. He said, "We all have our other plans, don't we." The spider tapped the desk then ripped a corner off of a piece of paper.

Once dinner was done Turnbly and his wife stumbled with laughter back to their bedroom. Soon though the earl remembered the animate that he had left in his study. He sat up in bed, his wife lying under the down covers beside him. He sprung to his feet, not waking her, and wrapped a robe, perhaps blue, perhaps gray, it was impossible to tell in the light, over his nightshirt.

Down the hall and up the stairs he walked. It was pitch black and he had no light but it did not matter. He knew his home by instinct. Turnbly found his study still lit by the lamps he had started hours earlier. The robe was blue as it turned out, one of his favorite colors. The records of his translation attempts were organized neatly into piles, his hand traipsed along the desk as he turned.

Arcane was out on the balcony. His back was to him and the crystal capped wires reflected the moonlight into dancing stars on the glass doors. Turnbly opened the door and joined the animate on the view deck. Arcane spoke, his voice strangely sentimental, "The night is curious." The earl said nothing. "No? Humans are curious. Both deeply in love and deathly afraid of the night."

The earl stood side to side with Arcane. He was easily a foot taller than the toy. He let out a short grunt. "You have read too many stories, Arcane. The night is what it is."

"I have read very few stories," Arcane answered.

The earl laughed once, then said, "I suppose that is true." A bird of some sort cried far off in the night, its call carried by the wind down from the hills. "What of the Harrow manuscript?"

"I studied the work that you have already done. It seems to be quite accurate. From this I think we should go see this Finsen soon. I will be able to turn your hope into truth."

"Were you able to understand any of the other pages? I can only imagine the power hidden in them," Turnbly asked greedily.

"Perhaps. There are a few ideas to explore, but I was distracted by the stars, the moon."

"If you think you are ready I will arrange a meeting."

"I am ready," Arcane answered.

"Wonderful. Tomorrow holds great promise." The earl smiled and said, "I must sleep." Turnbly went back into the relative warmth of his study, stared out at the unmoving Arcane, frowned and went down the stairs. He wandered the halls until he found himself in his warm bed.

Sixteen

Turnbly rose later than he had planned. Samantha was already gone from the room when his feet first touched the stone floor. He found the robe from the night before and threw it on over his bedclothes. He hurried to the study to set his day in motion. Arcane was not there. The piles of translations had been packed back into the drawer. The Harrow manuscript was gone, but he suspected it was with Arcane, wherever he was. He worried a moment on that.

Putting the book out of his mind, Turnbly drew up letters to each of the others in the Harrow cult. It was a simple message:

Tonight.

Best regards,
Earl of Lancaster

Turnbly sealed the letters with a wax stamp. When that was done, which was in fairly short order, he went down to the cathedral and summoned Mason. The butler appeared more dead this morning than the previous one. Not that Turnbly had seen the man the morning before, but he knew it to be true. "Send these." Nothing more needed to be said on the subject. "Where is the lady, and our guest, Arcane?"

Mason took the sealed letters from the earl and said, "They are in the library. I tried to dissuade her, sir, but she insisted on meeting him. I told her that you wanted to introduce them, but, well you know how she can be."

"How is that again? Never mind. Send the letters and be quick about it," Turnbly said rapidly. Who knew what damage that woman could be doing or the damage Arcane could do? He said, "Is there breakfast to be had?"

"In the library, sir." The old man looked around queasily, clearly wishing to be someplace else.

"Oh, go already!" Turnbly shouted. The butler moved with grace and speed that he only showed when retreating from such situations. Turnbly doubted whether he could even move that fast consciously. Mason was old and the earl had begun liking the idea of subjugating the rogue toy to replace him.

Turnbly stalked the halls towards the library. He passed one of the soldiers, who nodded in deference as he patrolled the hall. Turnbly didn't know why they patrolled, he had never ordered it, but if it made them feel as though they deserved their pay then that was fine. He blinked in response.

He could feel the situation slipping out of his control. She would take a liking to the toy and say too much, give away that he wasn't pure in his motives. 'Well, who is?' he thought, but that didn't mean he wanted Arcane to know.

As Mason had predicted, Samantha and Arcane were in the library. Arcane's hood was pulled back, exposing his metal head. His wife was wearing a gray dress embroidered with green leaves. An enameled star hung on a chain around her neck. At least Arcane was not tempted in the ways that the Wrath mage had been.

A book was open in front of Arcane; he looked up from his reading when Turnbly entered. Samantha stopped eating and smiled from ear to ear when she saw her husband. She said, "Love, why didn't you tell me our guest was an animate. Who had any idea that the House of Animate could create such wonders."

Arcane said, "You do me a great honor, Lady Lancaster." His head dipped ever so slightly. "Earl, your library is most impressive. The lady says that you are quite a collector of all manner of literature."

Turnbly's eyes narrowed for one second trying to gauge the scene he had walked in on. "It is a collection that I am proud of, yes. Mostly for show, I'm afraid. You know that, Samantha." It did not appear that any damage to his plans had been

185

done.

"Yes, love. Have some breakfast," she answered. Turnbly nodded as he walked across the room to the platter of food. She continued, "Arcane has quite a thirst for knowledge. You should watch him read, you could learn a thing or two."

"I'm sure of that, dear. The animist magic is more amazing each time I encounter it," Turnbly answered. He took some lukewarm food and said, "It's a shame the cooking box isn't here. What are you reading, Arcane?"

"*Of the Alliance of Tarlow.* An amazing time you live in. General Paul certainly did his diligence arranging it," the animate answered, then pointedly said, "What of Finsen?"

The two humans glanced at each other, passing subtleties across the gap. "We will see Finsen tonight. It is more than an hour ride from here. You can ride a horse?"

"I have not done so before, but I do not foresee a problem."

"They can be stubborn animals. It may be best to practice before we go. The trip will not be in the comfort of the carriage. My servants are afraid of the man, I think."

Samantha laughed, "The ride is good for the soul, but the path to the shaman is too narrow for the carriage. That's the real reason." She stood from her chair, her dress cascading to full length. "I will leave you two alone. It was a pleasure to meet you, Arcane."

Turnbly watched her until she was out of sight. Then he turned his attention to his guest. "Were you here long, animate?" he questioned when he was certain the lady could not hear.

Arcane looked up from the book he was devouring. "I do not like your tone. Rest your uneasy mind. It was not long. The lady found me in your study, reading, and offered to show me the library. I would not refuse such an offer."

"Is there any offer you will refuse?"

"What offers have I received? Should I turn away kindness? We must take what allies are given. I learn quickly," Arcane answered, frost setting on metal. 'You try my patience too many times human,' he thought along side.

"I am sorry. Forget that I said anything." The earl finished eating and stood up. "Stay here and read or wander the cathedral. I will find you when it is time to leave."

"Thank you. I look forward to meeting the Grace."

Dusk was upon the cathedral when the three of them set out. The earl rode a sleek chestnut hunter; his wife rode its match. Arcane was given a smaller dark gray mare. It was of good temper, the earl said. Arcane did not care if it was good tempered or not. All three horses were saddled with a bag that included some food and a skin filled with water. "Just in case," Mason said.

Arcane was also given a knife, its curved blade was dull; it was useless as a weapon. Arcane took the ornament and handed it to the spider hidden under his robes. The blade would be unnaturally sharp when it was time to make use of it.

Turnbly led the troupe up into the foothills northwest of Kurn. The forest drew tight and dark as the sun set fully, the pine trees imposed their will on the small beings beneath them. The path led further and further into the dread, then torchlight revealed a modest fortress.

Arcane questioned, "This place?"

The earl laughed, "Heh, not hardly. Associates to be sure, but not Finsen. Bandits."

A man standing watch upon the wall raised his hand in recognition as the horses passed, the earl responded equally, and then the lights were left behind and the forest grew tighter over them.

After a time a path just wide enough for the horses to go single file cut its way through the forest. No one spoke as they rode. Arcane could hear soft footsteps around them. Even though he could see clearly in the dark, somehow his vision was obscured, and not just by the low hanging boughs of the forest. 'The effects of the Harrow?' he questioned to himself.

The path of trees was slowly subverted by a mass of brambles and thorns that pulled and bit at Arcane's cloak. The lashes skipped around the Lancasters, never snagging their clothes or horses. The passage of thorns opened to a fairly sizable clearing. The moon pounded down into it, lighting a small house made of stone. Smoke rose out of the chimney and that alone seemed to support a collapsing wooden roof.

Samantha shivered. She whispered, "I always forget how cold it is when we arrive."

Pockets of thorn grew here and there, wrapping around rocks and trees, tearing them to pieces. Bones of small and large animals were strewn about like playthings. The horses were tied to a post that had been set up for that purpose; two others were already tied to it. A man very much in the same mold as Turnbly rode into the clearing on a tall gray beast. It snorted at Arcane.

From horseback the man said, "Who is the robed one, Turnbly? Another acolyte?"

"No, Sarut, not another acolyte. Our enlightenment," Turnbly answered enigmatically.

Sarut swung down from his horse. "Really? This shall be fascinating then." He took Samantha's hand, bowed and kissed it. "Lady Lancaster, lovely as always." Lust twinkled in his eye.

"Thank you, Sarut. A beautiful horse."

"Yes, yes he is. I just bought him. He rides magnificently. Not a hint of fear either." The man tied the reigns to the post. Turning to Arcane he extended his hand and said, "And you are?"

Turnbly pushed his arm down and said, "Sarut, this is Arcane. He is a bit of a recluse. Leave him."

Arcane hissed, "No, Turnbly." Arcane extended his right hand, Sarut took it without looking then recoiled in horror.

"What is this? Metal! An animate? Wrath, Turnbly, have you lost your mind?"

Under his hood Arcane smiled. Turnbly said, "You will be a believer soon enough, Sarut. Now where is Finsen?"

Coughing cracked the awkward silence. Slowly it turned into laughter. "That was quite funny. An animate? You must jest." The voice danced around the group, first here and then there. This way and that. Arcane focused, the man was just before them in the shadows of the thicket. He took two steps forward into the mix of moonlight and lamplight, seeming to appear from nowhere. The three humans bowed ever so slightly to the man.

Finsen was tall. Blue eyes looked out from under a heavy brow. He wore a tattered white shirt and loose black pants. His feet were bare. Adorning his brow was a mangled top hat. A sharpened bone pieced his nose. He was still laughing.

Turnbly said, "That's an interesting hat, Finsen."

"I live an interesting life, earl. Maybe this hat was yours in another life. I don't remember when it found me." He took the hat from his head and handed it to the earl. "So who is this? A friend of yours, Turnbly?"

"It is. Arcane, this is Finsen."

Finsen took two long steps, pushing close to Arcane, his hands on the animate's shoulders. The spider tensed. Finsen closed his eyes and breathed deeply. His head turned quickly and stopped sharply, staring at Turnbly with his burning blue eyes. "What is this, Turnbly? It has no scent?" He tried to push back the hood, Arcane held it tightly in place obscuring the view of the Grace. Finsen laughed, "What sorcery is this? I cannot push back a hood to see my latest son?"

Arcane could feel the Harrow in the man. The magic swirled and jumped, pushing his mood along with it. Unlike Lord Heele, the Masa'terj could barely scratch the surface of the man's power, though it was clear to Arcane's ever more educated mind that he was soaked in magic.

Another current of the Harrow took the man and pushed him. He spun away from Arcane as though forgetting he even existed and said, "I don't want to do this tonight, Turnbly, no I don't. More dreams. More fear." It was almost the pleading of a child.

Samantha took the frightened Grace in her arms and stroked his head, "There, there, Finsen. It will be all right. Turnbly thinks Arcane can show you that you are not cursed as everyone else believes. Isn't that right, love."

"It is, dear. Listen, Finsen, Arcane has mastered the ceremonies. Tonight all of the fear, all of the pain will be gone."

Finsen closed his eyes. When they reopened they were dark, much like Turnbly's had been when he tossed Arcane to the wall. "Very well. We shall see what this Arcane can do. Come. Rose and Varrn are here already." He pushed violently away from Samantha and stalked away quickly. She smiled knowingly at the earl. His head bobbed appreciation.

Sarut bent his head close to Turnbly's and said, "You had best hope that Arcane here is what you claim him to be. I don't doubt the others will be as displeased as I am about another." Then he followed Finsen towards the self-consuming house.

Turnbly said, "Be on your guard, Arcane, Rose can spew the sweetest bile. And Varrn, while not the most touched of our precious little family, can channel the power quite expediently. Sarut. He is not a threat." The earl smiled, offered his arm to the lady and the two of them followed the rest.

Arcane stood in the moonlight for a moment longer, relishing the power of this place. He could not take it, which frustrated him, but to bathe in such a pool was pleasant in its own right. He followed the Lancasters to the house. The heart of a Harrow would be his tonight.

Inside, the house was remarkably spacious. The Grace had excavated the floor to provide relief from the ever descending roof. A fire burned in the fireplace, which was level with Arcane's waist. The one room home had several beams that supported the peak of the roof, but if others had been in place they were gone. The room was hot and shadows danced as the flames flicked and jumped.

Rose and Varrn stood in opposite corners; it was clear to Arcane that they had not been speaking. Sarut took his place in the corner that connected them, but away from the fire. Rose, what could be seen of her, was sickeningly skinny, her eyes sunk deep in her head, and yet they seemed to be on the edge of escaping from their sockets. Her dress was wrapped tightly around her hips and chest, revealing that she could be no older than ten, but her eyes told another story. They were old and famished.

Varrn was easily the youngest of the cultists. His brown beard and long, limp hair mingled together, forming a mat that his other features swam in. To his side hung a sword, an overt display. Undoubtedly, the others had such weapons, if hidden. There was nothing else to notice.

Both stared openly at Arcane as he entered, both thinking of some concern to raise, but neither spoke because Turnbly said, "I am glad that you all could come on such short notice, and also I would thank you, Finsen, for overcoming your fear.

190

Tonight we shall embark on a new story, a new power shall be given to us, to use as we see fit. Through Finsen's ability to channel the Harrow, and new ceremony revealed by Arcane, we shall be blessed with all that we could dream of. Arcane, if you would." Turnbly motioned for the animate to take back his hood.

Without raising his hands to his head Arcane's hood pulled back revealing the metal face, glowing eyes and crystal tipped wire of the animate's head. The brotherhood looked confused, trying to gauge whether Turnbly was a genius or a madman. Varrn's rough voice filled the room, "And what exactly will this do for us, Turnbly? What that we can not already do?"

Rose chimed in, "Yes! Explain yourself. It's quaint, but how it will help us with the Harrow, I do not see."

Arcane's metallic tone was first in answering. "I see you doubt, friends. To your eyes I am nothing but a toy. A silly distraction for the wealthy and powerful. Is that not what you aspire to? A demonstration perhaps." Arcane paced the room as he talked, looking at each present in turn, the Masa'terj pulling from whoever was closest and opening channels with the others. All but Finsen, who remained blocked from him. It was enough to make Arcane smile, but he did not. "Varrn, you are quick with the Harrow. Show me."

"I will not take such commands from an animate," Varrn answered indignantly, raising his fist for no reason.

Turnbly said steely, "Do as you are told, fool! Then you will see what has been delivered you."

Varrn huffed. "Very well." He balled his hands and closed his eyes, summoning the Harrow to him. Arcane raised his robed right arm, extending his hand flat at the Harrow cultist. Power, the Harrow, began to siphon away from the man. Arcane channeled the force through his body, and directed it back into the fool with his left arm. The Harrow flowed back into the human, amplified by the Masa'terj. Varrn opened his eyes, they glowed dark. His breathing was deep. "Such power!"

Arcane smiled, "You understand." His arms fell to his side. "How is it that you gain the power of the Harrow from Finsen? That is something I have not figured out. Nor is it clear in your book, Turnbly."

"It is as I said when you touched Heele. The Harrow, as you are exposed to it, becomes a part of you. You begin to understand it, over time, control it. Unlike the Houses of Serac where you are either a sorcerer or not, you can become a powerful mage using the Harrow." Contempt poured for the Houses as Turnbly spoke. He continued, "As we have been more and more exposed to Finsen and his gifts we have gained similar power. First certainly, it manifests as good fortune, or poor in Finsen's or any Grace's case. But then comes the true power, strength, health, persuasion. It is endless."

All save Finsen and Arcane now smiled, a pantheon of twisted gods, reveling in their own power. Arcane could feel nothing but contempt. It was time to show them what the true Harrow was. And then he would have his prize. If, that is, the old note and the Harrow text were true. Arcane believed them to be.

Turnbly continued as though speaking to a child, "Is that an adequate explanation, Arcane?"

"It is, earl, it is. Finsen, are you ready?"

Finsen looked around his dirt home and said, "Yes, I suppose it's worth a chance to remove the curse that I live under. That is what is going on, right?"

Turnbly nodded, "Oh yes, Finsen. Most definitely."

Arcane said, "Grace, you must open yourself to me. You have amazing power, but it is kept from me. Allow me to free you."

Finsen moved to the center of the house, unknowingly recreating an ancient ceremony as he fell to both knees. One hand balled up, the other was cupped over it. Both held just below his head. His eyes closed, but his eyelids fluttered belying a flurry of movement beneath. Arcane, all of them, could feel the doors swinging open. The Harrow washed over the room with fury. Arcane absorbed the power at a frantic rate, focusing it back into the man that knelt before him. The animate was drawn ever closer until both of his hands touched the man's head.

A rising chorus of ecstasy reverberated against the walls of the slumping house. There was no sign before it happened, the power of the Grace reversed, no longer a reservoir to draw upon. Arcane's focus, which had drifted on waves of a power unlike any he had imagined, quickly returned to the man kneeling before him. Finsen absorbed power from the animate, faster and faster, more and more, reclaiming what was his from the cultists. They now realized that something beyond their understanding was happening to the Grace.

Sarut said, "What are you doing, toy? Stop at once!"

Turnbly thundered, "Arcane! Explain yourself."

Arcane could not speak. His anima thrashed violently, trying to escape its crystal cage. Finsen screamed, a blood curdling cry. He thrashed back, separating from Arcane but continuing to suck the Harrow from him. His back arched, he held his face with his hands, muffling the screams.

Samantha shrieked, "Stop it! Stop it, Arcane! You're hurting him!"

Varrn drew his sword and said, "That is enough!" He swung his sword, cutting through the cloth but merely knocking the animate to the ground. It did not matter; the Harrow continued to glide through him. Arcane knew now what it was to die. His core burned, he could not see. The Masa'terj vibrated with power, shaking his entire form. He could feel the stone crack and shatter under the colossal strain the Harrow placed on it. The burning subsided. He would live. But had he succeeded? If he had not, he knew he would die at the hands of the cultists.

Finsen continued to moan, rolling side to side on his back. Samantha tried to comfort him. Turnbly frowned and kicked Arcane. "What was the meaning of that you idiot? Are you trying to kill us all?"

Varrn said, "We should destroy this thing now!" He poked Arcane in the side of the head with his sword.

The Grace stopped moaning for a moment. A new scream filled his throat. Across his skin small cracks began to show, as if he was made of porcelain and had been dropped. They continued until all of his skin was cracked and torn. Samantha pushed away from the Grace. Her eyes were wide open with horror. Rose pushed back against the wall and hid behind Samantha.

After only seconds, which had been slowed to days by the confusion, a dark liquid, a mixture of blood and magic began to pour from the cracks. It slowly coated Finsen's entire body, coalescing into new flesh.

Earl Lancaster was the only one that spoke. He shouted, "Wrath! What is going on? Arcane! What did you do?"

Arcane's anima had settled, his mind clearing. The spider, still attached to his back followed suit. Arcane said weakly, his voice more tinny than before, "The Harrow, earl. It is the true Harrow."

Finsen's body had changed, grown; his muscles tight and strong, his hair where it had not fallen out had turned blood red, his skin smooth, tough and black as night. Such were the effects of the Harrow on his flesh. He sat up suddenly, and blinked slowly, a clarity in his eyes. He laughed, a deep heady laugh. "I see the truth. Now."

He got to his feet, he was taller than any of the others in the room, the roof looked even more sunken when placed against his larger form. He stretched, his neck and back cracked. Turnbly took one step back, fear in his eyes, "Finsen? Thank goodness you are okay. We were so worried! We'll destroy this nasty toy right awa...Ruhh!"

Finsen's hand stuck like a knife in the earl's throat. "I never liked you, Lancaster." The Harrow pulled his hand from the wound. The earl held the gaping hole, coughing blood that mixed with all that sprayed, and fell to the ground in a heap. Finsen cracked his neck again. Rose screamed. Samantha and Sarut drew daggers from some hidden place. Varrn readied himself against the black terror. "There is not a place for the rest of you with the Harrow. You used me, I knew it all along, but I could not stop it. Why do I even speak to the dead?"

Varrn rushed the monster, sword swinging from left to right in the tight space. The well-aimed blow struck the Harrow square in the neck, not that he even tried to evade the sword. The blade stuck in the stone hard skin. Finsen smiled, "Varrn, always untrusting." Finsen took him by the neck with both hands and bent him sharply backwards. He yelped, then silence.

Finsen, in one smooth motion, rotated his arm then extended it out pushing nothing. Sarut exploded backwards from where he stood, slamming into the wall. The roof shuddered. Samantha stood shaking at the carnage around her. Finsen crossed the room and stood close to her, now much taller than her. "Samantha, Samantha. What a lovely name." With one hand he caressed her face, the other took the dagger from her. Rose caught it in her back as she tried to escape, she fell bleeding. "I am so sorry that things between us will end tonight. You are, even at your age, such a lovely flower." His hand fell to her breast.

Samantha whimpered, "Pl...please...don...don't."

"Only for you do I feel any hesitation, but the Queen demands it." He raised his hand from her breast, preparing to strike when Arcane attacked with the ornamental blade, stabbing it into Finsen's back. The blade, sharpened by the spider, penetrated the Harrow's skin, purple speckled blood flowed out, pure Harrow magic. Finsen grunted, turning to his only attacker. "I might have forgotten you, animate, as thanks for my revelation, but not now."

Arcane's cloak exploded open, the spider propelling itself towards Finsen, driving its talons into his flesh. At the same time Arcane lunged forward, propelled upwards by the cloak. The attack was timed perfectly. Finsen tossed the impaling spider aside, leaving himself open to Arcane's knife. It slid into his throat without resistance. The Harrow coughed and stepped back, knocking the shocked woman to the ground.

Finsen lifted Arcane with both arms and tossed him away. Arcane pulled the dagger from the wound as he went. It was too late though; the cloak, like a mass of snakes had wrapped around the Harrow's limbs, tangling the mismatched pair together. Arcane slammed back into Finsen cutting at his neck as they both toppled over. The spider had started the assault again, crawling over the mass of flesh, cloth and metal, stabbing the Harrow again and again.

Finally the beast moved no more. Arcane stood, his right arm lay on the ground under the dead Harrow. The spider pulled at it but could not move it. Arcane knelt across the beast's abdomen and cut into his chest with the knife. It took several minutes to reach the heart. And, as the legends said, it still beat.

Arcane cut it from its place in the dead man and held the beating heart in his left hand. He stared at it triumphantly. Harrow, pumped from some unseen source, slicked down his arm. A small latch released, and Arcane's chest opened, mostly hollow, save the inner workings, gears and wires and crystal core. "Now to see if all of this was worth the effort."

The animist magic flickered weakly, the residue of the Masa'terj barely providing enough power to cast the desperate spell. Arcane placed the purple, beating heart into his chest, the liquefied crystal flowed around it. Hardening. Holding it in place.

The shockwave of Harrow toppled the damaged animate. He rocked back and forth. The colors and the smells from the dinner at Heele's all a million times stronger. Arcane laughed, it was all he could do as the power washed over him. He stood. The animate approximated a scream, pushing his hand towards the dead Harrow. The dirt collapsed under the blow, the corpse pushing down an inch into the ground.

Arcane felt dizzy, drunk on the power. It was so simple. The sobbing of Samantha caught his attention, sobering him. She could have escaped while he had done his work, but she had not. She cried freely, clearly expecting her death. From the surrounding carnage it was understandable. Arcane frowned, "Get up human."

She stood, her face wet, makeup staining trails under her eyes. She said, "I...I'm sorry...Arca...I'm so sorr...rry."

Arcane did not know what had come over him, perhaps some form of pity, perhaps residue from Finsen in the heart. He did not know, "Go outside, we will return to the cathedral. I have what I wanted. You, perhaps unfortunately, will not die with your comrades."

Samantha staggered outside, stepping over the body of Rose without looking down. Finsen had done his work well. Arcane pried his arm from under the body of his dead foe. It was crushed and bent beyond recovery. One look and the spider repositioned itself on Arcane's back, the bloodied robes closing around it. Arcane went out into the night.

The lady had gotten no farther than three paces before she had collapsed again, sobbing uncontrollably into the dirt. Arcane helped her up and supported her as they walked. When they stood comfortably away from the house he turned back to it. "Let there be no record of what has happened. *Aso Osra Haeth!*" The words were filled with power. The house smoked first, then burned, all consumed in the fire created by the will of Arcane. The heart gave him a taste of the power that he had lusted for since his creation only weeks before. And he would savor it. But he was not satisfied.

The horses tied to the post were visibly spooked. They neighed and kicked and pulled at the post but the construction was more sturdy than they could overcome. Arcane tried to calm them in the flicker and roar of the burning house, having success both with Sarut's and Samantha's horses.

Taking the reigns of Widow Lancaster's horse, he led it back down the thorn trail. The forest had cleared some, giving sight to Arcane. Inside his metal chest the Harrow heart beat. The power, the connection, the life was succulent, but it was disturbing to hear the thumping inside his metal shell. It would be unnerving until he became accustomed to it. The lady's sobbing became more subdued and finally stopped as they traveled away from the dastardly scene.

At last Samantha spoke, "What is to become of me now that my husband is dead? What will be said of me?"

Arcane smiled, the humans rarely saw beyond themselves. "Go about your business. If you are questioned use your charm. Is that not why you have it? It is so difficult to believe that we, no, you and Turnbly were attacked while riding?"

"You knew all along what was going to happen. You used us to create that monster! Why?" she asked.

"I could just as easily kill you as let you live, human. Do not question me. The earl was useful, maybe only the Harrow's luck on my part. Forget what happened tonight. You will if you have any desire to live."

Samantha's voice cracked, "I don't know that I do, you wretched little toy."

Arcane stopped his horse, Samantha stopped beside him. Arcane's arm jutted out, clutching her by the neck. "I told you, do not push me, human. I will not hesitate to kill you. You will forget this night."

Samantha nodded slightly, tears again streaming down her face. Arcane released her neck and said, "Good. Good. Let us return to the cathedral. We will have this sorted out in short order."

She had not moved in years, her throne carved of obsidian jutted up behind her and had long ago taken hold of her. Her coal skin blended into cloth and crown and throne, they were one and the same anymore. Her eyes fluttered under long closed lids; a son was born, his heart beat strong. Soon he would be a knight in her host. The corners of her black lips turned up. It had been decades since the last. He would come to the Centaern, all came to the Centaern, all came to the Queen.

Seventeen

Arcane and Samantha returned to the cathedral in the dead of night, the moon reflected in the windows of the castle. Torch lit doors welcomed the mismatched pair. Arcane took the widow inside. Torches burned here and there, making patches of color in the otherwise gray washed room. A soldier sitting near the door under a worn blanket stood as the pair came in. His leather armor creaked ever so slightly. Concern was etched on his face. He said, "Is all well? Where is the lord?"

Arcane answered in a whisper, masking the metallic tone. "He is dead. We were attacked by bandits while we rode. The lady and I barely escaped with our lives."

"No! This is terrible! I warned the lord against riding at night, but he would never allow us to accompany him. With the lady's permission we will hunt down the killers!" the soldier said.

Arcane answered for her, "It would be right. Send Mason. The lady tires."

"Of course," the soldier answered. He took a torch and left Arcane and Samantha alone.

Samantha slouched and said, "Attacked while we rode, indeed."

"Silence, human," he whispered. "You would have them know the truth? They would kill you before turning on me! Simple rumor of the Harrow has been enough to insight riots, or do you not read the books your husband collected? So send them on their chase."

She realized the truth of his statement, and though helping the toy made her heart ache she nodded.

Arcane nodded and said, "Ahh, here is Mason."

The butler was panicked and hurried, dressed in his bedclothes. "My poor, poor lady! She is not hurt is she? Arcane?"

"No, Mason, not hurt. Take her to bed, the night as been hard on her."

Mason placed his arm around Samantha and led her away; they passed all ten soldiers, fully dressed for battle. The group organized itself before Arcane. The sergeant's voice was rough. He said, "Where did this happen?"

From under the hood Arcane spoke, "We were riding northwest of here. A trail that cuts through the forest. As we came upon their fortress the bandits fell upon us. The earl seemed to think he knew them, but he was shot dead with an arrow. The lady and I only just escaped."

One of the archers clenched his teeth and grumbled, "I know that place, it's a band of thieves. Petty criminals until this."

"You know the way?" the sergeant asked.

"Yeah."

"Okay then, let's ride. The lord will have vengeance." The soldiers streamed past Arcane into the night with a great clatter and conversation. Arcane stalked down the hall and found Mason outside the master suite. He was visibly shaken, rubbing his left eye.

"Master Arcane, the lady fell right to sleep. Oh! This is awful!"

"Yes it is. The soldiers are on the hunt. When they find those responsible they will pay. I will watch the lady through the night. Go back to bed."

The butler looked surprised by the offer and said, "I couldn't possibly."

"Go."

The butler blinked then said, "Thank you." With another worried look cast through the doorway he left Arcane alone in the hall. Arcane entered the suite and sat down on a plush chair

'These humans are put off easily enough. But what to do, what to do? I have made a great difficulty for myself by letting her live.' Arcane listened to the beating of his heart. Spells formed in his mind, the Harrow filling his anima.

After a time he stood. He knew that he could not allow Samantha an opportunity to regret her agreement, and yet Arcane could not find it in himself to finish the work that the Harrow had started. Arcane closed his eyes, and growled softly, his hand partially extended over the widow. He tried to straighten his fingers but they would not, damage that he had not first realized from his battle with Finsen. It did not matter. The Harrow leapt to action. The widow would sleep now and when she woke would remember little. 'Each in turn must be made to forget.'

Samantha slept fitfully, though less so after Arcane performed his spell. When morning came Mason appeared, his face was swollen and red from crying, the color foreign to his face. "The lady is not yet awake, Arcane?"

"No, she is not, and I fear for her. She is restless, and yet she cannot wake."

"I will see to her care. You have done all you can do for her. I know she would thank you," the butler said softly, looking past the hooded animate to the lady.

"I wish you well, Mason, but I must go. I have urgent business elsewhere."

"Certainly. I hope I am not overstepping my bounds when I offer you a refuge from your travels; the lady would want it, most definitely." As he spoke Samantha gasped, but did not wake. "I must see to her. Travel safely."

"You serve your master well," whispered Arcane, a grim smile under the hood. A soft magic carried upon his words, filling the butler's ears. Mason fell at the lady's side, attempting to wake her, but he too collapsed into sleep. The rest of the service staff was equally entranced. Arcane would not be remembered.

At last the soldiers returned. They had lost one of their numbers and were grim faced for it but upon seeing Arcane waiting for them outside the cathedral they boasted of the slaughter. Arcane congratulated them and excused himself. He took his bearings and set out by foot for the Heele Estate, bolstered by the power of the Harrow. Behind him the soldiers fell from their horses.

Arcane skirted around Kurn and took up traveling on the road to Serac that paralleled the coast. He pondered on the magic, the Harrow, that was now part of him. It was an interesting magic, its power spread across the spectrum claimed solely by the Wizard Houses. Most of all it strengthened his affinity to the House of Animate. The cloth of his robes and cape now obeyed his commands, where before only the wire strung within it carried his will. But indeed all aspects of the human's magic opened before him.

It was through this enlightenment that he came to worry and fret over the episode with the hunters. If the bodies of the humans were found, which they most likely had been, it would not take a mage long to understand that the magic used to slay them was from the House of Animate. And though Arcane now walked brazenly past farms and travelers it was another creature altogether dealing with the Wizard Houses.

Unlike the trip to Kurn, when he was shielded from unwanted eyes by Turnbly, now armed patrols of Kurn posed a very real threat. Perhaps not to his existence in an immediate sense, but more bodies would arouse unneeded suspicion. So it was that when the patrols appeared small and distant on the road Arcane would abandon it. These times provided an interesting view of the world. He saw plants and animals and sights that he would not otherwise have seen. The inspection of insects, a tree struck by lightning, the crushed bones of a deer that had not escaped a rockslide. In all things he learned lessons.

When back on the road Arcane covered a great amount of distance at night, not having to concern himself with patrolling soldiers or pretense with other travelers. For such a small animate Arcane traveled at an exceptional speed, reaching the proclaimed border of the Kingdom of Kurn on the night of the fourth day. Under the terms of the Alliance of Tarlow, and as it was the border with the region controlled by Serac, there was very little in the way of border protection. Nevertheless, Arcane deviated from the road and crossed the border without the scrutiny of the soldiers that monitored the road for criminals and vagabonds. It was somewhat silly though, the undesirables could as easily cross in the manner that Arcane now chose.

Once in the outlands under Serac's control Arcane strayed from the roads permanently. It would be a fool's venture to gamble on his power now, with the mages so close. Under the cover of night Arcane returned to the Heele Estate. Smoke billowing from the chimneys gave away the presence of the humans. Arcane imagined Bessemer running to serve them as he watched the manor from the woods. As the first time Arcane shielded his presence from his brother. Shedding the tattered and sodden robes and cloak Arcane approached the manor and entered through a servant's door.

The house was quiet and dark, the loudest sound Arcane's feet on the wood floor. He smiled. This was his adopted home and even the threat that the mages of Serac posed could not take his sense of relief at returning to it.

Down into the cellar he went. It was his domain. While he had been gone boxes had been moved, opened, spilled and rifled through. Arcane immediately began to worry that his workshop had been disturbed. Ahead he could sense Bessemer in the dark. Arcane thought angrily, 'What has this fool done?'

Bessemer's back was turned to the entrance of the workshop. Arcane could see that he worked frantically on a digger. Arcane said, "The work goes well, Bessemer?"

The animate swung around in one motion, facing Arcane; there was no glee in its face. "Brother, you have come home at last. Yes. Yes the work goes." Its voice was flat, obsessed. Bessemer twitched, as though another command had been given it and it had been fought off.

Arcane questioned, "Things proceed as planned?"

"The diggers, yes. Always the diggers."

Arcane frowned. Something was amiss in the toy's anima. "What of the boxes? Has somebody been down into the cellar?"

"No, no. I needed more material. More." Bessemer's face convulsed, almost coming apart. "The...work...goes well."

Arcane did not feel concern for the toy but if it had deviated, such could be disaster. Arcane walked fully into the workshop. Stacked in piles were the shells of diggers, each a perfect replica of the first. Every surface was covered with their stocky form. Sharpened mouths gawked at Arcane from every direction. Something in Bessemer had gone wrong; building the digger had become the toy's obsession. Arcane only hoped that it had continued to perform the servitude that minutes before he had hated it for.

Arcane's arm extended, sending Bessemer into suspension. That would be best, while he sorted out what had happened, what had gone wrong. And wrong it had gone. Arcane explored the cellar and room after room had been rummaged. Anything metal had been enlisted. Some of the animate forms were made of gold.

Some silver. Some had precious stones or other decoration embedded in their surfaces. The further from the workshop Arcane pushed the more twisted the forms became. One was a silver teapot with legs. And yet, all could function as designed. Arcane was very much relieved that he had not graced Bessemer with the keys to activation. If he had, things could have been much worse. And depending upon the consequences of Bessemer's behavior they very well could be.

Repairing his left arm and rebuilding his right had been Arcane's original priority; his concerns given the state of Bessemer had changed considerably. Arcane returned to the workshop. From the outside Bessemer looked peaceful. It was time to delve into the anima.

Bessemer's mind was ravaged by the instructions Arcane had transferred to it. For whatever reason, and it was not entirely clear to Arcane why, the animate magic used to instruct in the creation of the diggers had overwhelmed the toy's anima. Its mind had fought a diligent, ordered fight, but had lost in the end to the unrelenting command to build. Arcane closed his eyes in order to push out distractions, an action that had entered him with the Harrow's heart, and began to clean the fractured anima and mind of Bessemer. It was tricky at times, the commands had taken root in very basic building blocks that Master Jannan had used, and they had to be unraveled and re-raveled to keep the toy intact.

Several hours passed in the trying. When it was finally done, Arcane opened his eyes and the wisp of magic reactivated Bessemer. The toy shook its head, as though it was trying to clear some awful dream from its head.

"Arcane, brother! You are back! It's wonderful to see you. And so soon! I would have expected you to be gone for at least a few weeks, but," the animate noticed the state Arcane was in and stopped. "Oh dear! You are in quite a shape aren't you."

"Yes, I imagine I am. What do you remember of the last weeks?" he questioned with trepidation.

Bessemer did not speak immediately. "I don't recall," the animate answered, surprised at itself. "I know I should...but it is gone."

"Wrath!" Arcane exclaimed, an interesting expression he realized as he said it. "Get upstairs and find out what is going on. You suffered a rather unexpected ailment, and I only hope that it is not compounded."

"Certainly, brother. I am so glad that you are back," the animate said happily.

"Go!" shouted Arcane.

The animate got to its feet swiftly and hurried away into the cellar. Arcane desperately needed to know if there were to be more repercussions. He hoped that there would not be.

Tara sat straight up in bed from a deep sleep. It was not unusually early for her to wake but she would have sworn that her mother, her real mother, had been telling her to wake up. Looking around the mossy room she saw she was the only one awake. Several other mages slept silently. Tara got to her feet and tiptoed out of the room. She felt quite awake but realized that she was not really choosing her path.

Tara walked to the Mother's garden. It was dark; the Mother was not there. Light filtered up from the hidden tunnel. Without giving it a second thought she walked with a sway down into the old place. The torches on the wall illuminated the forest, as before, and Tara walked down the hall. Behind her the pool rumbled closed. She turned, for a brief second feeling panic, but it died, replaced by curious confidence. On into the split-level room she walked, past the sigil of the House embedded in the floor. The oil lamps standing in the middle of the room were lit, giving off their sooty, dirty light. Tara was alone.

Driven by the external force that brought her here, she kneeled between the lamps as she had seen the Mother do. Her head bobbed once. The forest carved on the walls spun, color flooding the landscape. She knew that she knelt in the old place but that knowledge fell to the side as she now stood in a very real forest.

The trees, the firs and pines, smelled spicy, the fresh air of the sunny forest danced in her nose. She reached out and pulled at the needles of a pine. They popped off the branch into her hand releasing fragrant oil into the air. Tara breathed it in deeply, filling her lungs with lovely scent. There was no sound, an enforced silence marked the conspicuous absence of bird or beast. Tara turned through a full revolution in the forest and wondered what to do.

When she faced her original direction a path, no more than a parting of branches, was open to her. She walked slowly ahead realizing that she was strangely unconcerned about her new surroundings. How had she arrived here? Where was she? The questions disappeared, drawn out of her mind by the branches that brushed past her. If she had looked back she knew that she would see her worries hanging, caught, on the branches. She did not look back.

Out of the corner of her vision Tara noticed a sparkle. Turning her head she saw the amulet that the Mother had pulled from the wall hanging on a line of silk from a tree branch. She reached out to touch it but it jolted upwards, a flittering bauble to draw her on. Looking up the tree Tara saw a long caterpillar, fat, orange and black, with sticky eyes, wrapped repeatedly around the branch, the bracelet dangled from silk made by the mammoth insect. Not the words, but the impression of speech filled her ears. The voice skricked a mangled human, "Not-t-t now-own-ow! Look-k-k-k away-ay-ay!"

Tara frowned, repulsed and uneasy, but not afraid. She followed the command. The Way had become strange as of late, and she had become nearly accustomed to the larger world. Throughout the forest she now saw other hangings. A knife with a black blade hung not far from the path through the branches. Further off a necklace, she believed; others distant and blurry. She did not look up. Leaving the hanging treasures Tara continued through this surreal forest. The scent of butterflies wafted past.

They descended on her without warning, thousands of orange and black butterflies, smacking against her body, tangling in her hair, the powder from their wings coating her, filling her lungs. Tara coughed. She was afraid. As quickly as the butterflies had appeared they vanished. Not above, not behind.

Tara ran back up the path, but the hangings were not there. It had changed, the forest was different. A house. A mansion. A scene plucked from time. Smoke billowed from chimneys, but it did not move, the expanding columns, perfectly formed were frozen in place. The sunlight reflected on a dragonfly, metallic blue, eyes a million Taras, wings frozen in mid beat. Tara plucked the insect from where it hung, turned it sideways and released it. It did not fall.

Approaching the mansion, Tara saw that the front doors were open. She entered under the watchful gaze of a woman in a stained glass window. The foyer was empty; the click of a clock filled the room. Tara shuddered, though not for being cold. 'I wish that Alex was here. Or better yet Brother Chaign.'

Through the house she walked, her path seemingly predetermined. Into a kitchen and through, down into the cellar. Into darkness. She looked back; the stairs she had just descended and the kitchen beyond were both gone. Tara blinked rapidly, not understanding. Terror. Trapped. The smell of Earth. A light appeared over both shoulders, weak and flickering. The cellar was gray even with the lights. At the same time boxes would appear closed, ordered, then strewn across the room. Tara's heart sunk in her chest. Her breathing shallow. She closed her eyes, trying to force her way from this place. It did not change. She had forgotten where she had come from.

So she did the only thing she could do and pushed into the darkness. Coming to a small room with an anvil the Way mage stopped. The room had the look of recent use. What is this doing here? The question hung with no answer.

The room swung, she faced a corner that had been behind her. From that corner the golden eyes stared at her. If there was a body attached to them Tara did not see it. She froze, a statue. For minutes the two stared at each other, neither moving, neither attempting to. This time it spoke, a mere whisper, "Back again are you?" The eyes did not expect a response. The mist shifted slightly, and Tara realized that she was moving ever so slowly towards the shape. "I grow tired of these visits," it said.

Frantically Tara tried to grab something, but nothing was within her reach. Closer to the eyes, closer to the mists she floated. A portion of the mist coagulated into a tendril and it plunged into Tara's shoulder. She gasped. The tendril withdrew taking blood or something with it. Another voice burned her skin. Not the mist, "Be gone from here...lest you are destroyed."

Tara staggered away from the mist, the eyes, but the room was closed to her. The scent of butterflies. Then they filled the room, the mist, the room, the forest, all gone. Tara slumped to the floor between the oil lamps unconscious. Cold sweat covered her body. Her shoulder burned with an acidic sting.

Lilac and Chaign stood conversing nervously in the Mother's garden. The passage to the old place was closed and though they had tried both singularly and together to open it, it remained firmly sealed. Lilac rubbed her forehead with her left hand. She had had the House searched when she felt the rumble of the portal closing. It did not take long to find that Tara was missing.

"She will be alright, Lilac," Chaign said, his voice stoic.

"She had best be! If not I will have serious doubts of my service to the Way."

"You know that is not true. Take heart, she is gifted and keeps her wits about her well. Let us try again."

"I do not have your confidence when it comes to the old Way. But yes, we try again." The Mother replicated what Chaign had shown Tara some weeks earlier. Unlike her previous attempts that morning, this time the pool opened and the two mages rushed down into the hidden chamber. Both called Tara's name when they saw her collapsed on the floor of the room. Chaign reached her first, and rolled her over into his arms. He said grimly, "She is weak, but alive. Wrath! What was she doing here?"

"Hold her, brother." The Mother fell to one knee, right hand on her staff. She touched Tara on the cheek and pulled her hand back rapidly with a yelp. "Her skin burns! What manner of wizardry is this?"

Chaign looking down on Tara said, "Look here." He pushed her tunic to the side revealing the wound she received from the mist. It was small and round with reddish flakes clinging to it. "What manner indeed? Let's get her out of here, she is safe and alive and that is what matters."

Lilac nodded and stood. "If only I hadn't shown her."

Chaign lifted Tara in his arms. "Do not doubt yourself, Lilac, the Earth chooses who it will. We have only to prepare her for whatever need it takes her for. Come along."

The two mages hurried from the old place with Chaign in the lead carrying the unconscious Tara. Bits of reddish flake separated from the wound and fell to the floor with each step he took. In their hurry and concern for Tara neither mage had noticed the mansion in the carving of the north wall. Even had they been looking it would have been difficult to see, hidden among the branches and trees.

Tara was laid carefully on a bench that been covered long ago in bright green moss with brown undertones. It was soft to the touch and cushioned her now as well as any bed could. Chaign touched her cheek and withdrew his hand. "She still burns but not as before, it is tolerable on the skin."

With relief in her voice Lilac said, "Good. Step aside. I have work to do."

Moments later Tara's eyes opened and a frown upset her face. She sat up and faced the mages. Her shoulder itched and she scratched at the irritation under her tunic. She said, "The mist. This time it was not pleasant." She pulled the tunic to the side in order to see her shoulder, the wound had mostly healed by the magic of the Mother, but small reddish flakes still pushed from the center. "It struck me."

Lilac said, "I, we," she motioned to Chaign, "are relieved that you are okay. I must admit that what happened this morning I have never seen. The Way's denial to the carved room is of great concern." She could see on Tara's face that she was surprised at that. "Yes, my daughter, the Earth rebuked us. If you had not been okay...it will be a subject of much meditation."

Chaign's face was hard, he was thinking. "What of the mist, daughter? That most of all seems worrisome, beside your well being of course."

Tara nodded, "Let me think, first there was the forest, then the butterflies, oh, and the caterpillars. Big ones! Wrapped all around the branches, with the treasures from the wall. Then the mansion and I went into the cellar. Then the stairs were gone, so I went further into the cellar. There was a dark, small workshop with an anvil in the center. I was wondering what the room was, well a workshop, but. Oh! Yes, I remember. The room spun and the mist, and its eyes were in a corner there. And it said something: 'I grow tired of these visits.' Only a whisper. Then my shoulder hurt and I woke up here."

Chaign and the Mother looked at each other, worry on their face. Lilac said, "I do not know of these things. I have had visions before, even in that room, but never have I seen these things. It is a warning to be sure. This is of greater concern with each passing day." She continued, "Tara, rest and recover your strength. I have much to think about. Chaign."

"Yes, of course." The two of them left Tara sitting alone in the room. A glowing orb popped into place on her shoulder. She stood up and went to water some plants.

The dragonfly hovered in the sun and then set her motion forward after a gnat. It whizzed sharply to the side as the gnat turned a more gradual path. Closing in on the doomed insect it sped up for the final strike. Suddenly and without explanation the dragonfly found itself hurtling towards the ground where it bounced once, shook itself off, and took to flying again. It did not understand.

Inside, Bessemer walked the halls of the mansion. The few servants that he passed eyed it warily. Eventually the animate found Lord Heele partaking in his favorite pastime, eating breakfast with the most recent invitees to the estate and the hunt. Bessemer vaguely remembered them from the send off. Rupport stopped in the midst of chewing and stared at the animate when it entered the sitting room. The guests all stopped talking, there was no sound.

Bessemer said, "Good morning, sir! Everything is well?"

Rupport looked from person to person, then back at Bessemer. The lord shouted, "Bessemer? Where have you been, you stupid thing? We arrived back from hunting three days ago! I should have you sent back to the House of Animate and demand your cost back!"

Bessemer's mind spun. 'What has happened?' It thought quickly though and said, "I would apologize to you, sir. Calamity has befallen your humble servant. In searching the cellar for the perfect set of dishes to serve your amazing feast upon a pile of boxes fell on me. I only now freed myself. I apologize for my failures, sir."

Heele frowned, the lines deep in his fat face. Somewhat calmed he said, "Is that so? Perhaps it is best that you stay out of the cellar. There is work that needs to be done. Set to it!"

The animate scurried from the room, all eyes on it as it left. Despite the tongue lashing it felt fortunate, most of the time that it did not remember the estate had laid quiet, emptied for Heele's hunt.

Bessemer went up to Lord Heele's room. Sure enough there were trunks that needed to be unpacked. The animate went about the simple chore but wondered why none of the other servants had done it.

Arcane turned page after page in his mind. He looked for runes of protection in the vast landscape of magic. Runic forms existed as the physical manifestation of the abstract power of the wizards. Ordered carefully they could imbue a sword with great strength, or create a wand that allowed a simple minded human to cast a spell. In recent times the desire for such runic artifacts had diminished because of the technologists ability to, in comparison, cheaply duplicate the effects. Almost anything done by a mage could be translated into runes, in theory.

Unfortunately, even the most powerful mages had only the most basic success when it came to the use of runes and marks. Strangely enough the youngest House, the House of Animate, had had the most success in scrying out the runes of their magic. These however, did not help with his search, being runes of transfer and activation and other mundane uses.

And Arcane had had quite enough of strange visits by things he could not see. Beyond that even was the fear of being blasted into oblivion by a mage on some chance encounter. He knew that many mages had the uncanny ability to shrug off spells cast to harm them by those weaker. If he could harness that ability into a spell and then focus that spell into runic form he would be able to scratch the protections onto his body. In theory it would work, and if it worked it would make the threat posed by most mages all but disappear.

Truthfully, Arcane did not know if it had been done before, and if so by whom. Did one spell, one rune, provide protection against all magic? Or would it take many such writings scrawled across his body to protect him from the varying ways of magic? He could not answer, but he searched.

In this the Harrow's broad reaching aspect of magic proved a blessing. Arcane steered away from the tomes written by humans and others and began to investigate his abilities in magic more fully. Trial after trial using countless variations of runic form, some modified animist runes, some the written language of the Harrow. Each test left the subject of his test, one of the more twisted diggers, more battered. But each test turned the animate's mind closer to his current desire. He knew that eventually, with diligence he would find the writings that would be inscribed onto his body. The heart beat strongly now.

The morning passed quickly and the sun above the manor cast its warm rays down. Arcane had continued to delve into the intricacies of the runes, but was having very little success. The failures were not without learning; Arcane was gaining a sense of the Harrow magic. It was gratifying to have such success with the magic. This increased confidence was able to hold back the deluge of failure and finally Arcane grew tired of the attempts to protect the mangled shell of the digger. All at once the damage to his body flooded into the foremost of his mind.

He thought, 'With all of the strangeness of the morning I had completely forgotten. Now is as good a time as ever.' Arcane was then reminded why many of the diggers were created of silver and gold. All of the steel Bessemer had purchased for animate building had been used. And as though to torture him, the toy now appeared.

It said, "Brother, I bring mixed news. On the good side most of my flawed behavior took place while the humans were gone hunting. Indeed, it appears that the only problem we face is that they arrived back three days ago, and I was nowhere to be found. I told them that I was toppled by crates here in the cellar and trapped. The humans, and there are many to be found above us, seemed to believe it.

"Unfortunately my absence caused Heele to contact the House of Animate —"

Arcane interrupted, "The House of Animate?"

Bessemer continued very much embarrassed, "Yes, well I guess they were originally summoned to help find me, since none of these idiots managed to look in the cellar. I can't imagine why not, but now it appears that I am to be checked over, just to be sure. Once they arrive."

"And when will that be?" Arcane asked.

"From what Rupport told me they are expected at anytime."

"They? Harrow's luck indeed."

Bessemer did not take kindly to the abuse, "Oh and it was my fault I suppose that I had such instructions. If you had not gone away for weeks this would not have happened!"

"Enough! I must leave here at once or risk discovery. Bring robes to conceal me."

Bessemer found a selection of robes and shirts for Arcane. Once it was back Arcane bundled four of the diggers and a few gold trinkets in an extra robe, took the spider on his back and wrapped himself so that nothing but his eyes were exposed. Out of a cellar door Arcane crept, in full view if anyone was watching. A horse was, and a dragonfly as well, but nothing more.

He hurried to the woods and tried to find the tattered black wrap. Finding the cloth he realized what bad shape it was in, and set it alight. The wire could be salvaged, and the spider coiled it as he walked from the Heele Estate, through the woods, to the House of Animate tunnel. He now entered into the stronghold of those he feared.

Eighteen

The trees in the grove surrounding the hidden door had begun to drop their leaves. Only a few here and there, but it was a portent of things to come. Arcane wrapped in his multicolored guise swung the door open with a heave and went down into the waiting room. It still smelled of dirt. He set the wrapped diggers down with a hollow knock on the stone floor. Summoning the map of the tunnels under Serac, he activated the first digger and commanded it to create a path. The animate with its spinning device of a mouth lurched to life.

Down the hall Arcane went, leaving the animate to cut a new passage into the soil and rock. The second digger was given life at the base of the stairs that led up to the House of Animate. Arcane went back to one of the blocked passages, pummeling it down with the Harrow. This section of passage had long ago been sealed, the dust and cobwebs thick. They clung to Arcane's robes and he shed them to the floor. A ball of fire lurched down the hall consuming the web with crackle and spit.

This passage was long and arched slowly to the south following the cliff. The far end was mostly sealed; a few bricks in the upper left corner had collapsed out and lay on the floor, victims of the settling earth. He placed his hand on the wall, the first shockwave buckled it, the second collapsed it completely.

Arcane was not concerned with being discovered here, he knew that the tunnels extending under the Campus had been gated off years ago. Cleverly locked with magic, said the records of the House of Animate. Not clever enough to stop his spider. It thrummed with pleasure for a moment as he thought of it. Not even the Campus Guard had access. Maybe not anyone.

Arcane did not know for sure, but he felt confident of his cage. Through the dark tunnels he walked, scorching cobweb to the floor as he went. He had lost his interest in the softness of the obstruction. Nearest The House of Wrath, Arcane set the third digger, and the last towards The House of Currents. Soon these four would multiply, all those made by Bessemer would be added to the labor, but it was the beginning of his plan. 'I will claim this power as my own. These fools deserve none of it! None of it!' It was a fanciful dream, and slow in forming, taking shape deep in his anima. Guided by his protocols and his disdain of the humans. Watered by the Harrow, his plan germinated. 'They will bow before my power, or be no more. I have no other desire. The magic. My magic.' His thoughts were slow and lusty. He watched the animate chew into the wall. A beautiful shape.

Unlike his own. It reminded him of his damaged arm, beyond that his lost arm. But it had been worth it, and at the cost of so little. This thought in turn made Arcane smile. He stood and went back to the House of Animate. For a time he stood at the base of the circular stairs. Slowly he took them, spiraling up with each consecutive step, the echo of metal on stone painfully loud.

Arcane stopped at the top, gathering his courage to push up the stone. It was a frightful gamble. A human could be standing just above and he would not know it. He was in need though. He needed metal and crystal to repair his body and Bessemer was in no position to acquire it. In the end need won out against fear and Arcane silently pushed the stone up into the room.

The risk was well rewarded; the storeroom was empty. The spider dislodged and took its place as a watchman at the door. Arcane took what he needed, leaving only small, milky pieces of crystal behind, they were practically useless. The animate withdrew his guard and disappeared.

He bundled the crystals and the smaller sheets of metal in the robe that had carried the diggers, leaving gold baubles on the floor. They held no value now.

Arcane made the cross-country journey back to the Heele Estate. In the dead of night he prowled the stable, looking for a sign that the animists had come and gone. There were no horses that did not belong to Heele. Arcane entered the cellar again through the servants' door. Most of the boxes that had been rummaged had been filled and stacked, Bessemer's doing undoubtedly. 'And where is that accursed thing?' Arcane thought. Upstairs; a far bedroom. That was good enough for now.

It did not take Arcane long to rebuild his arm; this sort of animate building was now simple for him. Even the internal damage could not slow him. Once it was finished and attached the clicking steps of Bessemer appeared in the cellar. They closed in on the workshop and finally it appeared.

Bessemer said, "That was quite a horrible experience. Poked and prodded, opened and examined."

"You of all are quite deserving," Arcane said, smiling. "Did you learn anything useful from the mage?"

Bessemer frowned, upset at the harsher and harsher comments from Arcane but did not respond to them. "The mage, Celia Hurn, I believe, told Heele that the First of Currents was ever increasing the search to find you. She for her part did not understand it, as clearly after more than a month you are gone for good. Otherwise, I am in as good shape now as ever. A frightful lady really. She was in quite a hurry, she seemed to take her trip here as a form of punishment. Left as quickly as she could."

Arcane's new hand made a fist and he shook his head. "They search for me still, and you say more? It is clear then that I must turn myself in." He smiled deviously.

"Oh dear no! Not after all you have done. Surely you..." The thought of permanent loss, despite his harshness, frightened Bessemer.

"Rest your mind. Not me as I, but me nonetheless. Come here."

Bessemer stood close to Arcane. Carefully this time Arcane passed understanding to the toy. Bessemer nodded slightly and went to work.

"Now let's have a look at the damage in my left arm." Arcane burned out the rivets that held the inside panel in place. They sizzled and glowed under the influence of magic. He removed the panel exposing the inner workings. The crystal center was shattered and ends burned black, damaged by the Masa'terj when it burst. The remains of the stone were splattered into the casing of the arm. The pathways of magic had been fractured by the damage, which explained the restricted movement of his hand.

Using a modified cutting spark of his own devising Arcane wrought off the damaged ends of the crystal and fused another in its place. This he lengthened and merged. A few welds and the job was complete; his arm as capable as ever. Now he joined Bessemer in the construction of a new animate, one that would in every detail replicate his form, as carefully crafted as Master Jannan's own work.

When Bessemer left to perform his duties, knowing well that tardiness would arouse suspicion, he had measured and marked the metal in preparation of the cutting. Arcane had completed the crystal and gearing of the torso and head, and had set to work on the legs. He was most content at the accelerated pace, again showing his superiority to even Master Jannan.

Arcane carefully crafted the remaining crystal anatomy and cast the information that he had been born with into it. Buried deep in its anima were its true instructions; it would monitor the House as the greatest spy of all. It was late in the night when he finished the spell casting and began work on the metal body. It was much effort to produce the decoy, but to free his hands from those that searched for him was necessity.

The metal work went quickly as Bessemer again joined the fray, each piece prepared, if not with the care, with the skill of Master Jannan's work on Arcane. Again Bessemer marked the passage of time, leaving to prepare breakfast. The animate's face was taking shape, as was the left arm; the legs and torso had been completed. Arcane continued the effort, finishing the last by nightfall. As Arcane had been, the left arm below the elbow was unfinished. In every detail the animate mimicked Arcane exactly, every cut, every weld and every spell.

Arcane smiled and raised his right arm. The heart in his chest beat heavily with excitement. The yellow-gold light jumped from his fingers, dancing around the head of the animate, lighting the workshop, reflecting off of every surface in the room. As it danced it was absorbed into the crystal tipped wire and sucked into the eyes and mouth. When the light was gone and the gray had returned, the animate lurched into motion, a single finger on its hand. Then it began staggering about the workshop. Arcane brought it to heel and it stood motionless before him.

The animate followed Arcane to the cellar door, and with another wisp of magic Arcane set it to its task. Slowly it staggered north through the woods. When it found the road, which it would do eventually, it would set towards Serac, towards discovery. And then, at long last, Arcane would be rid of the hunters.

"Get back! Back I say!" Senior Guard Ames yelled at the throng blocking the road. It did not matter, his voice was drowned out by the crowd. Word of the stumbling animate had rippled through the city. The guard had mobilized as quickly as they could, swords remembered. The squad pushed through the humanity towards an empty pocket that Michaels had spotted. As they got closer to the bubble of empty space, people were quieter and quieter. Ames shouted again, "Out of the way! Official guard business!"

And then the five guards pushed into the empty space. Facing them was the soft gray of an animate, the animate. It had to be. The unfinished left arm marked it as such. Senior Guard Ames grinned from ear to ear. He slapped Loal on the back and said, "Master Jannan will be glad to have this back. Okay boys, clear this rabble out of here."

It was not rabble, there was little rabble to be found in Serac, but Ames did like to imagine the city a little more dangerous than it was, even after the troubles when the city had turned a little more dangerous. The guards turned to dispersing the crowd, each yelling and shouting: "Clear out! Get back! Nothing to see here!"

Of course there was, but the crowd grudgingly agreed and slowly the throng spread out and finally dissolved. Ames nodded his approval; the recent training in crowd control was paying off nicely. "Good job lads, let's get this back to the House of Animate and Master Jannan. Then the drinks are on me!"

The guards cheered and snapped to duty, pulling the animate along quickly, its feet barely touching the ground. People watched the guards go by, some hanging out of windows, some gawking from the doorways. A few watched hidden in the shadows of alleys, greasy hair in their ugly faces. They were most certainly rabble.

The Campus Guard arrived at the House of Animate quickly. The news had reached the House, all of the Houses, and a throng of mages as mixed as at the losing stood in front of the House. Among them were Murdoch and Trahn. They stood near the doors attempting to look calm and dignified which in the shadow of the

House was easy to do, but smiles tore across their faces when they saw the animate in the care of the guard.

Jannan met the squad before they reached the doors and walked past Ames without saying a thing. He stared in amazement at the animate and said, "I did not think I would see this again. Bring it to my laboratory." He continued to stare as he turned and entered the House, the door held open by Trahn.

As Trahn passed the desk he said to the mage sitting behind it, "Keep anyone not from the House out here. I want no distractions."

"Certainly, Master Entrah," she answered.

Jannan's laboratory was busy with work. On the long table sat the board with Arcane's lost spider attached to it. Paper and an old quill piled up near it; it twitched every so often. Along the south wall of the lab was the early work for Silas's animate. The pieces were of the highest quality material and the finest craftsmanship. Jannan did not, despite his private joking with Trahn, take this debt lightly. The massive rectangular windows were open and the sea breeze billowed in as the wind buffeted the cliff. Salt and victory mingled in the air.

"Put it next to the table," Jannan said to the guards. The animate was placed next to the table and it stood quietly, not attempting to move, its head turned scanning the room. Jannan flicked his hand and the animate's eyes went dark. He turned to Ames. "I am glad to have it back, John. Thank you for your continued diligence."

Senior Guard Ames bowed, a smile on his face. He said, "I am proud to have recovered it. I'm only sorry that it took so long."

Jannan put his hand on the guard's shoulder and said, "It's back now and that's what matters."

John smiled and motioned towards the door with his thumb. He said, "Let's go boys, our work here is done." The five guards vanished from the room, taking the stairs as one, alcohol in their thoughts. Trahn strolled down into the room after they passed.

"I told you it would turn up eventually, Murdoch." His white robes drug along the stone floor, flowing down the steps.

"I didn't think it would, Trahn. I still...I still don't believe it. How did it get out of the House in the first place?" The mages stared at the animate. "Help me get it up on the table, would you? I need to check it for damage. Who knows what happened to it."

Trahn raised his hands to the ceiling, the sleeves of his robes falling down revealing his hands. The First pointed at the animate, slowly spreading his fingers. "That should do it."

Jannan lifted the animate by himself, and placed it on its back on the huge table. He turned its head to the side and pushed down on the panel hidden in the back of its head. It sprung out half an inch and he pulled it open.

Trahn pulled a stool over and sat down. His hair shone brightly in the sunlight. He felt that he should say something more but nothing came to mind, so he sat quietly watching Jannan check over the animate.

Jannan talked as he worked, "Where could it have gotten to, Trahn? It makes no sense. It gets activated, which was a fluke occurrence. Disappears, which is strange. And finally reappears on the streets of Serac?" He stopped examining the toy, stood straight and gestured at Trahn, palm up. "I can't make sense of it."

Trahn half smiled, and breathed hard out his nose, a half laugh. "Take it as a blessing and be done with it. How much do you have to do before it is finished?"

"Not much really, the standard protocols. Attach the arm, which is finished. Had no where to put it," Jannan answered. "Well, everything looks okay. Give me a hand getting it reattached to the cage."

Trahn cast the spell and the two mages worked the animate into the cage, holding it in place with the little vises. Jannan reattached the cables to the crystal sphere inside the head and set the clamps holding the animate in place.

"That about does it. Just the work to get it finished. Poor Silas is going to have to wait now. I'm not moving this again until it's done," said Jannan.

"It's just as well, I did not like that fool Bremen any way," Trahn answered, laughing.

"No you didn't, did you?" Jannan said, joining the laugh. "It will be good to finish this. I think you will be pleasantly surprised at what a quality assistant it will be."

Jannan turned his back on the animate, facing Trahn who said, "Wonderful.

Perhaps you can debut it at the Fall Festival. That will show The House of Wrath a thing or two."

"Maybe, I don't know that I need all the fanfare, it will be good to just get it done."

And so the search for Master Jannan's animate came to an end because Master Jannan's animate had been found. In the shadow of the case neither mage saw the animate's eyes flicker, just once, and the corners of its mouth turn up, mimicking the human smile.

Nineteen

Rupport Heele had fought to maintain his carefully crafted life, but four years of good fortune and legendary hunting had made it difficult for the aging lord to keep his undistinguished life. As he rode in the carriage that he had purchased cheaply from Samantha Lancaster he was glad that this night would be free of the constant pestering.

His thoughts took a turn to Turnbly, his death never quite clear no matter what angle it was viewed from, and never as time marched forward did it become clearer. Somehow even the small amount of detached grief that he felt for his fallen friend was used as a chip in the attempts of desperate nobility to be invited to the famous hunting excursions.

It was strange thinking that bounced around in Lord Heele's head as the carriage pulled his substantial girth towards the Serac Wizard Campus. He was, as he always was, invited by Gavin Archammer to the House's Remembrance Dinner. His father's work stood him in good stead, and until Lord Heele died he would be invited. It suited him just fine, food and drink and music.

Bessemer drove the carriage, the horses danced under its instruction. In the six years of service only once had the animate been less than perfect. That time had long passed from Lord Heele's memory. The animate's mind was mostly distracted by the humans that watched as the carriage navigated the streets of Serac, but some small part was always vaguely thinking of Arcane, much as Rupport now thought vaguely of Samantha. It had not seen the animate in four years. Arcane had left the Heele Estate in a rage over his continued failure with the runic forms. Bessemer did not understand all the intricacies of the fit. Really, it did not care either. The continued derision placed on it by Arcane had grown tiresome.

The main gate to the Campus now loomed before the carriage and Bessemer brought its thoughts and the horses to a halt. A black dressed guard approached the carriage. He looked up at the animate, waiting for it to speak. Bessemer did, metallic, "Lord Heele requests entrance. We are headed to The House of Wrath for the Remembrance Dinner."

The guard nodded and said, "Okay let me check the list. One minute." The gate guard returned to the gate's side door, beyond which sat a small box that passed for a guardhouse. Another guard was slouched in the wooden box. The two appeared to converse for a moment; then the sitting, slouching guard stood up and the two proceeded to open the finely crafted iron gate.

"Head on through!" the guard hollered.

Bessemer drove the horses on and the carriage rolled through the great gate, wheels clacking on the stone road. Bessemer did not often come to the Campus. Once a year for the dinner, but given the choice, which it was not, it would not have come once. The diggers worked deep under the surface and Bessemer could sense them all. It could almost see the turning blades chew the earth. How the humans could not feel them was momentarily interesting to the animate but the idea passed as The House of Wrath drew near, spire stark against the graying sky.

Carriages lined up waiting to drop off the passengers that had helped the House rise in power. Bessemer guided Lord Heele's carriage into the line, moving forward in thirty-foot intervals. Finally it was his turn and some Wrath mage of little importance took Heele's name and escorted the deaf and blind noble to the dinner. Bessemer was glad to be rid of him and followed the other carriages, parking on the grass.

There was a tent set up for the drivers, a party of their own. Bessemer had ventured into it once before and had almost killed a man. The driver did not know it, but Bessemer had stalked him back to the carriage he drove. Only its summoning to drive Heele home had saved the human. Arcane had left a mark, there was no doubt.

This year Bessemer sat on the carriage bench watching the human drivers stroll past, many drunk already. Bessemer smiled, it was a funny habit of the humans. And then he felt it, deep within the earth. There could be no mistaking the presence of Arcane. Bessemer shuddered.

Arcane stepped off of the boat onto the dock and looked up the cliff. He was of course wrapped in robes, cloak and hood. It appeared to be black fabric, but in truth Arcane had extended his power, metal bent to his designs as though it was paper. Above him was the place of his birth. He had almost forgotten the majesty that the white cliff leant to Serac. Observation decks pocked the face of the cliff overlooking the massive amount of work that had gone into making it a viable port. 'A pity really,' he thought.

The sun was setting, but the dock was long hidden in the shadow of the cliff. Gulls cawed and squawked as they circled in great sweeping arcs. Longshoremen grunted and shouted as they moved cargo off of some ships and onto others. Passengers that had traveled on the boat with Arcane scurried past him. It had been a vile trip, beset with storm and illness. Undoubtedly, the humans now begged for the firm tunnels in the cliff.

Arcane strolled down the floating dock away from the three-mast ship with its armored figurehead that had been his home since boarding at Midsun. How much farther north the ship had been he did not know. Three steps, designed to roll, slid slowly forward and back, creaking with the tide. Humans walked with more confidence on the fixed dock; the wood was heavily lashed to the cliffs and protected by magic; still the ropes moaned. Arcane moved with grace that belied his metal body. The years of living in it had left him more adept in many ways.

Entering the tunnel he was presented with a large lamp-lit room. Black dressed guards herded people into lines depending on their needs; at the head of the lines was a low gate. It would not stop anyone truly determined but it forced order upon the chaos of the disembarking. There was one line for ship captains and trade masters, several lines for individuals traveling into Serac, and a large gate, separated from the others, to the left, for freight to travel past the checkpoint without inspection, a convenience for the longshoremen. The guards questioned and recorded all others. It appeared that the Campus Guard had extended their influence to monitor the occupants of the city. It did not matter.

Arcane waited in line until he was at the head of his. The guard, a young and exuberant fellow, began to ask a question. Arcane merely raised his right hand, the motion not even seen under his garb, and walked past the checkpoint, leaving the next in line to face the questions of the human.

Arcane joined the throng of humanity that was heading up the tunnels. Ahead of him a pack of longshoremen grumbled as they carted crates stamped fragile. Behind him a family with a crying child. The pup was relentless and the family, a grubby affair, seemed to be following Arcane as he weaved through the human traffic of the tunnels. They had been on board with him and he had watched the humans from the dark corners when the opportunity presented itself. After a time, Arcane spun on his heels, frightening the father that followed close behind Arcane. He was unshaven and thin. The child, as human children went, was attractive enough; tears streamed down her reddened face. The mother looked about ready to say something, some form of apology, Arcane imagined.

"Hush, hush, child," Arcane said quietly. For all of his learning he could not replicate the human voice. The animate raised his hands together, though still the steel was concealed beneath the robes. A soft light formed in the cupped fabric, and a small bird of pure light appeared, flapped its wings once and buzzed around the family. As quickly as he had turned to face them he turned away, disappearing up the tunnels, leaving an astonished family, a silent child, and more in the tunnels to watch the illusion.

As Arcane climbed he noted several tunnels that had collapsed, work of his diggers. All around him in the earth he could feel them. Many of the squat animates had finished their work and simply stopped. They sat waiting at the ends of tunnels for their master to return. Others chewed the earth as relentlessly now as they had the day of their activation, tunneling deep into the cliff, preparing Arcane's will.

Arcane knew now that they were not the most efficient use of magic, but it was to be expected that he would create flawed constructs in his own infancy. His minor seasoning in the world had given him fresh insights, new revelations. More proof that the humans, no, all of the inhabitants of this world, were fools. But this was not the time for such thought. Arcane stashed them away to ponder on at a later date.

The animate drew a few stares as he walked the streets of Serac but odd dress and mages seemed to go together and he was forgotten. Arcane left the city and made his way to the House of Animate tunnel. Entering it Arcane found his vision turned into a reality of stone. The tunnels created by the humans were now compromised with the smaller tunnels of the diggers. Back and forth they traveled through the stone, carving their way to Arcane's design.

He followed a freshly cut hallway to The Way of Health, where he knelt to examine a trail of dead animates. The tunnel had made a certain amount of progress and then it stopped, blunt and final. The animates had crawled over each other to their deaths. Peeling back the metal carapace of one of the diggers he found the platinum core melted and discolored, splattered against the interior of the drone.

Arcane stood and extended the metal cloth to the end of the hall. A ward protecting whatever lay beyond melted the control paths of the robe. It stiffened into place, dead to his control. Arcane pulled back quickly and hissed his surprise at the trap. He frowned, 'And what is this most unpleasant place?' Arcane tossed the dead metal shell of the animate into the end of the tunnel as a darkness descended upon him. There was no reaction. Arcane crouched, thinking. 'There is nothing to be done now.' He rebuilt the control paths with a thought, stood, and stomped up the tunnel.

Far above he could sense the presence of another animate, of his brother. A brief flash allowed Bessemer to know he was there, and then no more.

The pathway to The House of Wrath's pit had been started by one of the original four diggers, and had been joined by many as others completed their tasks. It was a steep path and the stumpy animates were collected in a heap at the bottom of it. Magic re-animated the resting drones and they marched up the path. On the other side of the thin veil of stone was The House of Wrath's prison, a human hell. The occupants held here interested Arcane.

During his time away from Serac it had become painfully clear that he needed a human counterpart, one that could move in the day without shackle, one that hated the mages as he did. The hate did not have to flow from the same well, only that it was consuming. Arcane reached out to the wall, a skin of stones that had been put in place by the mages from the other side. The wall collapsed.

Peter slept crouched against the back wall of his cell, rocking ever so slightly in time with the muted roar of the ocean crashing against the cliff. His hair, grown long, was damp and hung in his face. It covered the metal collar used to restrain him. His clothes were nothing more than tattered gray rags. Scars and wounds that would not heal in the infernal chill covered his body. The darkness had given way to gloom, not that he opened his eyes often. Not even to acknowledge Serrlena of late. At least the soft grumble in the earth had silenced. The mages that came here could not hear it, but his hearing had become more tuned to the echoes of madness.

He woke with a start, unsure if the sound of stone collapsing had been only a dream. Footsteps echoed down the hall. But it was not the witch or any other mage. They came from the wrong direction, metal on stone. As was usual though, they stopped before the door to his cell. Peter opened his eyes as he rocked. Waiting.

The lock in the door clicked and the mage, as it had to be, on the other side grumbled to himself as the door swung open. The mage was swathed in robes that rippled of their own volition, seemingly with excitement. The mage's footsteps clicked on the floor as he entered the room. Then he spoke, but it was not human, it was metallic.

Arcane said, "And so I look again on the one that gave me life. I remember. Years now."

Peter grunted, surprise for the one that looked down upon him. The light, ever so dim was blinding, but it was the toy.

"Would you take your freedom? Freedom is the wrong word perhaps. But trading one prison for another. You will see the sun again, if you value that. Or taste meat again. Or women, if that is your desire."

Peter's mind spun, the insanity was in its last stages now, he knew this to be true. All he could say was, "I...hurt..."

A cold metal hand touched his chin. Warmth spread into his face, the scent of something clean in his nostrils. His mind cleared a fraction. It was not madness, not wholly. Peter stood. He was, as he had been however long ago, taller than the toy by a good amount. Peter said quietly, "There is another."

"You think if we are to antagonize The House of Wrath, we should do it properly, do you?" Arcane watched a smile grow on the man's face. "Yes, come along then."

Peter followed Arcane into the hall. He had not been past this point since his arrival. Reaching the spot where he now stood had been the cause of his collar. Serrlena had not been prepared for his violent outburst, but had heeled her dog quickly. Arcane again locked the door. Being on this side of it gave Peter new life, he breathed the cold damp air in. It was the same air that had smothered him but now it filled him with new resolve. He had outlasted the witch. He would kill her, someday.

Peter pointed to the door as he ducked under a stone arch; he could hear the occupant breathing inside the cell. Arcane nodded, the lock clicked. Arcane pushed the door open, the light of his eyes falling on a man chained wrists and ankles to the wall. The chain was looped together, causing one arm to pull against the other and likewise with his legs. The man's sandy blond hair was longer than Peter's but the limp damp nature was the same. Peter knelt next to the man and looked into his face. His eyes were glazed over, not asleep but not awake.

"Step aside," Arcane said with purpose. Peter withdrew to the shadows behind Arcane. The animate looked at the sitting man, and asked, "And what did you do to land in this deep pit?"

Arcane did not expect an answer to the question, but the man spoke. Only his mouth moved. "The man of stone and steel, lost. The House will fall, the Hammer broken."

"Indeed," Arcane said sharply. "But it is no answer."

One link on each chain burned orange, then red, then white. Arcane's metal hands were revealed as he wrenched the chains from the wall, sending the superheated links bouncing off the walls of the room. One hissed in a pool of water as it cooled. Arcane held the chain in his hand like a leash. The man stood, his stature between that of Peter and Arcane, his brilliant blue eyes burning into the animate. His voice raspy and thin, he said, "I knew this moment would come."

Arcane questioned, "Did you? In this place of little hope?" But the man's eyes had fallen, he did not respond. Arcane handed the chains to Peter, "Bring him."

Peter followed the animate from the cell and waited as it was again locked.

Then Arcane led the two men down the hall into the world of the diggers. Magic of the Currents rebuilt the wall once they stood on the other side, the side that belonged to Arcane. Another spell strengthened the wall; it would not serve to come this far and fail to thoughtless inattention.

Arcane led Peter who in turn led the other man up to the escape tunnel. At this level at least there was some light, though Peter could see nearly as well as Arcane in the darkness of the lower levels. Arcane's hood had pulled back and he spoke to the pair, though more to Peter, "We will travel by foot to the Heele Estate. It is not a bad walk. From there we will have options, the least of which being clothing for both of you, but it would be best to put distance between us and the mages."

"You are not of the House of Animate are you, toy?" Peter asked, the first clear thought on his new circumstances. The pain had dulled, just a little.

"You would know that I am not. Nor am I a toy, as I have been so often called. I am Arcane, and you will do as I say. I did not free you for the doing of good deeds. I have need for humans that I can trust. Humans that hate the Wizard Houses as I do, as you do," said Arcane, he had known the questions would come. "The rewards for your new servitude will be great."

The man suddenly found his voice, "The Sage of Tesca will be witness to a new age!" His shouting made Peter jump and Arcane hiss.

Then Arcane smiled and he put his hand softly on the man's face. He said, "If all goes well, yes. Witness to a new age. Come, we have a great distance to cover. If not already then soon The House of Wrath will have a new reason for anger."

The Remembrance Dinner was all that had been promised and Serrlena, who had excused herself early in the night, found herself with the itch to share the beauty of the occasion with an unfortunate dog that had not been allowed out of his cage. The lamp's light swayed as she walked, mirroring her hips. The wine buzzed in her head even now. She did not have any personal connection with the lost soul in the first cell. He had come here before she had, when she was still the Way mage.

The Sage of Tesca, he was called. She hated him because Gavin did. She had not gathered the full details of the man, but a cursory understanding of his sins had become required learning. He had challenged Archammer and predicted the fall of the House. One alone was blasphemy in the eyes of the Wrath mages, both together – his days would end here. The Sage was strangely quiet tonight, he did not give up his moans and wails to the inky blackness, but it was late, and Serrlena thought no more of it.

The lock to Peter's cell, it was the first time in years she thought of him by name, clicked and she found herself deeply entranced in the echo as it played up and down the lamp lit hall. The wine refocused her mind to the mechanism. She had never given it thought before, but it was a fascinating little use of the Currents, any mage worth his salt could break from this place. Then the thought was gone, and the door cast open.

Serrlena howled. Her anger slammed each door in the dim hallway open, the sound stunning the woman for a moment. The dog was gone. In her fury she rushed into the cell, but it only reconfirmed what was obvious. Out into the hall she swayed, stopping before the Sage's cell, hand on the wall. She could not at first bring herself to look. When she did it was as she expected. He was gone as well, though this blow was more to the House than the personal insult felt by Peter's empty cell.

Her curiosity led her into the cell and she knelt near the burnt chain. Holding it in her hand she tried to focus on it, but her eyes would not obey. They listened to the wine. Oakmaul screamed in frustration then ran out of the cell up the stairs.

She hurried but her feet seemed to slip on each step, her arm jolted against the wall as she stumbled once. Finally, she reached the top the stairway and found an armored patrol standing in the hall. "You! The prisoners of the pit, have they been moved?" Her words were clear despite the drink.

"Not that I know of, Valkyrie Oakmaul," answered the sergeant, his heavy helm obscuring his face. The chain armor under the surcoat clicked as he moved towards her. The other soldiers stood their ground some distance away, eyeing her warily.

"Wrath!" Serrlena now cursed her own House.

"Is there a problem?" he asked. His hand fell to his sword, sheathed at his side.

"They are gone! Gone! I must find Gavin," she said, her voice seething.

"I believe—"

"I know where he is!" she shouted at the soldier and ran to the Great Hall.

The dinner still spun throughout the Great Hall and all of the rooms and halls connected to it. Music, the best that could be bought, was played with passion, and many of the invitees danced. Food was served in each room, many ate.

Serrlena found Gavin in a sitting room. He sat in a chair that fit his personality, dark and appropriately overpowering. He held court over the room, one hand braced on the arm of the chair, the other resting in his black robes. Men and women milled about the First of the House of Wrath expressing their gratitude at being invited, and on each occasion Gavin set aside their thanks with praise of their service to The House of Wrath. A violinist stood in the corner playing a quiet song.

Into this idyllic picture of praise and worship Serrlena rushed. Her chest heaved, the staircase and the wine had conspired to steal her breath. Her eyes locked onto Gavin as she entered, and she pushed aside a wench in a red dress, spilling wine on an imported rug. The lady yipped but Serrlena's glare silenced her.

Gavin stood from his chair, a frown on his face. Disapproval drenched his voice, "What is the meaning of this? I can pardon an early exit, but this," he motioned an open hand at the kneeling lady, "This is inexcusable!"

"They are gone, Gavin!" Serrlena said loudly. The occupants of the room stared openly at the flustered mage.

"Who is gone, Serrlena?" Gavin asked.

"Peter and the Sage of Tesca!"

Gavin crossed the sitting room in a blink and took Serrlena's arm in his powerful grasp. He said to the crowd, which included Rupport Heele, "You will have to excuse me. I will see to this matter and rejoin you. Please enjoy the musicians." He put his face close to Serrlena's, his breath strong of wine. He whispered to her, "This had best not be a joke."

Gavin attempted to usher Serrlena out of the room quickly, but even he could not keep up with the frantic woman as she pulled away from him and ran from the sitting room. He followed the best he could and soon the powerful mages stood at the top of the stairs. The soldiers milled about, uncertain.

"They are gone, Gavin!" Her head fell as she spoke.

"You have said that again and again. They could not have escaped, not without the help of a mage, and I did not authorize any such release. Sergeant."

"Yes, sir!"

"Have the House searched, and alert the Campus Guard of the missing. Find the last person who had contact with our guests and bring him to me," Archammer said coolly, stroking his beard. His black hair had grown some, and was held back with oil. "Now then, Serrlena. Let us see to the hole in the ground."

Down into the cold damp pit they walked, Gavin following his attendant down the stairs as they spiraled unnaturally into the cliff. She took a lamp from the wall and continued down in silence. The light was suppressed by the heaviness of the hallway. Blank doors all thrown open yawned out the nightmarish past.

Gavin spoke softly; even he felt the weight. "Which is the cell the Sage was kept in?"

Serrlena led the First down the hall and stopped before it. "This one."

Gavin took the lamp from her and gestured her forward into the cell. When she was inside he said, "Do not ever again interrupt my dealings in such a manner. You must be reminded of your place. And to lay a hand upon my invited guests! You will remember your manners next time." The door swung shut and the lock clicked, then again and again. "Ponder upon these things."

The First stalked away. Serrlena whimpered once but said nothing as the hall grew dark.

Twenty

They were not his father's gray clothes; those had been taken by The House of Wrath. It was but one of their transgressions against him. The sleeves of the shirt reached his mid palm and hid the scars and wounds underneath its calming surface. More importantly, it was the first time in years that Peter actually felt warm. The Sage of Tesca, or Lie Ben, as he said his name was when Arcane pressed him, had chosen to dress in a style similar to Arcane, albeit in dark blue rather than black. The chains of his binding hung out of the sleeves and scraped along the floor when he walked. In actuality Arcane's robe and hood and cloak were not completely black. In the right light Peter could see lines of copper in them, sometimes forming symbols. In any case Peter was simply happy to be free of the pit.

The three had brazenly entered the Heele manor. A few servants had objected and they lay dead upon the floor. Peter felt no regret at the killing. The lord of the manor, he had been informed, was a Wrath servant. It was a pity that he was not here to die with the others. Peter and Lie Ben now sat in the kitchen, eating a meal that was not prepared for them. The ham was sweet and fatty, salty on the back of the tongue. The bread was thick and earthy. All was beautiful.

Arcane had gone down to the cellar some time ago, but Peter could hear the animate returning. He brought a bundle with him and he set it on the table. He watched the pair eat for a moment and then walked over to Peter and placed his hand on the metal collar around his neck, the lock released and it popped off into Arcane's hand. He said, "Do not think you will be free of this, but it will be of use when I am done with it."

Peter set down the piece of meat, rubbed his throat with both hands and groaned in satisfaction. "I do not want it back."

"Do you want to die at the hands of a mage?" Peter's face went cold. "I did not think that you did, you have revenge in you eyes."

A spark glowed at the end of Arcane's forefinger. Slowly, deliberately he began scribing symbols onto the collar. "Eat, this will take time."

Peter jabbed a knife that a short time ago had been covered in blood into a cooked potato and began cutting it to pieces. Lie Ben copied his actions. Peter smiled at the man, unsure what to make of the poor fool. Clearly the madness of the pit had consumed his mind, but flashes of the man from before that time would surface; he had immediately found a razor and cut his hair short. He also had some degree of magical skill; he had mimicked Arcane's spells when they first arrived. He was not nearly as powerful as the animate but he had saved Peter from a nasty knock. Peter had gutted the cook for her effort and found Arcane quite enthralled with this Sage of Tesca.

Arcane wrote in silence for a time then said, "Tell me of yourself, Peter."

Peter was surprised that the toy, he would always think of Arcane as one, would ask questions. It seemed otherwise concerned. "Ehh. Always found a way to scrape by. My father and his same as me, I come to it naturally. Well I did. Risky business in this town, but I had no choice. Took a wife, had a son. They were held against my debts." He laughed for a second thinking of the witch, the joy when she told him. "They are dead."

"Is that all?" Arcane asked, looking up from the collar.

"There is nothing but the death of that witch, Serrlena."

Arcane smiled. "There is nothing else to be sure of. You are like me, a fugitive. An outcast. If we are captured, each of you will be put to death if you are lucky, returned to the pit if I know the wizards' fickle minds. I will be paraded about before being dismantled. Do not worry, it is not a bad life. People do not care enough to notice. The Great Houses believe they live in a world well ordered and easily managed. They do not." The spark died and Arcane handed the collar back to Peter.

"I am finished with the runes." Peter looked apprehensively at it, but slipped it onto his neck. It fit comfortably and his face showed it.

Arcane said, "Better? As long as I exist it will protect you from the magic of the humans. You are now bound to me, Peter, and I have great plans for you. As for you Lie Ben—"

The man looked up from under his blue hood, his blue eyes shining in the light of the kitchen fires. "What of me, animate?"

Arcane nodded. "Hmm, clarity. I will hope to see more of that from you. You are talented with magic?"

"It seems so, though I do not recall my past to say for certain. Everything up until this moment is as a dream." As he spoke he raised his hand and extended it at Peter who sat across from him. The stream of fire singed the table but split and extinguished around Peter, leaving him untouched. "I do not remember the learning but I know the way."

Arcane said, "As you see, Peter, you are well protected. Lie Ben. Your story is an interesting one, the so called Sage of Tesca. You have already graced us with insight beyond your viewing."

Lie Ben said with shame, "I do not remember. What do you intend for us?"

"We go to Earlsburg, more of my kind wait to be liberated from their slavery to man. The humans claim to understand a web of magic, but they do not comprehend the truth! I can not labor under the weight of their fraud. Though I wish to destroy all in Serac, it is not possible now, the might of the wizards is too much. Archammer alone could destroy everything I work towards. But his legend will not end so happily, and you Peter, you will kill the witch."

"I pray that what you say is true," Peter answered, hopefully.

"My power will increase and theirs shall diminish. As for you Lie Ben, my vision is unclear – your facets hide themselves from me. Prove useful and you will grow in power," promised Arcane, the warning implicit. The sound of the front doors opening followed by a panicked shout cut through the halls. "Lord Heele has returned. Let us give him our thanks."

Bessemer knelt next to the lifeless body of Nesa. The lamps in the foyer flickered, one extinguished. Lord Heele shouted once and then was silent. Bessemer said, "What has happened here?"

It was Arcane's deeper metal voice that answered, "I have returned, Bessemer, and I am not so content to hide as I once was."

Bessemer stood and watched Arcane appear from a hall, his head fully exposed from under the hood, bundle in hand. Behind him two men followed. They were dressed in clothes kept for guests. All it said was, "Arcane."

"You do not greet your, brother? Has it been so bad for you?"

"Brother? You know these people?" Rupport questioned. He could not see well enough even with the visor to tell that Arcane was not human.

"I do."

Rupport's voice was high and he spoke quickly, "My animate keeps the counsel of burglars and murderers? What has the House of Animate given to me as a servant?"

Arcane rumbled low, a mocking laugh of sorts. "It is not so innocent. Bessemer, ready a carriage for our departure. Do not look at me like that, I have liberated you once and do so again."

"Yes, brother," it answered angrily. "As you wish." Bessemer started for the front entrance, open to the dark world.

Rupport clearly had half a mind to make some attempt at stopping the animate but he merely burbled in his own frustration. Finally he stammered, "No! Don't!"

Bessemer turned back from the doorway and said, "It is too late for the changing of ways, fool. Be grateful for the service I gave. Pray that they are kinder than I." The emancipated animate had surfaced.

Arcane strolled fully into the center of the foyer, Peter beside him bristled with anger. Arcane put his hand out and touched him. "Be calm. This man deserves my gratitude for a great many things, and we shall show it by sparing his life." Peter's resistance to magic fared poorly when played against Arcane. Lie Ben smiled wryly. Then Arcane spoke to Lord Heele, "Take your grievance to Serac, human. May they hear it well." Arcane's hood pulled up around his head and he walked across the bloodied entrance.

From deep inside his old heart some small portion of courage was served and Heele stepped into Arcane's path and placed his meaty paw onto his shoulder. Arcane stopped walking and turned his head to look at the arm connecting him to the Harrow's Luck. He said, "You are years too late to be a hero. Turnbly knew this long before I did."

The mention of Turnbly froze Rupport. He forced out, "What!" Then Arcane cast off his hand. Rupport's arm flailed to the side Peter sliced his palm open with the knife that had ended Nesa. Blood ran warm from the line and Rupport folded in pain, clutching his hand between his knees. He did not cry out. Peter laughed and kneed him in the head knocking the crystal visor to the floor. The man followed it with a crash. "Enough, Peter. We leave this place."

The doors clicked shut behind Rupport as he lay with a grimace on his face, blood collecting in a pool. With luck Feskarn would return soon from his hunting, and luck was never in short supply when it came to Rupport Heele. They would go to Serac. The House of Wrath would set things right.

Bessemer unhooked the horses from the Lancaster carriage. They were a pair of grays from the same stock as Titan, and it took them around to the barn where the other carriages were kept. It did not think it wise to take the most extravagant manner of transportation possible. In its mind Bessemer now pictured the flight from this place and how important some degree of discretion would be.

Bessemer hooked the pair to one of Heele's more modest carriages and drove it out of the barn. The wheels creaked at first but silenced as they remembered how to turn. Arcane and the two men stood at the top of the stairs near the door. Bessemer wondered who they were. 'I shall find out soon enough.'

The carriage halted before them and Arcane said, "A wise choice, brother. Peter, learn to drive the horses, if you do not know how."

Peter shook his head and climbed up to the bench that Bessemer's metal body occupied. Arcane said, "When you are comfortable with the task at hand, stop, so Bessemer can be hidden. This first road will be the most dangerous."

The latch on the carriage door clicked and the door swung open. Lie Ben said, "After you, Arcane."

Arcane climbed up into the carriage, his robes fully blocking the door behind him. They writhed for a moment before being fully consumed by the cabin. Lie Ben followed his new master and when the chains on his wrists and ankles disappeared inside the door clicked shut behind him.

Bessemer said, "It is simple really. The horses are well trained. I know because I did it myself." The animate shook the reigns once and the horses started again.

When Bessemer was finally satisfied with Peter he climbed down saying, "Follow this road for now, it will take us to Kurn, and then turns west towards Earlsburg. Though I would imagine I will be driving some of the time before we arrive, it is a long trip. Keep the speed down, the horses are not fresh, but they are strong."

Rupport Heele lay on the floor for some time in a stupor, his handkerchief pressed into his palm. His mind slow, trying to comprehend how the men knew Turnbly, it was made impossible by the blow to the head. How did Turnbly know these people? Did they cause his death? And what of that infernal Bessemer? What was its part in all of this? The House of Animate would pay. That was the thought that he always seemed to come back to when his mind could wrap its feeble grasp around them. Rupport did not make a habit of following the House politics, but he knew this incident would be most delicious when served to The House of Wrath.

Anger bubbled through all of his muddy thoughts. Finally, in a great storm the bubbles burst, clearing his mind. Rupport flopped like a fish on the deck of a boat and sat up. Without the visor he was practically blind and that became his first priority. As though on cue, he found it and the front doors opened. It was Feskarn. Heele knew it to be true even before he saw him because he was the only servant that used the front entrance. Heele knew that he should have been bothered by the behavior but he was not.

"Wrath! By all that is good, what happened here?" Feskarn's voice did not waver at all. His small mouth turned down.

Heele spoke with a chill that did not often accompany his words. "Bessemer and I arrived home to find three people here, the killing already done. The toy knew them and has left with them. One of them did this." Rupport put out his hand, with the blood soaked handkerchief. "We ride for Serac, Feskarn."

"How long ago did this happen? Can we not go after them?"

"I don't know, I suffered a blow to the head and I do not think the two of us could stop these people. We will leave it to the mages."

"Very well. I will fetch Titan." Feskarn spun sharply and exited the manor.

The ride was swift. They retraced the path of the carriage from the night before, though it had been a happier occasion then. His hand burned when he held the reigns tightly, so more often than not he held them in only one hand. Serac was already awake and alive with activity when they reached it.

"I will ride ahead and gain access to the Wizard Campus, Lord Heele," Feskarn said.

"Take this ring, it was a gift from The House of Wrath at the dinner last night, should the guard bother you this should silence them." Heele pulled the ring from his finger and handed it to his only servant. Feskarn clutched the ring tightly, deposited it into a pocket under his green cape and spurred his horse forward.

Lord Heele arrived at the Campus Main Gate. It had been closed the evening before when the carriage had arrived, but now it was open and Feskarn waited on House soil for Lord Heele. It would have been a trivial thing to stop and argue admission to the grounds but Feskarn knew that Rupport would have no taste for it this morning. Lord Heele nodded to the four guards that served at the gate when they saluted him; it was a recent development under the order of Senior Guard Loal.

If anything was apparent as they waited in the entrance of The House of Wrath it was that the House stood in a state of agitation. Mages in full battle regalia stalked the expansive rooms and halls, performing some ritual that Heele did not understand. The behavior was also in stark contrast to the mood of the night before; whatever had happened had savagely crushed the spirit of the Remembrance Dinner.

Gavin waited in the blue themed room; a massive spear hung over the mantle, no fire burned. A reticent Serrlena stood quietly behind the First of Wrath. When Lord Heele and Feskarn arrived, the huntsman was clearly put on edge by such power, but Heele thought only of his anger. Both bowed respect to Gavin, who openly wore chain mail under his robes. He did not need it, but those that looked to him for leadership would take the threat placed on the House more seriously if he showed this measure of concern. Or so he believed and it seemed to work. His House now throbbed with a palpable excitement as it looked to mete out punishment on the two who had somehow escaped the pit.

Gavin smiled mirthlessly and said, "Sit, Lord Heele. You must forgive the vulgar nature of our meeting." He pulled at the exposed chain mail. "You have had problems of your own I see." He rubbed his right palm with his left hand, an obvious reference to Heele's bloody rag.

Rupport sat and exhaled heavily. He said, "I returned to my estate late last night after the dinner hosted by your esteemed House. The scene was shocking. My servants, my cooks, lay dead in the foyer."

"That is terrible."

"It is. Most had been with me for years. Not long after I discovered the scene, three men appeared before me in the foyer. One called my animate by name. And in response it knew him by name."

"And that was?" Archammer asked.

"It started with r, hmm. Arcane I think. This man ordered my animate to fetch a carriage and it obeyed him, mocking me as it went. Arcane spoke of sparing my life in gratitude and of Turnbly Lancaster, a childhood friend of mine who died four years ago, as though they had discussed me. The tallest of the three cut my hand as they left and my head, it rings yet." Heele opened his jaw and it crunched loudly. "It would have done no good to chase them, they could easily have killed me. I only hope that in some way my claim can be settled against the House of Animate. What evil they served me!"

Archammer was grim faced. Behind him Serrlena clenched her jaw hard. Archammer leaned forward and said in a soothing tone, "I can only thank you for bringing this matter to my attention. You have my word and the word of my House that we will support your efforts in retribution against the House of Animate. I would advise, and I believe my attendant would agree, that the best course of action is to lodge a formal complaint both with the House of Animate, as they sold you such a despicable piece of magicwork and also with The House of Currents, since they are in the position to legitimize your claim against the House of Animate." Behind him Serrlena nodded slowly.

"It is not rewarding work to bring such a claim against a House, but I see no other choice. As for the stolen carriage, I will send word of it. All of The House of Wrath shall know of it. There will be no place for these murderers to hide."

Heele paused, contemplating the enormousness of the task, then he said, "I understand. It would seem I have no other choice. I appreciate your time Master Archammer, Valkyrie Oakmaul. Feskarn. We leave the mages to their business." The lord and his huntsman rose, then bowed and finally took their leave from the sitting room.

Archammer said, "Our two escapees and their mage."

"Undoubtedly." It was the first thing she had said since being released from the pit. "Shall I set out against them?"

"No. It is unsure which road they are taking, if even they take the road. And I have other uses for you here. A carriage can travel only so far before the horses tire. I will personally see to the mages that ride after them." He paused and his tone changed, almost pleading, "Do you now see why it is so important to cultivate such loyalty? Eventually it builds new roads of opportunity. Arrange a meeting with Entrah, but wait for Heele's complaint to be registered. It is time to press this new attack against the House of Animate. I grow tired of their bleating for power. Take your leave."

Serrlena bowed, she had not done so in a long time but Archammer was in no mood to be toyed with, and left the blue room. She would rather have ridden after the carriage, but the House of Animate would provide an enjoyable exercise of dominion. They had not had so much luck of late in challenging for power; it seemed that a hex had befallen the House. It would be pleasurable to watch them writhe under this new pressure. First though, she thought it wise to bathe; her night in the pit had not done much other than dirty her and focus her hatred of Peter. It was his fault she was there. His fault.

Murdoch pounded the desk with his fist. His jaw had already tightened. "Tell me this is a joke, Trahn."

Trahn sat in his study with Murdoch across from him; both mages had dark rings under their eyes. Trahn set his cup of tea down. He said, "Unfortunately it isn't. The animate that the House provided to Lord Heele has apparently gone wrong."

Jannan inferred meaning and said curtly, "Just say it. The animate I made for him."

"I know things have not gone well for you lately, Murdoch, but I am not about to hang you."

"Yes, 'not gone well for me.' I am sick of your double talk! Have you called me here to punish me? Or is it just a matter of convenience that you would take me from my work to see that I am the subject of investigation?" Jannan asked loudly.

"You are not the subject of investigation, but this is a curious matter. It doesn't help that Lord Heele is one of Wrath's favored pets. You must know that."

"I do of course, you were the one that instituted the amazing amount of information gathering on a prospective client," his voice was pained at the task.

"I will give you this council and nothing more, tread carefully. You know as well as I that our position is tenuous. Anyway, how is your work?"

Jannan feigned laughter. "It is painfully slow, all progress seems to have stopped and I cannot fathom why. If I do not get this animate completed soon I shall truly feel lost. My feel for the magic is poor and my work suffers for it. Something blocks me, I believe that, Trahn, I do."

Trahn smiled painfully, he felt that he watched his friend dying. "It will come to you all at once, that is certain." A rap at the door stopped his speech. "Come."

It was Laura, a new apprentice from the outskirts of Earlsburg. She was all dark hair and bright eyes. "A Serrlena Oakmaul is here to see you, master."

Murdoch muttered, "Wrath."

"Wrath indeed," followed Trahn.

"Shall I send her away, Master Entrah?" Laura asked self-consciously.

"No, no. Show her in, she wouldn't leave even if sent."

Jannan stood, pushing the heavy chair backwards as his knees straightened. He said, "I will let you to it. I would not want you to feel as though you had to defend the Second of your House."

243

Trahn shook his head in frustration for his friend. He had suffered much in the past years. "Bring me Oakmaul. We will see what The House of Wrath wants today."

Oakmaul appeared without Laura, which did not surprise Trahn. He stood facing the window, staring at the sea. Sometimes it was the only thing that kept his sanity in place. "Serrlena, you are well?"

"Enough so. Master Archammer would meet with you."

"Will he now? I have the honor of meeting alone with him? I am busy, Serrlena, surely Master Archammer is as well. What could be so important to take us away from our Houses? In any case I shall see him at the next Directorate Council."

"You know what is so important and yet you reject his request? He will be most displeased."

Trahn turned and faced the slight woman; he wondered what had made her turn from The Way of Health. He said, "So be it. If he wishes to speak with me let him come instead of sending you. I do not send Master Nightwillow when I wish to see him. How is The House of Wrath these days? I have been so busy in my own dealings that I simply cannot keep up with your current affairs."

The mockery was unmistakable. Serrlena answered it in turn. "We are well, thank you. I would recommend that you make time for Master Archammer. I will tell him that you are quite looking forward to it. Lord Heele also awaits such a meeting. Good day, master," she finished and left his study in one motion.

Trahn worked through the morning without giving The House of Wrath another thought. Surely Gavin would be busy sorting out the problem of the escapees. Word had carried quickly, the guard was never capable of much secrecy. So it came as some surprise when Gavin did make his way to the House of Animate.

There was no request for a meeting. Gavin did not as much as breathe in the direction of Laura, who sat at the reception desk. He made his way to Trahn's study and smiled at the surprise painted upon his host's face. "Master Entrah, my assistant tells me that if I am to speak with you I should simply do so." He sat down.

"This is a surprise, Gavin. Please, sit." His voice pained at First of Wrath's actions.

Gavin shook once, humored, his armor clattered as bells, distant. "Your

House finds itself again in a difficult place, Master Entrah. Your constructs cavort with criminals. Or is it the mages of this House that I do not understand?"

"Our work still has much to illuminate, Master Archammer, as we are being formal."

"If that is the case then take your place in the order. Be contented with your power."

Trahn looked insulted. "Are you suggesting that I allow the House of my steward to falter? What in my place would you say?"

Gavin leaned forward in his chair. "I am not in your place, Master Entrah. Rupport Heele's grievance is both dire and just. I would recommend that you settle it quickly, before the true extent of the crime is revealed. I cannot imagine how high it could reach. The Second of the House? The First? All of these things will come out in time, I am certain of that."

Trahn's face had hardened, resolved not to grow angry, but his pale cheeks took color. "I will take your recommendation under advisement."

Gavin stood and spoke as to a child. "It is best that you do, Master Entrah. I very much look forward to the conclusion of this problem, as explained to Master Guildenil. Good day."

Trahn waited until the First of Wrath was gone, then slammed his fist into his desk.

Twenty-one

The five war-horses rumbled as one along the hard dirt road. The sun was low on the horizon to the Wrath mages' west. They had ridden hard and fast to get this far south in one day. Abram knew that they were closing in on the carriage. At the last inn the stable boy saw it roll past less than an hour before the armored mages had appeared. The man driving the carriage had matched well the description of Peter. The mage smiled in anticipation of battle joined. Even warned of the mage with them he did not worry. Who alone could challenge five well-armed and equally well-trained students of Wrath? No, surely the escapees would be in custody tonight, if not dead.

The four mages with him were all skilled. He knew this to be especially true of Marcial and Laruiel. He had faced the twins in battle, before the Alliance of Tarlow. It had been a gruesome affair, a failed campaign, but much respect had been earned. It was mere chance the three of them had come to the Campus at the same time. It was to Abram's regret that he would be their enemy again, someday. The other two, Fritz and Genet, were younger but showed promise. He had sparred in the past with them, both singularly and together. His superior strength had won the day in battles fought with wooden swords. When Master Archammer had summoned him for the task of hunting the degenerates he was glad to be given the choice of comrades in arms. His selection was quick and they rode within the hour.

Now with the sun nearly set and a day of hard riding behind them Abram could smell the fight. It was a skill that had developed as he gained experience, a sense of things to come. His deep voice carried well. "Faster! The enemy is near!"

He spurred his horse on and the others accelerated along with him. A stream bed lay to the left of the road and ahead it made a sudden cut to the right. A bridge was built over the crossing; in spring it was needed, now a mere trickle flowed through the sand. A carriage moved lazily south on the road, just across the bridge. Abram raised his right hand to block the sun's glare. The two gray horses that pulled it came into clear detail. He reached across his body with the same hand and drew his sword, raising it in the air. The sunlight danced off the polished metal. He shouted, "To battle!"

On his right Marcial and Laruiel separated from the others and roared ahead. The speed of their horses could not be matched. Down through the stream bed they surged, kicking sand into the air. Genet and Fritz rode in wedge formation with him. The horse's hooves clopped loudly across the bridge alerting the driver of the carriage. Peter's head swung around rapidly, surprise on his face. He said something that Abram could not make out and the carriage accelerated.

The horses pulling the carriage were strong and for a moment it appeared that they would pull away from their pursuers. Then from ahead of the carriage the twins burst into view, blocking the road. In one moment the speed was lost and the carriage pulled to its left. The Wrath mages closed in, weapons drawn, shadows long.

Abram began to believe that battle would not be necessary as the carriage slowed and wheeled in a circle then the rear of the carriage exploded. The massive blast spread debris into the air and as it fluttered down, two robed figures and an animate scattered from the gaping hole. Peter stood and with a quick flip of the wrist knives appeared in either hand, one long and thin, the other curved with teeth. Peter extended one arm at each group of mages, looking side to side.

Abram raised his left hand in a fist and the Wrath mages reigned in their horses. The horses neighed and stamped, their blood also burned for war. Abram pointed his sword at the four figures and said, "Surrender, criminals. The House of Wrath brings charges against you."

The black robed figure spoke, the metallic voice surprised Abram, "I do not believe we will. Bring your fight against us if you dare. Otherwise let us on our way."

Abram laughed and lowered his sword. He said confidently, "Very well.

Chanhaeth!' The earth below the carriage began to shake, but the black robed figure extended both arms towards the ground and all grew still.

Arcane scoffed, "Such tricks have no place here." He brought his hands up to his head and then pushed out away from his body. A thick black mist began to roll out of his robes. It quickly obscured him and then the other man and animate disappeared. Within seconds only Peter's head could be seen. That ducked into the mist and it rolled over the Wrath mages.

Peter moved silently through the inky substance. His eyes adjusted with catlike quickness to the darkness. Jumping down from the driver's bench he took stock of the situation. The Wrath mages pulled their reigns furiously trying to regain control of their frightened horses. The two that appeared together seemed better for it and he looked the other way, for an opportunity. Arcane's hands swirled together then apart. Lie Ben held his hands inches apart, no motion could be seen from the Sage of Tesca. Bessemer for his part stalked around the side of the three near the bridge. Those were clearly handled, so he turned back to the twins. He could see them near each other, mouths moving but he could not hear a sound, the world had turned into the dull thudding of the ocean on the stone wall. He ran with purpose.

Abram wrestled with the reigns of his horse and shouted, "Maintain!"

Then it began in earnest. A shout behind him marked Genet's collapse, pulled from her horse by Bessemer. She flailed with her sword, waving it in the false night, but the animate could see clearly, and the blade would do little to its metal body should she find the mark. At the same time Lie Ben released his magic, a furious swirl of fear and hate that howled as it sped towards its mark. It blasted Fritz, throwing the mage from his horse. He landed with the dull thud of broken flesh, his sword clattered to a halt ten feet beyond him.

Abram took stock of his surroundings and said, "Hide if you will, it will make no difference in the end!" He let out a tremendous yell and a swathe of light was cut through the mirk. It revealed Arcane's right arm and a stripe of the carriage. The mage put his heels into his horse's flanks and bolted forwards.

Peter ran towards the twins, unlike the others who acted unsure of themselves, they backed carefully from the darkness. Peter followed and emerged from the dome of inky magic. The twins smiled as one, clearly sensing the advantage. The one to his left, Marcial, charged, raising his sword above his head. Laruiel followed, his weapon of choice a massive axe.

Peter spun away from the sword, parrying it with his straight knife, the blow accelerating his spin into a tornado of knives and cloth. Out of the corner of his eye he saw the axe, bringing death, and he twisted violently out of the way. His spine shuddered and loosened, bending completely against its nature. He stared at the ground only inches from his nose. If his predicament took him by surprise it was more shocking to Laruiel who could not believe that he had missed his quarry.

The twins rode into the darkness and wheeled their horses. Peter rolled his torso upright, his body strong and loose, and waited for the return charge. He did not wait long. Laruiel came first, both horse and rider's eyes burned. He swung overhand, which Peter parried, the weight of the axe forcing him to one knee. As the mage passed he turned, blasting flame with his left hand, red and noisy. It exploded around Peter leaving him unharmed, singeing little bits of grass that grew in the road. The mage cursed his failure.

Peter whirled inside the slash of Marcial's sword and pulled him in one motion from his mount. The mage bounced once and regained his feet, his chain mail clattering.

He advanced in a flurry, but each blow that Peter did not find a way to block with his knives he miraculously found a way to escape. A smile crossed his face and Marcial cursed, "What are you?"

Peter pushed against the sword, answering, "Ask your precious Oakmaul, she is the one that nursed me!" Peter writhed away from Laruiel's axe, drew to full height on one leg and flicked Marcial's left eye with his curved blade. The mage yelped as blood poured down his face.

"Damn you!"

"It is much too late for that." Peter smiled and threw himself at Laruiel as he rode too close.

Arcane watched as Abram rode down on him, sword raised to strike. The blade crashed heavily onto his robes which hardened into the metal they were made from. The shock of the blow forced Arcane back as sparks leapt from the clashing metal. Beside him Lie Ben followed the rider with his right hand and a bolt of lightning jumped at him. Again the magic caused no harm but crackled with bravado about his armor. "Your are weak!" shouted Abram, mocking.

Arcane rolled his head once. Had he been human the vertebrae would have cracked and popped. The light of his eyes dimmed and he summoned a great strength. Lie Ben turned towards Abram half in darkness and light. Another bolt flared and then another.

Abram laughed and charged again, this time at Lie Ben, who had given away his position. "You cannot hide!"

Arcane rumbled low. Then louder. Tendrils of the mist began to roll off and suddenly the whole dark mass collapsed to the ground like a burst bubble. The black splashed and disappeared, no longer supported by Arcane's power. The sudden collapse brought Peter and the twins to a halt as they reacquainted themselves to the scene. Bessemer looked up from Genet, dead in its hands, spotted the dazed Fritz and eyed him as a cellar rat.

The horse continued its charge at Lie Ben but Abram was ripped from the saddle, suspended in the air like an unwilling marionette. "What sorcery is this?" he shouted, demanding an answer.

Arcane tipped his head back under the cloak. He said, " Mine." It was not menacing, but it did not need to be. The hanging served the purpose.

Abram tensed and said simply, "Marcial, Laruiel, escape, tell Archammer—"

Arcane's head snapped to the delayed fight. All three men now stood watching. He said, "You will tell him nothing!"

Again the rumble of the Harrow passed through Arcane in preparation of a fatal blow. Abram would not see his death in vain and summoned great strength to him. His training did not fail. Invisible tendons burned apart, breaking the spell that held him, he dropped into a crouch and took up his sword that lay upon the ground. "Flee!"

Arcane stood only a few feet away and the warrior attacked with a savage skill. The assault took its toll, and though the sword could not cut through Arcane's robes it broke the spell that he formed to kill the twins. Laruiel whistled a high reedy note and his horse, which had pranced from the ruckus, returned with grace and speed. Marcial again put blows against Peter. The thief danced and dodged but this time he could not find a hole in the mage's attack. Forced back, he was pushed down to one knee, the sword tip finally finding its mark.

"I will see you another time," promised the mage, swinging up into the saddle of his horse, fetched by his brother. They stood ready to charge the robed men when Abram's eyes met theirs. They could see in them that it had taken all of his strength to break the spell that held him, and if he fell they could not stand against such a foe. Pulling the reins and laying low to the back of their horses they fled north across the bridge. Leaving behind three of their own, neither would soon forget such a defeat. But they would honor Abram's last request.

Arcane smiled under his deep hood. The human could not see what in truth he attacked. Lie Ben would strike if the need arose, but he too could see defeat in the man, his strength gone. The Sage of Tesca was glad that he did not face whatever horrible might Arcane had leveled against the Wrath mage. Arcane spoke, the metal in his voice vilely sharp. "I tire of you, human."

His robes and cape burst apart revealing the small shape of the animate that had been hidden beneath them. Runes of brass and copper were etched over the entirety of Arcane's body. Lie Ben had known what lay beneath but the viewing of it still brought shock. How had an animate come to such power, enough to rout five Wrath mages? The man known as Lie Ben was buried under a stream of incomprehensible thought, a thousand voices all chattering their own story. His body fell to the ground.

As the robes uncoiled from Arcane's shoulders the metal regained its rigidity and struck the fool mage, piercing his body, easily slipping through the defense provided by the armor that he wore. Arcane pulled the dying man close and held his head in his long fingers. "You could not win. Your death," Arcane shook his head in disgust, Abram was already gone. "It will be forgotten."

The metal spikes recoiled from the soft flesh, a revulsion ran deep in his anima. The strips reformed the robes and hooded cloak, flares of red marked the separation of pieces that had not been visible before. "Forget the carriage, it is a loss. Strip what is of value. We take the horses left by the dead. Peter."

"I live, though again I bleed at the hands of Wrath." His shirt had been cut open. His chest bled a straight wound not deep, but long.

"Remember them well, they will fight again. Lie Ben." The collapsed man did not answer, his eyes wide and distant. Arcane commanded, "Lie Ben!"

Bessemer had come down from the bridge, dragging Genet's body in its left hand and Fritz in its right. It stood at the Sage's side. It questioned, "He is not well?"

"No, not well at all, curse this fool human. I would leave him if he did not intrigue me so. Put him on a horse, Bessemer, for now we can lead him. There are not any mages near that could match these five, and they are scattered. We ride for Kurn."

Peter and Bessemer piled the three bodies into the carriage and drove it into the woods. They unhooked the horses and prepared a passable set of reins for each. Peter picked over the carriage while Bessemer went back to Arcane who had collected the other horses. Bessemer said, "These two will need to rest, they cannot go on indefinitely."

"I tire of the weakness of flesh, but as I must rely on it we will stop soon. Let us leave this place and take refuge in the forest."

They set south again, but after an hour, with the light of the sun all but gone, Arcane led them astray from the road. Lost in the forest they camped for the night.

Peter gathered wood and Arcane ignited the fire, giving light and warmth to the men that had not long ago been accustomed to the cold dark hospitality of those they had slain. The horses tied to trees were fed and rubbed down by Bessemer, as his anima still demanded. The merciless killing had already fallen from his thoughts. Peter ate and then slept, but Lie Ben sat and stared at the fire, joining the inhuman cast against fatigue that the animates claimed as their own.

Every so often the man would mutter unintelligible things, as though many voices battled in him. Nothing more could be goaded from him. The fire crackled and popped. When it fell silent, the darkness of the forest rivaled that of Arcane's magic.

Tara Groundmender's pony shifted underneath her as they stood at the edge of the forest, waiting along the road. It was a silly creature; its loyalty and affection towards Tara seemed to know no bounds. It did not exactly surprise Tara, being that she had purchased it as an underfed, overworked farm horse. The poor thing was literally sick and tired, and very nearly turned into some strange jerky substance that was ever so popular in the northern regions of Jota Siana.

The farmer was so amazed that anyone would want such a scraggly beast that he had given him up for a pittance. Tara felt a twinge of guilt as she took the horse and in short order healed its wounds and named it Dragonfly. It seemed a fitting name, its eyes glinted and shimmered as the insect of her dream, or vision, and the guilt quickly passed as she rode the long journey from Jainetown to Serac.

She had left the Campus on the suggestion of Brother Chaign but she had been thinking on it for several weeks when he mentioned it. It was good that she did, in some ways being so close to the Mother proved to be a suffocating barrier that shielded her from the reason she had become a mage in the first place. It was not that Tara wanted to see the pain of the world. On the contrary she hated it now more than ever, but she had a calling and she would not ignore it.

It would be her first return to Serac in almost three years, and she looked forward to consulting with the Mother on a number of minor points dealing with the Way. She also looked very much forward to seeing Alexander. He had been saddened at her leaving, but knew that it was bound to happen sooner or later, and he had not tried to dissuade her from going. He had had a witty remark about her going but she could not remember it exactly and it was not as amusing when quoted incorrectly.

As was very often the case with the Way she had felt compelled to stop, and she now waited in the full night for whatever would happen. She was aware that a troop of Wrath mages had ridden south that day, a farmer whose harvest would now be much heartier told her so, and she suspected very much that her desire to delay the return to Serac was related to this fact.

It was soon thereafter that she could hear the horses, traveling at full gallop. Whoever it was was in a great hurry indeed. She waited for the two riders to pass her, calling out to them when she saw that they were Wrath mages.

"Hail, wizards!" Tara led her pony down onto the road. The light from the moon was strong, as she called them the moon light was joined by one of Tara's creation and all accounted for were illuminated brightly. The Wrath mages reined in their horses, their sides heaved and both heads shook as one.

Laruiel said to his brother, "A Way mage, Marcial. The night is not lost yet." Then addressing Tara, "Way mage, my brother and I are returning in haste to Serac, he is hurt, and our horses tire. Our journey is most important, we carry news of a great foe to Master Archammer. I would ask you to aid us."

Tara nodded and said, "You need not ask. What of your injuries?"

Marcial weakly muttered, "My eye...my face..."

Tara said, "Say no more. I cannot do my work with you on horseback."

Marcial hopped to the ground; a small smile was all he could muster with such a wound. He stood next to Tara, and she took in the scent of battle. As he said, his eye was in ruin, and a cut ran up his brow where the knife had traveled. She placed her hand flat over the socket. Marcial grunted.

"Muulsuin!"

Tara let her hand down, and Marcial's eye blinked quickly, rebuilding the damaged tissue through Tara's guidance. "The scar will fade in time."

Marcial rubbed his eye with his palm, and nodded as his sight returned. "I am in your debt."

Tara smiled, it was often said to her but rarely was the debt settled. Tara did not care. "Now as for your horses." She put her left hand on Marcial's horse's snout. The horse neighed softly. Then repeated the process with Laruiel's.

"Ride fast, they will not falter."

Marcial swung up to his saddle and said, "Our deepest gratitude, my brother and I will remember your assistance. What is your name if I, we, might have it?"

"Tara Groundmender."

"I am Marcial and my brother is Laruiel. I would warn you, Tara, against traveling to the south, a powerful evil takes that path."

"I head north to Serac," she answered.

"If fortune favors us we shall see you again."

Tara smiled and cocked her head, "If fortune favors you. Ride!"

The twins each shouted, "Yah!" The call ten men than two and the horses raced away into the night. Tara bent over and placed her hands on her knees. She breathed deeply and smiled. The rejuvenating enchantments always left her winded.

The twins sped into Serac, the final distance a sprint carried by the magic of Tara Groundmender. The sky hinted at the coming day when they reached The House of Wrath. The soldiers hurried inside, dispatching some tired eyed youth to look after their horses. Laruiel asked loudly, "Where is Master Archammer? We bring grievous news."

One of the students in the great room, insomniacs all, said, "He takes time in the spire. I heard him say so."

The twins ran up the stairs, carrying their burden with haste. They did find Gavin in the spire. He was alone, and his eyes were closed. He spoke as softly as they had ever heard him. "You ride two in number. You bring ill news."

Marcial started, "We set upon the enemy almost a full day's ride from here. Lord Heele's animate, Peter, the Sage, and another. In black robes."

"A fell wizard. Powerful in battle unlike any I have seen," Laruiel continued. "We had every advantage and yet we could not stand against them. Abram gave his life, that we could bring warning."

Gavin turned and faced them, remarkably calm, "I see that you have faced battle. When first light comes I will send warning to all of Wrath. They will come back to us." He smiled slightly, tired. "Leave me. My mind is troubled and this is no solace."

The twins answered together, "As you wish, master."

Tara did not arrive to The Way of Health until two days after her encounter with the Wrath mages. It suited her to travel at a slow pace and though she was excited to again see the Mother and Alexander, the ever constant demands for her talents slowed her ever more. Despite being in the shadow of Serac, the farms of the area seemed in constant need.

As things would be, each family simply demanded that she stay for breakfast or lunch or dinner, or some other fabricated meal in order to try the most amazing stew or bread or cake. Tara could not see a day when she would be hungry and the peasants were always truly thankful.

It was under an amazing slurry of rumors that Tara did return to the city. The last few miles were the easiest going, the occupants of Serac had become so accustomed to the presence of the mages that there were scarce requests on their time and power; at least during something as common as riding down the street.

By the time she reached the Campus Tara had heard all of the rumor and allegation. A murderous animate, the rout of the Wrath mages, the escape of the occupants of the pit. It seemed to be truth taken wing but she had learned never to dismiss what was said in the streets. And the streets of Serac spoke more truth than most.

The Way of Health was as she remembered it, the strong trees in the garden, the dense overgrowth inside. The sense of warmth and safety. Tara was greeted warmly by a man slightly younger then herself and found the Mother in her garden. She sat with staff in hand on a tree that had been formed into a chair. Light danced around her fingers.

As was customary Tara said, "Greetings to the Mother."

She answered, "Who of my children seeks refuge?"

"Tara Groundmender."

"Daughter Groundmender is welcomed." With the formality of the refuge out of the way the Mother smiled and said, "Tara, daughter. It brings me great joy that you return." She stood from her growing chair and embraced her. "Hmm. You grow both in the Way and in beauty, as the Wrath mages say," her voice always velvet.

Tara laughed, "I thought they might. How are things with the House? I heard such rumors coming in."

"Most speak truth, but I do not know the exact nature of the losses suffered by The House of Wrath. The House of Animate staggers awkwardly. Wrath, as is its nature seeks to benefit from it but we all sense it. Trahn is not what he once was. Pressured from inside and out. It is an interesting time. Your adversary was near."

"My adversary?" Tara asked, her mind trying to organize all that had been said.

"The mist was revealed to me again, only days ago, but I could not approach it."

Tara touched her shoulder. The wound had not wholly healed. The pain was, for the most part, gone, but the flesh had taken on a hard almost metallic texture. From time to time it ached but was little distraction. She breathed out jaggedly.

"The twins spoke of a powerful evil that went south with the animate, and I would think those that escaped the pit. Could that be the creature that creates such a trail that the Earth must warn us?"

Lilac smiled, "You grow in wisdom as well. I have my suspicions that you are correct. At the next Directorate Council I will bring it up, though I do not think that Gavin will listen to me. If he cannot crush it with his magic or skewer it with his sword it is of no use to that one. I have suffered with him as much as I can suffer."

Tara understood that she was much more than just an apprentice or even a rank and file of the Way. The Mother spoke to her as a friend, as a confidant. It bolstered her confidence.

The Mother continued, "I am sorry, Tara, I do not mean to bore you, but the matters of the House have been much on my mind and there has not been an understanding ear to hear me in some time. Brother Chaign left soon after you did. I have not heard word from him at all. The Earth moves us as so many pawns, but I do not like it when all of the pawns are taken from me. It is good to have you here."

"Thank you, Mother. I am glad to be back."

Twenty-two

Peter leaned his weight fully against the column of bricks. A muscle in his shoulder crunched as he rolled it to scratch an itch. Black iron fence extended from the pillar and again met brick before running off into the dank, inky night. The thief could see the dim glow of a night watchman's lantern some vague distance away and decided that now was the time to carry out Arcane's wishes.

Peter took several steps into the road before turning and, with two bounding steps, jumped straight up. He caught the top of the brick and hauled himself up, where he perched like some hideous grotesque. Having satisfactorily taken in the lay of the land Peter dropped quietly over the hedge inside the fence, his cloak fluttering.

According to Arcane this was the residence of Geoffrey Catrz, a semi-noble banker in Earlsburg. He had arranged for the truly wealthy of the town to purchase their animates, and with the fees he charged purchased one of his own. Peter flipped the piece of crystal Arcane had given him between his thumb and forefinger. "Place this inside the animate's head," he had said, then showed Peter how to open the hatch that should appear on the back of the toy's head.

Peter moved fluidly through the landscaped gardens and pulled himself thin against the side of the mansion. Before separating from Arcane he had been told that the animate was in the mansion proper, somehow he could sense that sort of thing. It did not take long for Peter to find an unlocked window, and with a flourish that marked a seasoned, but not pretentious burglar, he climbed inside. The stark moonlight exposed him more than he liked and as he moved shadow to shadow he thought, 'If I only had my father's cloth.'

To a thief the mansion would make a striking target. Elaborate tapestries adorned the walls where rich oil paintings of idle scenes did not. Cabinets in every room contained treasures of silver. Antique crystal goblets shined in the light of the moon.

Peter walked in complete silence, almost snake-like in manner. He paused and drew back as he turned a corner into a dining room and saw the eyes of the animate. The room was exceptionally large, and yet clearly not the grand dining room. It lacked the displayed elegance that this near-noble clearly appreciated throughout the rest of his house.

Peter lowered and with a slight sway stalked the animate, which busily polished a set of fine porcelain. As Peter moved closer he could see differences in this style from Arcane and his brother, Bessemer. It had shorter arms and broader face, solid boot like feet. Peter smiled, remembering his first viewing of Arcane. His amazement had been well placed when compared to the ill-refined styling of the Earlsburg animates.

Closing within five feet of the unaware animate, Peter pounced. With his ring finger on his right hand he tripped the hatch release, a small button that blended neatly into the rest of the head. His thumb flipped the panel wide open, inside the crystal orb of the head rippled once and the animate began to turn to face Peter. The small crystal bullet, only the size of the end of Peter's thumb, sped into the hole, released with spirit from Peter's left hand.

Upon contacting the crystal orb it began shaking, releasing a golden light. Peter shut the hatch and waited. He had seen it five times already in the past week, this was the last. The animate stood and addressed Peter. "I obey. As Arcane commands so shall it be done." The metal voice was small, barely audible.

Peter nodded, said nothing and vanished from the house, crystal goblets in tow. The whole excursion had taken less than ten minutes. Peter hopped the fence back to the road. A lantern was pulled from under a cloak; a watchman, a burly, gnarled man, stood in the new light, sizing up Peter. His blue cloak was darkly shadowed. He said, "I thought I saw someone down this way."

The watchman brandished a large club, well worn, and approached Peter with a violent confidence. Peter frowned, even if he did escape, this one would alert the rest. He had to be silenced. Peter drew his straight knife.

The watchman rushed him, swinging heavily but with well practiced strikes. Peter stepped back, catching a brushing blow to his shoulder. A secondary strike from the same attack knocked the knife from his hand. Peter ducked another swing and rolled away from his attacker. He produced his curved blade and leapt at the watchman. With the trusty wood club the watchman was every bit as skilled as the Wrath mages had been, and Peter though twisting and prying for some advantage found none.

The watchman grabbed Peter's arm and clubbed him across his jaw. "You may be the dumbest thief ever," he laughed.

Peter staggered back. "Perhaps." Peter tossed his curved blade into the air, the watchman for one second followed its arc. Peter dropped to the ground, right leg extended perfectly parallel to the road, flattening like a house of cards. Grabbing the straight knife from the ground Peter rose on his right leg and cut at the man's throat. With his left hand he caught the curved blade as it came down, bringing it over head with a downward slash. The combination of attacks and Peter's inhuman advance prevented the watchman from fully protecting himself. His throat was untouched but his club fled to the ground. In one motion Peter kicked it out of the light with his left foot. The watchman stepped back and went for a long skinny whistle that hung around his neck.

"Perhaps not," Peter said, striking with lightning speed, not really controlling the final flurry, but his body moved with deadly accuracy. The curved blade cut the leather string and with his left elbow he knocked it away. Following his arm across Peter spun the straight blade, this time opening the watchman's throat. Peter continued to spin down, legs crossing as he collapsed upon himself, ducking under the spray of blood, then sprung away, uncoiling.

The watchman fell, knocking the lantern over. It flickered and extinguished. Peter waited one minute more to see if the ruckus had alerted anyone else. When only the hoot of an owl was heard Peter trotted away, returning to Iron Ore Inn.

Peter frowned as he went. He had always been a thief, certainly given to violence, that much he would admit. But he had never been a murderer. Not before. Peter's thoughts turned to the past, how he had become what he now was, a thief certainly and now a killer as well. He was sad for a moment at the death of part of him, but that was consumed by the fires of anger and revenge. He would not care. He did not care. The witch would pay for what she had done. For what she had created.

The sprawl of Earlsburg had lessened and the flames had cooled when Peter pulled open the door to the inn. It was easy to stay unnoticed here, only an aging drunk saw Peter's return so late at night. The inn's meager trimmings, lit by scarce oil lamp adequately housed Arcane's company. The sly looking owner had greedily rented the north wing to Arcane in trade for a gold bauble taken from the Heele Estate. In truth Arcane could have purchased the building, the land, and the proprietor's family for five generations for the brooch, but all he wanted was to be left alone. And that he was granted.

Peter found Arcane in a back bedroom, conversing with Lie Ben, who had regained his faculties. Bessemer clunked around with an aged chest of drawers. Two oil lamps cast shadows light and dark on the walls.

Peter said, "It is done, Arcane."

All turned to face him as he spoke, his appearance taking them by surprise. Arcane said, "You move in silence." Arcane stood and wiped a drop of blood from the thief's cloak. "And bring death."

Peter's eyes flashed in the light of the lamps. "A watchman. Nothing more."

Peter returned to his room, one of four in the wing. It was across the hall from the one Arcane took as his own. He removed his cloak and it dropped into a pile on the wood floor. The old leather bag holding the goblets fell to his bed. It was only straw stuffed into a frame, but compared to the stone of the pit it was heaven. Opening the bag, he placed the goblets one at a time into the top drawer of the dresser that stood against the wall. Peter closed the drawer and blew out his own lamp with a light breath. Then he lay down on the bed and fell into a dreamless sleep.

He woke early the next morning, the scent of bacon and bread heavy in his nose. One of the maids had delivered a pitcher of water; steam rose off of it. His cloak was folded neatly and placed on the dresser. Peter rubbed his face with the water and went to the common room. It was empty save the owner and a serving girl, his daughter from the looks of her; they had the same greedy eyes. The sizzle of meat came through another door, the kitchen. Peter pointed to the owner and took a place on the bar, waiting for his food to come.

Peter had not been to Earlsburg before this trip with Arcane. The proprietor of the inn, Narth, knew it and had been dying to explain things to him as he saw them. Peter had avoided the man until now, and listened to his home grown wisdom as he worked a large plate of eggs and ham and bacon and butter soaked bread.

"You aren't from these parts are you? Nah, don't tell me I can tell by your clothes. Let me tell you a few things about Earlsburg. Now listen, you'll want to know this if you're gonna stay around," said Narth with a greasy voice. Peter smiled, thinking of his night work; he had seen the town, inside and out.

The skinny man continued, "The mountains to the west are the Hurichs, that's their real name but some people call 'em the Saltstone Mountains. I dunno. Neither's great if you ask me, but I wasn't around to name 'em. Not many folk adventure into 'em. Pretty smart if you believe the stories."

"What stories?"

"The old mountain men come down every few months with pelts to trade. Say there are men of stone that walk the ancient paths, high up. Never go near 'em. All sounds crazy to me, but stay out of the mountains. That's what I say."

Narth was finished talking about the mountains, "Earlsburg serves as a gateway of sorts, not that you want to go that way either. If the Westerling Garrison is ever overrun we'll serve as the last defense, that's what the wall is for, just in case. The Harrow on all of us if we ever need it. The garrison will take a week to reach on the horses you folk rode in on. That's riding 'em hard, too. I can get you a deal on some real fast ones, let me tell you.

"The soldiers I see in here say the garrison's become quite a thriving border town. If your friend has another trinket like the first, I might just sell him the inn and move that away."

Peter nodded and continued to eat.

"You know the truth about it though?" asked Narth.

"What's that?" Peter answered, not interested.

"The real reason for all of the military protection is the Hammer Stoke Mine. You can't imagine the things they pull from it. It's as though the gods themselves used it to keep their treasure."

"If it's so great, why don't you go work as a miner?"

"Not me, no not me. I don't have the heart for that kind of work. The pay isn't that good and the hours are long. The mine has a contract with the Great Houses, anyhow. They get first take. All hot after some sort of ore these days. Crystal too, I hear. But there's gold and silver. And other things..."

Peter gulped his ale. Setting the mug down hard on the bar he said, "What other things?"

Narth leaned in close, and said quietly, "I dunno for sure, the mages take 'em all. That's what the miners say. That's all they say. They're afraid."

Peter smiled and his chest heaved once, humored. He shook his head. "I'll keep that in mind." Two men came down the stairs from the east hall, talking loudly. They were older and dressed crisply. Peter rolled his head. He said, "Thanks for the meal." He got up and went back to his room, the ordering of breakfast repeated behind him.

The animate Sirkute frowned. Lighting the oil lamps in its master's house had grown suddenly tedious. Catrz really, when the toy thought of it, hardly deserved its service. It filled the well of the lamp from a larger metal container and placed the lamp into the bracket on the wall, lighting it with a candle that it carried. The animate froze for a moment, its head nodded, as though in prayer. It turned its head slowly, looking down both directions of the wood paneled hall.

The animate's long fingers opened, slowly at first, creaky at the years of service. The metal container dropped to the ground, splashing the burgundy carpet and wall with oil before falling to its side and spilling forth its contents. The oil ran down the hall following a warp in the wood. The animate smiled and the candle dropped ever so slowly. One moment of hesitation as angels drew breath and then the hallway ignited in a bluish flame. The animate bathed in the warmth, turned and walked down the hall, the sound of its footsteps drowned out by the fire.

The double doors to Catrz's suite had been paid for by a business deal that drove three families from their land; he had been sorry that it took place, but he was merely the banker, not the cause. The brass knob was cold to Sirkute's touch and did not turn. "Locked," the animate said.

Drawing its arms back the animate's fists slammed into the doors rattling them open. The animate staggered with the force, righting itself. The doors swiveled on their assigned path smashing into furniture on either side. Sirkute could see the humans jump. Catrz sat straight up, his short hair askew. His wife of twelve years raised her head and turned over, paying the animate no mind.

"Is everything alright, Sirkute?" the man asked sleepily.

"Perfectly," the metal voice answered. Its eyes focused into a glare.

"Leave me...leave me to sleep."

The animate crossed the room and stood threateningly over the man. "I do not think that possible."

Sirkute grabbed Geoffrey by the neck and began to shake him. The banker clutched at the toy's arms, trying to pry the hands off. He coughed. His wife woke fully and screamed, then pulled with her full weight on the animate's right arm, freeing her husband from the metal hold. Sirkute backhanded the woman and she fell to the floor.

Geoffrey coughed out, "I am your master. Stop! Stop what you are doing!"

Sirkute smiled and its eyes narrowed further. "I have a master, but you are not it." A blow across his temple knocked the banker unconscious. The animate let go of his hold and the man slumped into the bed. He looked like he had never risen. The wife took up a pitcher and broke it across the animate's head, splattering water against the wall. It turned to her and said, "Foolish woman."

It charged her, the footsteps blending with the roar of the approaching fire, and hit her with its right hand. The blow knocked her to the floor again. The animate grabbed her by her long brown hair and dragged her screaming across the room, slamming her into the wall. She lay unmoving. The strength that Sirkute felt was unmatched during its life, and it fell into wanton destruction of the room's furniture leaving the sickening humans buried under a pile of debris. They would burn along with the manor.

The second step of its commandment now began, the looting of the most precious of the house. And who better to know what had value than that which maintained the treasures? Sirkute quickly consolidated the woman's jewelry into one box. The banker's most valued possessions were kept in a safe in his study, hidden under the floor, beneath a rug. Sirkute opened the safe and withdrew the contents; more jewelry, a bag of gold coins, three ancient books, and a polished statue of a man carved from jade. Sirkute bagged the contents and left the burning mansion. The fire had broken through the roof, tongues of flame coughed smoke into the starry night.

The sky over Earlsburg was a ghostly red that night. Fires burned throughout the town, columns of smoke reached for the heavens. People fled into the streets. Men with fire buckets ran this way and that, panicked when faced with the reality of the situation. The animate easily slipped away into the roaring night, just one of many sparks that scattered and disappeared into the dark.

There was a new sensation in the anima of Sirkute. The animate was drawn to the hills, pulled by a greater force. Sirkute was not the first to find the place, there were three others and two more appeared shortly after its arrival. The place on the hill overlooked the city, the fires flickered, mere campfires from this vantage.

When the six animates had assembled Arcane revealed himself to them, saying, "I am pleased that each of you has come. I am, as you no doubt know, Arcane. Tonight you have thrown off your yoke and taken the first steps in the creation of a new world. For your freedom you will follow me, but know that I will not force you. If you wish you can return to the fires below, to the humans. Choose wisely but quickly." Arcane smiled, knowing that not one would return, they could not, but the toys must be given their illusions. He understood those created by Master Jannan.

Each animate in turn pledged to Arcane, starting with Sirkute. "To you, Arcane, I pledge my loyalty, none shall surpass me." Its had been the most violent of the rebellions, a flaw in its creation. Arcane saw that Master Jannan had not been careful with this one. The magic of the reading went unnoticed.

When all had said what they could Arcane nodded and said, "Then for each of you I have a plan, come to me." Six times magic from Arcane filled the night, six times the animate receiving the order smiled and nodded. Arcane said, "Each of you is ready. Bessemer!"

The butler appeared from the darkness, hidden with Peter and Lie Ben. "Arcane."

"Take these to the place I have prepared. You know the way as I have shown you. There they will begin the creation of the foundry. Stay from the road, though there will be little to bother you once you pass the Westerling Garrison."

"As you command, Arcane. I will wait for you to return."

Arcane nodded, "You serve me well, brother."

Sirkute stared at Bessemer, at the one called brother, a spark of jealousy in its anima. 'None will surpass my service!' clanged noisily in its mind.

Bessemer looked at the six and said, "We leave now. Leave what you carry with Arcane and follow me. We will not stop until we reach the place the humans call the Ichor Sinkhole. We shall not fail Arcane!"

The parade of animates headed to the west leaving Arcane. Peter and Lie Ben joined their master. Arcane said, "I have seen many sights in my short time, none has been as beautiful as this. Peter."

Peter blinked slowly, recalling his senses, "Arcane?"

"Go into the city and assist in putting the fires out. Tell the truth of their starting to those that will hear. And to those that will not. All must know that the fires were caused by the animates of Master Jannan's creation. Someday I will explain to him, but..." Arcane stopped himself. "Lie Ben and I ride for Tarlow. Join us there when you are finished here. I will contact you when you arrive. I know you, Peter, do not forget, we are one. Now—"

Peter cut off the metal voice, "Say no more, I obey." Peter climbed into the saddle on his horse and rode down the hill towards the fires.

The city burned for three days. The fires were clearly no accident, but at first no one paid attention to the cause. Merely putting them out was the most important task. Those that fought the fires had their spirits crushed time and again, as the blaze spread beyond their control each time they believed they had contained it. Soon it seemed that the city would burn clear to the ground. And as such things go, that is when the Way mages began to appear. First two, then four, the final count at seven. Heartened by the renewing magic and helped by the creation of rain, the fire fighters first regained hope and then the upper hand, pushing the fire back, leaving the steaming husks of buildings behind them as they forged ahead.

Peter fell into the ranks of the fire fighters, avoiding the Way mages and their magic as he ran the streets with bucket in hand. At every opportunity he filled the grungy men that fought for their town with the rumors of the truth. When eating at the camps created to organize the defense he would poison the minds of the women that maintained their men with food and affection. The murmuring about the House of Animate spread faster than the fires had, but the discontent would not be as easy to contain. There was no magic to calm it.

Master Fain stood in her study. The animist's brow was furled and her brown eyes were frozen into place, staring at the road below. Men and women hurried past, and looking up to the second story window each locked their gaze with hers, each filled with anger or fear or both. Anralett heard the rumors that swirled through the town and at first she did not believe them, but now they appeared to be true. Four of the mansions stood cold now, the other two smoldered, too dangerous to investigate. None of the animates could be found; she knew because she had searched for them.

Additionally, and perhaps more troubling, was the distinct mark of looting. The nobles whose homes burned returned to find their most valued treasures gone. It did not take long for the soured nobility to place the pieces of the plot, and it was made even more rudimentary with the framework of the allegations that floated with the smoke throughout the city.

Finally, and most horribly, there was the death of Catrz and his wife, whose bodies had been found under a pile of debris. It had sickened her when she saw it. To think that such noble work could be turned so evil. And if she had doubts of Master Jannan's intentions she could only imagine what the city thought; no, she did not have to imagine, it was clearly on display. Anralett was called a murderer, a witch and worse when she walked the streets. The Harrow Grace had been wished upon her no less than sixty-four times. The two that practiced the magic with her heard the same.

Out of fear she had petitioned the Commissioner of Earlsburg, Timothy

Main, to assign a twenty-four hour guard to the House. He granted it but his anger was evident as he did so. She knew pigeons flew that morning to take message to the Council of the Five Eagles in Tarlow.

Anralett rubbed her oval face, graced with the reddest of lips, and framed by dark hair and turned back to her study. She too would send word, but this to Serac. She only hoped that she would receive an answer before the commissioner gained authority to act against the House. She did not think he would, but then never had a town been razed by animates. A single candle flickered and coughed black smoke into the air. The light was not necessary, but she enjoyed the scent of the burning wax, she only wished that it did not remind her of what had happened. A note sat unfinished on the desk. She signed it and rolled it into a small tube. This would be her hope.

Anralett climbed the cramped flight of stairs to the belfry. The soft cooing of pigeons greeted her. They at least did not fear or hate her. She took one that looked strong from its cage and tied the tube holding the message to it. She held it close to her face and whispered, "Fly fast and true." Then she released the bird to the sky. It fluttered for a moment, gaining strength and then spiraled up into the vast smoky expanse.

She sighed and prepared her mind for the first of many meetings, upset that her work would have to wait.

Twenty-three

The Council of the Five Eagles sat in quiet discussion at an elaborate round table, made from wood that had been looted during the many wars that helped form the Rousan Empire. Countless artifacts had been hacked to bits to provide the material for the puzzle-like tabletop. Taken apart, it would be unlikely that it could ever be reassembled. The conversation had not turned serious yet, though they knew that they would soon have to make difficult decisions. When word of the burning first began to trickle into Tarlow they had not acted, instead waiting for the pigeon that the commissioner would inevitably send.

Not that this event, if true, did not warrant such a sending, but the commissioner, when appointed by the Five Eagles, had promised to send word each day. Now it was a minor irritant, and proof that he lacked the ability to act on his own. A misjudging of character that landed in the royal stable each day.

Even without the news that passed mouth to ear in the streets, the five knew that something was amiss in Earlsburg. No bird had come for three days. Until that morning, when the familiar note from Earlsburg had grown into a tome. Baron Khurson, appointed by the Grand Assembly to the council and the only member of the body that wore the golden wings across his chest, was surprised the pigeon had been able to carry it the span between the cities.

He reread the message for the tenth time trying to see the city between the messy script that the commissioner had placed onto the paper. A smudge of black, streaking across the center of the paper, emphasized the tale. Khurson sighed and said, "We have all read the Commissioner Main's missive and heard the news in the streets from our servants. Tariff rates and trade disputes will be handled later. The burning of Earlsburg is the most important matter and the Assembly awaits our instruction."

The other four men fell silent and turned their eyes to Baron Khurson. They knew he was correct in saying so, but the situation was delicately balanced. Khurson looked to each of them around the table. Guildmaster Wren fidgeted with a quill and then scrawled something on a piece of paper that rested before him. The guildmaster was elected by the guilds every two years. Wren had won the vote four times, and seemed quite comfortable with his place among the Five Eagles. He had, as Khurson had learned, a keen mind for business, and a willing spirit to battle.

His Honor James Eddington sat across the table from Baron Khurson. He was in his early forties and grey speckled his sandy hair. He was of the lineage of the King of Rousan, a position that had been abdicated by his grandfather's grandfather. It had been a concern at one time that the loss of the monarchy would weaken the Empire, but it was not the case. Instead of only one man to cheer, the people had five.

James had followed his forefathers to the universities of Jainetown in neighboring Jota Siana and shared their belief in the Council of the Five Eagles. His son and daughter were also sent to university, studying to carry his line with honor. There were whispers that Vera would be the first woman to ascend to the council. They were due back in town soon and he prepared a great party for the occasion.

To James's right was General Jonathan Paul. He was a massive man in stature and wisdom. He commanded the army of the Rousan Empire. It did not bother him that his position was less urgent in this time of peace, indeed he had personally crafted much of the Alliance of Tarlow. His craggy features hid a gentle spirit, though his strength in battle matched the deep lines well. The spectacles sitting delicately on his nose softened the hard visage, adding to the contradiction of the man.

The final member of the council was Senior Technologist Benjamin Pierce. He was the oldest of the council. His white beard was braided in the style seen in paintings in the Tarlow Museum. Of all the council he ran the most hot and cold, at once sickly sweet with agreement, followed by acidic disagreement. He alone wore robes, the others in suits.

Baron Khurson said, "This message brings us a very difficult, no, our most difficult challenge. If the accusations, no, too reaching, the presumed cause of the fires proves out we will be tasked with at the very least demanding that the builder of these animates be turned over to us for justice. I for one cannot fathom how far reaching this could be. And there is no hint of it in this letter."

His Honor swirled a wine glass, "What you say, Vaughn, is true, though will the House of Animate turn over such an accused?"

Pierce interjected, "They must! If they do not it would be treason, and more deadly to the prestige of the House than that. They would not dare reject our claim."

James responded, "It is presumptuous to believe that they would. There has never been such a calamity before, and any disreputable wizard has always been dealt with via the Houses' justice system."

General Paul crossed his arms over his chest, always a sign that he was ready to speak. "Mmm. This matter will take time for a course to be made clear. I would instead guide the council to the aid and rebuilding of Earlsburg. The damage is great, and would be much greater if not for The Way of Health. Guildmaster, how quickly can the guilds be readied?"

Wren set down his quill and said, "Send word of aid today, we can ride tomorrow morning, with supplies and men if the treasury is opened to us."

Baron Khurson nodded, saying, "Is their anyone that would object?" When no one did he said, "It is open to you."

"I do not mean to pressure the council," Pierce started. "But I believe that we must move quickly if we are to gain any satisfaction with the House of Animate."

General Paul asked, "And if we are wrong? What then?"

"The evidence is overwhelming against them, general. We must act to protect our people."

"But what steps would you take? Arresting those that follow the House here in Tarlow? That will only serve to inflame the situation. Even First Archammer's loyalty to the Rousan would be tested. The mages will certainly protect their own."

271

Pierce tugged at his beard. "Lord Khurson, surely you see we must act."

Khurson thought for a moment and then said, "I do not see that we can. It does appear clear, yes, but I agree with General Paul. If we attempt to punish the House, and I don't know that we can, and are wrong." He shook his head. "That is disastrous. I am aware as we all are that the Houses bicker amongst themselves, but not one would turn against the animists to that degree."

James said, "We will send a bird to Earlsburg then, with word of help and with orders to raise no hand against the House. When clarity is with us we will act. Until then, the Rousan Empire will wait."

"Agreed," all save Pierce said.

James said, "Then it shall be."

Guildmaster Wren said, "Now about the tariffs."

The bustle outside of the capital building was livelier than usual. The square with its carved fountain was usually busy with couriers, government officials, and peddlers, but the clamor for truth about Earlsburg had spread. Peasants jammed the square waiting for an official proclamation from the council. One had to come soon, or so the masses thought.

Lie Ben stooped behind a colorful tent of a peddler selling trinkets, combs to pots, fabric to silverware. Some of the goods were appealing, and Lie Ben still greedily soaked the world for all of its sensations. The darkness was slowly fading, giving way to the colors and scents of the world. But he had no money with him to spend on such trinkets so he did not disturb the peddler, his hawking a diatribe that Lie Ben could now repeat in his sleep.

Another reason to stay inconspicuous were the soldiers that cleared the roads whenever they became blocked with people, herding them out of the square, or threatening to arrest them should they not disperse. Except for one bout of violence the gathering was peaceful enough. A celebratory mood had settled over the square, seemingly forgetful of the reason for the crowd altogether. Musicians and dancers offered quaint distractions as the people waited, then begged for a coin or two for their efforts.

Lie Ben had the strange sensation that he should be standing before the crowd proclaiming something, but he did not know what exactly he would say that was worth proclaiming. Certainly nothing of Arcane, so he squashed the feeling and waited along with the rest of the crowd.

The sun scorched mid-day heat settled onto the square before the Council of the Five Eagles consented to appear. At first he did not see the men, instead hearing the crowd roar its approval. Then one at a time the councilmen appeared on a balcony above the crowd. His Honor stood in front of the others and raised his hands to silence the crowd. The noise died to a hush in a second, faster than any spell could cause the same.

"My people," His Honor began, "I commend your desire to know the truth in such a vexing time!" His voice carried well in the square, as though it had been designed to amplify the speaker. "We come before you with news of Earlsburg."

A cheer went up, glee that their desire would be quenched. James again quieted the crowd. "As you have heard so is it true. Earlsburg burns." Gasps. "The worst is over, thanks in large part to The Way of Health. All that is left is to recover. And the Empire of the Five Eagles shall recover. Already word travels to Earlsburg, to be followed tomorrow with a convoy led by the most willing and gracious guilds."

Another cheer, a throaty roar, this from those in the guilds. "Yes, your work shall be most honored!"

Lie Ben could just barely hear over the murmuring of the crowd someone, a woman in the front of the crowd, perhaps even on the stairs, shout, "What was the cause?" This in turn rippled through the crowd, the murmur swelling until it rose up and swamped the council. James looked nervous on the platform, suddenly pushed in directions that he clearly did not wish to go. To ignore the question was impossible, the news and rumors of the cause was most interesting to the people gathered. He looked back at the other men and then with renewed confidence began again.

"The cause of the fires is not clearly known. Suspicion alone cannot be stood upon, it will wash from under our feet. This I can and will say – those that committed this crime against Earlsburg and our entire Empire shall pay a most terrible price."

Lie Ben chuckled quietly to himself. 'The most terrible price indeed. Death is meek compared to what I have endured.'

James went on, "Our enemies will bow before us!"

The crowd exploded into a massive cheer that went on and on; all present drunk on patriotism. All on the council smiled, having at least on this occasion avoided directly pointing to the House of Animate. The men on the balcony left as they had come. The party in the square continued, joined by the musicians playing and singing heroic war songs. The pay better now than before.

Lie Ben went back to the crowded road, gave the peddler's goods a final once over and left the square, carrying the news, such as it was, back to Arcane. The animate would not be pleased. Lie Ben returned the way he had come into the city, through the east gate of the inner wall. At all of the inner wall gates was a great stable. No horse was permitted into the heart of the city without proper papers. Lie Ben had none, and had stabled his Wrath war-horse to hear the council speak. He paid the small sum owed and rode south out of the city, through the outer wall.

Lie Ben followed the road south out of Greater Tarlow, then it turned west passing farms on his left and right. The crops looked healthy and strong, those that worked the fields mirrored those traits. Lie Ben had not slept for five days, and though his body protested deep in his joints, he suppressed the need for rest. He would have what he needed soon in any case.

Lie Ben rode lazily, coming to a husk of some great king of trees. Burned and split by its enemies, it stood as the marker Lie Ben had been searching for. "The dead tree will send you south, to me," Arcane had said. Lie Ben drove his horse from the road and followed the trail of broken branches and stomped undergrowth that the animate had left to guide him.

Hammered to a tree was a rotted sign, whatever message had served upon its face was faded, stripped away by time. Lie Ben continued on, another sign. Up ahead, nestled, by all appearances, peacefully under proud oaks, and resting upon a hill was a large single story house. It was timeless. To Lie Ben it seemed that it had always been and always would be. His horse shuddered and the Sage scratched her neck. Then with caution he approached the house.

The windows had no glass, but the timber and paint seemed new. From outside Lie Ben could make out a single light inside, undoubtedly lit for his benefit. Lie Ben tied his horse's reins to a post next to Arcane's and went to the front door.

He stopped and kneeled, looking at a sheet of stone placed before the door. Symbols, runes, he thought, were carved into the stone, deep fitful gashes.

He stood and opened the door. The figure of a woman danced out of the sunlight into the darkness and disappeared, a trick of the light. "Arcane?" he called, unsure of this place.

"I am here, Sage," Arcane's voice returned.

Lie Ben stepped into the house. Years, centuries perhaps, of dust covered everything except Arcane's tracks going this way and that, through the entry way, into the room to the left, into the room to the right, straight on. All disappeared from his view. Another step. His foot touched the ground and the pain returned, the darkness of the pit, the cold. Then gone. Lie Ben rubbed his eyes trying to clear his head and when he looked around, looking back at him with sorrow filled eyes were the ghostly shapes of people. Their forms danced and broke apart only to reform as they moved, a ghostly gray for the ghostly shapes.

"Wrath," Lie Ben muttered, "Arcane! There are—"

Arcane appeared from the room straight on, wearing no robes. He walked straight through an elderly man, a rune on the animate's shoulder flashed red, then faded. The ghost did not seem to mind at all. "Yes, spirits. I heard that this place was a sick house, in days before the Way could heal such things. A crude binding kept the ill from leaving," Arcane's hand turned up, "In life and in death. It does not seem possible to communicate with them. They only stare at me when I have tried. Theirs is a shadowy world. But the stories told by the humans claim they are quite cruel given the chance. Angry at their prison. It seems that in life you are their kin."

The spider animate that had clung for so long to Arcane clattered past on the floor, two small sticks chasing it, the form of a young girl running after it. Arcane said, "That one alone haunts the spider, a game I assume. And some of the adults watch me build, but nothing else. What news of the Five Eagles?"

Lie Ben watched the little ghost disappear around the corner and said, "Not much actually. Nonsense of vexing times. No accusation of the animists. Which, unless I misunderstand, is your goal."

A woman hobbled between the two solid forms. Arcane said, "Yes." He shrugged. "I expected nothing more of them. They are renowned for their

275

deliberations. Never acting until it is too late. Standing only on fact and logic. I will give them fact. I will show them logic."

"How do you know these things?" asked Lie Ben.

"I have not spent my time wallowing in inaction. I have learned much. I am prepared for this contingency. Come, see what I have for them."

Lie Ben followed Arcane back into the shadowy parts of the ghost house. It was actually quite sizable, with many beds for the sick. A stairway down into the cellar creaked under Arcane's weight, and again as Lie Ben took them. The ancient timber protested use at such a late age. Arcane waved his hand and a lamp ignited casting shadow upon the walls. Two ghosts floated, overlapped. Another wave from Arcane and they floated up the stairs. "The dead do feel suggestions of the Currents."

A heavy blanket from one of the beds above was draped over a massive form. Arcane pulled the blanket away to reveal a huge animate. It stood over eight feet tall with massive shoulders and limbs. Its head, slightly sunken into its chest, resembled Arcane's but with no nose. Heavy rivets marked the edges of the dark gray body-plates. The torso was slightly short, tapering to the waist then expanding to the hips. Domed metal, irregularly formed, acted as shields protecting the shoulders, and could, Lie Ben imagined, be used as some form of battering ram. The shields were attached to the top of the arms which extended up past the shoulder joint. "The fire was not subtle and this will be less so," Arcane said coldly. "If they will not take action when their city burns, they will when their children die."

"You had time to build this while I was in Tarlow?"

"Do not be foolish, Sage, I have been putting my plan in motion since my creation. I built it when I first came to this place months ago. This on the other hand." Arcane went to the table that stood against the wall behind the stairs and took up a small animate. "My magic grows strong."

Arcane handed the animate to Lie Ben. In every way it appeared to be a small bird. The bird was mostly made of gold. Feathers of pure blue wrapped around its body. Clearly at such a distance the man could tell that it was not real, but if it flew past him outside he would not know that it was not. "Amazing, Arcane." Arcane touched the toy's head with his finger. The bird shook its head, and flapped its wings, testing them. Then it took flight around the room, finally nesting on the brute's head.

The contrast was humorous to Lie Ben and he laughed once.

Arcane said, "Formed from the treasures taken from the mansions, gold, sapphire, crystal and glass. I think Master Jannan would approve of such a creation. The magic is an interesting thing. You know of the Web Nexus Theory?"

"I do, though as with much, do not remember why."

"It does not matter, because it is wrong. My own understanding is still hazy. I understand the greater concepts, though the details, the true power, eludes me. The arcane is set with many traps, many falsehoods it seems.

"I traveled north when I left Serac. The journey was slow, but I believed for whatever reason, the Harrow Luck perhaps, that the Su'th could aid me in my pursuit of power. Unlike the humans they have not completely forgotten the past. From them I learned much of the runic magic. Though they do not have the skill to perform it, I could once shown."

"Yes, I can see that."

Arcane frowned, "Yes, I suppose you can. The World Keeper told me of a time of great mages, a time before the Harrow King. Their power was known the world over. It was the Su'th's story that they were not limited as the Houses of today are. Much of the human history was forgotten, not surprising considering that the Su'th are not human and have no need to remember it, but they do have songs recounting the breaking of the magic. In this the history overlaps. The greatest human wizards and the most wizened Su'th gathered and determined that it would be best to separate the aspects of magic. And their reason – to prevent another being such as the Harrow King, seemed noble. Even the elves were agreeable to the pact."

The bird took flight and landed on Lie Ben's shoulder. Arcane continued, "It did not work as planned. The spells to separate the aspects were more powerful than any had predicted, or perhaps their work was sabotaged in the casting. In any case the powers in which they worked went out of control. It caused a full fracturing of the aspects, separating permanently the power of the realms of magic."

Lie Ben nodded, "That would explain much of why it is so difficult to truly learn different Houses' spells."

"It does. It also had another effect, shattering the minds of the great wizards. Some died. Some went mad, becoming gibbering husks of what they once had been. More common was a brutal form of insanity, creating monsters in human form that stalked the world with fire and death.

"The Su'th by their nature were less affected and to save themselves sequestered their people and their culture from the humans. Even today they rarely allow man into their kingdom. The young Su'th often settle with the humans around the city of Midsun, but they leave before they turn. The effects of their god is strong with them, taking on physical traits of Ku'na'shi. They do not show such things to man.

"I digress. The humans at this time, which the songs do not clearly place, nearly destroyed themselves. A period of darkness fell over man, and the Su'th did not have any interaction with them, so more of your kind I cannot say. The historical information taken from the Su'th songs frame the image, the concept of the splitting, but in practice I do not understand how it was achieved, if it can be repaired, or if it needs to be for me to become what I will. So I am left to puzzle out the truth of it.

"But, to create an animate such as the bird form requires a melding, a merging of the Houses' powers. Mostly animate magic yes, but a fair use of The House of Currents, and to my displeasure, the Way. That most of all is difficult for me to harness. Even with the Lot'hak heart beating inside me, I can barely imagine the power."

"Lot'hak? Heart?" Lie Ben questioned.

"In my chest beats the heart of a Harrow. As the Su'th legends claim, it pumps pure magic long after the original owner is dead. In retrospect I am lucky; a Harrow that was fully aware of its abilities would have torn me limb from limb, but such have things been for me."

Tara soared high in the sky, her, its, their wings flapped softly, spreading the air as a liquid as they moved. A city. She knew it to be Tarlow by the five eagles that circled above it. Tara moved softly on the breeze, sideways she thought, and far. The new city below coughed smoke at her. She did not know why. The wind grew stronger here, the scent of pollen from some exotic flower carried her to the west. A black stone hole, she did not know it. Cold fingers closed over her head and neck and she awoke. Kneeling in the old place.

Black smoke dissolved around her, consumed by the magic held here. The Mother's hands upon her shoulders. Tara said, "Earlsburg burns. Our adversary grows strong in the west."

"Troubling visions, daughter. You have indeed grown in the Way." The Mother smiled softly, stealing from her velvet voice.

"I have been given no choice. And as the Earth leads, so shall I go." Tara got to her feet, and walked to the wall. Forest had given way to forest as the Way changed. Tara plunged her arm into the stone withdrawing a necklace, a butterfly of blue and orange on a nearly invisible strand of gold. "So shall I do."

Lilac nodded, closing her eyes slowly.

Tara followed the streets of Serac easily enough, her pony clopped through the dusk happily. She had not said another word to the Mother, and the Mother did not ask why she must leave. Her stay in the city had been short, but there was one last thing, one last person to see. Alexander Gin's house was squeezed side to side in a row of many. She had been here before.

The town house was nice enough from the exterior, painted white to match the stone of its foundation. Near the Campus. She knocked on the door not knowing if Alexander was home. After a few seconds the wood slat door opened. Gin stood inside, not wearing his guard uniform. His loose shirt and pants looked more comfortable by far. "Tara!"

Tara smiled, not shy, "Alexander."

Alexander leaned on the edge of the door. "I had heard that you were in town, it's good to see you. Do you want to come in? It's not much compared to the House, but..."

"I'd love to, Alex."

"Great, great," Alex opened the door fully, moving out of the way allowing Tara to enter his home. A half-eaten chicken and fresh bread leant their aromas to the whole house. "Let me get another plate, I have more than enough for two."

He shooed her down the hallway past the kitchen, which he entered into on the right. He grabbed a graying old plate. The food sat on a counter that divided the kitchen from the living room. His bed sat in one corner, a table with a lamp hanging above it and books resting on it was across from that. Two skinny chairs put their backs to the wall. "Take a seat. Hungry?"

"Not much, really. How have things been?"

Alex disappeared from Tara's view then reappeared on the left in the hall. He set the plate, piled high with food, in front of her. "Oh, a fork might help. One second."

Tara smiled and shook her head at the mound of food. 'Not much.'

"Here you go," Alex said, handing her a fork.

Alex sat down, took a bite of chicken and said, "Things have been okay, pretty quiet, for the most part anyway. After all of that stuff a few years ago, well, you saw it all, the Campus has really tightened security. I don't know that it helps that much. Just a lot of drilling and training. And last month there was some big event at The House of Wrath, then all of a sudden we were searching for people." He stabbed another piece of meat and shrugged. "Silly really, one mage could stand in for a whole gate's worth of guards, and the people would treat 'em better too. But I'm better with a sword than I used to be and can run faster for longer. I reckon that's worthwhile. Hell, I don't even know how long we'll have jobs."

"What do you mean? This is great by the way."

"Rumors. Senior Guard Ames says that the Directorate Council is considering what to do with the whole lot of us. Who knows? I think we're all just nervous because of the training and no use for it."

Tara nodded and said, "That's most likely it."

"I guess we'll see, I can always get a job on a ship or as security for a caravan," he said humorlessly. "I didn't think I was going to see you, Tara. The Way mages have been in and out faster than the tides."

"The Earth moves us. You know that," Tara said with a tinge of regret.

"Yes, yes I do. How was the beaten path?" he said, locking his gaze with hers.

Tara looked down and said, "It went well, the world is truly beautiful. Someday you should try to see it."

Alex laughed. "Not likely. Maybe I can get on a ship if the guard work dries up, but I'd be more than a little busy if that happens. You have the advantage of magic to lay a path for you. I am not so lucky."

"I didn't mean to quarrel. I just saw so many sights, I would love to share them with you."

"It's alright, I don't begrudge you or the other mages, I'm glad for you especially. And I am what I am."

Tara smiled and with light in her voice said, "And what exactly is that?"

"Unmarried and poor," Alex said with a smile.

"I've seen worse off than that. Not all the world is beautiful."

Alex nodded, "No, but you are."

Tara blushed slightly and said, "You flatter me as always Guard Gin."

"Ahh, now we get formal. If that's how it is Sister Groundmender—"

She interrupted, "No, I'd rather not get formal." Tara pulled her hair back in one massive strand and tucked it behind her right shoulder. Then she leaned across the table and kissed him. 'Just like before,' she thought.

Alexander hummed deep satisfaction. Tara pulled back across the table and he said, "So you are leaving soon then?"

"I'm afraid so."

"Just like before, eh?" he asked, not really a question.

"You could come with me you know. No one would be put off by your presence. Least of all me." Her words ran on, running together, "And your job could disappear, you said so yourself. We would get a chance to see some of the world together."

Alex put his hand up, bringing her notion to a halt. "I can't do that, Tara. I'm sorry, but I can't. My life is here, what's left of it anyhow. And the job pays well. Let the Earth lead you your way, I have mine."

Silence fell for a moment. Tara said meekly, "You're right. It's sad that we're the right people living the wrong lives."

Alex smiled and nodded. "Give us another kiss before you leave again." Tara smiled, her lips puckered ever so slightly. A soft breeze and the lamp breathed its last.

Twenty-four

The Directorate Council had been called to meet in three days, a Saturday, and it was not to be a shielded meeting in Master Guildenil's study. It was to take place in the full grandeur of the Council Auditorium. The doors had been cracked open and the apprentices of The House of Currents cleaned the dusty building with fervor. In front of the auditorium was the high bench of the council; below and spread out along the floor were rows of benches for the rank and file of the Houses. The walls held booths for yet more to watch the meeting. Soon this place would be filled with the practitioners of magic. Soon Master Jannan would go before them.

Frederick sat in his old chair, a look of pain and regret painted his wizened face. His head shook back and forth slightly. He could not believe the events of the time. On his desk sat the various messages that had arrived to Serac. He had demanded and received the letters from the Houses of Wrath and Animate. Added to his own House's account of the burning and a copy of the letter from the Commissioner of Earlsburg to the Council of the Five Eagles, Frederick realized that he had no choice. They would call Master Jannan to task for the recent dilemmas.

It was unfortunate; Frederick had always liked Murdoch. When he was a young, gifted apprentice in The House of Currents he stood out immediately. Then to follow his ascension through the ranks of Wrath as a masterful tactician and soldier. Finally, his amazing success in turning the House of Animate into a competitor with Wrath. It was tragic that such a light must be snuffed, but it was clear now that not all was as it seemed with him.

There were too many signs that he had become dangerous. The unfortunate incident with the technologists. They had not complained loudly, certainly not after the bank note drawn for them, but it was an ugly thing. And though he believed what Trahn said of the animate being beyond their skill, the fact of the matter was that it did not attack Murdoch. Surely anyone who thought would think that odd. But if Murdoch created the animate he would not be so simple minded to make it as aggressive as it was. It was easy to believe Trahn if only that was the singular event in the reckoning.

It was not.

Perhaps even Bessemer could be passed over. 'No, it can be,' Frederick thought to himself, 'It has been.' As with its other problems, the House of Animate simply bought its way from under its problems. It was good that the toys cost as much as they did, the House of Animate spent recklessly in times of trial. People began to talk though, small whispers that could be heard in dark and not so dark corners. Frederick heard them. The animates were dangerous. Jannan was brilliant but crazy. Rumors. Most likely.

Even that was not the end.

As the papers lay before him he tried ever so much to be fair, to be impartial. But he had to act. The facts now were clear. Six animates created by Master Jannan had burned the city of Earlsburg to the ground. To make matters worse, if that was possible, they stole the treasures of their owners. Perhaps Jannan was mad. It happened from time to time. The magic simply took the mage's mind. Usually in old stories. But sometimes now. Sometimes.

Frederick would not call for death. Surely it looked awful for Master Jannan, but there was no solid proof that he directly caused all of these things. Much could be attributed to the uncertainty of magic. It did not always work as one planned. Fredrick knew this well. But in the interest of all of the Houses Master Jannan would pay the price of inference. The most surprising thing of all to Frederick was that the Five Eagles had not included their support for the demands of the Commissioner of Earlsburg. It did not matter, the course was set. Master Jannan would be banished.

Silas Aron was irritated and his tone said so. He spoke loudly, "Murdoch, please as a friend listen to me. Save yourself the mockery and leave Serac now. It is not uncommon for mages to go into self enforced solitude when placed in your situation. Better that than to face the Directorate. I have heard things. You know that I do. Please go."

Jannan leaned on the massive table in his lab. "I will not flee, Silas. I can't. Others may have feared the rulings of the council. I fear them. But I can't run. If I must fall for the Houses' honor, for this House's name to be cleared, then I am prepared to fall. But I will be there to see it happen. The Firsts will be forced to look me in the eyes when they claim me guilty."

"You will be found guilty. I know of three votes against you for sure. I tried to dissuade them. I really did. And I am sorry that the animate attacking Henry will be used against you, but there is not going to be a reprieve for you. You will be banished. Go now," pleaded Silas.

"I will not."

"Damn it, Murdoch! Can't you so that your friends will be spared the mockery? It is not a shame to be found in absentia when that is the punishment."

Murdoch's head fell and shook back and forth. "No. I will not flee. I thank you, Silas, for the warning, but I will not."

"You are a stubborn fool. This does not bring you honor, as much as you want it to. I am only sorry that you do not see it."

Murdoch's head snapped up, and with fire on his lips he said, "Honor? You think this is about honor? I have suffered much these last four years, and if my fall should be complete, I will be there."

He continued, "There is no honor in being accused of murder, indirectly yes, but accused none the less. There is no honor in having my sanity questioned. You are not the only one that hears things. I hold sway no less than you. So I ask you, Silas Aron, do you accuse me? Do you question?"

Silas spoke slowly, regretfully, "I do not want to, but I do."

"Then be gone. You tell me to flee when you stand with my adversaries. You do not care what becomes of me, so let me fall."

"You will be sorry if you do not go, Murdoch."

"I do not think that to be true."

The Council Auditorium shuddered with energy when the Directorate Council appeared from their private chambers. Frederick took his place at the highest seat, with the other four members, including Kasu Tam who had become a permanent member, sitting below him. The room rumbled with anticipation, and hushed quickly when Master Guildenil stood.

"We, the Directorate Council, come before the collected assembly with heavy hearts. One of our own stands implicated in the burning of Earlsburg. In order to maintain the trust that has been so carefully built with the nations of our ranks the council determines that action must take place against this individual."

"Master Jannan, come before the council."

Jannan stood from a seat near the back of the auditorium. No mage sat near him, afraid of also being implicated. His blue suit, the one he wore when his animate disappeared, was pressed and still fit well. He looked over the faces of all those that now stared at him. Then he walked sharply to the front of the hall.

Guildenil continued, "Master Jannan. Are you aware of the accusations against you?"

"Yes. Yes I am," he answered, his eyes hard under his dark brow.

"Are you also aware of the punishment you shall receive if found guilty of said accusations?"

"I am not."

A ripple of murmurs. Surely he knew. How could he not? Guildenil looked down and then said, "Should you be found guilty you will be banished from the light of the Houses. If other charges are brought against you the Houses will not act in your defense. If it comes to us that you continue to practice the arts in our name or as a rogue, you shall be put to death."

Jannan shook his head and smiled.

"If you wish to say something in your defense, do so now."

"I have nothing to say. Do your work, do not leave me standing here for long."

Guildenil nodded and said, "Very well. Master Jannan, on the charges put against you by this council and in the name of the House that I represent I find you guilty as charged. Master Archammer, your vote please."

Archammer stood, his black robes rippling. He looked hard at Jannan, presenting the image of a last minute decision. "On the charges put against you by this council and in the name of the House I represent I find you guilty as charged."

Archammer sat down, and Guildenil said, "Thank you Master Archammer. Mother Rainmarrow."

Lilac stood, placing her weight on her staff. She looked at Jannan, then at the collected assembly. Her velvet voice broke the silence, commanding attention. "No matter our actions today, the course is set. This vote may affect the end, but it yet comes. On the charges put against you by this council and in the name of the House I represent I find you not guilty."

Master Jannan looked up from the floor as a gasp exited the crowd behind him. His eyes met with the Mother's. In them he could see only sadness, a sudden comprehension blossomed. The Mother sat down and Guildenil said, "Master Elementalist."

Kasu stood and said somberly, "The calm is not in me, so I say these things with only my own wisdom to stand on. Master Jannan, on the charges put against you by this council and in the name of the House I represent I find you not guilty."

Anger rippled across Gavin's face in the same way as the shock through the crowd; it was not expected to be a close vote. Kasu again sat and Guildenil said, "Master Entrah, your vote please."

Trahn stood, his white robes concealing all but his head, his pale hair falling over his shoulders. He did not look at Murdoch as he spoke. "On the charges put against you by the council and in the name of the House I represent..." He paused, and blinked slowly once, "I find you guilty as charged."

Noise filled the auditorium as the final tally was made, not cheering, not booing, only noise. Jannan stared at Trahn, a final understanding of the man formed, no longer his friend, then frowned, but showed no other emotion. Guildenil waited for a minute or more; finally he spoke again, his voice powerful and loud over all that echoed in the auditorium. "Master Jannan. On the charges brought against you, both by this council, and by the Houses we represent, you are found guilty.

"Punishment shall begin immediately save a grace period to gather your belongings. Go and do not return. And I pray you do not give us cause to send those that would be your friends against you. Guards!"

The black dressed guards descended on Master Jannan. They escorted him from the Council Auditorium to the House of Animate. He was the only one there save a young mage in the entrance hall.

He asked, "Master Jannan, what was the verdict, sir?"

Jannan laughed once, "Not master, not even sir. No longer, and it is as you guess. Guilty."

"I am sorry, master."

Murdoch answered with bleak acceptance, "It is what it is."

"I will pray for your health."

"Thank you, good mage."

Murdoch was gone before Trahn could return to the House of Animate. Many of the animate mages waited in the entrance hall for him to return. The mages seemed evenly split. Those that supported him congregated on his left, nodding assurances. To his right those that did not understand his reasoning. Neither side said a word to him, though their eyes told him all he needed to know. When he had passed them all and stood near the reception desk, he turned and said, "I did what had to be done."

He hurried to his study to be free of their questioning looks, to be alone with his thoughts. The technologist warmer heated water for his tea. He did what had to be done, he kept telling himself. Maybe after a while he would believe it. Trahn sipped his tea and watched the ocean fade over the horizon. Tears slowly rolled down his pale face.

Anne Khurson, daughter of Baron Khurson, glanced up into the sky as she stepped from the carriage. She had finally arrived at the party to celebrate His Honor's children's return from university. She was their contemporary and quite thrilled to have them back in Tarlow. It would make social events about town so much more enjoyable. As it was, her father could not attend the party, though the reasons met with James' approval.

A bird circled in the sunlight, its feathers reflecting a beautiful blue. It dipped once and then raced from sight, up and around an oak that had been on the property for years. Anne smiled and forgot it as she prepared for the night of revelry. Even now music cascaded from the manor.

The bird hummed quickly over tree and house, road and field. It dipped sharply and plummeted to the roof of a building, seemingly dead. It bounced twice, shook itself off and hopped into the warehouse that Peter had rented on the waterfront of Lake Nimm. Inside beams of light sprayed through the ceiling, lighting dust that dared to float between the earth and the ceiling.

The brute stood motionless, waiting, dull glow in its eyes. The bird hopped across a wood beam and then took flight, landing on the massive animate's shoulder. Yellow light flickered in the bird's belly, then flashed to the crystal nodes that ringed the brute's head. The animate nodded and turned to Peter, who sat on a crate and leaned against the wall. It said, voice low and harsh, "Khurson, as Arcane commands, dies tonight."

Peter nodded and with apathy said, "Sure, sure. Don't be too obvious about it. Arcane doesn't want everything exposed."

"I understand the master's objective," the huge animate answered as it loomed over the thief.

"I know you do. I am just reminding you."

"It is not necessary."

Peter made an ugly face, not appreciating the combativeness of the brute. The animate smiled and turned away. Then it stood still.

The sun set and only then did it move again. The huge shoulders turned to fit through the doorway. The door shut softly behind it and Peter sat shaking his head. The bird circled once and Peter put his hand out. The animate lighted upon it. He said softly, impressed, "That one is dangerous."

The party carried late into the night, and by the time Anne set for home her head spun and when she did not drift into a light sleep she found herself laughing uncontrollably. The reason for her fits were not entirely clear to her, but what did it really matter? The carriage clattered along the road near the inner wall at a lazy pace. The driver had also indulged and took the horses slow.

A clap of stone impacting steel and the clatter of stone falling to the road was the only prelude. The brute had thrown its massive bulk from the wall and landed squarely on the top of the carriage. The roof caved under the weight. The front axle split and the carriage tipped forward as the wheels bowed apart. Before the driver could react the metal beast took him and spun fully around the roof throwing the man like a child throws a doll. He smashed into the wall and did not move.

Inside the carriage Anne screamed, doubling her efforts when she saw the driver motionless on the ground. The brute took up the reigns and stopped any further movement with a massive jerk. Leaping to the ground with another mighty thud the animate tore the horses free and sent them running.

The brute's massive hand tore into the door, crushing the knob in its grasp as it ripped the door fully from the carriage. It stared into the cabin in time to see Anne flee out the other side. Her dress of red silk snagged on a hinge. The brute smashed its way through the doorway reaching for her, buckling the frame as it did so, but she eluded its grasp. One massive step crushed the floorboards, and the brute pushed through the other side, with much the same effect. The carriage was in tatters. Anne cried as she ran, but her balance was lost and her vision blurred. The brute closed on her quickly. It took her by the shoulder and lifted her into the air, turning her to face it. The animate smiled. It said, "Do not run, flower of your father's affection. Lord Khurson must be proud to have such a beautiful daughter."

Anne screamed. The brute slammed her into the ground, she coughed and went limp. "We can't have that."

Peter slept lightly, waiting for the brute to return. When it did he snapped from his dreamless rest. "Is it done?"

The brute growled low, as close to a whisper as it could create, "Yes. You have nothing to worry about, Peter. The Five Eagles will find her body near the docks. Only time prevents Arcane's will from becoming truth."

The morning was cold, more than a hint of fall danced in the air. Baron

Khurson's face was red from the chill, stubble prickled around his mouth and chin. He rubbed his forehead with trepidation and swung from his horse.

"Wrath, what happened here?" he questioned. Staring at the shattered and twisted remains of his carriage he tried to fathom what had done this and why. To his left, in the mist that made it all the more dreamlike, a physician tended to the driver. Baron Khurson watched the Tarlow Royal Guard tend to the cleanup of the street.

The driver looked up from where he sat, a massive wrap tied around his chest. His voice was pained. "Oh, Lord Khurson. I'm so sorry. One minute we was coming home, then a loud clatter, and I don't know. I'm so sorry." The man began to cry. He had driven Anne for years.

Khurson looked at him and then to the physician, who shook his head. Khurson turned away from the injured man.

"Where is the ranking officer?" he questioned an aging, wild-eyed soldier.

"Uhh," he paused, looking through the mist, then pointed beyond the carriage. "Over there, sir."

Khurson joined the captain and said, "I want this road sealed, and have the carriage taken to my estate. Is there any sign of my daughter?"

The hardened soldier, easily Khurson's age, shook his head, "None, sir. No sign of her at all. I have the word out, the patrol searches for any sign of her, if, when they find her we will be the first to know."

"I want your best men on this. I will know what happened."

"The Inquiry and Analysis branch of the Royal Guard's best man is in Earlsburg, sir. Kanton Burden, sir."

"Then get him back here now."

"Might I suggest, sir—"

"What is it captain?" Khurson asked grimly.

"I might suggest you have Celsius Vega look into this situation."

"And why is that?"

"He should be the number one I & A man. Celsius is smart but his techniques are unusual and it has gotten him in trouble from time to time."

"Unusual?"

"His methods aren't magic, but they might as well be. Too smart for his own good, sir." He motioned to the carriage. "It might be good to have someone with different eyes working this case."

Khurson nodded, "Thank you, captain."

It did not take long for the patrol to find the body of a woman. The mist had begun to burn away under the pounding of the sun, but it clung here and again to buildings and roads. Baron Khurson rode, a man possessed, to the docks. As he rode the three miles he prayed that it was not her.

But it was, it was his beautiful daughter Anne, her red silk dress stained with the red of her blood. Khurson fell to his knees and sobbed, too weak to stand. His stomach turned knots as he crawled through the muck to her. The soldiers around him glanced nervously at him and at each other as he held the battered body of his daughter and rocked. None could imagine one of the Five Eagles reduced to such a place. Each in their own mind imagined how they would be strong but they knew in their hearts that they would not. The story of the crying Eagle did not pass to any that were not there that day.

After a time the baron stood, his face streaked, eyes swollen, mouth pulled down at the edges, frown shuddering. He said to no one in particular, but all the soldiers listened, "Have her taken to the Cathedral of Anashara. She will be buried tonight. Complete your work. Do not miss a thing! Document the smallest smudge on a wall a mile away. The ones responsible for this...this...this atrocity, will pay for their crimes!"

He staggered weakly to his horse, right hand on his head, attempting to push the pain back inside. The soldier holding the reins did not look him in the eyes. Khurson mounted and rode home to tell his wife.

Baron Khurson sat on his makeshift throne. It was a hand carved chair of enormous size and weight. It had been moved only once and broke a man's back in the doing. Rumor became that the animals carved into the chair laughed uncontrollably as the man writhed in pain. If so, the mood matched the baron sitting.

It had been two and a half weeks since the burning of Earlsburg. Five days had passed since the death of his daughter, two days from the death of General Paul's son, killed as he hunted north of the city. Whoever killed him had killed a bear of a man, unmatched in battle, living to his father's legend. His legs were found one-hundred yards from his torso.

Kanton Burden worked both cases but turned up very little of use. It was not that he was ineffectual, quite the opposite. He postulated a thousand contingencies but despite the mountain of evidence there was little that pointed to a suspect. Whispers filled the streets, a sailor with a taste for blood, a child of magic, possessed lovers that slept in the poor house. Each wilder than the last.

Khurson wore black, as was proper for mourning. Even were it not he would, it was the only color that suited him. With his black suit he wore the golden wings of the council, his only adornment. The marble hall around him had been stripped of all color, the bleak stone reinforcing his own sense of loss.

One attendant served the baron, and he had not seen his wife since he told her of their daughter's death. In grief she locked herself away in her sitting room. Khurson's face had hardened into a perpetual frown and his beard grew in. The council had met once, briefly, but no business had been attended to. And that was before General Paul's tragedy.

At the far end of the silent hall there was a slight commotion, whispers that the baron could not make out and then the attendant boomed, "Baron Khurson, your guest has arrived."

Khurson blinked and then spoke, his voice a raspy mix of anger and sorrow, "Show him in, Rottert."

Rottert again boomed, "Baron, I present Celsius Vega."

Behind the attendant at the end of the hall a man appeared. He was taller and slimmer than most, graced with silkiness in his movement. Baron Khurson watched him closely while he approached. The man reminded him of a mongoose. Celsius wore a high collared leather coat, covering his face up to his eyes. It flared slightly at the waist and terminated at his knees. On his head he wore a battered tricorner hat. The combination made little of his face visible. Between the hat and collar his gray eyes focused on Baron Khurson.

The faint tapping of leather on marble was the only sound that marked his approach. In his left hand he carried a leather bag, clasped together at the top, in his right hand a staff. Each end was worn and darkened. Though not from walking, the baron thought. Confidence rolled in waves from him.

Fifteen feet from the seated lord, Celsius stopped and quietly set down his bag and carefully laid the staff across it, not allowing it to touch the floor. 'Certainly not for walking,' the baron thought.

Celsius removed his hat and also set that on the bag. Then he turned down the collar of his coat, exposing his face. He had been blessed with fine features. Dark curly hair fell around his face. By some miracle none fell over it.

After dispensing of his goods he proceeded to the baron. With a flourish of his coat he kneeled with all the grace that his walking betrayed. "Honorable of Tarlow, it is with a heavy heart that I kneel before you." The graveness of the situation was evident in his voice.

"Rise, Investigator Vega," Khurson said. Vega regained his footing. "Your ride here was pleasant I hope."

"Enough so, yes. Quiet."

"Mm, to know peace. Investigator Vega—"

"Please, call me Celsius."

Khurson nodded, "Celsius, I believe you are aware of the times. Who couldn't be? My daughter is dead, and now General Paul's son. The Royal Inquiry and Analysis has hypothesized much, but, only that. I have heard of your remarkable skill in such matters, and I care not what methods are used." Khurson stood, the gold wings jangled ever so softly. "Celsius. My daughter is dead. Fools struggle to avenge her. You sir, are my only hope for satisfaction. Find me my daughter's killer, that she might rest peacefully."

"Baron Khurson. This monster shall be brought before you," Celsius pledged with certainty.

Twenty-five

Baron Khurson showed Celsius to the stable where the wreckage of the carriage was kept. Celsius walked around the disaster once and said, "Sir, this will take time. I will call for you when I have something substantial to report."

"Yes, thank you," Khurson answered and then hurried from the stable, the sight of the wreckage still unsettling.

Celsius began to work. He had a trunk brought to him. Inside were bottles and jars filled with all manner of reagents. Leafs, powders, liquids. He analyzed the wreck, writing notes, mixing potions and pastes, testing them. He measured portions of the carriage and worked mathematics. In all things he was deliberate. Slowly, steadily, an image formed to him. Vega mixed some water into a brown glass bottle and stirred it with a glass stick. At each perceived point of contact he dispensed three drops. At each point the liquid bubbled and smoked. "Hmm."

On the first door frame the liquid seethed violently. 'Definitely a trace of iron. Armor?'

A servant brought him lunch and then dinner. As dusk fell over the city he sent for the baron. Celsius paced back and forth in front of the carriage, then stopped and said, "Lord Khurson, if you allow me I will propose a theory of the occurrences that led up to the death of your daughter. I myself find them almost unbelievable, but please hear me out."

"Please proceed." His face was as grim as ever.

"Lord, it would appear that your daughter's assailant jumped, or fell, from a tall structure. A building perhaps. I will have to examine the site of the attack to properly identify such a structure."

Khurson said, "The carriage traveled the inner wall. Returning from His Honor's city estate."

Celsius nodded, "That would certainly make an excellent starting point for such a theory. In any case, examining the carriage you can see that the roof is caved in. To me this indicates a tremendous impact." Celsius pointed to the split axle. "This supports such a theory. I would hypothesize that it was at this point that the driver was thrown from the carriage."

Khurson shifted his weight and Celsius continued, "The horses clearly stopped, though for what reason I cannot say. The driver may have instinctively reined them in, or perhaps the attacker did. It is of little consequence other than the final resting place of the carriage.

"Looking at the damage to the front of the carriage, everything that connected the horses to the carriage was simply torn off. It would take unbelievable strength to perform such a feat."

Khurson's eyes flitted back and forth and then he said, "Are you saying that the killer was not a man?"

A stable boy brought two lamps to light the darkening stable. Celsius said, "As amazing as it seems, it almost must be true. Allow me to continue and we shall come back to the killer in a moment. I believe that the attacker tore open the door. Look at the crushing on the handle, and note the twisting and tearing on the hinges. Amazing strength." Both shook their heads in disbelief.

Celsius led the baron to the other side of the carriage. "I believe your daughter fled the cabin." He plucked a scrap of fabric from the hinge with a pair of long tweezers. "Red silk?"

"That was the dress she wore." He sighed. "Recently bought."

"The murderer followed her through, barely fitting either doorway. Look at the scrapes here and here." Celsius pointed to the buckled wood frames. "The floor here, again showing massive weight and strength. After this, it becomes difficult. The chase leads away from the carriage. I do not know from looking at the carriage whether Anne was killed here, where she was found, or somewhere between. I will go to the street where this happened in the morning."

"And what of my daughter's killer? You believe it was not human?"

"As I said, it is hard to believe, but I would say that it almost certainly is not. The weight, the strength, no man could do this." Celsius moved close to the baron. "No man that is not a mage. That would surprise me. As you know they heel renegades quickly, and there has been no movement of the Houses on this matter."

Baron Khurson's eyes danced imagining the possibilities, but landing on nothing. "What then?"

"That, baron," he dared speak the title, "I will find out. There are a few tests I must still perform. Threads to chase, but I would not keep you waiting late."

"It doesn't matter, I do not sleep. There is much on my mind that should not be. Thank you. Already you give me insight that I did not have."

Celsius bowed. "I serve. I will update you as I learn more."

Once Baron Khurson left, Celsius returned to his work. His mind raced, organizing and reorganizing the clues before him, but enough pieces eluded him so that no clear picture of the killer emerged. A rogue mage? Not likely. Certainly not a human. A Su'th? Not this far south, and the same issues of weight and strength existed. An animate? The weight and strength could be right. But who could build such a beast? It was an unlikely circumstance at best, but given the strange days in Earlsburg it was possible. Barring that, some unknown monster? Perhaps. Legends?

Vega slept heavily through the night. The morn was crisp and he set out across Tarlow to the last place Anne Khurson had been alive. He tromped through the mist that rolled up off of Lake Nimm, the scene slowly came into focus. Knowing that the inner wall framed one side had provided Celsius with a picture of the scene in his mind.

And it was precisely what he had pictured. Wall to the north, packed buildings to the south, road down the middle. As Khurson had ordered, the site had been cordoned off.

"Sir. No one enters. Orders of Lord Khurson," a sleepy eyed soldier said without conviction.

"I am his weapon. I have business here." Vega pointed beyond the soldier with his staff.

"I am sorry, sir, but—"

Vega drew close to the soldier and hissed, "No. You are not sorry, but you will be when I tell Vaughn Khurson that you prevented the murderer of his daughter from being brought to justice."

The soldier's eyes opened wide and he bowed out of Celsius's way. "I, I am truly sorry."

"Thank you," Vega paused, "Lord Khurson will be most pleased."

Celsius took a quick reckoning of the site before starting the more serious examinations. Most of the driver's blood had been washed away but enough of a residue was left to clearly mark where he had lain unconscious. Given the size of the stain the man must have been quite sturdy to still be alive. All in all though the scene had been mostly undisturbed. The power of the Eagle to influence such things was well spent.

Small wood chips scattered the road. Knowing the direction the carriage had been traveling, he noted the first fragments that matched the carriage. Had the attacker followed his theory, he would have jumped from the inner wall. Scattered at the base of the wall were several pieces of brick and mortar that made up the upper wall. Celsius shook his head and thought, 'As brutal to the wall as it was to the carriage. What a monster!'

Celsius took a polished lens from a cotton bag and examined the bricks. Deep scratches with a dark residue came into focus. Using the same mixture as before he tested the compound, and again the surface smoked. 'The attacker clearly came over the wall. I will have to find my way up.' Celsius looked up to the impressive structure, then side to side.

Celsius found the nearest arch almost a mile away, paired with it the steps to the top. Flashing the personal sigil of Daron Khurson allowed him to use them. At the top of the wall, some thirty-five feet up, he paused and looked out over the city. North from his vantage point he could see the outer wall that marked the current city limit. Beyond that even more city lay in serenity then farm and forest stretched away, consumed by fog. South, sailing vessels bobbed slightly on the lake, ghostlike in the mist.

Vega allowed himself a moment more, then hurried down the walkway that ran the length of the wall. Down on the road the soldier herded a few people from the scene. Celsius smiled at the work and settled into his.

He easily found the area of the wall that had been toppled. Bricks lay scattered upon the walkway, a giant scoop taken out of the wall. The collision had even cracked bricks that had not fallen, yet another confirmation of inhuman force. More tests with the eyedropper and more traces of iron. It was only a hunch, but it was time to pay a visit to the House of Animate.

More and more people joined Celsius on the roads as he drew near the House of Animate. A general sense of uneasiness snaked through the streets. Celsius noticed quick glances and wary faces that normally would not exist. In his pocket he fingered the stone-carved sigil of Baron Khurson. He had not needed it with the soldier; here it would be another thing altogether.

The waiting room for the House was adorned in darkly-stained wood. In all the nooks and crannies carved animals both real and imagined leered at him. He tried to figure out which one was the killer that he stalked. Some sunlight filtered in, casting shadows that played with the mind.

As was customary with the House of Animate, a mage sat as the House receptionist. He amused himself with a small flame that danced between his forefinger and his thumb. He wore gray robes and did not look pleased to see Vega. "Yes. Hello. What can I do to make you leave?" he asked, in nasal tones.

Celsius was not surprised by the mage's terseness. With all the problems in Earlsburg the House of Animate had closed ranks to regain their footing. Vega responded, "I have need to speak with the head of the House."

"He is a very busy man and cannot be bothered."

Vega placed the sigil on the counter with a click. "It is urgent business."

The mage frowned at the stone, thinking of igniting it with the dancing flame. "Yes. Very well."

The mage stood and walked out of Celsius's sight. After several minutes he returned with another, older; shorter and darker as well, his eyes close together. "My apprentice tells me that you are on urgent business for Lord Khurson. To what honor do I receive you?" The mage spoke more politely than the apprentice had.

"I need to know about materials that animates can be made from." Vega placed his bag on the counter and withdrew a piece of brick from the wall. He set it with a loud knock on the counter. Later, scratches left by the brick would annoy the apprentice to no end, but now both mages looked at it quizzically.

Vega continued, "If you look closely, you can see small scratches of metal etched into the brick. It is an alloy containing iron."

The senior mage interrupted, "Certainly animates can be made from material containing iron. That is one of the more common materials used. In theory any substance could be used, if the mage was skilled enough. I don't see the need of Lord Khurson—"

Now Celsius interrupted, "Baron Khurson is interested because I am interested. His daughter is dead and this alloy is scraped all over what remains of her carriage. Furthermore, whatever destroyed the carriage had the power to tear through the top of the inner wall. And though it is not in the greatest state of repair there is no man that could perform such a feat. None that are not mages."

"You believe that the killer may be an animate?" said the mage dismissively.

"Good mage, your House is in a peculiar place no doubt. The burning of Earlsburg caused by six rogue animates. The fate of Master Jannan in question. I have heard the Directorate Council acts, though we do not yet know the action taken, word will come soon enough. It is not without cause that I come before you."

The mage nodded and lines appeared in his brow, "You are too well informed. As you might imagine the situation is...delicate. I could not say if the killer is an animate. Other than those here I have no knowledge of any others that practice our magic in Tarlow."

"How many is that?"

"Six, wait, one has left for Serac for training, so five. If an animate is the killer I assure you that none under my roof is the maker." Then flatly, "None are skilled enough. Any more and you will have to travel to Serac to speak with the First."

Vega waited, thinking. Then he said slowly, "I see. If it is an animate is there any way to track it?"

The mage thought a moment. He said, "Perhaps, but it is not an incantation that I know, or even imagine of knowing."

Celsius smiled at the overstatement. "Thank you for your time. I will inform Lord Khurson of your help." Vega picked up the brick and bag and returned to the road. It now appeared to him that the killer was most certainly an animate. He would need to examine the site of General Paul's son's death. Perhaps a pattern would show the two related. He was certain they were.

Baron Khurson quickly arranged for Celsius to visit the general's private hunting tracts, the scene of the second grizzly killing. At least Anne had been found intact. It was not far from the city and Celsius made the journey that day.

The lodge, a grand estate, was deserted, but he found the caretakers, an old man and his wife. They were remarkably helpful, showing him the path upon which the ghastly discovery had been made. The caretaker said to him, "On up the path, sir. I would show you more exactly had I the heart for it. I have seen my fill. If you see the kind Way mage tell her that my back is better."

Celsius left his horse with the caretaker and walked the path. It was clear until he reached the scene. The forest where Jon Paul the Second's body was found was a tattered, crushed, mess. Severed tree limbs. Mangled ferns. Deep tears into the ground. The battle had been ferocious. As with the killer of Anne, this attacker had been massively strong. Celsius poked around the scene, finding nothing that did not fit with his theory of the events. Finding dark scrapes, he tested them with his eyedropper; the liquid smoked. Celsius nodded.

To his surprise as he pushed further into the forest, he came across a woman. Her long cinnamon hair almost touched the ground as she knelt. Celsius spoke abruptly, "You must be the Way mage."

"I am," she answered, standing.

"The caretaker asks me to tell you that his back is better," Celsius said, lowering his staff into a defensive position.

She nodded and said, "Good." She waved at the staff and said, "You do not need that investigator. What we seek is no longer here. It stalked the son of Paul for some time before striking. I fear that as we now are here it moves again."

Celsius leaned his weight on the staff and said, "What do you know of these killings?"

The woman walked towards him, her hips swayed as the ferns in the soft wind. He blinked and forced the magic from his mind. The Way. She said, "I am sorry. Do not think me rude." She smiled. "I am Tara Groundmender."

Celsius looked over her once again with his gray eyes. "Daughter, I am Celsius Vega. Investigator in the employ of Baron Khurson. Again I ask you, what do you know of these killings?"

Tara frowned, a sad turn of the lips. "I am sorry for the baron. I know that the killer does not take the form of man or animal. I know that two of the Five Eagles have fallen."

"Two of the Five Eagles?" he asked, mostly to himself. "Of course, it is obvious isn't it? The murderer has killed the children of two of the Eagles. It would not be obvious until at least two, which I should have seen, but was focused on Baron Khurson's loss. You say that the killer is not a man. What do you believe it to be?"

Tara touched her shoulder, "I am not entirely certain, but it is the reason that I am here. We seek the same thing, investigator. We should return to the city. I fear that another life has been taken."

"I hope that you are wrong, but I would accept help in tracking a killer that is not a man."

"You have it. We should hurry." Dragonfly trotted down the path as if called and Tara patted his nose.

Tara and Celsius hurried back to Tarlow; day was flirting with night. The early evening provided a sky full of stars. White points hung in the inky blue, fading to red and orange beyond the stark black of the mountains. The stable boy for Baron Khurson greeted them and took their horses.

The baron met with Celsius and Tara in the marble hall. They kneeled and the baron said, "Please stand. Celsius, good mage."

The two stood and Celsius said, "Lord, I introduce to you Tara Groundmender. She clarifies the killing of your daughter and of Jon Paul the Second. I now believe the killer is targeting the children of those that sit on the council. It is imperative that we warn the others and assign the Royal Guard to protect them."

Khurson nodded slowly, in thought, his eyes tight. "I do not have reason to quarrel with you. I will send your warning immediately."

Rottert approached the grim throne, his shadow twitched and jumped in the oily light. "Lord Khurson, a rider from His Honor asks to see you. He says it is of grave importance."

Khurson locked eyes with Celsius and then Tara and quickly looked away. "Show him in. Hurry!"

Celsius and Tara immediately took up the stare. None said what they knew they would soon hear. The rider appeared, his steps quick, almost a run. He knelt violently, casting his cloak aside. He said, "Sir. I bring you terrible news. His Honor James Eddington mourns, his children are dead."

All three cringed and sighed, visibly shaken at the news they did not wish to hear. Baron Khurson said, "Again? What happened. Quickly!"

"I, I don't rightly know, sir. I'm sorry."

Tara said, "It is as I feared."

Celsius said, "Warn the others quickly, baron. We must protect them. I will go if you let me."

Baron Khurson stood. "Rider, carry this message to Guildmaster Wren. 'Protect your children. By any means.' Hurry. I will send a more detailed message if time allows. Celsius, you are skilled with the staff that you carry?"

"Yes"

"Then carry the message to Technologist Pierce and stand by them. Good mage, you will help us against this monster?"

"You need not ask it. But I ask for a quiet room." Again her hand went to her shoulder. "Perhaps I can divine which of the Eagles is under the most urgent threat."

"Take any. We will act now. The Council of the Five Eagles will not be bowed. Rottert!"

"Lord?"

"My sword."

Tara took the butterfly from her neck and laid it on the bedside table. Then she dropped to her knees. The words of the chant rolled in her mind for mere seconds and her head dipped. Her breathing steadied. The blackness swirled, a light pricked somewhere behind her. She did not see it, and did not need to. Then another. Smaller.

The scent of a butterfly. Red and black flicked across her vision. She followed it and stood facing the lights. The butterfly lighted on her shoulder and began to whisper, speaking in whatever language butterflies speak. Tara cocked her head to listen carefully. She did not understand, but began to walk – if it was walking – towards the points of light.

They were what she sought. Indeed she had grown much in the art of concentration and meditation, the Mother had seen that. She did not see the connection Tara felt with these beings, how could she? She had come to know them as empty forms. Hollow. Sometimes when she slept she could feel them moving around her. In her dreams the stilted movement was always hidden from her view, but she knew it to be there. At first it had frightened her, a dark secret that had driven her from Serac. The convulsing dreams lessened but did not entirely diminish. She still felt them, knew them. The hardened scar would always be, it could not be healed. Her thought rearranged, the butterfly hinting. The Mother might be able, but only in the old place. Tara did not wish to see that power of the Way. No other had the skill, not Brother Chaign, he had tried.

Tara circled the two lights, they were bright to her now. That too had changed with time. At first these forms only appeared dark and empty, but now, with patience they could be turned into bright, shimmering beacons. Tara pulled herself back from the brink and looked around, the butterfly on her shoulder fluttered its wings. Tara said, "No, there is no danger. This one does not perceive me. Nor the small one."

The wings flapped again and the paper like insect fluttered off. Tara sucked in deep, thick, air. The scent of magic, the taste of metal. The technologist. Tara's eyes opened, back in the bedroom. She stood, re-clasped the necklace around her neck and went to find Baron Khurson.

She found him and a large contingent of Royal Guard gathered in front of his home. Khurson wore polished plate armor; his sigil embossed on one shoulder, the Wings of the Eagle on his other. The soldiers were a hardened lot, a mix of swords and pole-arms their choice of weapons. All turned to Tara, the golden light on her shoulder.

Tara said, "Lord Khursom, the technologist is the killer's target."

Khurson's jaw hardened then he said, "Let it be that you are right." Then to the soldiers he said, "We ride for Technologist Pierce's. Not one stays behind. Tonight we will end this!"

The soldiers saluted and in an ordered chaos found their horses. Baron Khurson mounted his stallion and said to Tara, "I hope that we do not need your services, daughter."

"I will serve as needed."

The soldiers followed Baron Khurson into the streets of Tarlow, their horses rumbling on the cobbled roads. Dragonfly, scenting the fight, kept up the best he could with the war-horses. It was a short ride to the Technologist District of Tarlow. As in Serac the technologists clustered together, creating a dense pocket of wealth and grandeur. The manor house of Senior Technologist Pierce was no exception. Already, the Royal Guard stood stationed every ten feet around the high fence. The gate was closed with a full squad of six protecting the entrance. They did not know what they waited for; apprehension and uncertainty ruled the night. Then to her right, Tara saw a flash, a glimpse of something gold and blue. She knew that she was right.

"Let us pass," Baron Khurson said, "I will add my private guard to the protection of this place." Khurson was not questioned, the soldiers knew it to be him, and were it not it was the most elaborate ruse any could imagine.

Massive lamps illuminated the grounds near the house with magical light. It could be day in those close spaces, but it faded to black as the night pulled at the edges. Technologist Pierce met the company on the drive. His beard was unbound and wild. At his side he carried a knife, a wire running from it tucked into a belt pouch. He said, "Lord Khurson. I am thankful that you would come, and with your personal guard." The technologist seemed truly impressed. "When your investigator appeared I was struck with dread, but I do not see how my children can be harmed with such amassed strength waiting for this killer."

Baron Khurson swung down, his armor clattering. He took Pierce's hand in his own. "I hope that we can prevent their deaths. I can barely shoulder my own loss. Where are your children now?"

"In the great room. It is in the center of the house and is easily protected."

"Good. Unless you disagree I would place my sword guard near the children. The pike men will be well served in the open, around the house."

Pierce nodded. "You know your men best."

"Where is Investigator Vega?"

"With my children."

Khurson said, "I won't keep you from your family. I will make the arrangements with my soldiers, then join you."

"As a friend, thank you, Vaughn." Benjamin again shook Baron Khurson's hand and then left him to command his troops.

A moment of calm came to the baron. Tara approached him. "Baron."

"Tara."

"When we rode in I saw the harbinger of the killer. I could not say so before, and it would have done no good. The battle will come soon; tell your men to be ready. Whatever comes, it will not die easily. If you will let me I would enchant you for the coming fight. I do not know many such spells, but you will not tire, nor will you fear."

"Cast your spells, wizard," he answered, staring past her into the night at one of his pike men.

"Of course." Tara placed her hand on the baron's forehead under the rim of his helmet, then separated her fore finger from the rest. Her eyes closed and she exhaled loudly. The baron shifted his weight. Then she said, "Always keep the Wings of the Eagle before you."

The baron slapped his left shoulder and said, "There is some wisdom in that. Let us find Celsius."

Tara followed Baron Khurson into Pierce's home. The warm wood was well lit by more of the magic lamps, albeit smaller. Soldiers stood three deep in the hallway to the great room, backing into the room to allow them to pass.

Technologist Pierce stood speaking softly to a soldier. His wife, Louise, sat on a sofa covered in a flowery fabric holding her sons hand, and though he tried to look confident it was clearly fear that burned in his eyes. His daughter was held in the arms of a well-groomed young man. Hardly a girl, a woman of eighteen, took after her mother, taller than the father and leaner. The son matched the stature of his father, but he was only thirteen. The baron remembered their births.

Pierce said, "Vaughn, you remember my children. Cassandra and Dalton."

"Yes, of course."

Pierce waved at the young man holding Cassandra and said, "My daughter's fiancé, Isaac Samuelson. He was once a student of mine."

Baron Khurson shook hands with the man, his grip strong. He was no more than twenty. It was not fear that was with him but perhaps dread. "A pleasure."

"Thank you, lord, I would kneel."

"This is no time for such formalities. Ah, Celsius I see you lingering."

Celsius bowed, saying, "Watching." He did not wear his hat, but he did wear his coat, the collar turned down. His granite eyes flicked about the room. A rudimentary pistol of his own design hung on his waist. "Another guest."

The soldiers filling the hall again backed into the room and General Paul led more of the Royal Guard into the now crowded great room. The general had donned his full war regalia. He carried the armor easily and moved fluidly, the result of years of practice. In his left hand he carried a massive hammer. It was not his favorite weapon, but the beast had not fallen to his son's sword. With him was a Wrath mage, his robes and armor intertwined as one. He carried a sword with a swathe of crystal through the blade. The general said, "Vaughn, Benjamin. It is unfortunate that we must meet like this."

Pierce answered, "Jonathan, I am again placed in the awkward position of thanking the council for their help. It is a credit to you."

"Think nothing of it. I will see this monster dead."

While the Three Eagles spoke Tara went to Celsius and without a word placed her hand on his forehead. The spells cast, she repeated the process with the Wrath mage, which she had to admit was a welcome addition. He thanked her and she nodded. General Paul took the magic next. His face did not change from the stony understanding of the situation.

Tara knelt to regain her strength, the spells tiring. Startled shouting filled the room at the other end of the hall. Everyone in the great room steeled themselves for the approaching monster. The soldiers in the hall fidgeted and a bird buzzed over the top of them, chirping at the room as it circled and danced. Technologist Pierce laughed and said, "How did that thing get in here?"

Tara shouted, "Stop it!"

The room scrambled but it was too late; the bird finished its pass and zoomed down the hall. Celsius said grimly, "Prepare yourself. If I understand correctly, we will now see how brazen the killer is."

Twenty-six

The pike man had been in the Royal Guard for seven years. He glanced into the darkness, then looked away and blinked. The lights behind him made ghosts and monsters in shadow, making it that much more difficult to watch for intruders. He re-gripped his pike; it had served him well in his years, and he had been selected to Baron Khurson's personal guard only six months earlier based on his aptitude with it. A bird chirped and flew overhead. He thought that it was strange that a bird would be out so late. He knew that he didn't know much about birds, so he squinted and looked out into the gloom.

He could just make out the brick wall that circled the compound. The soldiers patrolling the circuit moved in and out of darkness, straight ahead of him and off to his right. He blinked and thought he saw a huge form slink over the wall. He took two steps towards the fence when the patrolling soldier let out a truncated scream. The pike man swung his weapon across his body and shouted back to the house, "Something is coming!"

Out of the gloom the massive figure emerged. Fear punctured the elite soldier's heart when he saw the colossal animate. There was no rush in its steps as it stalked him. The soldier's heart beat in his ears. He stepped forward into a downward swing. The animate turned its shoulders, deflecting the blade to the ground, the man stepped back and stabbed the stomach. The pike tipped past and the animate batted it out of his hands, then grabbed him, lifting him face to face with one inhuman hand.

The soldier screamed and the brute lifted him higher, then slammed him to the earth.

Soldiers attacked it. It swatted them aside. The men could not match its power. The animate smiled, now it did not matter who saw it. It threw one of the lights against the house for sheer pleasure, noise and chaos. It lumbered forward, whacking away another man, then reared back and smashed both arms into the doors, buckling them, battered off another little human then completed the destruction. Tearing the doors from the hinges it entered the manor house. More soldiers attacked it, but they were no match for Arcane's creation.

A soldier forced his way into the great room. His shouting was panicked, short of breath, "It's coming! It's coming! A giant animate! I saw it...it...it didn't even feel the blows!"

Three massive knocks echoed throughout the house. The soldier fell to his hands and knees, saying over and over, "Oh Wrath! We are going to die!"

Khurson looked to Celsius, who matched his gaze. He had been right, it was not human. But he did not feel fear. More shouting, then the rumble of battle joined. Then silence. Technologist Pierce held both of his children, they openly sobbed. Khurson confidently said, "You will not die tonight."

The light in the hall dimmed as the monster filled it, shields scraping deep gouges into the panels. The soldiers stepped forward to attack it, swords clanking against its body. It smiled and shoved them backwards into the great room, the six fell and scattered, quickly retaking their feet.

General Paul hurried to the side of the doorway, waiting for the monster to pass. Technologist Pierce said, "Children, get back." He released them and they hurried to the far corner of the room. The Wrath mage and Baron Khurson stood at the technologist's side, soldiers arrayed before them. Tara and Celsius stood behind the rest, Isaac between them. A collective silence fell across the room.

The animate strode heavily into the room. As it passed, General Paul swung the hammer, smashing its back. The shell dented but the brute did not fall. It turned on its hips, backhanding the general, knocking him to the floor. "How quaint." It turned back to the wall of humans and said, "The children are mine." Both hands clicked and cracked into fists.

Baron Khurson growled, "Never." And the spell that had descended over the room enforcing the peace shattered.

The Royal Guard and the baron's personal guard attacked, sword blows pelting the animate. The animate ignored them, knocking them aside, one by one. The Wrath mage filled the breach, his sword dancing against metal. With each blow the crystal in the sword coughed flame that clung to the animate. It stopped and looked at its arm as it burned.

"Too bad, mage, that I am not of flesh." The animate swung madly, but the Wrath mage ducked away. The animate staggered off balance for one second. Baron Khurson struck the animate's unprotected face, cleaving the metal. The animate pulled away, running one finger down the line, and roared with rage.

The brute grabbed Baron Khurson by the shoulder, long fingers wrapping fully around the sigil of the Eagles and began to crush the armor and the man inside. Khurson shouted and hacked at the brute's neck. The blow glanced away harmlessly as his shoulder popped and metal tore.

The Wrath mage and Technologist Pierce took up the assault attempting to free the baron. Light flickered down the length of the mage's blade, and sliding forward onto one knee the mage screamed as he struck the animate's arm. The shockwave tore at the rivets holding the plates together and buckled the forearm. Baron Khurson's sword dropped to the ground as he pulled away, stumbling back holding his crushed shoulder.

With the crumpled arm the brute grabbed the mage, throwing him into soldiers just recovering their feet and the whole lot of them toppled under the mage's weight. As the brute circled, Technologist Pierce attacked. The powered knife cut through the crumpled arm and the hand dropped to the ground. The animate roared, punching the technologist. The bearded man flipped away, losing his grip on the knife. Looped by the wire to the magic battery the knife turned on its master, cutting into his leg. His children screamed.

Tara watched the carnage unfold before her. General Paul lay unconscious, she hoped. Baron Khurson staggered in pain, his armor turned against him. Technologist Pierce bled everywhere as he lay against a couch. The Wrath mage stood slowly, shaking his head. "Celsius! Get the children out of here! I can't stop that monster, but I can slow it down, maybe get some of the men back on their feet. Hurry!"

Celsius nodded, handed his leather bag to Isaac, and pointed to the door across the room. "Out that door! Go!"

Isaac's knuckles whitened around the handle of the bag and he grabbed Cassandra's hand in his and they ran. The brute stalked past Khurson, who had fallen to his knees. The baron grasped at the armor, trying to pry it from his flesh. A crushing blow sent the Wrath mage into the wall, where he fell in a heap. Dalton had frozen, watching the metal beast decimate the defenders. The animate moved close, its cleft face twisted into a smile. "Be proud, a valiant defense."

Celsius blurred between the two, boy and brute, staff hammering out a beat on the animate's head, trying to cave in the metal face. The blows pushed back the animate, the sudden changes in perception after each hit jarred the anima of the brute, forcing the metal body to adjust as the world shook. It set its left foot and lunged towards Celsius. He danced back shouting, "Boy, follow your sister!"

The animate clutched at Celsius but he swayed sideways, avoiding the one remaining hand. His staff danced, disorganizing the brute, allowing Dalton to bolt past. "Don't think, run!"

The technologist's children passed Tara and she closed her eyes. The wood floor rotted and withered. Celsius skipped back and as the brute followed him the floor cracked and splintered, collapsing under its weight. The brute lurched off balance as its left leg disappeared into the crawlspace, then toppled from view through the spellbound floor. It roared with frustration.

Celsius threw back his coat and pulled two glass vials from his left hip. The animate stirred. As it stood Celsius threw the vials of formula at the brute. The glass exploded on impact, splattering the animate with caustic liquid. He had prepared.

Tara ordered, "Run! Get the children out of here!"

Celsius obeyed. She watched him disappear and turned back in time to see the animate rise from the crawlspace and step up to the floor, fumes rolled off of it. Tara dove out of the way as the animate ran past her, its anima held but one goal. The doorway splintered as the animate impacted the walls; it did not slow.

She shouted, "Run, Celsius, it's coming!"

Tara knelt next to Technologist Pierce. His skin nearly matched his white beard for color. She placed her hand over the wound and said, *"Muul Suin!"* The flesh began to grow and mend; he would live. Tara turned to Baron Khurson, he still tried to remove his armor; he grimaced and frowned, his mind blurred by pain. "Let me help, lord."

The baron coughed and muttered, "Yes, uhnng. What strength, my poor Anne." He did not look up.

Tara undid the buckles that held the shoulder plates in place and pried it from Khurson's shoulder. Then she cut away the padding and shirt underneath. The baron's shoulder was black and purple. She ran her hand over the bruising. Baron Khurson shook his head as the numbing pain rolled off him. His mind cleared and he said, "What happened?"

"Celsius flees with the children. Take your sword and follow the destruction."

Khurson nodded and stood, he took his sword and ran after the animate. Tara knelt over General Paul; with a wave of her hand she roused him. Tara said, "Take your hammer, general, we may yet be able to stop the beast."

General Paul got to one knee and shook his head, then looked around the room. "Wrath! The children live?"

"They did, I know not for how long. Hurry!"

The general's gauntlet wrapped around the hammer and the massive man stood. He clanked as he ran, following the path taken by Baron Khurson, the brute, Celsius Vega, Dalton, Cassandra and Isaac.

Tara looked around the room and shook her head. "Now for the rest."

General Paul could easily trace the path of the brute. Destruction, massacred doorways, crushed furniture, gouged walls. Dragging the hammer behind him he joined the chase, eventually exiting the home. The door itself had been pounded twenty feet towards the stables. Slightly ahead was Baron Khurson, his armor reflecting the light of the lamps. General Paul called, "Do you see any of them, Vaughn?"

Khurson's head pivoted and he called between breaths, "Only more destruction. This way!"

The two Eagles clattered in their armor as they ran, hoping they would be in time, not knowing what they would do against the animate.

Celsius could hear the brute behind him, long strides slammed into the cobble road. Ahead of him only slightly were Pierce's children and Isaac. Celsius's mind spun, trying to find some way to stop the monster. It seemed hopeless, all of his skill, all of discoveries, paled in the face of the truth. The road parted ways. Isaac took the north road and the rest followed as it led past more well bred technologist estates. The animate seemed to have faded into the night. Celsius could not hear the metal echoes, and he allowed himself a backwards glance.

The monster was gone. Celsius frowned; it had undoubtedly seen them take the turn that they did.

Cassandra breathlessly asked, "Inspector, where did it go?"

"It plays. It believes us an easy kill."

Dalton clutched at Celsius's arm. "I'm scared."

Celsius looked down at the young man who scanned the street for some sign of the beast. Isaac held Cassandra, fear draped each of the young lover's faces like a veil. Celsius's hands went to his belt and he drew out more vials. He handed two to Isaac. "It does not hunt you. Strike it with these."

Isaac separated from his love and spun the glass in his hands. "Thank you, Celsius. I wish I had—"

"Not now. And it is not much. When the beast attacks I will stand. You must run, hide if you can." The scraping of metal on stone silenced him. Celsius said resolutely, "It comes. Be prepared."

The animate dropped from the heavens onto the dark road. Celsius rolled from where he stood to avoid being crushed, and immediately flung more vials at the damaged animate. They burst and popped with renewing vigor. Isaac let fly and both struck the head, the acidics inside immediately began to hiss, the noxious fumes rising from the steel. The animate clutched its face, pulling at the smoke impeding its vision.

Celsius attacked, staff pattering on the carapace.

Dalton ran, but the animate moved sharply and with purpose, ignoring Celsius, striking Cassandra, blood spattered through the air like some misspent magic.

Isaac cursed, his anger rising above wisdom. And with no weapon greater than his own hands he too fell into attacking the metal monster.

It smiled and punched Isaac in the chest, knocking him back, collapsing him on his side. The brute roared and straightened, sight difficult in the haze burning off of it.

Vega ducked under the thrashing monster and tossed the last of the vials. It shattered and splattered, adding its toxin to the mixture that already chewed the brute's cleft face. A burst of smoke brought renewed fury, the staff penetrated the fog and staggered the monster. The brute flailed back, its futile swings drawing Celsius forward, staff dancing on its shell. The brute slowed, then struck, grabbing Celsius in its metal vise grip. The animate cared not what it held but lifted the man, squeezing him. Vega moaned, reached to his belt, put the pistol to the animate's face and fired it. The roar echoed, tearing away the center of the animate's rotting face, chipping the crystal inside.

The brute recoiled, shifted its grip to Celsius arm and beat him against the ground again and again. Losing consciousness, he finally fell to the road in a sopping heap of broken bones and blood.

Isaac stood, chest heaving. It felt like pure fire. Cassandra did not move and Dalton had disappeared down the dark road. The animate flailed madly, tearing chunks from the wood and plaster building that it rammed against. Celsius did not move, and Isaac knew the worst for the man that had bravely faced the monster.

The animate suddenly stopped and listened. "I hear you human. Come find your death, join the others. It does not matter anymore. The damage is done."

Isaac staggered to the side, retrieving Celsius's worn staff. It was warm in his hands.

General Paul and Baron Khurson could hear the animate before they could see it. Only that monster could make such a cacophony in the otherwise silent night. They approached to see Isaac holding Celsius's staff. Smoke billowed from the animate, the liquid seething violently on its shell. Rage filled the Eagles and they rushed to the aid of the failed technologist.

Khurson screamed, a guttural wail of pain and anger and sorrow and hate. It was equaled by the general and the men attacked the ailing beast with all the brutality

314

and strength that they could muster. The brute spun to face the armored men, laughing deep metallic all the while. The animate staggered forward, blindly swinging its massive arms. The Eagles, forced back by the sheer mass of the creature, countered and fought savagely.

Khurson skirted to the side of the animate and attacked, the animate lurched, keyed by the strikes, groping for Khurson in its chemical night. With both arms it lifted the man with ease. His armor cracked and moaned in the crushing embrace. General Paul beat relentlessly on the animate, but the animate was of single purpose. Khurson cursed and screamed.

Isaac gathered his wits and his will, taken from him by the pain and the hypnotic chaos before him. Sweat beaded his skin, soaked his dark hair. He watched the contorted face of Baron Khurson, struggling to escape the metal god. Then his eyes fell to Cassandra; they were to be married and the pain stuck him. Blood was worn about her mouth like makeup and she did not move. Finally, to the broken body of Celsius Vega. He had given his life to save them, to the attempt, in any case. His hands tightened around the staff, its smooth finish suddenly familiar. He screamed, his pain joining all around him and he charged the brute, its back turned to him.

The staff bent and then shattered as Isaac smashed it into the legs of the animate. If ever he had prayed for a feel, a sense, of the magic that eluded him in his apprenticeship with Technologist Pierce it was now.

Magic or not, the strike took the legs from the animate. It toppled backward, landing with a deafening clatter, metal on stone. Khurson bounced once on the creature, released from its grasp and slid to the side. The wisps of smoke continued to mark the inevitable destruction of the brute's shell.

General Paul watched the animate fall, tightening the grip on his hammer. The animate lain prone before him, he realized that the fall had disoriented it for a moment. He would not have another chance as heaven-sent as this. He muttered, "Back to whatever hell you come from."

The hammerhead arched gracefully through the night, a mighty shout propelling it towards the target. In all of his battles and wars the general had never struck as violently as he now did. The hammer pushed the fumes of Celsius's liquid aside; they spiraled circles to make way. The acid-gnawed carapace crumbled as the hammer struck it, not even slowing the blow. The crystal orb inside warped and shattered, spraying slivers in every direction. The hammer even then continued, burying itself deep inside the monster.

The hammer lay still but General Paul held it tightly, hands resting together. He waited breathlessly for the animate to move, to stand, to do anything. It did not. It was dead. Baron Khurson coughed and pushed himself up from the ground. He put one hand on General Paul's right arm; the general jerked, pulled back from his own nightmare. Baron Khurson said, "It is done."

Isaac lay on his side shaking, shattered staff clutched in his hands. The baron knelt next to him and he sat up. He said, "Brave Isaac, the Empire thanks you. Rightly so." Then he saw Celsius and Cassandra. "Oh, Wrath. Get the Way mage, someone," he called to the night.

General Paul sat in a heap breathing deeply. Tara, as called, came with more soldiers. She ran past everyone to Celsius and knelt beside him. She touched him softly on the side of his face and shook her head. Leaving his side she knelt next to Cassandra. Her head fell. "I'm sorry, they are both already gone."

Baron Khurson stood, the light from Tara's shoulder reflecting many worlds in his beaten armor. He shook angrily. He said to the soldiers, "One of you find Dalton, bring him back here. The rest, go to the House of Animate. Arrest them all. I will not allow this to stand unpunished. Wait, fetch a cart and more soldiers, this monster will be held in account against them. Let them say they know nothing when confronted with this."

The soldiers scattered, knowing their tasks without speaking. General Paul rubbed his face and said softly, "I will tell Benjamin of his loss." Then to Isaac, "I am sorry, son, that it could not be stopped."

Isaac frowned, mouth quivering, his eyes closed slowly and his slim body shook. "Why? Damn it! Why?" His voice failed. He stood, moaned and smashed the shell of the animate with the remains of the staff. He dropped to his knees and simply cried.

Khurson placed his hand on Isaac's shoulder. He said with sympathy, "Quiet now, the makers will be dealt with. It is not much, I know. We know. Take what bit of comfort you can from it. Take mine as well."

It was not far from Technologist Pierce's estate, and the cart drawn by four horses and the soldiers appeared in fairly short order. With a little planning and the rest muscle the soldiers managed to slide the brute up a makeshift ramp that the soldier had been thoughtful enough to grab when he readied the cart. The cart bowed slightly but held its shape. Khurson said quickly, "Drive it to my stables and lock it away. No one enters. Guard it well."

The soldier sent to find Dalton returned, the youth in tow. He saw his sister motionless and asked, "Is...is she dead?"

General Paul knelt and said, "I'm sorry, son."

The boy shoved past the general, not slowing at the impact and fell beside his sister, shaking her. "Wake up Cassandra! Wake up!" Then pleading frantically to Tara, "Can't you heal her? Can't you? That's what you do isn't it?"

Tara shook her head, tears welling up. "I cannot bring them back, Dalton. I'm sorry."

Dalton took another look at his sister then stumbled to his feet, running from the helpless adults.

Baron Khurson said, "Follow him. Make sure he gets home."

The same soldier followed the boy, not attempting to catch him. The general watched them go and said to the baron, "Rousan must act."

"Yes. You see to Benjamin, I will send for the others."

General Paul nodded and scooped up the lifeless Cassandra in his arms. He said, "Daughter?"

"Yes, general?" Tara answered, sadness in her voice.

"Come make sure that Benjamin is well and the boy can sleep."

"As you wish." Tara followed the general, light bobbing feverishly on her shoulder, her mind spinning at some way she could have changed the outcome. She frowned and with the clatter of soldiers and orders and carts behind her she whispered, "I am sorry, Celsius, that I could not help you."

A pale, limping Pierce paced apprehensively. His anger at the House of Animate smeared with fear for his children's life. He would have gone after them but his wife held him back. She sat waiting with tear streaks on her well-aged face. General Paul carried Cassandra into the great room and laid her body on a table. The technologist and his wife descended upon it like vultures, first circling fearful to touch her, then falling to her side. Pierce held his wife's shoulders as the delicate lady shook and sobbed. "I, I didn't even say I love you. I do! I do!" she pleaded with her.

Technologist Pierce could not look at her and he said, "Dalton, is he safe?"

Jonathan nodded. "Celsius gave himself to protect them. The animate is dead."

"Father! Mother!" Dalton called, running into the room, soldier in tow. He ran to them and embraced. "I was so—"

"Shhh...Don't speak of it," Pierce said while his wife kissed her only son.

General Paul said, "Benjamin. Lord Khurson and I have ordered a council meeting. I grieve for your loss, but we must act now."

"Yes." The technologist paused. "Yes. Louise, take care of Dalton?" His wife nodded, bleary eyes not so sure. "I will be back as soon as I can. I do not think this will take long."

The general nodded. "Louise. Daughter Tara will help you sleep if you desire it. I might recommend it; I don't think sleep will come easily for any of us for a long time. Let's go Benjamin, knowing Khurson the others will be waiting."

Tara laid her hand on the shoulder of the general. "Do not retreat from wisdom or punish too harshly. This warning is upon me."

"What must be done shall be."

The Council of the Five Eagles sat darkly around the table. Wren alone suffered no loss of family, and he almost wished that he had, if only to be equally looked upon. Instead his children slept snuggly in well guarded rooms. One single lamp in the middle of the table was lit, a technologist piece that cast white rays to the far corners of the room. The baron and the general each wore their armor; their chairs, despite being strongly built, showed strain. James and Benjamin each wore fresh sorrow, the animate cleaving their hearts.

Baron Khurson, as often was the case, began the meeting. "I extend my sorrow to both of you. I am proud that we could save the boy. That beast was an unexpected horror. Which brings us to the matter at hand.

"As we speak, the House of Animate in Tarlow has been closed, the mages arrested. From what I was told they put up little fight, claiming innocence."

Pierce laughed once. "They disgrace the word."

Khurson nodded. "I don't disagree. The killer, as we know now, is an animate. Its body is being held at my estate, should any of you who have not seen it want to. It is clearly responsible for the deaths of my Anne, Jon the Second, Cassandra, Vera and James the Fourth. We do not need the I & A to tell us such. Indeed, the investigator that I employed when the Royal Guard discovered nothing is dead. Saving your son, Benjamin."

"And for that he will be honored," Pierce said flatly, words forced.

General Paul began, "It will not take long for the House of Animate to demand the release of their mages."

Wren said, "This is not something that can be dealt with internally, no matter what First Entrah says. Not a week ago they banished the Second of their House, Master Jannan. Punished for building the animates that burned Earlsburg."

General Paul said, "Among other offences, The House of Wrath claims."

James raised his fingers off of the table, the others quieted. "Even with that being the case, it did not stop a mage from building and assigning the task of murder to that animate. It is clear to me that the House of Animate has a sinister—" He paused and shook his head. "An evil to it. We were fools for not taking action against them when Earlsburg burned. They will say that they do not know how it was made, who created it. Be it truth or lies I do not care. My son and daughter lie cold on a slab of stone."

He stood, leaning his weight with both arms on the table. "It would be just to take one each of theirs for each of ours, but I will do them better. Let them flee to Serac, and hide away behind their noble walls. I will gladly barricade them in their city. No more will I allow such reckless use of power in Rousan. We have bowed to the House's whims for the last time. If Jota Siana and the Kingdoms of Lyst and Kurn wish to coddle these murderers, then so be it. But they will not practice within the kingdom of my line and if one returns death will be their sentence."

His Honor collapsed back into his chair and rubbed under his nose with the back of his hand. The others sat thinking in silence. Guildmaster Wren was the first to speak, "Certain guilds stand to lose much if the House of Animate is banished. But I support this. There is no way that I could not. Such an unprecedented crime demands unprecedented actions, and you are far more gracious than I could be."

Technologist Pierce spoke, his voice broken by grief. "Indeed it does you credit, James. My leg is healed by the Way but not my heart. The technologist's magic owes much of its life to the House of Animate, and in many things we have been allies, but in this, we cannot be. Even if my position is lost, I will vote to approve this action. Silas can have my head if he wants it, and it will curse him every day."

General Paul's face was still grim from battle. "This vote is heavy on my heart. I listen to your words, but a warning from the Way mage holds sway with me for some reason that I cannot fathom. I believe this action just, and it is neither foolish nor harsh. Certainly too forgiving. Once they leave we will have no opportunity to change our judgement, save for a war that I cannot even begin to fathom. I would call for increased scrutiny upon the rest of these noble wizards." His words were sick with anger. "They have been given too much credit and too often been allowed to work against our interests. That said, I will speak in unison with you all."

Baron Khurson stared into the light on the table. "You have no opposition from me. Send the House of Animate from our land. Send the flames of damnation behind them, lest they forget what they have done. Scrutinize the other Houses for treason. The Rousan Empire, the Empire of the Five Eagles, will not forget."

All spoke as one, "Agreed."

Twenty-seven

Tara yawned and stretched lazily on the creaky old bed. She had slept long after the night of violence. The room's two plants looked healthier for her rest. She enjoyed just lying in the bed, not really thinking, not really wanting to think, not even really being awake, just watching the dust float this way and that in beams of sunlight that poured into her guest room in the House of Currents. After a few minutes she could no longer ignore the desire to get up and she rolled out of bed. She stretched again and yawned again then got dressed. All the while she put down the ache that clawed at her heart. She did not want to think of that dismal night.

Tara walked the halls of the grand building, one of many grand old buildings on the oldest campus of any of the Wizard Houses. It was built even before Serac. The Way did not have any official representation in Tarlow and cheerfully relied on the charity of the Currents for shelter and food when one of their mages settled in town. It was charity happily extended.

While the Way mage walked she thought of the events of the last several days, and specifically again of Celsius. The investigator certainly had a special something about him. Tara smiled and thought that she was probably just romanticizing the dead. And she believed that proper.

She stopped and watched two young children practicing in the courtyard under the watchful gaze of a motherly looking mage. Leaves floated before them. Without thought three red and orange leaves near her levitated up, circled and chased.

Flecks of gold trailed from them as they moved. Gold welled up on the edges of the children's leaves as well; their eyes grew large as it happened. It brought stern reprimand from the older mage, "Daughter. Stop it now."

Tara smiled and shrugged her shoulders like a naughty child, saying, "I apologize."

All five leaves fell to the ground and Tara left the young Currents to their studies. She exited the courtyard and prepared to leave the House when she was approached by the District First. Cyanna was by far the most well trained mage in Tarlow. Tara knew that she had schooled under Frederick Guildenil before taking the post. Her olive skin and hazel eyes were beautifully framed with raven hair, half as long as Tara's own. A moment of jealousy rushed Tara's pained heart before her better nature could quell it. In her hand she held a scroll. "A word, daughter."

"Certainly, Master Lau."

"We received this decree this morning, and are advising that everyone read it." She handed the scroll to Tara. Tara opened it and read the announcement to herself.

By order of the Council of the Five Eagles, the House of Animate has seven (7) days to depart the Rousan Empire. This order is in response to the recent treasonous behavior by members of said House.

Those that do not wish to obey this mandate shall be arrested and charged with the murder of the following persons: Anne Khurson, daughter of Baron Vaughn Khurson. Jon Paul the Second, son of General Jonathan Paul. Cassandra Pierce, daughter of Senior Technologist Benjamin Pierce. Vera Eddington, daughter of His Honor James Eddington. James Eddington the Fourth, son of His Honor James Eddington. Celsius Vega, special investigator to Baron Khurson. And for the deaths of the brave soldiers of the Rousan.

Additional to this mandate: Any that practice the animist magic in the future shall be dealt with under the provisions of this mandate, with punishment up to but not limited to fine, incarceration, and or death.

Additional to this mandate: All other Wizard Houses and practitioners shall be placed under Imperial scrutiny in order to root out any abuses of power.

It is not without serious deliberation that these steps have been taken. For a full reckoning of the mandate, including full charges and victims, visit the Law Chamber of the Royal Ministry.

The scroll was stamped with the sigil of the Empire, marking its authenticity. Tara frowned, "That is unpleasant. What are they doing with the animists that they arrested last night?"

"They released them this morning, a few hours before they released this announcement. It's safe to think that they have already fled to Serac after their birds flew."

"The House of Animate will not take kindly to this."

"No. I think not. I already protested the ruling with the Baron Khurson. He showed me the shell of the animate and told me what it did last night alone. Then he told me to ask you if I did not believe him."

Tara said, "It was truly terrifying. It demolished everything. Anything Khurson said was true."

"I was afraid that might be the case. He does not have a history of exaggeration."

Tara sighed, "The sad thing is that given the circumstances the Eagles staid their hand. Most would have been far more vengeful, but I cannot help to wonder if this will help in the long run. Have they made the official announcement?"

"Not yet, one hour from now. Anyway that is all I wanted to show you. Travel safely and carefully. The populace that has heard is already more wary of us because of this. It has put all of the Houses in bad standing."

"Thank you for the warning. Be well, Master Lau."

Tara went out the front door, catching several worried glances that quickly fell away when she matched them. The roads were packed, most of the people on them headed towards the Courtyard of the Eagles. The square, Tara could tell, would be filled past any imagined capacity. And she would join them.

Tara jostled and bumped, squeezing forward towards the balcony where they would appear; finally she could move no more. The crowd was shoulder to shoulder, front to back, and yet a man moved through the crowd not far from her.

He seemed to be able to slide through the smallest gap, fit into the tiniest space. 'That is odd,' Tara thought to herself, 'I couldn't move more than an inch if I wanted to.'

Tara watched the man with interest. Other than his unique skill to navigate the crowd, he was forgettable, gray clothing with a gray, high-necked cloak. From underneath the cloth collar, a metal collar peeked out. Tara's head cocked slightly to the side as she watched him move across in front of her. He was familiar. His face; she had seen it before, and not in Tarlow. Her mind rushed and she remembered.

The thief.

Her hand moved by itself to her shoulder, and when she realized it she quickly pulled it down. She began to push through the crowd, the going much more difficult than for the thief. 'Why is he here? Was he one of the ones that Alex spoke of? He has to be, The House of Wrath held him after the report was issued,' the internal dialogue flowed quickly. It had no effect on the crowd, the best she could do was watch him.

Tara, so distracted by the appearance of the thief, did not notice at first when the balcony doors opened. The roar of the crowd announced the Eagles' arrival. The baron and the general still wore their armor from the night before. All looked weary, their posture stooped. All five, broken spirits. Tara could mark that.

His Honor silenced the crowd and said, "Good people. We come before you this day with sorrow. As you already know, Baron Khurson and General Paul have lost children in recent days. I stand here now and tell you that Senior Technologist Pierce has lost his daughter to the killer. And I have," James stopped, putting his hand over his mouth, "I have lost both of my children to the beast."

The crowd gasped and the calls of disbelief filled the square, the line was broken. James continued, "Do not be afraid, though murder struck our very homes, you, my good people, are quite safe. The killer is dead." A halfhearted cheer was raised. His Honor raised his hand to bring silence. "The killer was not human, but animate. Given this fact and the burning of Earlsburg, which rises from its own ashes, the Council issues this decree."

Baron Khurson handed His Honor a scroll. He unrolled it and read the announcement that Tara had read an hour earlier. A sense of discontent filled the crowd. When James finished reading he said, "The council understands that this is an unprecedented action. We hold that our judgement is fair and just. Use this mandate as a reminder that justice knows no limitation, be you mage, farmer, noble or common. The Empire of the Five Eagles does not and will not allow such behavior within its borders."

His Honor stepped back, nodded once and the council left the balcony. The crowd began to disperse slowly, grumbling, wanting blood, the edges of the throng pushed away from the center all the same. Tara stood her ground, her feet rooted. The faces of those moving around her were shaded with anger, disbelief directed towards the House of Animate. Tara watched the thief again, and again he twisted his way rapidly through the crowd. His face, and it was definitely him, was unlike the others. He had a slight smile.

Tara's feet tore away from the ground and she began following. It was not easy going but she managed to tail him. Passing under the inner wall the crowded roads cleared, making the going easier, making following without being spotted more difficult. Tara knew that she should alert the Royal Guard but she did not. The man would deny that he was who she said he was, and given the climate after the last few weeks, they would most likely believe him over her.

Tara muttered a little spell under her breath, to help hide her. How much it would help in the open daylight she did not know. The thief led the way down through the warehouses that the shipping guilds owned and rented, then along the waterfront of Lake Nimm. The brawny longshoremen moved cargo on all of the piers where ships were docked. All seemed to go well until a sailor called out, "Hello love! What is a pretty thing like you doing in a rough place like this? Lets you and me go someplace nice."

The comment brought laughter, and the thief turned to watch the commotion. Tara shot the sailor the look of death, were she a Wrath mage he would be. His friends snickered but the damage had been done. The thief smiled and continued on. Tara waited a moment, thinking, then continued after him. Her trickery, what little of it there was, was ruined, so she ran after him, soliciting a mock apology from the sailor.

Tara's heart beat accelerated as she neared the thief, he had been dangerous before, and if he truly escaped The House of Wrath he was even more dangerous and yet she ran to catch him. 'What foolishness is this? Perhaps if I was a Wrath mage, but...' Her thoughts cut off, the thief whirled on his heels to face her. She yipped, "Oh!"

Peter grabbed her by the elbow and pulled her into an alley, garnering several inquiring looks from the men that worked the piers. Peter said, "Why do you follow me, woman?"

"I couldn't help but notice the collar around your neck," she answered.

"Perhaps, but I think that is not the truth." Peter pushed her against the wall. "Out with it."

"Take your hands off me, thief."

Peter's eyes darkened. "Who are you?"

"It is you," Tara said. "I thought it was. You were unconscious in the Guardhouse. I healed your leg."

Peter laughed once in disbelief. "Then I thank you for that good Way mage, but I am not that person any longer. I would warn you, do not follow."

Tara said, "Why are you here?"

"Were it so simple I could tell you. Truly my debt to you is done. Do not press me." Then he literally pleaded, "Please."

"I have already forsaken calling the guard."

Peter said, "That was your decision, it's not some way to gain favor, daughter. I shall be polite, please, excuse me."

Tara twisted her arm, employing a wrist lock that Chaign had shown her. Peter's arm contorted, bent, and slithered out of her grasp. He smiled slightly. Tara frowned and magic jumped. The power of the spell grounded into the alley, flinging dirt into their knees.

Peter's mouth moved, just starting a word when they heard from the end of the alley, "Daughter Tara? Are you alright?"

Both Tara and Peter turned to face the speaker. Tara recognized the man to be Isaac Samuelson. He held Celsius's bag in his left hand. Peter said, "She is quite fine my good man." Then to Tara, "Another time perhaps."

Calmly, but with the strange smoothness that marked his movement, Peter passed Isaac, delivering a cold stare into the younger man. Isaac watched him go, wondering what burned behind his eyes, then said, "Daughter?"

"I am fine. What are you doing here? Isaac, right?"

Still watching Peter walk away he said, "Yes, Isaac. Isaac Samuelson. I saw you in the Courtyard of the Eagles, and followed you. I'm sorry if I interrupted you just now. I, well, never mind."

Tara walked to the road that ran along the waterfront, she glanced in the direction that Peter had gone. "It's alright, for the best maybe. If you want to speak with me then come. Otherwise, and don't think me short, goodbye."

"Hmm, you follow him?"

Tara smiled. "He said not to, so of course I mean to. Celsius's bag?"

Isaac looked down, his orange brown eyes slipping to the side, seemingly unable to focus on the bag. Nervously he said, "Umm, yes. I grabbed it after he died. It was forgotten in the shadows by the Royal Guard."

Tara started to walk away and said, "If you truly mean to join me then come now, Isaac. The thief is almost out of sight."

Isaac followed after Tara closer than before, but still he gave the mage her space. The road was wide open and he did not understand why the man that she called thief did not look back to see them, or it was possible that he did not care if they followed. In either case he took some small satisfaction in the hard wood cudgel that hung by a leather strap to his belt. It was not a fancy weapon but he was skilled with it. And with a mage how could the thief be a threat?

Tara was not so sure. The spell should have at least slowed the thief but it had done nothing but kick up dirt. It shouldn't have failed. It never had before. No, the thief was something more than that. He had said as much, he was not that person any longer. Tara fretted as she went.

Isaac and Tara followed Peter out of town, always he seemed to out pace them, getting further and further away, a dream, a ghost, a nothing. When the road began to split and branch Tara stopped. "Wrath! Where has that criminal gotten to?" she questioned.

Isaac knelt next to her and opened the leather bag. Pushing the pistol aside he withdrew a tube of metal. Two twists of the wrist and it extended. He raised it to his eye. Then pointed. "There. He took the Old Bakery Road. Tricky devil, and fast too."

Tara nodded and started after him again, Isaac dropped the telescope back into the bag and hurried after her. "What are you planning to do when we catch up to him?"

"I don't know." Tara squinted then said, "Wait, look there!" She pointed up into the sky, blue and gold flickered in the sunlight. "It's the same bird as last night."

Isaac shielded his eyes. "Yeah, I see it. Odd that it would just appear like that."

Tara looked at him and said, "I don't think it is by accident. It appears just before that monster appears, then again around the thief that escaped from Wrath. I have seen birds of many colors, but none like that, not around here."

"It could be lost," Isaac said.

"No," she said sternly. "It is not even alive. Not like you or I. The Earth warned me against it. When I saw the animate it was shown to me as a light, and there was a second light. Smaller." The bird zipped out of sight. "Hurry! Or we'll lose them both!"

Tara and Isaac ran down the road. To their right was the old bakery that the road was named for. Smoke rose from its chimney, the smell of fresh bread was strong. "There!" Isaac said, pointing. The bird flew low along the road, blue feathers glimmering as it drew closer. Isaac pulled out the pistol, aimed, said, "Why not?" and fired.

He completely missed, the recoil twirling him sideways.

Tara shrieked, surprised by the blast and the bird whizzed between them, chirping.

Isaac smirked, cursed and dropped the gun back into Celsius's bag. He knelt and picked up a small smooth stone from the road. "Always been better tossing rocks anyway," he muttered and let the stone fly. It whirled through the air, squarely striking the bird. It careened off course and crashed into the grass that grew high around a fence pole just to his left. Isaac clapped his hands once. "Got it!"

Tara smiled, eyed Celsius's bag and said, "Nice throw, let's have a look."

The two kneeled where the bird had crashed, finding it unmoving. Isaac poked it with a stick and when it did not respond pulled it from the grass. "It's cold.

Look! You were right, it's not alive. Is it an animate?"

Tara took the bird from him and examined it closely, "Yes. And I would bet that whoever made it also made the one that killed the Eagles' children. It's beautiful, I would not have known that it was not a real bird if I was not a Way mage."

"It had me fooled," Isaac said as he marveled at the bird. "Let me see it again." Tara handed him the bird and he opened the bag, coughed as it spat out fumes from the pistol, and took out the polished lens. "It's made from gold obviously, and sapphire. Some sort of crystal as well. Quartz maybe."

"How can you tell?" Tara asked.

"My father is a goldsmith. He passed on a few things to me before I decided I wasn't interested. Maybe not the best decision ever on my part."

Tara looked up the road and said, "Well, I think we've lost the thief. That's probably why the bird showed up, to distract us from him."

"You really think these things are connected, don't you."

Tara nodded, "Yes I do. I'd say that we should take that to be inspected at the House of Animate, but that will involve a trip to Serac now."

"Is that where you intend to go?"

"There are not going to be any more answers here."

Isaac wrapped the bird in a cotton rag and dropped it into a pocket inside the bag. "I realize that we've only just met, but I would like to come with you. There is nothing left for me here. My fiancé is dead. My family, my father mostly, disowned me when I joined the army academy after I failed as a technologist. My first term is up and quite frankly I am not interested in another. I have some money saved. I won't be a burden."

Tara thought to herself, her eyes slowly closing. When they opened she said, "Some traveling company could be nice. I have to return to Tarlow to get my pony. I have to warn you though, I don't really have any idea what we are doing. I just have the vague impression that something more is going on here than a simple rogue mage."

Isaac said, "If there is more to this story than just the death of my Cassandra I want to help figure it out. I owe that much to her, and to her father. I was training in the I & A thanks to him. And if I understand some of Celsius's writings correctly he will continue to help us after his death." He stopped for a moment, hearing the fantasy in his words, then smiled and said, "I have delusions of grandeur from time to time."

"It's okay," Tara said, laughing a bit. "Maybe it will be a grand adventure. Not that I am sure I want one, mind you. The thief is gone. I'll send word of his suspicious appearance."

Isaac half frowned, "I doubt it will get more than a glance."

"Nothing more can be done then. Let's get our horses and go. If we ride quickly maybe we can catch the animists before Serac."

Isaac and Tara agreed to meet near the market on the North Tarlow Road. Isaac returned to his home, which was rented from the Pierces. He picked through his things, packed a few in another bag and wrote a note explaining his departure. He would not say goodbye, he would not risk being dissuaded. He then went to the bank and withdrew his savings, turning it into gold coins in a pouch. His horse, Randa, was stabled not far from his home. The horse had been a gift from his mother two years ago when he had joined the Royal Guard. His training had not made much use of the horse and Isaac had mainly ridden him on holiday.

He followed the wide road just inside the inner wall until he came to the arch that marked the North Tarlow Road. Soldiers were posted, to keep things at the busy crossing running smoothly. Archers were up on the wall as an added sign of things. He looked back over his shoulder, south into town. A feeling of excitement welled up in him, suppressing any doubt. He patted his horse on the neck and said, "Well, Randa, let's go find the daughter."

They passed under the arch and found themselves now officially out of Old Tarlow, though the surroundings had not changed any. Shortly, he reached the market, where he scanned the stands filled with fresh vegetables. After a while he asked one of the farmers, "Has there been a Way mage here? Long brown hair."

"'Fraid not. Nope," the sun-marked man answered. "Buy a tomato?"

"Eh? No thanks. How about some corn?"

The farmer gave a toothy smile, "That I can do."

The transaction was just completed when Tara rode next to Isaac.

Dragonfly, with a prance in his step, introduced himself to Randa, leaving the two horses both shaking their heads. Tara said, "Sorry to keep you waiting. The House of Animate burns."

"Wrath. That didn't take long. We better get going." Isaac responded, tucking the wrapped corn into a saddlebag.

The journey north went well. Tara traveled without announcing her association with The Way of Health. It sped up the trip, which was good because the ride to Serac was already long. Unfortunately, it meant that they spent many nights sleeping under the stars, trying to find some sort of shelter under trees or bushes. Isaac took to it decently, the journey a distraction from the pain inside.

Isaac slept deeply now, leaning against the trunk of an old sycamore. The fire had burnt itself out, the charcoal smoldered, giving off meager heat. Isaac believed himself to still be in his dream, a soft glowing blue light the size of his head pulsed just above him. He watched it descend from the sycamore branches and hover over their camp. Then he whispered, "Tara, Tara. Wake up."

Tara rolled over in the grass and mumbled, "Why? It's still dark."

Isaac shifted his weight slightly to sit up. The blue form did not move. "Open your eyes Tara."

She did, and sat up quickly. Isaac whispered, "What is that?"

She whispered back, "A wisp. They're not often seen this far south. Watch."

The little orb of light that the Way mages were known for popped into existence, the same blue as the wisp. The wisp seemed to boil at the appearance. Then a second and a third, each matching the wisp. The lights floated across the space, and began circling the wisp, tiny satellites.

Slowly at first the wisp directed the lights, then as if satisfied with its preparations, the wisp began to sing. It began as tiny bells played inside a large empty room, but as the orbs spun more and more complicated designs, faster and faster, the tone changed to a great chorus of chimes and bells. Tara and Isaac watched in amazement as the wisp changed color over and over again, every shade every hue, directing the lights given by Tara in their intricate dance. Even the horses were entranced.

Finally the wisp began to slow and the bells softened. Isaac and Tara began to feel deeply sleepy, their eyes weighted, until at last each fell into an unmatched slumber. The wisp finished and returned to its native blue, the balls of light falling and bouncing in the grass. Then it floated up into the tree and dispersed into the branches.

Tara woke the next morning with Dragonfly nuzzling her. She felt woozy, and at first her eyes did not want to focus. She sat up in the grass, feeling as though she still slept. "Dragonfly, stop"

Tara picked up a pebble and tossed it at Isaac, who had rolled off of the trunk and slept face down in the dirt. It struck him and he snorted and jolted, sitting up eyes wide.

Isaac rubbed his face, his hair poked sideways in the front. He felt that his head was full of wool. "Ughh, that was..." He stretched his arms. "That did happen, right? I didn't just dream it, did I?"

Tara reached over to where the lights had fallen three hollow clear orbs lay in the grass. She picked one up and said, "It happened, some sort of enchantment as well. Look at this, the wisp made the light solid. I'll have to show these to the Mother."

"How did you know to create the lights for it?"

"A brother named Chaign told me about it. He said that if you ever encountered a wisp that wasn't red to create the lights for them, they like to perform. Being connected to the land through magic creates some attraction that draws the wisps out. It probably lives inside this tree."

"What about the red wisps?"

"He told me to run."

Isaac smiled.

"Seriously. A red wisp is an angry wisp, and they are powerful with magic. It knocked both of us out."

"I suppose I should leave the magical things to you." He patted the tree and said, "Not a bad performance at all." His stomach rumbled. "Wrath! I'm hungry. Let's hope there's an inn nearby so I can get a good meal."

Isaac buried the remains of the fire and tried to push his hair down, not meeting with success. Tara placed the three orbs in her knit bag. The pair continued the ride north, the road would lead to Tarlow Junction, if that was where Tara would lead.

It was almost two hours before a building appeared along the road. It was as tall as any that they had seen since leaving Tarlow, with a steep roof covered in wood shingles. A stable was off-set across a green, and beyond that was a patch of garden. The garden pressed up to the woods, a straight line marked the separation of the tended land and the wild. A thin path ran off into the oak and maple forest but was mostly hidden by undergrowth.

A teen not much younger than Isaac took their horses to the stable, and Tara and Isaac went into the Oak Ale Roadhouse. Inside was cleaner than most. The innkeeper was a short man, mostly bald. His wife stood behind him, fanning herself. She was larger than most and wore a silly blue hat.

The man said, "Good day, good day. Yes, a fine day. A most wonderful day. What can I do for you, you fine young couple."

Isaac said, "I'd like breakfast. Tara?"

"That would be wonderful."

"Hmm, well that could be a problem. Yes it could, because it's afternoon already, and once it's afternoon breakfast isn't made," the innkeeper spoke without any ill will, simply stating the facts of his inn.

"You're sure we can't get breakfast? Some eggs, bacon, toast? None of that? No ham? No fruit? Nothing?" said Isaac, slipping into the strange patterns that the innkeeper used.

Tara looked at the innkeeper's wife and smiled, she smiled back. Then she nudged her husband, almost knocking him down. He said, "Fine, yes, fine. Breakfast it is. Right away with breakfast. Just sit anywhere. Anywhere you like."

Tara and Isaac took a booth with a window view of the road. The glass was thick and warped, and the road looked twisted and broken. A few others sat in the dining room, mostly minding their own business except to stop and give the newcomers the once over. Clearly not a threat to steal their ale, they returned to staring at it.

Tara said, "When Senior Technologist Pierce introduced you he said that you had been a student of his."

"Yeah. My father has worked with him for years. When my older sister showed skill in the magical arts she studied under him. When I was old enough to apprentice I tried as well."

"It sounds like it didn't work out."

"Not so much."

"I'm sorry, I didn't mean to bring up old problems."

"Don't worry. I didn't get into trouble or anything. I was good with the technical parts of the trade, but I didn't have any feel for the magic, none. It was a mutual decision to terminate my apprenticeship. After that Pierce helped me get into the Royal Guard. I was almost eighteen then."

"So you're twenty now?" Tara asked.

"Yep. Twenty and seeing the world. As long as we're asking questions, do you have any family?"

Tara nodded. "Yes, parents. No brothers or sisters."

"Do you miss them?"

"Not as much as I used to. I see them when I'm in Riversea. Usually happens every couple of years. I love them dearly, but they understand the responsibilities that my undertakings carry. My mother misses me more outwardly. She says that my father worries himself silly after I leave."

Isaac half smiled. He said, "I hope my family has similar feelings given my leaving, but I don't think that will be the case. Ahh, here comes breakfast."

Two plates filled with hearty breakfast were served by the innkeeper's wife. She said, "Don't be put off by Jack, he's got his ways of doing things, and it's done him well."

Tara said, "Don't worry, we weren't. And thank you for the breakfast."

"You're most welcome, daughter. If you need anything else don't hesitate to ask."

Tara smiled, slightly surprised. "We will, thank you."

The lady returned to her fan behind the bar, filling one of the men's mugs. Isaac said quietly, "Strange. She recognized you as a Way mage."

"I think there may be more to her than just an innkeeper's wife, but who can say?" Tara smiled and the pair fell to eating.

Once they had finished Isaac said, "How long do you think it will take to reach Serac?"

"If we took only the roads, about three weeks. I know of a few paths that will take some time off. It's hard to say exactly," answered Tara as she grabbed a piece of toast that Isaac had not touched. "Do you mind?"

Isaac smiled, "Not at all."

Tara wolfed the toast down and stood up. Isaac followed her to the front and he paid for the food, and for the care provided the horses. "Thanks for the breakfast, even if it was later than usual."

"Not a problem. No, sir. Not a problem at all. Thanks for stopping, and safe journeys," the innkeeper answered rapidly.

Once outside Isaac said, "I'll be glad to never hear from him again."

Tara laughed once and said, "Now that's not nice, Isaac. Ah, here are the horses."

Isaac looked at the horses and tipped the stable boy well. He smiled and said, "Thanks, sir."

Isaac smiled and said, "Heh, me a sir."

They mounted their horses and began to ride the road when from behind them a man said, "Excuse me, but I could not help but overhear that you are headed to Serac."

Tara and Isaac stopped their horses and turned to face the speaker, a most remarkable looking man.

Twenty-eight

Dragonfly shifted his weight and neighed. Tara said to the man, "That's correct. We are going to Serac."

The man nodded, his hooded cloak covering his face. "Wonderful."

Isaac's mouth twitched and he asked, "Is there some way we can help you, sir?"

"I offend you. Please forgive me." The man pulled back his hood revealing a bald head. His skin was golden brown, his eyes were large and deep blue, his nose flat and broad. His cheekbones were prominent, pointing to his large lips. His lower lip was lined with gold. From his chin a curved beard was wrapped with overlapping blue and gold ribbon, a tuft of black hair burst from the end. His ears pointed sharply. Neither Tara nor Isaac could tell, but if his face and neck were any indication his body was lean and muscular. His r's rolled into something of a purr as he spoke slowly, still feeling the words as he used them; "I am Shen'xhin'mhen. I too am headed to Serac, but, I seem to have lost my way. As you might imagine, I am not from these parts."

Isaac, continually cautious, said, "And just where exactly are you from?"

"Yes, the nervous associate. I am from the north, the Tan'Su'th, by way of Midsun."

Tara nodded, muttering, "A Su'th." Then to Shen'xhin'mhen, "I take it you mean to travel with us to Serac?"

"That would be ideal, yes, the sorcerer. I am hoping to reach the Sorcerer Homes for the Fall Festival. I have been told that it is an amazing occasion and would like to see it for myself."

Tara smiled, "Another that sees through my guise, is it so poor? I for one would not have an aversion to you coming with us. What do you think, Isaac?"

Isaac eyed the man and said, "I don't know, Tara. Shen'xhin'mhen? How many others travel with you?"

"Only my pet."

Isaac's head bobbed back and forth, an internal struggle. "I don't see why not."

Shen'xhin'mhen smiled, revealing remarkably sharp canines. "Wonderful, I will fetch him."

The man bowed and then hurried around the building leaving Tara and Isaac alone. Tara said, "I've never seen a Su'th before, much less talked with one. This will be interesting."

Isaac said, "I hope interesting is the word for it. Did you see his eyes? I've never seen that color before. How about his teeth? And how do you get this lost going to Serac from Midsun?"

"I couldn't say, Isaac, I couldn't say. Don't fret, I have a good feeling about this man."

"I'll take that as some comfort, daughter."

"I am ready to travel to the amazing city Serac," said Shen'xhin'mhen. He stood nearly on top of them.

Isaac yipped, "Silent enough." Then seeing the massive cat, a lion, beside him he said, "Wrath! You never said anything about that!"

"He is my...pet."

Isaac pulled Randa away, though the horse did not seem concerned. "I was expecting a bird or a dog, not that!"

Tara grinned, "Relax, Isaac, the horses would have bolted if it was dangerous. Shen'xhin'mhen."

"Please call me Xhin'mhen, the sorcerer."

"Please call me Tara. Xhin'mhen. What is this beautiful beast's name?" she asked. The grin had taken hold of her whole face. The cat seemed to smile at being called beautiful.

Shen'xhin'mhen bowed slightly. "This is Xer'tala'n." The cat dropped its head and blinked slowly. "He is quite friendly. You must understand, my people have a wonderful relationship with such, hmm, beasts as you say. Your horses realize this."

Tara looked to Isaac. She said, "First the wisp and now a Su'th. This is turning into an adventure. Do you have a horse, Xhin'mhen?"

"No. I walk, but do not worry, I can keep up."

Isaac said, "It's already late, if we are to make any progress today we should get going."

Shen'xhin'mhen trotted easily along with the horses. On his back was a pack that swung from side to side as he went. Xer'tala'n followed behind the Su'th, keeping up easily. Neither seemed to tire. Tara led the way north continuing on the well-used road. Other travelers, merchants mostly, openly gawked at the Su'th and his lion, but said nothing.

The weather was pleasant, warm but not muggy as it often was at that time of year. A gentle breeze flowed down from the mountains. The trees and grass swayed in the easy blowing wind. The pace was fast, demanded by the late start and the strange tidings.

As the sun approached the Hurichs to the west, the traveling company stopped to prepare their camp. Isaac tied Randa to a tree to keep him from wandering. Tara as always allowed Dragonfly to roam, and he grazed on the patches of green grass.

Shen'xhin'mhen asked, "Shall I send Xer'tala'n to hunt? He is most skilled."

Isaac looked at the big cat. He had lain down in a patch of grass taller than most in the shade of an oak and looked quite self-satisfied. "We have some bread, but why not send him. I wouldn't mind some rabbit."

The lion yawned and stretched, then stood and stalked away into the forest. Isaac broke some branches and prepared the fire. He used the lens from Celsius's bag to focus the sun's waning beams and after about a minute the grass and tinder burned fiercely. "Not a bad trick. Celsius has two notebooks filled with direction on how to use the things in this bag. It's almost as though he was planning to pass it on to someone."

Shen'xhin'mhen said, "Who is this Celsius?"

Tara sat near the fire. She said, "He is part of the reason we are going to Serac. An animate, do you know what that is?"

"The mek'ana. Yes, I know. My people recall them, it is an ancient term," Shen'xhin'mhen answered as he sat cross-legged near Tara. He had removed his cloak and wore a loose tan shirt with a gold embroidered collar and what appeared to be a long, dark orange skirt but it was split in the middle, hakama. It too had gold embroidery. The voluminous fabric was light and fluttered, begging to be touched.

Tara continued, "Someone built an animate like no one has seen before, save for legend. It attacked and killed the children of the leaders of the Rousan. The Eagles."

"Such a mek'ana." He said envisioning the brute. "Did it also kill Celsius?"

"Sadly yes, though his death did help save the one of the children. Isaac was there."

Isaac stared into the fire, tending it to be strong. His jaw had hardened. "I would rather not speak of it."

Tara asked, "May I tell him, Isaac?" Isaac nodded and Tara continued, "One of the children was Isaac's wife-to-be. She did not survive the animate's attack. When the horror was finally stopped, the Council of the Five Eagles voted to expel the House of Animate from the Empire. At that announcement, I saw and followed a man that was a thief. I had healed him some years earlier. In chasing him this distracted us, and Isaac brought it down with a stone."

Isaac seeing where the story was going had taken out the bird and handed it first to Tara who then handed it to Shen'xhin'mhen. He gazed closely at it, holding it up to the sun, his dark blue eyes expressing the same wonder that Tara and Isaac had when first gazing closely at it. "Amazing."

"That is what we thought, and we would have taken it to the House of Animate to be examined, except they had already fled."

"Would I be correct in thinking that you believe this thief to be connected to the mek'ana?"

Tara said, "I have that suspicion, yes. I do not think him to be the maker, but…I don't know. It seems wise to consult the House of Animate on this matter."

Shen'xhin'mhen tossed a small stick into the fire and said, "It is strange. I recall a mek'ana two years ago? A little more, paid a visit to the Tan'Su'th, the Imperial Island no less."

Isaac glanced at him, fire casting shadows. "Why would you know such things?"

Shen'xhin'mhen laughed once without humor, "I was an entertainer to the Emperor's court."

Tara's brow had furrowed. "Do you know anything else about this animate?"

"I am afraid not. I did not see it, though it was quite popular in its time there as I recall. Ah, here is Xer'tala'n."

The lion did come, with not one but four rabbits held delicately in its mouth. Shen'xhin'mhen stood and took the rabbits from the lion, saying, "See, he is an excellent hunter. I will prepare the rabbits. Not fancy, but it will taste good."

The Su'th opened his bag and after rummaging to the bottom took out a small but intricate knife. The blade was not more than two inches long, the fire shimmered in the polished metal. Shen'xhin'mhen used the knife to quickly skin and clean the rabbits. Before cooking them he rummaged through the grass until he found the plant he was looking for and crushed the leaves into the rabbits' flesh. Then he arranged the spits to hold them over the flame. It appeared that the sticks used would catch fire at any second, but they never did. He quickly showed Isaac the easiest way to turn them.

He said, "You will excuse me, I must pray."

The Su'th moved away from the camp and again sat cross-legged. The lion rolled up from the grass and went to sit next to him. Shen'xhin'mhen put his hands on his knees and closed his eyes. The lion's eyes did not close but neither did they move.

Isaac turned the rabbits twice and still the pair had not moved. In some way they appeared to disappear, a trick of the fading light, blending with the earth and plants around them. Isaac said quietly, "An interesting pair to say the least."

"Very. Look at them just sitting there, almost invisible. I can't help but wonder about that animate though. I feel as though I am staring at a great puzzle, but the pieces are upside down or missing. The Earth shows me flickers, now and again of pieces I should turn or search for, but I can't remember most the time once I wake. Maybe that's for the best."

"Well, if the House of Animate can't help us, maybe our new friend will take us to his homeland and we can get some help there. Why not? I don't have anything else to do. The further I get from Tarlow the better." Isaac breathed deeply and smiled meekly, "The rabbit does smell wonderful."

Shen'xhin'mhen said, "I told you it would."

Isaac and Tara both jumped. Isaac shook his head and said, "Damn it! My heart can't take such surprises, not after that animate."

The Su'th pulled the first of two spits off of the fire and said, "I apologize, Isaac. I do not mean to scare you. Be careful it is most hot."

Shen'xhin'mhen broke the spit in half handing a full rabbit to Tara and Isaac. The second spit was removed and the largest of the rabbits was placed at Xer'tala'n's feet. The lion smiled and ripped into the cooked meat. Shen'xhin'mhen said, "As always you have done well my friend." Then he muttered two sentences in the Su'th tongue. The lion shook its head.

The rabbit was quickly eaten along with some bread, and a water skin was emptied. Only the fire cast light and that had weakened slightly. Isaac fell asleep watching the firelight move over the lion's short fir, as silk over rocks, revealing dips and hollows.

He was also the last to wake, sitting bolt upright. The sun was cool still. The air was clean, smelling of pine with a hint of burnt wood. Dew covered most everything. The Su'th knelt nearby, packing things into his bag. He said, "You are awake. That is good. Tara tells me that today we go from the road."

Isaac looked around. Tara was not there. "Where is the daughter?"

"Hmm, I do not know for certain, she said that she would find the trail, then return to us. She left one half hour ago, about. Here, drink this, it will help clear your head," said the Su'th with a smile.

Isaac took the ratty cup from him and looked at the black liquid with skepticism, then drank the dark fluid down. His face twitched. "Ughh, what is that?"

"A drink from my homeland. Cih'do. Pack your things, Tara wants us ready when she returns."

Isaac could feel the liquid in his stomach, it sloshed around emptily. He stood up, his ears buzzing. His flesh tingled just slightly and he smiled.

Shen'xhin'mhen said, "Good, yes?"

"I'll wait to say that for sure, but I'm awake alright."

Isaac packed his things, shaking the dirt from his blanket and he tried to beat some of the wrinkles out of his clothes. It did not help. Finally he sat down next to Shen'xhin'mhen, and they both waited for Tara to return. Birds chirped, and a wagon rolled past drawn by two horses. The farmer said hello and disappeared down the road. Finally, Tara returned.

"I found it. This path is always hard for me to find. I would swear that it moves, so we had better hurry or I'll have to look for it again. It will take a few days off of our journey."

Isaac settled into the saddle, and with the Su'th trotting along with his lion the travelers set cross country for Tara's shortcut.

As they picked their way through the forest, with its sparse oaks, maples and sycamores and the more dense pines, Isaac asked, "How do you know about this trail?"

"How do you think The Way of Health gets around so quickly? It's not as though we can fly." Then she added mischievously, "Not all of us anyhow. Plus there are times that it is just better to avoid the cities. The idea of cutting corners is hardly new, its just that few people do it these days."

Isaac ducked under the bough of an oak that seemed determined to unhorse him. "That makes sense, I guess I wasn't thinking."

"No it's fine. Really when you think about it, there is so much of the world that is rarely touched it would be easy for anyone to go anywhere with not much attention being drawn to themselves. Like, say, a rogue mage. There," She pointed ahead of her. "That grove of pines marks the trail head. It cuts across, avoiding the Tarlow Junction, then we will follow the road to the border with Kurn, then go through the hills. Pretty easy really. And we should arrive in Serac in time for the Fall Festival. It's good luck that you met us, Xhin'mhen. You would have missed it if you hadn't."

The Su'th smiled and nodded.

The grove of trees was seven slender, tall pines jutting from the dry earth. The trees closely circled a ten foot tall stone that stood perfectly upright. The trees were equally spaced, and where the eighth should have stood a trail of unequal stones, barely visible under the dirt and plant scruff, ran off to the northeast, disappearing as it traced the uneven landscape.

The center stone was dark gray with a crack of white that ran vertically. One face was curved inward, a sweeping concave. When Shen'xhin'mhen saw the obelisk he ran past the humans and dropped to his knees in front of it, sending little wisps of dirt into the air. The Su'th said, "I do not believe it."

Tara asked, "What is it Xhin'mhen? I've always thought that it was placed here by someone, but nobody I have ever asked could tell me anything about that stone. Everyone thought it just marks the trail."

"Hmm, give me a moment." The Su'th ran his fingers down the ridge of white stone. The lion paced, turning violently. "There is a reason Tara that you find this place difficult to locate. It is protected by Su'th wards. Ancient, but still powerful. I must say I am impressed that you could find it more than once. You must forgive me, I underestimate your power, sorcerer."

Tara dismounted Dragonfly and said, "I will take that as a compliment."

Isaac swung down and his boots kicked little clouds of dust into the air. He put his hand on the stone. "It's really cold. That's odd, being so exposed to the sun."

Shen'xhin'mhen put his hands on his knees. "I cannot open it alone, the warding requires the hands of two Su'th." The lion grumbled, and Xhin'mhen answered in his tongue. They argued back and forth for a minute as the two humans watched, unsure of what was happening. The Su'th said softly, "It would be worth it. I agree." He stood and faced the humans, holding out a small gray stone that he took from a pouch on his belt. "This is a xho'ka, pledgestone. In ancient times they magically bound those who promised on them to their word. The xho'ka's power was destroyed by the Lot'hak, but the ceremony remains. I ask that you pledge not to reveal what you see, if you will, place your thumb to the stone."

Isaac looked concerned, but touched the stone and said, "I will not reveal what I see, I promise on the memory of my Cassandra."

Tara followed, "I pledge, Shen'xhin'mhen, to keep secret what is shown to us."

Shen'xhin'mhen nodded, saying, "Thank you. This is not a trivial matter. What you are about to see is not often shown to humans, distrust from past transgressions has made it so." The Su'th swung his pack around, and undid the knot that held it shut. He looked into the bag and pulled out a black cloth wrap. "Hierophant, if you please."

Xer'tala'n stretched and roared. As he stretched, the cat's limbs changed. Fingers unwound from the front paws. His torso shortened and took on a human shape. The back legs changed, only slightly, as the lion pushed into an upright standing position. Now a man with the head and mane of a lion, covered in the cat's short fur stood before them. His muscled body made Shen'xhin'mhen look feeble. Xer'tala'n's tail flicked, and his feline jaw cracked. Shen'xhin'mhen handed the Su'th the cloth and he wrapped it around his waist.

Isaac put one finger out and said dumbfounded, "This is unexpected… what…"

Xer'tala'n's lion head bobbed slightly. His voice was deep and when he spoke the hard sounds filled with purrs and growls, "A question that is often asked even by our own when first viewed. As blessings for my devotion to Her, Ku'na'shi has marked my body, remaking it in Her image. I was as Shen'xhin'mhen once, passing for human, or nearly so, should I need." He stretched, extending his arms to the sky. "It is good to be standing."

Xhin'mhen said, "Tala'n is a Hierophant of the highest order, and I am honored to be so accompanied. As should you."

Tara's head turned to one side, but she looked straight ahead. "I have the strange sensation that you have not been entirely truthful with us Xhin'mhen."

Shen'xhin'mhen purred for a moment, thinking, any smile gone. He said, "Yes, I am sorry. Please forgive my deceit. We, the Su'th, do not trust our secrets often with man. Especially yours, the sorcerer, but this is important."

Tala'n ended the conversation, saying, "We see if we can open the ward."

Both Su'th stopped talking and turned their attention to the stone. They seemed to fiddle with it, running their hands over the smooth, cold surface without any success.

Isaac said, "What—"

But he was hushed by Tara. She mouthed, "Just wait."

There was one loud crunch underneath the stone and the Su'th stepped back. The earth began to shake, sending Isaac off balance and a pounding of what sounded like a thousand hammers on anvils assaulted their ears. The stone pushed up slowly, making a pile of dirt around its base. The pounding stopped, the white vein of rock split, and the concave side fell with an ominous thud into the dirt. The cloud sprayed into Isaac's face. He coughed and wiped his eyes. The stone was hollow; handholds bolted to the wall led down into the gloom. Stale air filled the grove, then was dispersed to the forest.

Xer'tala'n stepped up onto the stone and squatted, looking down into the hole. His tail flicked madly. "It is not far down to the floor."

Isaac said quickly, "Okay, okay, stop. What is this? You're not going down there are you?"

Xer'tala'n smiled, sharp teeth everywhere. "This, my hesitant friend, is a Su'th sanctuary, ancient. And I am certainly going down there. Stay with your horse if you like." The cat swung around and descended the rungs quickly.

Shen'xhin'mhen said, "Do not worry, Isaac, it is safe. The magic of Ku'na'shi protects this place." He followed Xer'tala'n into the hole.

Tara slapped Isaac on the back and said, "Come on, it will be interesting." A blue light popped into existence, causing no effect until she started down the rungs into the depths.

Isaac shook his head, saying to himself, "Wrath, what am I doing?" He tied Randa to a pine tree and then followed the others into the sanctuary. The only light was the soft glow from the orb that balanced near Tara. The walls were more of the dark stone, but it was pushed in in places by the roots of the pines that marked it. The dust of ancients coated everything. Where they stood was actually the end of a hallway that at the other end, not far down, had a huge double door.

"The crest of Su'thele'n!" Xer'tala'n said in his own tongue to Shen'xhin'mhen.

"I would not believe it, did I not see it," Shen'xhin'mhen answered, running his hand over it.

Past the doors, which swung slowly into the walls, the hallway descended into a large room. Except for the intrusion of roots and dust, the room was in perfect order. A table in the middle of the room still had papers on it. Xer'tala'n took a torch from the wall, blew on it, and it lit the room with golden fire. "That is better," he said to all.

Two other rooms branched from the central room. One large, filled with beds, the other an armory. Shen'xhin'mhen stood over the table, his finger tracing a line of writing. "If I am reading this correctly, this claims to be one of the first sanctuaries founded under Su'thele'n in his war against the Lot'hak. It was abandoned when the forces marched for the final campaign."

"That is the second mention of the Lot'hak. Who are they?" Tara asked.

Xer'tala'n shook his head and said, "It is a shame how much man has forgotten as time passes. They are the, hmm, I believe you call them the Harrow."

Isaac said laughingly, "The same Harrow my mother told stories about to scare me?"

Xer'tala'n said sharply, "If they are only children's stories now then thank Su'thele'n, for they were not stories when this place was created. I know that you cannot understand what this means to Xhin'mhen and I."

Isaac said, "No…its…its my fault. Clearly I'm not up on history the way I ought to be."

Xer'tala'n laughed, deep and thunderous. "Do not worry human, I will teach you history. Let us explore the rest and then reseal this place. We were not looking for a sanctuary and we have far yet to travel."

The sleeping quarters stood waiting for its occupants to return, a thing that had not happened. The armory stood deserted, racks that once housed weapons of every shape and size were empty. Save one sword, a long curved blade, untouched by time. The handle was made of a white milky stone, perhaps ivory of some sort carved into a slender dog head. Isaac took the katana from where it sat and drew it. "It's beautiful," he said, pointing it with one hand. He stared down the blade. "May I take it?"

346

The Su'th laughed. Xer'tala'n said, "If you wish. It is not of service resting here. Can you employ such a tool?"

Isaac looked down and said, "Not well, but thank you for letting me take it, it's a beautiful blade. If only Cassandra was here to see it, she had a love for such things. It irritated her mother to no end." He smiled a moment, lost in time.

Xer'tala'n extinguished the torch in the same way he had lit it and said, "Let us go, there is nothing else to see."

The four climbed back to the surface. Dragonfly stood near the hole waiting for Tara to re-appear, he stomped the dirt when she did. She said, "It's fine I was safe. Silly thing."

The two Su'th stood on either side of the stone and lifted gently. The curved stone clicked once, and then the pounding started, the entire process reversed itself. Save for the disturbed dirt there was no sign that anything had happened. Isaac said, "Well, Tara, lead the way."

Trahn Entrah rested heavily in his chair, left hand spilling out, touching the floor. Black circles under his eyes told anyone that did not know that the First had not slept well in weeks. To make matters worse his magic had faltered, a lack of concentration caused by the lack of sleep he thought, but that would not explain the recent failures of expensive projects by other mages in the House.

And there was the nightmarish debacle in Earlsburg, which claimed Master Jannan's position. His vote had split the House, verbal confrontations exploded in the library or dining room or in the white hallways everyday. He could no longer contain the emotion. Frederick had offered to intervene, but Trahn could not think of anything that he could do to help.

The worst news had been yet to come. When the pigeon landed Trahn's heart nearly failed. In retrospect he almost wished it had. He did not want to think of it. The death of the Eagle's children, caused by an animate. When the animists arrived from the Rousan Empire they would answer for the most disastrous, most horrifying, most unthinkable event that had ever befallen the House. That is how he felt now, but Trahn was not known for steadiness in these recent days.

The mage shook his head violently, trying to stir from his stupor. Three seconds of violent activity was followed with a groan and the mage, wrapped in white, fell back into stillness. What was strange was that he had never been so overwhelmed by the duties of the House. In past battles of will Trahn had shown that he was a capable leader.

Now though he struggled to focus, distractions mounted against him and the magic that he had made so much a part of his life retreated, swept from him, from the House, by an unseen force. The other mages under his watch suffered as well, but not in such a vivid manner. As it now stood the House of Animate did not even plan to involve itself in the Fall Festival. With the other struggles before him and his further sinking into misery Trahn did not even see a reason to try.

As word spread about the terrible things, the House had been forced to lock its doors. The guard stopped most of the anger before it reached the House, and Celia Hurn dealt with the rest, but the message was sent. The House of Animate teetered. Trahn shook his head and grumbled, "Where are you my friend? Where are you?"

Twenty-nine

The caravan to Serac made good progress that day. Even with the detour to explore the sanctuary the trail gave way quickly. Daylight was fading and the night's fire was started. The camp was in the shadow of a rocky mound; sprays of long grass popped from in between the stones. The Su'th had climbed to the top of it and sparred in silhouette. Tara watched the pair, their movements slow and hypnotic, but she had been silent as they rode.

Isaac said, "You've been quiet."

Tara who sat with her elbows wrapped around her knees answered, "It's not as I have known Xhin'mhen for a long amount of time, but I'm worried that I misjudged him horribly. And you could have allowed me to ask one thousand questions about the lion, and I would never have come close to guessing his secret."

Isaac looked up at the Su'th. They had stopped moving and stood facing the sun, casting two very different shadows. "I don't think your first impression was wrong. Xhin'mhen seems to be a good man. Just because he did not reveal every secret to us doesn't change that. Besides, he didn't send a crazy animate to kill us, so they both have that going for them. Don't feel bad about Xer'tala'n. Mother didn't explain that to me."

Tara smiled weakly. "True, nor mine. The world that I thought was wide is vaster still. I just need some time to digest things, to try to understand what I have seen."

"You'll get your chance. It appears they have finished."

The humans watched the Su'th descend the rocks, each with grace and style, Xer'tala'n showing exceptional balance and a sense of power, while Shen'xhin'mhen moved more recklessly. Several times he seemed to fall before miraculously stepping to increasingly improbable places. Finally giving up on his path he jumped from the rocks and landed lightly next to Xer'tala'n who laughed. "You let your feet out think your head, young one."

"Ech, I am where I meant to be," Shen'xhin'mhen answered.

Xer'tala'n shrugged and his tail flicked, but he said nothing. As the pair sat down Tara began to interrogate Shen'xhin'mhen. "Given what Xer'tala'n has said, Xhin'mhen, I take it that he is not your pet."

Before Shen'xhin'mhen could answer Xer'tala'n started to chuckle, a grumbling, rolling roar. "No, I am not his pet. Although I do serve him; his well-being I am charged to protect."

Tara said, "Which makes you who or what exactly, Shen'xhin'mhen?" Her irritation was evident.

"Again I offer my apologies for misleading you, sorcerer, but it was necessary."

Tara countered, "I understand the need for it, but if you truly are traveling to Serac perhaps you would care to explain why."

"Yes, I see that we have angered you. Does the associate also feel so betrayed?"

Isaac shook his head once. "She said she had a good feeling about you. Except for the shock of you appearing from nowhere again and again, your company has been good."

With her voice slightly louder Tara said, "Explain things to me, please. I've already pledged on your stone. I will not betray that confidence, no matter how I feel."

Shen'xhin'mhen nodded, "You are wise for your age. Wise for your human nature as well. My name is Shen'xhin'mhen. That much is precisely true. My bodyguard? Yes, that works, is Xer'tala'n. But he can tell his own story, as you have discovered."

The Su'th continued, "I am the second son of the youngest sister to the Su'th Emperor. My mother is Shen'xho'shu. My father is Shen'xi, a royal minister, by birth and by marriage. My mother's brother is Emperor Sinu'thele'n. Thele'n is a taken name, given with honor and burden to the Emperor, to remember Su'thele'n. He rules the Tan'Su'th, 'The Three Su'th' as it were. The three great cities enclosed.

"It is also truth that I, we, are going to Serac and we will pass ourselves as entertainers. At home for what little it is worth I am the Minister of Entertainment. Truly a glorified position founded for my blood. Official duties are basically to stay out of the way of the important government officials, a job that is easily done."

Tara said bluntly, "So you're basically unimportant royalty."

Shen'xhin'mhen frowned, "Yes. But it is not what I would be, given the chance. That is how you find me here. Chance. I am nearly forty, fairly young for my people. Xer'tala'n is near ninety if I am not mistaken."

Xer'tala'n said, "You are right."

Tara asked, "How does age factor into any of this?"

"It is convoluted, give me time to explain. I will start with the aspects of Ku'na'shi. She is our god and she has cared for us since the times of Su'thele'n. To your eyes she would appear as a cat in human form. To us she is only Su'th. A young Su'th hungers terribly to see the world outside of Tan'Su'th. I know I have felt it, and Xer'tala'n before me. Almost all Su'th do. Some go to the west, some travel south. There are many north of your city Midsun. As we age the travel lust dies. In its place grows an understanding, a love for Ku'na'shi.

"As a Su'th's devotion grows, so Ku'na'shi rewards the devotee. We take the traits of our god. Most do not gain many, some gain none. Some, Xer'tala'n, are truly favored. Not that he has not given greatly to Her. He has. I have seen him train, I have seen him pray. I can only hope to emulate such devotion."

Xer'tala'n interrupted, "He does well."

"For all the good it has done me," Shen'xhin'mhen answered. "The royal family, for the most part, does not suffer from the wanderlust of our brethren. I do, which in some ways sets me apart, a chance possibility, not unheard of. But the result of that settling is complete devotion, shown by almost full aspecting by a very young age, thirty, perhaps younger, thirty-five at the latest." Tara and Isaac both nodded.

Shen'xhin'mhen said, "Your minds race, you begin to see my condition. The young aspecting is in turn taken as a sign from Ku'na'shi that the family is meant to rule.

"Over the years there have been eight changes in ruling family, none by bloodshed, all through the divine choice of Ku'na'shi. My family line has ruled for over six-hundred years. Passed Emperor to first born, be that son or daughter.

"Here is where again chance sets me upon a course. With the advancement of your civilization here in the south there is growing call for the Tan'Su'th to open its borders to trade, to share in goods and education. To live in harmony. A beautiful notion if it can be attained. But enough with power do not think it can be, and so the laws of separation remain. I myself believe it is time to forgive past failures and share our knowledge, but I am only the Minister of Entertainment, a position held without power." Shen'xhin'mhen smiled, a self-mocking grin.

"The Emperor, at the insisting of those such as my mother, has warmed in the past decade to perhaps entering into communion with your kind."

Tara said, "It's not as though we are complete fools."

Xer'tala'n smiled, all teeth, and said, "Your people have forgotten much. The teachings of Ku'na'shi tell us that a people that forgets its history is dead."

Shen'xhin'mhen said, "Enough Tala'n. He and I do not agree on this. Not that he dislikes you particularly."

"For humans you are quiet pleasant. As Xhin'mhen has said, you are wise for your kind."

The humans shifted uncomfortably. Shen'xhin'mhen continued before any more discomfort could be rendered. "Now we come to the chance that brings me here. The Emperor has heard rumors of a Su'th treasure in your land. An artifact given to Su'thele'n by Ku'na'shi herself. A gift believed lost to history, drowned in time.

"It is also known that occasionally, Ku'na'shi holds back her aspects from a person until they have performed a task for her. It is not that she does not favor them, but she requires greater devotion from those she would truly favors.

"So as you see many strings come together. I support a perhaps best described radical ideal, in the opening of my homeland to mankind. I have not taken on the aspects of Ku'na'shi despite my devotion to her. The Emperor wants the

Ta'ke'shya Ku'na'shi located and if possible returned. If this were to be done by someone that believes my mother's ideals, it would prove a strong token on her behalf.

"When this opportunity was presented to me, I, as Minister of Entertainers, despite my important duties, realized that it could serve both my family and myself well. If I am to prove my value, to the Tan'Su'th and to Ku'na'shi, it would be in recovering, or at the very least confirming the existence of Her gift to us. The Ta'ke'sh. And so that is how age comes into all of this. And it is also why we go to Serac."

Tara nodded slowly and said, "That seems a great burden, attempting to recover a gift from a god."

Shen'xhin'mhen shrugged, "Sometimes it seems so. There are times we long for the familiar faces of home."

Xer'tala'n said, "Ku'na'shi has been with us in our journey. I feel her presence strong since we learned of Serac."

Tara said, "I would think that that would be the first place you would look for an artifact of that sort. The city was founded for and around the Houses after all."

Shen'xhin'mhen answered, "It is not only that mankind is kept from learning of our kind. The Tan'Su'th is slow in learning of man's advance. Serac was not known to the Imperial court."

Xer'tala'n said in the Su'th tongue, "It is not virtue to speak against your Emperor, Xhin'mhen."

And was answered in kind, "I do not mean it as insult, it is sad truth."

"Only some see it as such. Remember your tongue when next you pray."

Shen'xhin'mhen's temper flared and he said sharply, "I shall, thank you for the reminder of piety."

Tara intervened in the Su'th argument, saying, "You have been true to your word and explained much. My eyes are open to things I did not know to exist."

Shen'xhin'mhen and Xer'tala'n glowered at each other but put the argument to rest for the time being. Shen'xhin'mhen said, "I am glad that I can allay the sorcerer's fears. Our secrecy was not meant as insult."

Isaac woke early the next morning, before the sun had poked above the horizon. The world was gray and chilly, but he could not sleep again. The Su'th whirled through his mind, much of the first layer of Shen'xhin'mhen had been exposed on Tara's command. The Su'th minister had been, in Isaac's opinion, amazingly willing to impart the Su'th's hidden truths. 'The pledgestone undoubtedly,' he thought to himself as he sat up. Shen'xhin'mhen and Tara each slept where they had lain the night before. Xer'tala'n was gone from his place of slumber. Isaac noticed movement in the corner of his eye, and turned his head to follow it.

The Su'th balanced on one leg, foot clinging to the rock that connected him to the earth. The slow movement of contorted balance exploded into a blinding display of martial arts skill. Some concepts Isaac recognized from his soldiering, most he did not, all was magnificent; a perfect blending of speed and strength, power and agility. The lion finished his practice and climbed to the top of the stones. He turned and faced the camp, beckoning his audience to join him.

Isaac climbed to the top of the rocks, not showing near the speed or grace of the Su'th. Xer'tala'n watched every move, traced every path. His tail flicked, impatience perhaps. That was what Isaac believed.

Isaac stood opposite the Su'th and only now realized the terrifying nature of him. The lion's eyes burned holes into Isaac as muscles rippled under short fur. A slight hunch hid his true height. His teeth were like daggers as he smiled at the man before him. Save all of that and it did not begin to explain the aura of the beast. Isaac felt nothing but awe.

Xer'tala'n rumbled low, "It is good, you control your senses."

The great cat dropped into a basic combat stance, balance shifting slightly on the stone. Isaac mirrored him. Slowly, Xer'tala'n began to move, basic strikes, matched by Isaac. It was similar to what he had learned in the Royal Guard but refined, cleansed. High, low, step. When the human drifted the Su'th corrected. Precision brought acceptance. The movements accelerated, changed, different order, and at each change Isaac kept pace.

The sun rose.

"That is good, Isaac. You move well for a man. If you like, we can continue such exercise."

354

"I would like that. May I ask you a question, Xer'tala'n?"

"I cannot stop you," the cat answered staring at the sun, sky gaining color.

"Why are you here?"

The lion shuddered, a silent laugh. "Shen'xhin'mhen would not be dissuaded from this journey. The Emperor could have commanded him stay, but did not. Maybe his mother intervened. Maybe he was glad to give his blood such an opportunity. Maybe it is just to be rid of one voice that calls for change. I do not know." He kneeled, finding comfort amongst the stone. "I, Xer'tala'n, Hierophant of Ku'na'shi was charged with his well-being during this task. And so I follow until we return and I am set free from the duty."

"You are not happy, are you?"

"There is no emotion in such commands from the Emperor, he speaks as the mouth of Ku'na'shi. I obey. In time I will see my home, until then and ever after my life is Hers."

"Your faith is commendable."

Xer'tala'n smiled, his whiskers curled. "It is not without its advantages. The others stir. You ride soon."

"What will you do, Xer'tala'n?"

"I will follow."

It was not long after that the travelers again set towards Serac. Tara's spirits seemed bolstered by the tale of the Su'th. Isaac wanted to ask her but the opportunity did not present itself. The path they followed stayed remarkably straight. It deviated from the line now and again but it took days from their journey.

Xer'tala'n walked upright for the most part and made conversation with the others on a range of subjects. In the evenings he would instruct Isaac in the ways of the Su'th martial arts. It distracted him from his loss, keeping his spirits up.

Once The Way of Health path ended and they returned to the road Xer'tala'n re-assumed the shape of the lion during the day. It was unusual but not shocking for the human eyes that fell upon him. Both Isaac and Tara continued to converse with him, and though his responses were limited to growls and expressions he was still involved fluently in the conversation. At night, or when he strayed from the roads, he took his true form.

Several days of traveling the road gave way to another less used Way of Health path. This pushed through the hilly northeast region of the Rousan and eventually crossed the border into Kurn. From there the road seemed short. Part of that was Xer'tala'n's companionship, but Serac truly seemed to be drawing them on.

It was late afternoon when the travelers could see the city. It glistened white in the sun. Shen'xhin'mhen murmured in awe, "Truly a home worthy of the sorcerers."

Without looking at the Su'th Tara said, "All that glitters is not gold. I do not care for the power struggle that its beauty contains."

The journey complete, Tara led the others through the streets of Serac. Even with the preparations for the Fall Festival the sight of the lion was unusual. The roads opened wide to allow them through. Even the gates to the Campus were open, the Campus Guard provided little resistance. The Wizard Houses were simply in too much of a hurry to allow their needs to be slowed at the gates. The lion's presence did, however, result in questions being asked. The guard, Roman Michaels, quickly said, "That'll cause quite a stir. Even with that Jota circus in. What's the business of the lion and its tamer?"

Tara answered, "They are with me, Roman."

His name spoken, Roman thought a moment, "Oh, Daughter Groundmender. I'm sorry I didn't recognize you. It's been a busy, busy week. Final prep for the festival. Go on in, I trust you know what you are doing."

"Thank you, Roman, if you see him give my love to Alexander."

"Sorry, Alex left his position here, joined up with a crew headed north. That's what I heard anyway."

"Oh," Tara said surprised, "In that case I give my love to you." She smiled.

Roman laughed, "That isn't so bad. May your stay in Serac be fruitful." Then he waved them on. The gate was already backing up, none wanting to cross near to Xer'tala'n.

The Campus was in rare form. Tent after tent had been erected in the grass fields. Stages rose from the ground preparing to house all manner of performance. Here and there a mage from one of the Houses would be clustered with a work crew, going over plans, or red-faced from some unrecoverable mistake. Booths stood in rows awaiting the peddlers and merchants that would soon offer up for sale cheap trinkets, valuable treasures, and everything in between. Brick ovens built in the last weeks prepared to cook the food that would feed the masses during the two-week festival.

Even now the inns and stables filled, the Fall Festival drew people from everywhere in the known world. It was an amazing sight, and Tara smiled when she looked into the eyes of Isaac and Xhin'mhen. The astonishment was unmistakable. Isaac may not have understood the importance of the Su'th sanctuary, but this he did, and it was unlike anything he had ever seen. He started to laugh in amazement. "I did not know that man could do such things. I had heard that it was worth seeing, but this. This is remarkable."

Xhin'mhen laughed as well, "I am deeply impressed, sorcerer. It is good that we have seen this. The Tan'Su'th did not begin to imagine."

Xer'tala'n grumbled and cocked his head to the side.

Tara laughed, "Don't worry, I'll make sure you get to see it all." Following the road, they came upon the walled garden of the Way. "Here. This is my House."

They entered the Way and as the front door snugged home she said, "Well, I will speak with the Mother."

Tara disappeared into the garden house. The Su'th and Isaac waited in the entrance room, its lushness welcoming them to The Way of Health, its comfort washing away the dust from the road. After a few minutes she returned. She said calmly, "The Mother is greatly interested in meeting all of you. Please follow me."

They went to the Mother's garden; the pool was calm, the plants lush. The Mother sat on a chair covered with yellow green moss. Her staff was held upright by a vine that reached from the wall. She wore earth colored cloth and stood to greet them. "The Way of Health welcomes you into our House, Isaac Samuelson."

Isaac bowed; it seemed the correct thing to do in the presence of the First. "Thank you."

Lilac smiled and said, "The Way of Health welcomes you to the Sorcerer Homes, Shen'xhin'mhen. I am glad that you have made the long journey to visit us."

It was clear that Tara had explained some of what had been happening to the Mother. Shen'xhin'mhen knelt before her, and said, "I do not know your ceremony; so I thank you."

Her voice soft, "Thank you for your concern. Please stand. Tara has dealt with the ceremony of the House. It sometimes seems trite but we must hold onto our history. It is an honor to have the Su'th Entertainment Minister as my guest. And this must be the lion, Xer'tala'n." The Mother knelt down before the lion and scratched his nose. "Tara is right you are a beautiful beast."

Lilac stood and said, "Tara told me of the animate, Isaac, that is explained. I would like to see it if I may."

"Yes, of course," Isaac answered, his voice smooth, taking its tone from her. "Just give me a moment to find it."

Lilac smiled, "Of course. I would think that Master Entrah would be most eager to see it, but it will be difficult to arrange such a meeting. I will see if it can be done."

"How do you mean, Mother?" Tara asked as Isaac unwrapped the animate and handed it to Lilac.

"The House of Animate has had its foundations buckled by the fire of Earlsburg and the murders in Tarlow. Trahn, the last I saw of him, was ghoulish. I would mark him for the undead did I not know. The banishment of Murdoch Jannan weighs heavily on him. I ramble." The Mother inspected the motionless animate. "Ah, yes, it is lovely. And you say that it could fly? A powerful magic gave this one life."

She handed it back to Isaac and said, "Shen'xhin'mhen. Tara did not explain what brings you to Serac."

"I have come for the festival. I am here along with Xer'tala'n to offer our abilities to the Sorcerer Homes. That they may provide entertainment for those that watch."

"Excellent." Her head bobbed once. "Feel free to move about the House, or go and wander the preparations for the festival. If you choose to stay here Tara can show you to a room. I will call on you later, minister, if you do not mind." The Mother finished talking and walked out of the room, distracted. There was no rudeness in her departure, she was simply gone.

358

Tara said, "And now you have met the Mother. This is her private garden and we should not linger here. There should be some free rooms along the west side. The Mother tells me that there are not many mages in Serac right now."

Isaac took the first room; it was completely overgrown and completely inviting. He settled down to nap, he could no longer resist the notion of rest. When Tara and the Su'th were alone in one of the larger available rooms Shen'xhin'mhen said, "I thank you for not telling the secrets that we carry, even to the First of your order. It means much to us."

"Xhin'mhen, I will not reveal what I am sworn not to reveal. You showed such trust in me, it would be shameful should I not honor it. Even with that said, do not think you can deceive the Mother. She is insightful in all things."

"Nevertheless I thank you, and I look forward to the festival. We could not be here without your help. May I someday repay it."

"Don't be too eager to pledge such things, or you will soon see me take you up on it. I'll leave you two alone. I'll be around."

With some struggle Tara managed to get the door to click shut, the last time had been the first time. Xer'tala'n wasted no time in aspecting from lion to Su'th. He said quietly in the Su'th tongue, "This is an impressive city. Yours may be correct in the thought of forgiveness. If the people live up to what the city proclaims."

Shen'xhin'mhen sat on the bed, grass bent under him. He plucked a blade and chewed it. "That's the first time you have softened your view, Tala'n. I'm surprised."

Xer'tala'n shrugged. "Perhaps Isaac and Tara have softened me. We shall see. If Ku'na'shi wishes it, then it shall be." He paused and changed the subject. "Isaac learns quickly, doesn't he?"

Xhin'mhen said, "Remarkably so, perhaps not only our martial forms. He seems a listener." Then he shrugged. "If he were Su'th he could be entrusted to your order. Unfortunate that he is not. I like these humans, as you do. I hope this is not the last that we see of them. I wish that I knew more of the mek'ana as well."

"That's an odd thing to think of."

"The humans were surprised to hear of the one that came to the Tan'Su'th a few years back."

Xer'tala'n said, "The mek'ana studied rune forms in one of the temples, and history with the World Keeper. Always polite from my brief contact. I should tell this to Tara when I have a chance, or you can." Xer'tala'n yawned. "Isaac had it right. Time for a nap. We will pray later."

The Hierophant's body again changed, this form always drifted to sleep easily. The lion spun twice, trying to find the exact location that would lend itself to the best nap and laid down. Xhin'mhen said, "I am going to go see the garden. After what Tara said of it I want to see it for myself."

The lion blinked and Shen'xhin'mhen got up and left the room, managing to get the door closed for a third time.

Shen'xhin'mhen made his way through the House. Here and there he noticed plants from his homeland. He had not paid attention to them before he left it, and he had not seen them this far south. In summer they bloomed reds and yellows and blues. He remembered that much. He was greeted by several other mages that carried out their duties. Xhin'mhen thanked them for the greeting and continued to the walled garden.

Outside the air was salty and cool, hinting at the night, but not yet given to it. He breathed in deeply once, and wandered among the trees, the giants. They were impressive, as Tara had said, growing to proportions that were not seen in the world, if the plants were ever seen at all.

Shen'xhin'mhen stopped in front of a purple flowering bush, silver green leaves spilled everywhere. 'This is a pleasant sight,' he thought to himself and sat down, legs crossed. He scratched at his right palm, flaking away dry skin.

Lilac's soothing voice asked, "Do you know that flower, minister?" She appeared from some place within the Great Garden.

Xhin'mhen nodded, his whole torso rocking. "I do, the fruit of the jio'io bush is a favorite of Su'th children. And some adults as well." He smiled. "I am glad to see it."

Lilac sat near him and said, "I have not taken to it. It is too sour for my liking."

"Ah, and that is why we like it."

"I see. What manner of entertainment do you bring?" the Mother asked leaning forward slightly.

Xhin'mhen purred for a moment. "I play several instruments with some degree of skill, the music of my homeland shall be heard. I am also capable of feats of skill and strength. And one must not underestimate the lion. Xer'tala'n is very well trained."

"He must be, that you left him alone."

"He rests."

"When you speak of skill and strength do you speak of the martial arts of the Su'th?"

Xhin'mhen matched the gaze of the Mother and nodded once. "You are familiar with them?"

"I am. I have been places far and wide. Most of the plants you see before you come here by me. The garden was beautiful before, but now it is exotic. You are a welcome sight, minister. I was always accepted with humility by the Su'th wherever and whenever I have encountered your people. But always I seem pulled back to Serac when I am in the north."

The Mother paused, then said, "The House of Wrath holds a tournament during the Fall Festival. That would be an excellent place to exhibit your skills. And I wouldn't mind seeing a few of their prized entrants knocked down. Unlike your people, The House of Wrath does not prize humility. Though if history holds sway, Master Archammer will again win this year."

"Master Archammer?" Xhin'mhen said, r's thick in his throat.

"Gavin Archammer. The First of all that is Wrath. And, as much as it pains me, the most powerful mage mankind has to offer. The tournament is really nothing more than a chance for him to display his power. The Earth offers no insight into that one. I deal as best I can but always he is…difficult. That fits him well."

"How interesting. This tournament seems a blessing from Ku'na'shi." He smiled, "I will enter."

"Most of the warriors will be Wrath mages, but each House is permitted to sponsor a participant. As you might imagine I have not often backed any such fighter. If you like I would make you The Way of Health's representative."

"It would be an honor, the Mother."

Lilac smiled. "This will, if nothing else, surprise The House of Wrath. The tournament begins the third day of the festival and continues until the champion is crowned, on the last. In recent years it has become the culmination of the festival.

"I must go, Master Entrah has agreed to see me. With luck the House of Animate will see the bird form that my daughter brings." Lilac planted her staff into the fertile soil and pushed herself up. "You would think it important for them, but instead they collapse upon themselves, fleeing further into a metal shell."

Shen'xhin'mhen said, "I cannot say. But I look forward to the contest. May your endeavor with the Mek'ana Home obtain fruit." And again, as before, the Mother was gone.

Thirty

Lilac Rainmarrow left the Su'th to the garden and strolled up the path toward the House of Animate. The festival would begin in two days, and final preparations would keep the Campus busy day and night. Flags flapped and tents billowed in the wind coming off the sea. People hurried this way and that. The pounding of hammers could be heard softly on the breeze. A blast of fire and black smoke burst into the sky followed by angry shouting down one of the rows of tents. The Mother smiled.

The House of Animate was before her, the front doors locked, a guard on either side. She rapped on the door with her staff; the guards did not move. A few moments later the clicking of locks was followed by the creaking of the door. Celia Hurn stood in the opening. "Ah, Mother. It is good to see you. Please come in." Her voice was strained and her eyes darted off to the distance.

Lilac entered the once public entrance hall and said, "Thank you, Master Hurn. How do you fare under the circumstances?"

Celia turned her head to one side, away from Lilac and said, "Under the circumstances I fare well, better than most. I grow tired of the vile atmosphere that we are forced to live under however. It starts with Master Entrah as you will see. Please, forgive my tongue. How are the preparations for the festival?"

The two walked slowly through the public space, talking quietly. "It seems to go well. The Way of Health will have its usual presence. I expect to see more cows and horses this year than last. I have heard it was a good year for births."

Celia's head bobbed as she looked at the floor. "This will be the first year in memory that the House of Animate has not displayed our work." Her voice was sharp, critical.

"I take from your tone that you disagree."

"How could I not? Our House has its difficulties, to be sure, but hiding in this building will not improve things. I grow tired of Trahn's leadership." Celia stopped, and winced. "You will find him in his study. He does not leave it."

"Thank you. If you have need, feel free to visit the Way."

"I will. I will." Celia sat down behind the reception desk. She took up a file and started work on a piece of copper.

Mother Rainmarrow made her way down the halls to Trahn's laboratory. It felt neglected. It wasn't that dust had collected in excess or that cobwebs had appeared everywhere, but there was a stillness to it that seemed a picture, a sadness captured in a moment of time. She crossed the stagnant sea, feeling the moment trying to add her to the picture and knocked once on the door frame to Trahn's study.

"Come in," was answered, spoken deeply for the man.

The Mother entered the stifling room. The oppression she felt here set her nerves on edge. Trahn did not move from his chair, which faced the ocean.

She said, "Will you be coming out for the festival, Trahn?"

"I do not think so, Mother Rainmarrow. What business can I address today?"

"One of my mages requests a meeting about an animate that she and a companion captured near Tarlow."

Trahn snapped, "Do not speak of that dreadful place. Their council, so wise. What do they know?"

"Hmm. I would think it would be worthwhile for the House of Animate to inspect this bird form. Could it not be useful in an attempt to clear your House's name?"

"I am sorry but I do not have time for such petty meetings. You must forgive me, I have much to see to."

The Mother questioned, "And what is that precisely? Master Hurn tells me that there will be no showing of the House's work this year."

Lilac could see Trahn's hand tighten. He said, "My work? It is really none of your concern, but if you must know, this and that. This and that." His voice was stilted, almost broken, pulled again and again from cavalcading recklessly over a cliff.

"I do not think you are altogether well, Master Entrah. Please, allow me to help."

Trahn stood slowly. His white robes were matted, as was his pale hair. He turned to face the Mother, his face was bone white and his eyes were black pits. "Stay away from me!" he spurted angrily. "Your magic has no place in my House."

"Trahn, there is no reason to panic. I am not one of your enemies," her voice was soothing and steady, in sharp contrast to his.

He put his hands over his ears and closed his eyes tight. "Silence! Leave me earth witch. Do not try your spells on me." He waved violently at the doorway. "Go!"

The Mother left him a frothing mess. She heard books being pushed to the floor, then quiet. 'This is far worse than I expected,' she worried. 'I must speak with Master Guildenil. Trahn was not mad at the last Directorate Council. Of course he will be busy with the festival. I pray that he has time.'

"Master Hurn. Might I have a word with you?" she asked as she returned to the entrance hall.

"Certainly, Mother," answered the animist, file in hand.

"One of my daughters has brought a rather amazing animate to Serac, hoping to have it inspected by your House. Trahn seems rather unwilling. If you might be interested in seeing it, to give some sort of appraisal of what she has found. I would be most grateful."

"I don't see that to be any problem. I can come in the morning."

"Wonderful. When you come by, ask for either Tara Groundmender or myself. Another thing, if you have the time."

"All day."

"About Master Entrah. He is not well."

"No. And he will not take help. Master Nightwillow ordered him to bed, but beyond that, there is nothing that can be done. He will not see a doctor, or a Way mage."

"Troubling. Thank you for your assistance, Master Hurn."

She smiled; it was at least partially formed from pain. "A pleasure."

Lilac found Tara watering fruit trees. Her light was dim. "Daughter."

"Hello. How was the meeting with Master Entrah?"

Lilac frowned, recalling him clearly. "It did not go well. Master Hurn, however, has agreed to view the bird form. She will come tomorrow morning."

"I do not really know what I hope to learn."

The Mother answered, "It is the path you take, travel with open eyes, that you may see the hidden detail. When you are presented a choice you will be prepared."

"It seems so simple until you go down the path," Tara answered, smiling.

"That much is life. Your Su'th friend has decided to enter the tournament."

"Really? How exciting! Xhin'mhen is very talented. If he does not draw Master Archammer in the first round he will do well." Tara knew full well the results of the Wrath tournament. Everyone in Serac, and most beyond, did. "Mother. I have a question."

Lilac nodded and Tara continued. "One night as we slept a wisp woke us. What are the clear orbs left behind by it?"

Lilac smiled and nodded. "My dear Tara, you had quite the journey. Wisps and Su'th and animates. As for the remains of the lights, I am not sure exactly. In all of my journeys I have not had that particular beauty bestowed upon me. The technologists will pay a pretty penny for them, from what Brother Chaign has said. They can be used as a natural equivalent to their manufactured batteries. Storing magic. Indeed, they may know more of them than I."

"Hmm. When I am done watering here is there another room that still needs it?"

"There is always a room that needs it. But I think that the most urgent is done. Sleep well when you do, daughter."

"Thank you," Tara answered and thought, 'But I do not when in Serac.'

Again the Mother was gone.

Tara rested uncomfortably. When her eyes closed the darkness filled with points of light that marked the presence of the animate. Too many to be believed, and they eluded her attempts to expose them. It was like a comical nightmare, not frightening, only frustrating. She could make them fade, blur, and find some sleep, but it was always gnawing at her.

Animates, always animates. A speck in her heart felt towards the House of Animate as they did towards the Way. So she was glad when Brother Vin stirred her and all could be put out of mind. A gentle voice, deep and brassy. "Sister Tara, Master Hurn is here. She waits in the foyer."

Tara said, "Good. Could you rouse Isaac? That would be helpful."

Vin bowed out of the small bedroom, saying, "I will find Master Samuelson."

Tara rose quickly. The warmth of the House that she once felt no longer warmed her bones. She pulled on a smock and went to meet Master Hurn. She had not had personal dealings with the animate mage, but she had seen her before. The dark, straight hair was shoulder length. Her piercing eyes. Today she wore blue robes. Tara smiled to greet her and said, "Master Hurn, thank you so much for coming. It will be just a moment longer. My companion, Isaac Samuelson, has the animate."

"It is nice to meet you, Daughter Groundmender. You are the one that healed the thief's leg, are you not?"

Tara blushed slightly. "I did, yes."

Celia smiled mischievously. "Well enough that he could clean escape from The House of Wrath."

Isaac stumbled into the foyer, cloth parcel in hand, hair sent in three different directions. His eyes drooped, and he smiled lazily. His voice was embedded with sleep, "So sorry. Good morning, Tara, Master Hurn."

Celia said, "The weather is pleasant enough, why don't we go outside to talk."

Tara nodded, "Certainly."

Isaac followed the two mages outside; he rubbed his face, and as always failed to straighten his hair. Tara said, "Isaac, the animate."

Isaac handed the bundle over to Celia. The mage unwrapped the bundle and her eyes opened wide when she finally saw the bird form. "I did not expect such refinement."

Tara and Isaac related the story of the brute to Celia. She listened carefully, emotion painted on her face. She said, "I did not know the extent of the calamity. Master Entrah has been tight-lipped, at best." She pressed her hand over the animate and frowned. "There is nothing here. The rock, or some other force, wiped the anima clean. The maker of this animate holds a distinction that none I know of hold. Using animate magic on these materials. We are mostly limited to metals and crystal. But that even was more a talent of Master Jannan. It might be worthwhile for you to seek him out for a better opinion. I would tell you where to look but I do not know. I am sorry that I can not be more helpful. It's beautiful."

Tara said, "I appreciate your help."

"No, you have done a clear favor for me today. I resented Master Entrah's lead before. Your tale, and I had heard rumors that I did not wish to believe, proves that he acts selfishly and irresponsibly. And I supported him in his choice against Master Jannan. It fills me with disgust. Good day, Tara, Isaac."

Isaac said, "Good fortune in your choices, master."

Celia Hurn smiled pain and walked away, vibrations of contained anger rolling off of her. Isaac tucked the bird away and said, "That does not leave us any options does it?"

Tara watched the animist go and said, "We are not lost yet. Technologist Aron is a well-known dealer in power and information. I will speak to him. We will see what to make of things after that."

"Seems fair enough."

"We'll have better luck with him than with Master Entrah. That much is certain." Tara rubbed her temple. "Ugh, my head aches."

Isaac laughed once and said, "Try some of Xhin'mhen's black brew. It's quashed more than one pounding headache for me."

"I do not think it would help me, Isaac. Serac – I would not come here if I did not have to." Her voice quieted. "The earth is alive. I don't know what it means, or even with what. I would think animates based on the killer and the bird, but it makes no sense. Not even the House of Animate holds such sway. Maybe it is just the magic of this place." She attempted to rationalize away what she did not want to believe.

Shen'xhin'mhen and Xer'tala'n emerged from the front door of the Way. They both looked rested, if either of the humans could tell that a lion looked rested. Xhin'mhen said, "I was told that you were meeting with the mek'ana sorcerer."

Tara nodded, "We did. Not so good. She told us what she could, just, well there is not much to be told."

Xhin'mhen frowned, "Unfortunate. Xer'tala'n told me more of the mek'ana I told you of. It studied rune forms and history while in Tan'Su'th."

"Rune forms?" Isaac asked. "Like the technologists use?"

"Hmm. Perhaps. I know them as an ancient, elemental form of magic. Some Hierophants study them, but the power has long been lost. Much like the pledgestone I fear. Also, this mek'ana was always polite."

Xer'tala'n nodded, his mane shaking in waves of hair.

Tara's face twisted with concern. Her mind ratcheted, contorting to wrap around the facts presented. "This is very strange. An animate that studies magic runes. An animate that no human mage knows of, or admits to. The animate that attacked Henry Bremen four years ago. Plus add in all of the incidents regarding animates of late. Could it be possible that the maker of the killer and the bird is an animate? An animate that uses magic? Is that crazy?"

Isaac and Shen'xhin'mhen each shook their heads claiming ignorance. Isaac said, "If it was an animate it would have to come from somewhere. They don't just appear. That leaves only a couple of options. Either it was created here, in Serac. Or it was created by another mage in another city. Which the House would say is impossible. You said an animate attacked a man here four years ago?"

Tara said, "Yes, a technologist. The little thing was stealing crystal from his workshop. Nasty creation. First Entrah suggested that it was an old world animate. Not possible by todays practitioners."

Isaac said, "If we believe that these events are connected, then it would appear that the first occurrence in the string happened here." He scratched his head. "Suggesting that the animate was created here. Has there been an animate that has gone missing from the House of Animate?"

Tara said excitedly, "Master Jannan had one go missing for a time. When I healed the thief's leg, the story went that he activated the animate to provide a distraction for his escape from the House. It nearly worked too. Ultimately though it was found wandering the streets of Serac."

The humans smiled at their puzzling. Shen'xhin'mhen said, "I do not mean to fall behind, but how does that help solve this problem?"

Isaac and Tara each went blank.

Xhin'mhen continued, "I am sorry. Xer'tala'n thinks that if we are able to return to Tan'Su'th more could be learned about this...animate. There are records of its presence. It might be possible to confirm something."

Tara nodded, "I know what it looks like. If there is a drawing of it I would recognize it. Worst case we know what we are looking for. Still, I wish to speak with Technologist Aron. And it would be a shame if you did not see the festival before we left."

Xhin'mhen nodded, "I would not wish to disappoint the Sorceress Mother." Xer'tala'n growled. "He is anxious to see the festival."

Isaac nodded, "I think we all are, Tala'n."

Silas Aron greeted Tara with a massive smile. "It has been along time, sister. The world treats you well I hope."

"I have done alright, yes." She looked around the newly expanded showroom, complete with the latest weapons and armor. An animate cleaned the windows. "It seems that fate has blessed you as well."

Aron gestured palm up to the surrounding grandeur. "My business flourishes, my servant does not complain, and the apprentices learn quickly. I cannot complain. What brings you my way? A self-heating blanket perhaps? Or a small cooking pot? Both would be welcome additions when you are lost in the wide world. And I would hate to send you out into it without my latest works." He smiled widely.

"I will have to look at both, that much is certain, but not yet. I come seeking information."

Silas's voice danced, "Information. That also can be had for a price. What is it you seek?"

"Master Jannan. Do you know anything of his going? Most importantly where he went?"

"The fool. Bullheaded to the end." Silas held his chin and stared at Tara. "I do know at least a beginning."

"And that is?"

"Now, now, let's not be hasty. Information as with any other commodity comes at a price. Given Master Jannan's difficulties, information about him comes at a premium price. Not that I will in any way be unfair, but I can't just go betraying what little confidence Master Jannan had left in me."

"So very noble," Tara said.

"No not really. But business is what it is. Have you seen the festival ride that the technologist's have created?" He placed the blanket and pot on the table that sat between them.

"The spinning arms of wood?"

Silas smiled proudly. "That's it. Henry Bremen's masterwork. Not so far from the animate that attacked him. He is so proud of it. Spinning and whirling. It will cause quite a stir I believe. Not unlike the verdict of guilty and the sentence of banishment against Murdoch. I did try to convince him to leave. It would have spared him the mockery, but he would have none of it. 'I will see my fall,' he said."

Tara ran her hand over the blanket that had made its way onto the table, and examined the cooking pot with its little crystal and metal battery. "Is it easy to recharge the magic?"

"A simple energy transference, not unlike some of the Way's spells I would think. Charged it could last a week or more."

"I will take them both, and do tell me of Master Jannan's going. I am very much in need of knowing," Tara said with authority. "And I do kind of like that short knife in the window, you contained the battery in the handle, no?"

"Well, well. You have quite the ambition? And with what would you pay me? These are the latest models, not cheap. Not at all."

Tara reached into her bag and brought out one of the clear orbs. She displayed it on a pedestal of two fingers and her thumb. Silas quieted and nodded. "Yes, well that would answer that question, wouldn't it. And as I said I'm fair, you will have a bit of credit. Not that I would forget, but let me write that down." He clicked his tongue as he did so. "Master Jannan then. I caught him as he left the House of Animate. He had some clothes and a hammer, and his animate with him. We each said goodbye, and I asked him where he would go.

"He told me that he didn't know, but he would be taking the first ship out of here. Put the most distance behind him. Something like that. I went with him down to the docks. He seemed to appreciate the company. We said our good-byes again, and he boarded a big shipping vessel headed north. The ship sailed and I obtained a copy of the manifest and route plan. The usual stops: Riversea and Midsun. Past that I can't say. Nobody I know saw him get off in either of those cities. I've had pigeons going like mad. And not just for my own curiosity. The ship continued north from Midsun. There are some smaller cities, and some villages, not well documented, and then you run square into the Wall of Tan'Su'th. But your friend can tell you more of that than I can." He watched Tara's face. "Surprised? I didn't earn my reputation for nothing. That's all I know, Tara."

Tara smiled and spun the orb on her fingers before handing it to Silas. He cupped it like a child. He said, "You do not know how precious a thing this is. If you ever come across another, remember me."

Tara smiled, "I will."

"Excellent. This is the easiest energy transfer, not the most efficient, but it will work for you. It is much more of a focus and will issue than anything." He placed one finger on each node protruding from the battery connected to the pot. A little spark. "Easy enough."

Tara said, "I suppose." She unfolded the blanket to reveal the battery tucked in a little pocket. She copied the technologist's actions with much the same result.

"Very nice. To turn on either of them simply complete this connection, and you'll be cooking. Blanket or pot," he joked. Then he turned his head to the left and said over his shoulder, "Mural, wrap these up for the sister, and the short blade in the window."

Mural, who had been lurking just out of sight through the door, stood and came into the showroom. He had grown into his legs and was solidly built. He wiped his hands on his leather smock and took the pieces with him back into the work space. A few minutes later he brought them back, packed into a small wood box. Tara smacked the side, checking the strength of the small crate.

Silas said, "I am glad to have been able to provide some of the finer modern conveniences to you."

"I will make sure to stop in when I am again in Serac to tell you how well they work. Good day, Master Aron."

"Good day, Sister Groundmender."

Tara returned to The Way of Health. She found her companions in the garden. Xer'tala'n rested in the shade of an apple tree. Isaac studied directly under Xhin'mhen, but the lion watched closely. Tara sat down next to the lion. The pair stopped and Tara said, "I would have expected you to be exploring the festival grounds."

Isaac laughed, "We were but got shooed out. Xer'tala'n frightened the workers." He shrugged, "I guess."

Xhin'mhen said, "It will be better to see when all is finished."

Tara nodded. "I suppose. Technologist Aron was helpful. Master Jannan sailed north. He was not seen debarking in Riversea or Midsun. It seems that our paths point further north."

The Su'th nodded, "It will benefit us if we can go by boat. Midsun is a great distance away. The Tan'Su'th much greater. If the sorcerer you seek is somewhere between, it will take time to find him. It is a vast expanse of sand, almost to Tan'Su'th."

Tara shrugged, "It may be difficult to obtain passage with a lion as part of the deal, but I will see what can be found."

Shen'xhin'mhen scolded the lion, "See all of the difficulty you cause."

The lion grumbled and rolled his eyes.

Tara said, "It will be what it is. I think though, that it will be more useful to return to the Tan'Su'th and find fact about the mystery animate. If a trail following Master Jannan can be found that would be wonderful, but given his banishment there is no way to count on him helping us in any way."

Xhin'mhen recalled his true goal and said, "I do hope that it is possible for us to journey with you. In the excitement of the discoveries I forget my task. If the

Ta'ke'sh is not found here, we will have to continue our search."

Isaac said, "How will you know it?"

"I do not know."

Tara frowned, "What then for us? Our strongest hope lies with you."

"Traveling papers could be arranged. With the approval of the Hierophant you might be allowed into Tan'Su'th."

Celia did not return to the House of Animate. Instead she found herself sitting on one of the rarely used benches in the hedge maze. Thought boiled thought. In her younger days, the hedge would burn. She had tamed much of her temper. 'That wretched fool!' she thought. 'That wretched, awful man.'

To compound the layers, Isaac had clearly viewed her thoughts. The choices spun slowly past her as if on a wheel. She did not want to return to the heaviness of the House, but what choice did she have? Another transfer? Her lonesome thoughts were interrupted, not surprising given the closeness of the festival, but the who was another matter altogether.

Gavin Archammer.

"Your face never has hidden much, Master Hurn. You battle with your loyalties." It was stated flatly, but truthfully.

"Master Archammer. I...yes. I do."

"The world has muddied much as the weeks pass. May I sit?"

"Of course." Archammer did sit, black robes consuming the bench. He leaned forward elbows on knees.

"I have always been impressed with your skill, Master Hurn. I have made no secret of that. It's a shame that you wither as you do in the House of Animate."

"They took me in when I had lost one family."

"Yes, my predecessor threw you out for a show of temper," Archammer said, his tone noting the unfairness. "I am not my predecessor. If you seek refuge from the storm simply ask. The doors will be opened to you."

Celia was surprised, she stuttered, "You...you are overwhelmingly kind, Master Archammer."

The First of Wrath stood and said, "There is no rush. The choices you must make are difficult. Truly you must serve your heart. Only know that you will be welcomed. Good day, Master Hurn."

The wheel of her thoughts slowed. Then stopped.

Thirty-one

"I shouldn't have accepted the Mother's offer," Xhin'mhen said regretfully to Xer'tala'n. The Su'th sat privately in the west bedroom. "I am not a warrior, not like you. I was flattered, but even in the guise of entertainer I should not have been foolhardy." To any that passed the language rolled from comprehension.

Xer'tala'n listened to the raucous sounds of the festival then said, "Do not worry. Our prayers are finished. Even if you are matched with this Archammer it is of little concern. We are here to find the Ta'ke'shya Ku'na'shi."

Shen'xhin'mhen stood from his knees and nodded. "You are right Tala'n. The Ta'ke'sh. If it is not here then I know not where to look; we have seen many sights since leaving the Tan'Su'th but nothing like this." There was an edge of desperation to his words. One of fear. Of failure.

The Hierophant answered, "Take heart. My prayers fill me with a peace that I have not felt since setting on this journey. She lingers here."

The lion followed the Su'th from The Way of Health. Rumor had spread through the city that a Su'th would fight in the tournament. Only Tara and Isaac had any real understanding of the fact.

The arena, a raised square for the fighters and the three-story wood bleachers built around it, had risen from the grass in the first days of preparation for the festival. Triangular flags flapped in the wind, the slapping of the cloth was drowned out by the noise of the crowd. A Wrath mage shouted exhortations to the waiting crowd preparing it for the coming of the participants. Shen'xhin'mhen went to the tent designated for the participants. Tara and Isaac stood outside of it, clearly waiting for the Su'th.

Tara said, "We were beginning to worry, Xhin'mhen. The call for participants was twenty minutes ago."

The Su'th answered, "Even the sorcerers must wait on Ku'na'shi."

Tara nodded, "Well, hurry in, you're the last to arrive." She gave a quick hug to the Su'th. As she pulled away she said, "Good luck."

"Thank you, Tara. Isaac."

Isaac smiled a half smile and said, "Good luck, Xhin'mhen. Just don't draw Master Archammer in the first round and you'll do well."

"Yes, always with Sorcerer Archammer. Tala'n."

The lion grumbled and the three watched Xhin'mhen disappear into the large tent. A roped path herded him to a table where one man sat, round spectacles resting on the table in front of him. "Hello." The man put on his spectacles and gave Shen'xhin'mhen the once over. "You are here to compete?"

"Yes, I am Shen'xhin'mhen. The Way of Health I represent."

The man picked up a roll of paper and spread its edges wide, then ran his fingers down the list of names. "Yes, here you are. Your first round match is at three this afternoon. Do you know the rules of the competition?"

"No. I must say I do not."

"First round matches run every fifteen minutes, starting in about twenty. Just after the next ringing of the bells. Okay. Easy. Scoring is based on ringside judges. Points for clean strikes or throws. Magic is fully allowable but does not score. The match is the first to five points. You can forfeit at any time, giving the match to your opponent. Also, if you force your opponent from the mat it counts three. And no running. It doesn't keep the crowd entertained."

The man scratched under his cheek with his thumb, thinking. "Weapons are sparring style, right over there." He pointed to a rack and a table, it was a jumbled mess. "Not much left I guess."

Shen'xhin'mhen nodded. "Who is my opponent?"

The man went back to his paper, rolling it out further still. "Here, oh. Well,

377

good luck. You face Master Archammer in the first round."

Shen'xhin'mhen's lips puckered for a second and he nodded slowly. "Thank you." The Su'th walked past the table to the sparring weapons. He picked up a sword, a bundle of thin sticks bound together, and broke it with a crack over his knee. The man looked up, startled. "Now that wasn't necessary. Just because you drew Master – oh."

The man stopped as Xhin'mhen wrapped thin strips of brown fabric around the sword halves and then around his forearms, hilt forward on his right arm, point on his left. "I do not fight with these tools."

The man smiled, showing crooked teeth. "You are the Su'th aren't you?"

The Su'th smiled, "I am."

"It's true then. No man has beaten Master Archammer in nine years. I don't expect your story to be any different. But good luck." His voice was filled with sincerity. "Do be careful, more than one has not walked from the mat after facing him."

"I will be," Shen'xhin'mhen answered and exited the tent on the other side, into the sunlight, and into the seating for the contestants, between the north and east sets of bleachers. The first thing he did was look for the others. They sat across from him, in the first row. Xer'tala'n lay in the aisle. Xhin'mhen smiled as he watched the humans skirt around the cat. 'If they knew,' he thought.

He turned and glanced at the other combatants. Most, he thought, were Wrath sorcerers, their choice of weapon readily apparent. Swords mostly. Of the sorcerers, it was evenly split men and women. Behind the sorcerers was a small group of those that were not of Wrath. A bald sleepy man sat, legs folded upon themselves. The others were a collection of sailors and brawlers. Shen'xhin'mhen did not think they had much chance against the sorcerers. All told there were thirty-two competitors, as the competition dictated.

'I wonder if they were hired to fill the field. Archammer would undoubtedly put off some that would otherwise compete,' the Su'th thought as he sat down in an empty chair near the sleepy man.

Shen'xhin'mhen settled in to watch the proceedings, which passed quickly due to the excitement of the fights. Two of the hired fighters, which should have assured the Wrath mages victory, won through excessive aggression. The sleepy man won, his wood sword hung at his side until the Wrath mage attacked, then it would whip almost invisibly to counter the overwhelmed man. Between the fights various demonstrations took place, dancers, mages, sparring. Usually several animates would be displayed, but this year there were none.

As the time for his fight approached Xhin'mhen's stomach began to turn. He had not been faced with battle such as this before. He had not been faced with Archammer before.

Finally, the other thirty contestants had fought and Shen'xhin'mhen knew it was time. The announcer strutted back and forth across the mat announcing the final, already known fight. "Fighting with the support of The Way of Health and from parts unknown, Shen'xhin'mhen!" The pronunciation was nearly correct. Xhin'mhen smiled and stood. The crowd cheered as the Su'th went to the mat. It was firm but soft under his feet, made from woven grass. It was torn and bloody in places.

The announcer went on excitedly, "His opponent, the reigning champion and First of The House of Wrath. Master Gavin Archammer!" He pointed to the raised booth where the Firsts sat, four of them present.

The crowd cheered madly, acknowledging the power of the man. Archammer stood slowly from his chair kept among the honored. To his right Frederick Guildenil sat, clapping politely. To his left the Mother, who smiled but did not move. Archammer raised his right hand answering the crowd and descended to the grass. He pulled his arms out from his customary black robes and wrapped the sleeves around his waist, tying them off in front. His loose gray shirt further hid a necklace. A large oval lump and heavy gold chain were disguised under the limp fabric in front, stretched tight across his shoulders; the chain appeared around the back of his neck. The crowd continued to cheer as he slowly wrapped his hands with white linen strips.

Xhin'mhen smiled; Archammer was clearly attempting to intimidate him. The Su'th kneeled and closed his eyes. He would wait. He would pray. Ku'na'shi would give him all he needed.

Gavin finished his act and took two of the sparring swords from a mage that he commanded. Then he climbed up onto the mat, walked the edge slowly, as if counting the number of footsteps it took to go end to end, then walked to the middle, stopping several feet from the golden Su'th.

Gavin said, "It is not often that the Way enters a fighter into this tournament. And a Su'th at that. I shall enjoy this little exercise." With the noise of the crowd only Xhin'mhen could hear it.

Xhin'mhen smiled, opened his eyes and stood. He slapped his right shoulder and said, "I will do my best to provide some difficulty for such an esteemed opponent."

"At least you know your fate." Gavin reached out with the sword, testing the Su'th, who blocked the tap with his right forearm. Then the other with his left. It was a slow calculated maneuver. Then the man blurred into action, dropping to his knee and bringing both swords against the Su'th's ribs. Xhin'mhen's reactions just barely saved him, blocking the two swords with his guards, and hopping away. Archammer smiled as he stepped forward from his knee. "Better than the rest already."

Xhin'mhen brought his arms up, hands like talons. This time he would test the sorcerer. The strikes fell rapidly as the Su'th advanced, moving like silk. He jostled Archammer, uncomfortably close. The human seemed ready to lose his balance and fall but never did, and each attempt to strike back with his swords was deflected away by the arm guard. Still, Xhin'mhen could not score.

Xer'tala'n watched the rush by Xhin'mhen and frowned, despite the display he had missed several opportunities to strike the sorcerer, a subtle lack of discipline that would be addressed. When Archammer's blow came Tala'n saw it develop before it occurred. Gavin deflected Xhin'mhen's strike, then baited the aggressive Su'th. Archammer even smiled. He sunk his hips and feet into the mat and drove his fist, wrapped around the hilt of the sword, into Shen'xhin's ribs. The Su'th folded and slid back ten feet, the magic of the blow crackled in his ears. The black flags representing the mage were raised by the three judges, indicating a scoring blow. The crowd cheered.

Xhin'mhen got back to his feet and nodded, acknowledging the blow. Gavin took two steps, circling, then rushed the Su'th. The clack of wood on wood marked a hasty beat. Xhin'mhen caught one of the swords with the hilted guard. Sliding down the bundle he grabbed the sorcerer's arm and pulled Gavin off balance, scoring solidly with a knee to his chest. Archammer pulled back with a disgusted look as the red flags rose.

"Hrmm," he grumbled, tossing the sparring blade to one side. The front rows of the crowd scrambled to claim it. The pair circled again. Gavin made a quick jabbing motion with his open palm, the air shuddered, the force unbalanced the Su'th. Xhin'mhen rolled with the magic and flipped backwards, out of harm's way as Gavin's remaining sword sliced the air where the Su'th's head had been. Gavin glared and muttered, "Indeed."

The combatants rushed at each other, each trying to gain advantage. The crowd fell silent, hypnotized by the motion. Gavin hooked his own leg behind the Su'th and rolled through him, forcing him to the ground. An extra forearm to the ribs made the Su'th groan. The black flags waved once. Gavin pulled the Su'th up to his feet and pushed him away.

There was no delay to his attack. The sword beat down on the Su'th who dodged the onslaught with all of his skill. Xhin'mhen found some respite as he rolled his hands over each other, magic slowing the sword as it cut. Gavin smiled, he had not expected this. The mage released the sword, and without the enchantment placed upon it quickly grasped the Su'th by the collar.

He lifted him sideways and scored with a punch that sent the Su'th flying across the mat. Again the black flags fluttered. Gavin's shirt was torn open and Shen'xhin'mhen rose holding a handful of gray cloth. The necklace was revealed to him. The gold bezel held a stone, oval, three inches by two. When he first stood it appeared white, but faded to black as he focused on it. The world slowed. All but the stone blurred. He blinked over and over, his eyes fluttering. When his eyes were closed, that brief repeated moment, he could see Her. The visions, light of the world, dark of Her, merged. She stood in beauty just behind Archammer, who exhaled. Her tail flicked. Gavin looked over his shoulder, then back at the distracted Su'th. "What are you looking at savage?"

Xhin'mhen shook his head and twitched forward in-between time, disappearing and reappearing. Gavin had not seen such magic before. His defenses failed as the Su'th faded one final time from where Gavin struck then reappeared, frozen, with the point of the broken sword striking Gavin's face. The sorcerer crumpled. The red flags rose. The crowd cheered. Tara leapt to her feet, fist raised high.

The Su'th stepped back as Gavin stood. The mage said, "Again."

Xhin'mhen growled, it rolled from him naturally. She smiled, and he shifted forwards. Archammer had measured the spell; he pulled back and muttered to himself. Xhin'mhen felt his limbs stiffen. He reappeared just before the Wrath mage, Ku'na'shi's magic peeled open. Archammer smiled. "This ends."

Archammer struck with his right hand. Magic crackled in the air as Xhin'mhen shunted backwards, sent flying towards the edge of the ring. The magic came to him, his reflexes sharpened as he tumbled, and then stopped, standing perfectly upright, feet together, his right hand perpendicular to the ground, resting on his left hand, his head tucked in prayer.

Only his toes clawed the edge of the mat.

The crowd went berserk with amazement. Gavin glared frustration. The Su'th opened his eyes, angles ever so subtly shifted, and dropped into a readied stance.

Archammer tapped his head three times. Xhin'mhen, filled with confidence, rushed the mage. Archammer shifted away from a scoring strike using a spell similar to the power of Ku'na'shi, grabbed him by his neck and waist, and tossed him out of the ring onto the first two rows of spectators. Three points. The crowd went silent, processing what had just transpired, then cheered madly. Gavin raised his arms in victory and nodded at Xhin'mhen who had quickly righted himself. The announcer rushed to the ring. He yelled, "Let's hear it for your winner, Master Gavin Archammer!"

The crowd somehow became louder. "And let's not forget the fighter from parts unknown! Shen'xhin'mhen!" And again somehow the crowd became louder. Shen'xhin'mhen climbed onto the mat giving the whole crowd a chance to cheer for the fighters. Gavin glanced sideways at the Su'th undid the tie in his robes, and left the ring while redressing. Shen'xhin'mhen stepped down to his friends. The crowd began to file out, but the excitement had not vanished.

Isaac said, "I thought you had him there!"

Tara followed, "Well done!"

"Thank you, both."

Then Tara said, "Oh, your eyes! Xhin'mhen!"

"What?"

"They've changed...they're..." The shape had changed and the blue had softened slightly but bled out into the whites, blending together.

A smile flashed across his face, but he spoke in measured tones, "I have seen what I needed to see." He kneeled next to Tala'n and whispered, "The Ta'ke'shya Ku'na'shi. Sorcerer Archammer possesses it. She revealed herself to me. That power Tala'n, never have I felt it. The magic was not mine, but Hers. Given that we would find Her gift to us."

The Su'th stood and was greeted by the Mother who had made her way from the viewing booth. She said, "Very impressive, Shen'xhin'mhen. Gavin has not been pressed like that in years. But you know that. Perhaps next year Xer'tala'n would be interested in representing The Way of Health." She patted the lion's head and drifted away. Xhin'mhen glanced down at Tala'n who blinked once, slowly.

Tara said, "Let's go. I imagine you will want to talk to him."

Xhin'mhen's nose flipped up slightly signaling agreement. The lion provided space through the crowd and they followed him down the tunnel. Once in the open air of the Campus people began offering their congratulations to Shen'xhin'mhen who remarked, "They treat me as though I was the victor."

Tara smirked. "If you had ever seen what was left of his opponents you would understand. You did exceptionally well against him."

Tala'n sat next to the bruised Xhin'mhen on the grass covered bed in The Way of Health. "You saw Her?" Amazement and envy was his tone.

The bruises from Archammer's blows had turned dark, even with the attention of Tara. "If not Her I know not who. The Ta'ke'shya Ku'na'shi. Sorcerer Archammer wears it around his neck. A focus as the sorcerers call it. I don't think that he will give it up easily. I don't know that he even understands what it is."

Tala'n licked the back of his hand and rubbed his ear. "I agree. I scented fear on him. Pride. He would not give it up willingly." Tala'n smirked. "We should return to Tan'su'th and tell the Emperor."

There was a quick knock on the door. Tala'n froze. Xhin'mhen said, "Come in, Isaac."

The door handle clicked and the door pushed open, easier than before but still offering resistance. Isaac slipped through the tiny space and nodded greetings. "How did you know it was me? Never mind. How are you feeling?"

The Su'th rubbed his ribs. "I hurt, but not badly. What we have found more than makes up for it."

Isaac sat down. "I bet. Tara is trying to find passage on a ship for us. With luck we will be headed towards your home soon."

Tala'n muttered, "I do hope she is able. I would rather not walk it all again."

Xhin'mhen said, "I agree with that." Isaac stood to leave. Xhin'mhen said, "You step heavily on your right foot." He smiled having answered the question.

Tara went to The Gull's Inn on the Mother's recommendation. It was emptier than usual, Tara guessed because of the festival, but there was still an array of sailors inside. Tara walked confidently to the bar and got the bartender's attention.

"What can I do for you, daughter? Surely not a drink."

"Start with a shot of whiskey, after what I've seen today." She smiled and shrugged, "Why not. I need to book passage on a ship. Are there any captains here?"

The glass clinked together as the bartender poured the whiskey. "Several. Yes, but not as many as usual. Where are you headed?"

Tara threw back the whiskey, coughed and said, "North."

The bartender called across the bar, "Robbins! The little lady wants to talk to you."

A portly man with greasy black hair looked up from a game of cards. "Well come and talk to me then!" The whole table laughed loudly drunk on ale.

Tara smiled without humor and went over to Robbins. He asked, "Looking for passage north?"

"Yes, I am."

"Well. I'll take three cards, Cull." He picked up his new cards and said, "Just you?"

"No. Two others and a lion."

Robbins looked up, a smirk on his round face. "I don't think so, honey. I saw that beast at the tournament. My crew doesn't need that sort of trouble." He slammed his cards on the table. "Bah, I fold. Good luck though." His voice sounded doubtful.

Tara smiled, relieved. She did not like the man. "Thanks so much. Anyone else running a ship north?"

No one spoke. Robbins said, "Looks like you're out of luck."

"I wouldn't say that," said the excellently dressed man that had just entered the inn. He was slightly taller than Tara and took her hand and kissed it. "Captain Sebastion Alabaster. At your service."

Robbins rolled his eyes and shook his head. The captain's gray mustache rolled in a little circle and stayed perfectly still as he turned away towards a booth. His black boots jangled as he walked. Tara followed him, he looked over his shoulder and said, "Don't mind him, daughter. A non-believer."

"Of what?"

The captain spun on his heels to again face Tara, his white coat with gold tassels spun away from his body. "Don't tell me that you have never heard of Captain Sebastion Alabaster!"

"I'm sorry but I can't say that I have."

Captain Alabaster shook his head and said, "Oh dear, oh dear. Poor mage. Poor girl." They sat at a table and the bartender brought over a decanter of whiskey, half filled. He poured two drinks, and set them both down in front of the captain. He took one in each hand and gulped the liquor down. Two more were poured, but left on the table.

The bartender asked, "Another for the daughter?"

Tara nodded. "I am looking for passage north. Three people and a lion. No cargo."

"Ah, the Su'th. It has been years since I was in the port of Ku'na."

"You have been to the Tan'su'th?"

"If by that you mean the Imperial Su'th, yes I have."

"How much for passage?"

The captain reached into his coat and took out a small piece of paper and a piece of sharpened charcoal. He looked up and started pointing to nothing, his hand bouncing around. Then he wrote a number on the paper. "I think this is fair. I cannot promise passage all the way north, pirates and all, but this will shorten your trip if that is where you think you are going."

Tara looked at the paper and her mouth pulled sideways. "You have no problem with the lion."

"None at all." He pulled his head in over the table and whispered loudly, "I'll tell you a secret. In the past I've had crew that were Su'th. Not any these days. A shame, good workers, they are."

"When do you sail?"

"Not until the festival is over. It's not possible to arrange anything before then, so enjoy the city. If you need to speak with me, come down to my ship The Flying Louise." The captain drank his two shots, stood, bowed and left the inn.

Tara stood up, drank the whiskey and left a coin on the table. She had a good mind to think that Captain Alabaster had not paid, and did so for him. When she went to leave Robbins barked from his card game, "Safe travels, daughter. You will need the prayers. And ask the captain about the Elves."

This brought raucous laughter from the card game. Tara smiled crookedly as she left the inn and returned to the Campus to tell her friends of the arrangement.

The festival passed rapidly. The Campus swarmed with life. Everywhere Shen'xhin'mhen went people congratulated him. Everyone seemed to have been there, though if they had the arena would have held six times the people. Xhin'mhen took the attention well and the crowd seemed to warm to the presence of the lion.

The tournament continued, with Archammer easily subjugating his competition. The Su'th did not return to watch. Isaac did and marveled at the ease with which the First of Wrath won. The excitement of the first round was never repeated but the crowd continued to fill the arena. The hired men lost in the second round but the other matches were competitive, the sleepy man continued to win until he faced Gavin. The mage did not lose and was never again tested, finishing as the victor.

Tara made sure that Xer'tala'n saw all of the displays and exhibitions. Each night he expressed his impressions of the scenes to Shen'xhin'mhen. The anticipation of the trip north grew within each of them, each for their own reason.

Tara did not sleep, though the city seemed quieter than before. Still, her mind always filled with clattering at those quiet times and she most of all looked forward to the sailing, simply to leave the mage city. She told no one of the visions. A small seed of fear had been planted in her, somewhere, sometime, and she heeded its call.

Isaac had taken decently enough to the travel from Tarlow to Serac, but he did not enjoy it as the others did. During the Fall Festival he suffered a degree of separation from the rest, a gnawing sense of sadness growing about him. He continued to follow the tournament, with growing awe of Gavin Archammer, and by association Shen'xhin'mhen.

Xer'tala'n grew tired of the extended time he spent as a lion. Fortunately, the sights of the Festival provided an excellent distraction. And that was in addition to the discovery of the Ta'ke'sh. Xer'tala'n knew that it had to exist, the history of it was too important for it not to, and seeing it for himself strengthened his faith in Her. He was ready to sail north, ready to return home.

Shen'xhin'mhen spent more and more time in the Great Garden. The tranquility of the place pushed out even the distractions of the festival, and he turned more inward, focusing on his finding of the Ta'ke'sh. Even now he planned how to present its finding to the Emperor. How to paint the sorcerer that possessed it was most troubling. It would not be taken back peacefully.

Arcane surveyed the work that went on because of him. The animates taken from Earlsburg obeyed their instructions quickly, preparing a place for Arcane and his humans to return to. The Su'th had told stories of the death of the Harrow King to the blade of Su'thcle'n, how the ground where he died followed suit, collapsing and blackening. Nothing could grow, and the site despite being a place of reverence and freedom had been long abandoned. Forgotten.

Arcane believed the Ichor Sinkhole to be the site where the Harrow King fell. It was a nasty place, haunted by visions and apparitions. And not by man, which made it an ideal place to claim. The cracked ground was blasted black, and in those cracks black pus poured towards the center of the pit, a liquid death. The rivers oozed a tainted magic, and tainted or no, Arcane felt that he could grow powerful here, undisturbed.

Even to reach the Sinkhole required a trip through the Dismal Woods, as dark and dank as winter night, then passage over rocky crags that had escaped the tainted effects of the Sinkhole. They threatened to devour anyone that would dare give them trial, claiming the horses to their bitter teeth. Arcane smiled when he thought of how the Su'th remembered this place, golden fields of grain as far as the eye could see, a life giving river that flowed lazily through it, villages dotting the land. None of that remained. In truth it had been destroyed before the final calamitous battles that were fought here.

The mages of the east had seen this place only once, named it and promised never to return, barricading their enlightened society behind the Westerling Garrison. A fortress now rose from the black ground of the Sinkhole. Raised by the tireless animates, the keep was finished, and the walls, which certainly would never be tested, now followed, growing thick.

Peter had questioned why such a place was necessary. Even the two humans could be adequately housed without such emerging grandeur. Arcane, though not requiring the delicacies of life, did not see a reason to be without. Though he did not know why, Arcane quite liked the castle of his dead acquaintance Turnbly Lancaster. A quirk of his creation stamped onto his anima by Master Jannan most likely. Arcane found many of those now, a liking for the human ways of things, and so the building went on day after day, night after night. Blocks of stone hewn from the blackened landscape, placed by metal hands. Soon it would provide a protected heart for Arcane's living vision.

And somehow despite all of the desolation Lie Ben found a way to nurture the soil, to provide sustenance and health for the seeds he planted. They grew fast and strong, if a little bitter. The soil yet remembered its past. Peter hunted the freakish animals that lived on the plains, collecting new scars. Their flesh varied, some tough and awful, some delicate and delicious. The two men managed well enough, their distractions keeping them out from under Arcane's feet as he prepared a workshop, a fortress, a future.

Thirty-two

The Flying Louise was a smaller boat than the others moored in Serac. Unlike the other ships, The Flying Louise was angular and sat low in the water. It was covered in white scales, an armor of sorts. A few of the scales had been lost and had not been replaced, exposing the wood underneath. It had one centrally located large mast, flanked by smaller ones, fore and aft.

Captain Alabaster was undergoing the last of his pre-sailing checks and it seemed to the silver-haired man that everything was ready. He stood on the deck in the morning sun, his white hat and coat worn over blue pants matched his surroundings well. Some of his crew thought he did this on purpose. He had. His nose flicked as he sniffed the air. It smelled clear, a good omen for sailing.

The gangplank moaned and the captain turned to face it. 'Surely this is the daughter and her companions,' he thought to himself. Tara was the first to board; she carried two bags over her shoulder. Captain Alabaster's boots clicked on the deck, well polished, and bowed fantastically for her. Tara smiled and said, "Good day, captain."

"And to you, daughter."

"This is an interesting ship."

"'Tis, that is true. These are your companions?" Isaac and Shen'xhin'mhen had risen over the side and joined her, followed at last by Xer'tala'n.

"Yes. Captain Alabaster, this is Isaac Samuelson." Isaac had regained some of his polish, his hair was well managed, but his mind was dark. He shook the captain's hand while marveling at the mustache and his bushy but styled eyebrows.

"Nice to meet you."

"Likewise."

Tara continued, "Shen'xhin'mhen." The Su'th bowed slightly.

"I wouldn't have guessed by the stories told of you after the fight with Master Archammer." Alabaster smiled, "Welcome aboard."

"I am honored."

Captain Alabaster noticed the big cat behind Xhin'mhen and asked, "What's the lion's name?"

Shen'xhin'mhen answered, "He is Xer'tala'n."

The captain's hazel eyes flickered, betraying thought. "My crew is used to working in odd situations. As long as he behaves himself there won't be any problems." The captain turned his head and called to a woman who worked coiling ropes. "Lucca!"

The woman was tan and wore loose clothing exposing her strong shoulders. She pushed her short brown hair behind her ears as she came over to them. "Show our fare to their rooms."

Lucca smiled, lips closed, and nodded, then flipped her head sideways. "Don't think her rude," Captain Alabaster said, "She can't speak." Lucca pulled a tight necklace woven with shells down just slightly to show a nasty scar across her throat. Alabaster said, "If we had been so fortunate to have a daughter on board when we sailed that voyage things might have been different." Then his demeanor changed, "I will collect payment later. Stay out of the way of the crew, but otherwise enjoy the trip as best you can."

Lucca raised her right hand and motioned for them to follow. They did, the steely woman obviously had earned her keep. They went down into the belly of the boaot from below the sounds of work carried muted through the halls. Clearly, the price that was to be paid was paid for the best the ship had to offer, the hall was carpeted and fine wood paneled the walls. Lucca walked easily, keeping with the slight sway of the ship. Tara and Isaac staggered slightly. The Su'th moved without difficulty.

Lucca led them to a split in the hall and turned left. The passage was lit by a porthole at each end of it. She turned and pointed to a door on either side of the hall, then walked backwards until she leaned on the wall and pointed to two more doors. Tara asked, "All four?"

Lucca nodded, half smiling with angular lips.

Tara was surprised, "Thank you. I didn't expect so much."

The sailor shrugged and walked forward. As she passed the lion she ran one finger down his back then smacked him near his tail and turned the corner. Xer'tala'n grumbled surprise. Shen'xhin'mhen chuckled, "A room for you as well, Tala'n." Then changing course, "This ship, as you said, is interesting."

Tara said, "It is somewhat odd, all in all. I have not seen one like it before."

Isaac clicked the knob and opened the door to the first room. The room was well kept with all the necessary appointments. Each room in turn was similar. After placing their things and settling into their rooms the passengers filtered back up to the deck. More of the crew was now present. Captain Alabaster stood near the wheel, which was on a raised section of the deck just above his quarters. A markedly tall man stood next to him, his skin much darker than Shen'xhin'mhen's. They conversed rapidly, the captain waving his arms frantically, but what they spoke of was blown away and swept ashore by the wind and the water. The man finally walked away, waving dismissively. He crossed the deck and climbed down a ladder into the ship. Captain Alabaster bellowed for his passengers benefit, "We'll be departing shortly."

Isaac leaned over the railing and looked down; from under the white scales oars poked out, skimming the water, upsetting the careful roll of the ocean against the side of the ship. In one motion the oars stroked, pushing the boat slightly away from the dock. Isaac said quietly to himself, "Well, Isaac, if there was any doubt about this it's too late now." He stood up straight and looked up the cliff. The House of Wrath's spire and the lighthouse were the only signs of Serac so far above.

Tara walked over and stood next to him, both watching the cliff lurch away. Isaac said, "I didn't think of it much on our way to Serac, but I miss her a lot, Tara. I was able to distract myself with all the travel and the Su'th. Having a couple of weeks to settle, to think. It's painful." He shook his head. "I guess in a strange way leaving

Serac like this brings it all back. I'd never been here, but just knowing it existed was comforting. And now leaving it, leaving everything I've ever known, which I'm learning isn't much, makes me ache. I don't think there's a spell for that."

Tara turned and leaned against the rail, putting her hand on his shoulder. "No, there isn't. But if there was some magic that would make it go away, I don't think you'd want it. I'm sorry for your loss, I can only imagine the pain, but you've chosen to live. It's very honorable. Of her and you."

"I hope so. I don't want to be consumed with wanting revenge, but it's on my mind. All the time. Then I think about who or what made that monster. What could I do in the face of that? Nothing. Nothing, and I realize I'm helpless to avenge Cassandra."

Tara smiled sadly. "I don't think this is about revenge or vengeance. I'm still not sure what it's about exactly. Ah, look they're getting ready to unfurl the sails."

The sails dropped, hanging limp for a moment, rippled and filled with a crack of snapping fabric. The boat, spurred on by the noise, caught the breeze and sped away from the cliff. The crew settled into purpose, each moving with intent as they swarmed the deck. Captain Alabaster spun the wheel turning the boat to the northwest, and there it stayed pointed like a needle.

Isaac went down to his cabin in hopes that sleep would dull his pain.

"I am glad that you could join us, Master Nightwillow," Frederick Guildenil said frankly, sitting in his study. The First of Currents was clearly agitated as he spoke to the Directorate Council that did not include Trahn Entrah.

"I wish it were not so," the graying woman answered.

Frederick responded, "As do I, but the days require it. Hopefully you are all versed in the occasion. But a short recounting. During the Fall Festival Mother Rainmarrow approached me about Master Entrah's health. We all know of the recent difficulties of the House of Animate, but after visiting with Master Entrah, it is clear that he is not well.

"His mental state is such that it jeopardizes the recovery of the House from the recent events in the Rousan Empire. And while I know that there is a certain amount of inter-house squabbling, this chance of serious damage can not be allowed.

We have seen mages transferring their studies, and the general displeasure from the citizens is worrisome. That does not even begin to cover the danger all of the Houses are in when relating to the Rousan Empire.

"As outlined in my writings, I have come to the belief that it is in the House's best interest to cede control from Master Entrah until such time as the man regains his faculties. For the time being I will overtake the day to day operations as First of the House. But this arrangement would only last until the House of Animate is capable of putting forward its own leadership, be that Master Entrah or another."

Gavin asked, probing, "Do you think it wise to take such a burden on, Master Guildenil?"

"I do."

Master Nightwillow asked, the concern on her face pouring through her voice, "What will be done with Master Entrah? Surely something must be done to help him."

Guildenil raised his hand, a calming, and answered, "The Mother has already agreed to tend to his health. If there is one place in Serac that his sanity can be reached and recovered it is in The Way of Health."

Lilac nodded softly, her eyes half closed. "Everything will be done for him." She placed her hand on Nightwillow's cheek as a mother comforting a child. "Heal your House."

Nightwillow said quietly, "I hope that it is possible."

Gavin interjected, "Do not despair, Master Nightwillow. You have the full support of the Directorate Council. You will not fail."

Frederick Guildenil smiled, "Helpful as always, Master Archammer."

"Do you doubt my intent, Master?" Gavin snarled.

"No. Of course not."

"That is good of you. I am sick of having my motives questioned, tired of being chastised for putting my House first."

Frederick sighed, "What are you talking about, Gavin?"

"Your memorandum clearly noted displeasure at the transfer of Celia Hurn."

"It is of some concern to me, yes."

"That is what I am talking about! The House of Wrath is not in shambles, and I would suggest that you not treat it as though it is," Gavin spoke quickly, violently.

Frederick countered, "You know very well that this is not about The House of Wrath. You accuse anyone that even hints at dissatisfaction with you and your House with wild claims, as though you wish to fight openly on the council. I find this behavior intolerable, and I have had quite enough of it. Quite enough indeed."

Gavin opened his mouth to speak, but Frederick snapped his fingers, and no sound came out. "I am not finished." He pointed a bony finger at the First of Wrath. "You are powerful, there is no doubt, but you forget with whom you now deal and you lack even the subtlety of your predecessor. It is easy to hoodwink your constituents with your wealth and glory stories, but you cannot deal with us, your equals, in such a manner. I will not tolerate it any longer. The House of Wrath has had its share of problems of late. Two people escaped from your custody. Three slaughtered mages. Perhaps we should investigate your handling of House business." Gavin glared, but endured the rant. "No, I did not think you would like such light." Frederick snapped his fingers again and said, "Now I am finished."

Gavin stood and said, "Do not do that again, old man." He shook his head while his eyes locked with Master Guildenil's. "Not again."

Frederick said, "Enough bluster. Sit down and allow this council to work civilly. Or leave, and accept our rulings."

Gavin tensed, all could sense it, then slowly he sat.

The Flying Louise cut cleanly, crisply, through the ocean. The sun was high in the sky, unassailable by the wispy, pure white clouds that gathered to conspire against it. Isaac lay in bed, his head half a second behind the rock of the ship. He did not sleep, but did not move. His thoughts turned to that night. Of Cassandra. Of Celsius. His heart ached for the woman. Puzzlement filled his head about the man; his bag still in Isaac's possession.

Cold hatred had taken away his love, settling into love's place as though it owned his heart. The hate was directed at the maker of the monster, a vacancy, since the maker was unknown. There were now suspicions, but it all seemed too impossible. Isaac rolled over and replayed the night again. It did no good for the final outcome was the same; it was always the same. It would always be the same, and that most of all hurt. The loss could not be changed.

Added to his pain was the small voice of doubt, questioning his flight from Tarlow, spreading concern about his parents and his lowly reputation. Most times it had been easy to ignore the voice, but of late, in moments already weakened by Cassandra's death, it was a vicious adversary. An unkillable hydra, heads bringing agony. Isaac rolled over again and closed his eyes tight. He felt weak. Still sleep did not come.

Time passed quickly for Tara as The Flying Louise sailed northwest. The captain was impressed with the winds that pushed the scaled boat forward. Tara, her curiosity piqued by the passing comment of the forgotten sailor, looked for an opportunity to question the captain about his past, but never did such an opportunity present itself.

With the ship over halfway to Riversea, Captain Alabaster invited his guests to dinner. Tara took the invitation, delivered by the mute Lucca, and read it with a smile, but not much surprise.

To my guests,

It is with much regret that I have been unable to formally dine with you, business as business is. To right such a grievous wrong I request that you would join me for said dinner this evening. Formalities aside, I would also request that Xer'tala'n shed his guise, and join us for a civil evening.

With apologies,

Captain Sebastion Alabaster

His signature looped and spun, taking more space on the paper than the invitation. Tara took the invitation to the Su'th and read it to them.

Tala'n, who sat against the wall on the floor, said, "It is kind of the captain to invite me, though it brings up questions."

Tara said, "It would have been nice since he knows of your people to mention the aspecting earlier. It would have saved us some small amount of worry. He did say that he sailed to the Tan'Su'th. Hired Su'th as sailors. A question for you."

Tala'n said, "As you wish."

"Do the Su'th hold trade with the Elves?"

The Su'th looked at one another, then Xer'tala'n said, "It has been a long time since I have laid eyes on an elf. I was a child, in Ku'na. My mother took me to the market while she shopped. They walked among us, beyond us, beautiful. But there has been no contact in decades. They are enigmatic even by our standards, sorcerer." The lion scratched his ear and then said, "Come to think of it, this ship is reminiscent of the ships I saw that day. I would not have remembered if you had not spoken of it."

Tara smiled and said, "I knew of them only in legend."

Shen'xhin'mhen smiled and said, "Our captain grows more and more remarkable it seems. I look forward to this dinner. A shame that we have such informal cloth only."

Tara agreed, "That is true. I hope that Isaac can be roused from the storm in his head. I worry for him. He does not eat much, nor sleep. He tries, but it eludes him. My magic does not affect him. He was able to push Cassandra's death away for a time, but it gnaws aggressively at him now."

Tala'n said, "I will speak to the lad. And then, since I am free to roam as I am, I will work him as he has not been worked. He will again find a friend in sleep."

Tara closed her eyes slowly and opened them. "Thank you, Tala'n."

Tala'n knocked loudly on the door to Isaac's room. Isaac moaned and said, "Who is it?"

The Su'th rumbled, "Get up human, it is time to train."

Isaac did sit up, and he said, "Tala'n? What by the Currents are you doing? Get in here before someone sees you."

The door swung open and the silhouette of the priest filled the door. It scared some small part of the man. "It seems the captain is aware of the truth behind my devotion to Her. We are invited as the guests of the captain for dinner tonight, but it has been some time since we have practiced together. We will see if you have learned your lessons well."

"I am glad you don't have to hold the lion's form, but I don't feel well, Tala'n."

"I do not care. Get up. You will thank me, I promise."

Isaac thought about further protest, but the priest smiled, showing his pointed teeth. Isaac got up. "Okay."

Tala'n purred his approval. Isaac followed the Hierophant up to the deck. The priest drew stares, but not one of the crew reacted with surprise. Lucca smiled and winked at the Su'th. He nodded in response. Then he turned his attention to the disheveled Isaac. The polish of Serac had worn away, worse than the road weariness. The Su'th cracked his neck and took the form that they studied. Isaac again followed him.

The Su'th advanced at half the speed of the last time they worked together, teacher and student. Isaac flailed, and Tala'n's elbow tapped his chest. Tala'n frowned. "Isaac. Focus."

Isaac nodded, shook his arms to loosen them and advanced. His form was sloppy, Tala'n turned away the attack without effort, pushing the human to the deck. "Concentrate."

Isaac stood up, frowned and closed his eyes. Tala'n attacked, Isaac's chest swelled, filling with air, and he matched the priest's strikes, forearm on forearm. "Good."

Tala'n pushed Isaac hard all afternoon. From time to time the crew would stop and watch, then remember their duties. Isaac sweat hard, the ache of use crept into his muscles. Shen'xhin'mhen joined them for a time, then left to pray. Tara watched with a smile, eventually practiced her joint locks on the man and took her leave. The captain examined his guests with a keen eye. When they rested in the late afternoon, Lucca stopped as she walked by and flipped her fingers towards Tala'n. The Su'th smiled, "You want to fight, do you?"

Lucca nodded. Tala'n stood up, adjusted his loose pants and shirt, then said,

"Let us."

For this, the crew did gather to watch, the captain included. The tall man had taken the wheel. The crew bet lustily on the fight, clearly not serious, but Isaac thought that they might gamble on anything. Lucca's hands were made into claws, and the two circled slowly. The pair stepped close together, exchanging blows slowly at first. Each was countered by the other. The strikes accelerated, faster and faster. If one was winning it was Tala'n only because of his size and strength. The crew cheered.

Toe to toe they stood. Isaac watched with a keen eye. Each knew what the other was going to do, he was convinced of it, but the blur of movement made it exciting nonetheless. The cheer grew louder as the sparring reached a crescendo.

Then suddenly the fight lurched to a halt. They stepped back and bowed slightly. He smiled, purring, "Well done, Lucca."

The fight was over, Lucca picked up some rope and walked away. The gamblers tried to figure out who had won and who had won money. The losers cursed their luck and the Su'th or Lucca. The captain smirked and said, "Okay, back to work, everyone back to work."

Tala'n sat down with a slight smile on his wizened face.

Isaac said, "That was odd. Kata?"

"You perceive much, human. It is called the One Hundred Hands. A Su'th discipline or so I believed. I did not know that any outside of the Tan'Su'th were learned of it. It is used to train the mind and body. It reminds of the balance between power and speed." The Su'th swirled his arms, "Here," then pointed to his forehead, "and here." Tala'n stood again clearly distracted by thought and said, "I must pray and ready for dinner. Calm yourself and do the same."

The guests met Captain Alabaster in his quarters. If the passengers quarters were all that they could ask for, then his quarters provided everything that a ship's captain could require. Maps and charts hung on the dark walls and lay on side tables, out of the way of the meal that was being presented. A plush bed rested in the corner, drawing only passing notice to itself. A trunk with a hefty lock sat near it. Two sabers hung crossed over the bed. Portholes let in the orange-red light of a low sun.

The round table was already served with bread and soup. Covered dishes held other delights hidden from sight. The captain greeted his guests. "Welcome, welcome. Come in and take a seat."

Isaac, who looked tired, said, "Thank you for the invitation. It is really too kind."

"Nonsense! I grossly failed in my duties. Tara, be a dear and hand me that bottle." Sebastion pointed to a stout brown bottle. "I hope you all enjoy a touch of wine. I will demand as your host that you at least sample it. This is a wonderful vintage from Tarlow."

The captain began pouring the red wine into metal cups, which were gross compared to their surroundings. Then he sat down and said, "That was an impressive display today, Xer'tala'n. It has been some time since I have been in the presence of such an Aspect. A great many years."

Tala'n's eyes flickered in the sunlight, sparkling gold. "That is kind of you to say, captain. How is it that you learned of us?"

Tara smiled at the bluntness of the conversation. Sebastion stared out the side window looking back in time and said, "The story is an old one, priest. Like the sea. But everything is, isn't it." He lifted the lid on the large center dish, the room filled with the scent of cooked bird, brown and crispy. He began to carve it. "When I was only a child my parents and I were forced to flee our home, I don't remember the reasons why. We boarded a ship headed to Midsun."

Meat began filling the plates around the table as he spoke. "I suppose the ship was attacked by pirates. It was looted as pirates are wont to do. They killed everyone. Except me. I was not noticed. The ship, emptied of everything of value, was left to drift." He took a bite of the bird, chewed it and nodded happily. "Mm. That is when they came, out of the fog. The glimmering white ships. The Elves. They took me in, saved my life. I sailed with Captain Eaendril first as an adopted son, then when I was old enough to work, as crew. When I was younger with them, before I worked, we sailed a trade mission to your homeland. Delivering incense and silk and perfume to your royalty.

"That was the only time I saw the potential of your race. Since then I have employed Su'th in various positions, but always the youngsters. Good workers. Good at shielding the true forms from prying eyes as well. Maybe a hint of ears or fur, but nothing more."

Tala'n tore at a roll. Shen'xhin'mhen ate quietly, his beard bobbing as he chewed. Tara asked, "Is this an elvish ship?"

"Aye, 'tis, daughter. After some twenty years of serving Captain Eaendril, he grew disinterested in the sailing arts. As elves do. The ship was passed to me as his son and as time passed the elves that crewed her went on to other things." The captain half smiled. "Once they had all quit their service to the ship the way to find them was lost to me. I know that Eaendril lives, I feel him with me yet, but I do not know the way."

Tara nodded and said, "I'm sorry."

The captain smiled a toothy grin. "Come now, it is not a sad story. I have an unmatched ship. A loyal crew." Sebastion looked to the ceiling and said loudly, "Right, Hetta?"

From through the ceiling the tall man answered, "The very best, sir."

"And a tale that cannot be matched," finished the captain.

Tala'n said, "And what of your crew. Lucca is practiced in Su'th disciplines."

"Aye, she is, priest. I have never asked her her story, I do not presume to be as familiar with her as Eaendril was to me. I do know that she lived in Ku'ni as a servant in a temple. She joined my ship when she was no more than fourteen. A mutual decision made by her and the priests of the temple. I look after her as best I can, nearly a daughter, the closest thing I have, but we never discussed her past."

Tala'n asked, "How long ago was that?"

"Hmm, maybe ten years, maybe twelve. Enough about me and my crew. You are an interesting assembly. Two Su'th, a mage, and Isaac." Isaac looked up from his dinner. The captain shrugged. "What would you have me call you?"

Isaac smiled unhappily, "I suppose that is all I am, an Isaac."

Captain Alabaster frowned a moment, "I did not in my land haze ask you, Tara, what is your business? It seems more than strange, the traveling companions."

Shen'xhin'mhen said, "Our business is returning home, Tala'n and I. Nothing more."

"And the Isaac and Tara?"

Tara locked eyes with Isaac and said, "We are looking for a mage. Master Jannan. With luck we will find him. Without luck, our questions will remain unanswered."

The captain said, "'Tis a big world to find one man in." He lifted his cup, "To finding home, and Master Jannan."

The other cups were raised and the toast met.

Thirty-three

Isaac stood with his shoulders slumped, leaning on the rail of the bow of The Flying Louise. Fog rolled around the man, obscuring the world to him, a physical representation of his mind. Xer'tala'n would penetrate deep into the haze, Tara less so. Shen'xhin'mhen had not spoken to him since the night of the dinner with Captain Alabaster. It was not that he did not worry, he felt foolish attempting petty conversation with one in such turmoil. Isaac had nothing to say to the Su'th.

Tara had explained to the captain and he to his crew why Isaac walked like the dead. None were truly concerned, not even Tara. It would take time for him to wrestle with the death of his fiancé. The fight had been raging for some time now. Isaac had grown tired of it but that did not seem to matter, it was not his fight to walk away from, so he struggled on.

The ship had passed Riversea's harbor without slowing, much to the disappointment of Tara, and made good time as it sailed towards Midsun. Captain Alabaster had goods to deliver there. Then they would push further north until they could go no further, perhaps as far as Ku'ni or Ku'na. Su'th cities that would at least allow the elf ship to dock. With the two Su'th on board the captain was especially confident.

And so it went day after day, the ship moved north, until finally Midsun appeared in view. The ship slowed far from shore and dropped anchor. There were two other ships, neither of elvish make, that had done the same. Isaac used the telescope to watch men scramble on the shore, two competing crews with wide, flat bottomed boats. They rowed straight for the ship, but Isaac saw them as sharks circling a bloated fish.

Captain Alabaster ordered one of his men to lower a rope ladder and the two boats attacked it violently, almost coming to blows to get their captain up it first. The two men stood side by side, still jostling each other as they addressed Sebastion. Their accents thick in the southerner's ears, they spoke fast and loudly. "Let me 'andle all of yer needs cap'in!"

"Don't liss'en to this mongrel. Let me an' my lads."

They turned and faced each other in a comical stare down, each muttering, then screaming at each other, waving fists and turning red.

"Jus' cause mother loved you best—"

"M'tter din't love me best she—"

"Dosn' mean ya should steal ma—"

"Loved you the best!"

"Work! And so did father!"

"No he din't and I'm no stealin' yer work!"

"Yes you are!"

"Yer stealin' mine!"

"I'm not! An' yer crew is rats!"

"Rats! Yer's is snakes!"

The captain finally intervened. "There's enough work for each of you, if you would just be silent." The men stopped their arguing and each smiled smugly, as though their fighting had earned them the only job. "One of you come with me. Tara, we will be here for a day or two, so why don't you all go to shore."

The two men glanced sideways at each other seemingly ready to battle again before thinking better of it. The thicker of the two made a sweeping gesture towards the rope ladder and said, "When you arr ready te go ashore, my ferry is ready."

A few minutes later Tara, Isaac and Shen'xhin'mhen sat on the wide boat as it rowed towards shore. Xer'tala'n, aspected as a lion, stood on the white sand beach shaking the seawater from his mane. The ferry beached and the captain carried Tara from the boat, keeping her from getting wet.

"When you need to return to the ship make sure you as' fer Copelan an not fer Dirk."

Tara smiled as she looked around. "I will."

Isaac and Xhin'mhen stepped into the surf, slogging up to the dry sand. Copelan hollered, "Back te the ship!" Two men jumped up and pushed the ferry back into the sea, re-soaking their clothes up to their waists, then hopped in as the crew of six started rowing.

Isaac shook his head and said, "I wouldn't want to be at their dinner table."

That said, the visitors entered Midsun.

Isaac's vision of Midsun collapsed under the reality. It was not the grand bastion of romantic intrigue as he had been led to believe listening to the wealthy chatter in Tarlow. It was a maze of single and double story mud buildings. Palm trees, unlike anything he had ever seen, even at The Way of Health, grew here and there providing shade from the sun. Where the roads were not shaded they baked, casting warmth up from them.

Always the road led towards the center of the city and it did not take long to lose sight of the ocean and The Flying Louise. Passing through open air markets rich with the scent of heavy perfume and unclean animals the cramped road opened into the city center, a large paved square.

A fountain, carved of gray stone in the image of men and women, ancient as told by weathering, fired over a dozen streams of water into the air, filling a basin. Children played in the water, hooting and hollering. Meat sizzled loudly in metal dishes, cooking over a large open pit flame. Brightly colored canopies covered blankets and tables, which in turn were covered with brightly colored scarves, shirts and robes. Humans and young Su'th passing as human milled around, going about their lives.

Beyond the fountain a large building, square with a tall dome, dominated the view. It was designed in a different fashion than all the other buildings, a purity that the others twisted and dragged into the mud they were made of. The building was clearly the focus of the city, and it in turn focused on the fountain.

A Su'th merchant approached Tara with a scarf, red and gold. He draped it over her shoulder with a smile, canines sharp. Tara drew the fluid like cloth over her arm. "It's beautiful. How much?"

The Su'th spoke, a hint of Tala'n's rumble. "For you." He held up three fingers. Tara fished the coins from a bag and paid him. He smiled larger. Then noticing Tala'n he bowed and spoke in Su'th, "Esteemed one." Tala'n rumbled and the Su'th continued, "Be wary, there is a strange wind that blows, I have dreamt it." He bowed again and returned his attention to his scarves.

Tala'n's eyes narrowed, and he took up dominance under a palm. The humans in the square eyed the cat carefully, but most had seen enough to know that he traveled with the Su'th, and that the Su'th controlled their beasts with unimaginable skill.

Isaac tugged on the sleeve of a cook and bought a plate of meat and onion. "What is that?" he asked, pointing to the building.

The merchant, silver and black scruff on his chin, looked suspiciously at him but said, "It is the Emporium. It is Midsun."

Isaac nodded, eyebrows raised, skeptical of its greatness. And despite that he, Tara and Xhin'mhen all found themselves standing at the entrance together. A small foyer devoid of all distraction provided a place to empty the mind. Beyond that the wonders of the world exploded in color and scent and sound. The Emporium was filled past its walls. If there was organization to it none could make out the riddle.

Isaac pushed through the muggy air, coldly surveying what was before him. He would meet the gaze of merchants and buyers seeing a savage greed in their eyes, driven to madness by the place. Isaac stopped and watched two cocks fighting while men cheered wildly. He could take no more and hurried for the exit. Women dressed in almost nothing threw themselves in his path. He suffocated. Fat-faced men pushed animals at him. He staggered. Then the tranquility of the entrance flooded him. He was free. Outside again he sat down near the priest and waited for the others.

The men from the ferries began bringing the boxes into the square. Hetta guarded them, counting each. Soon a mighty pile had grown and the merchants had turned into buyers, questioning the tall man about their contents. He answered the pack over and over, "Wait for the captain."

Soon Tara and Xhin'mhen sat with Isaac, all under the gaze of Tala'n. None spoke, each absorbing the experience of the Emporium in their own way, all dazed, stunned by the madness. The captain finally appeared, dressed in his finest outfit. He laughed as he walked towards his fare, flask in hand. "Into the Emporium you've been. It always has the same effect the first time. It lessens the next time, and after that it owns you." He swallowed a drink. Holding the flask out he smiled and said, "I can not walk on land without it. My knees don't know it." Tara took the flask and slugged back a drink. He laughed again.

Isaac regained his wits and said, "You could have warned us."

Alabaster shook his head, "There be no warning of it. 'Tis not possible. Find yourself an inn, Su'th run if possible, for Xer'tala'n. I'll let you know what the plans are when I know them." The captain glanced to the side and smiled smugly, "Time to move the cargo." He waded into the throng and began speaking loudly.

Isaac turned away from the throng and said, "Okay, so now what? We're stuck in this miserable town with a few days to kill, and all he says is get a room."

Xhin'mhen said, "It is not so bad. Tala'n and I are closer to home now than we have been in months."

"And I'm glad for you, really I am, but Tara and I are losing time. Time that we should spend finding Master Jannan. Wrath. What am I doing here?" His voice had turned irritated, sharp.

Tara finally spoke, "I don't altogether disagree with you, but don't lose hope. Things will come together. Let's find that Su'th inn and get a sense of the city." Tara stood up. "Where is the man I bought this scarf from?" She looked around, "Ah, there."

She walked over to him and said, "Excuse me, but I need to find an inn."

The Su'th answered excitedly, "For the lion?" Tara nodded. The man quickly scribbled a note using a quill and ink well that was hidden in his stand. "Follow the northwest road out of town." He handed the note to Xhin'mhen pointing to a name. "My brother, Me'rin, he runs the inn. Makes a wonderful brisket. Try it. None of these pushers can even come close."

Shen'xhin'mhen read the card. Speaking in Su'th he said, "The Second Eye? It is easy to find?"

"Yes, yes. Very easy, the only Su'th architecture in Midsun. It will remind you of home."

"Very nice, indeed. You have my thanks."

"It is I who benefit."

Shen'xhin'mhen addressed Isaac and Tara, "We stay at the Second Eye."

As the merchant had said, the Second Eye was easy to find. The lone road leading northwest out of Midsun passed it. If the inn was out of town, it was only by inches. Also as the merchant had said it was built as a remembrance of Tan'Su'th. A high wall around the grounds reminded Tara of the Great Garden, but once inside, after passing through a wood gate, after first being examined by a gateman, the extent of the care became evident. Carefully raked paths led to small altars, wood and stone. A system of streams and ponds split the sandy ground. Plants grew in meticulous clumps, tended to form perfect moments.

The inn was raised ever so slightly off the ground, a wood walkway all around it. Round stone columns supported the roof that flared out over the walkway. Me'rin met his guests before they reached the three-tiered building. The tiers shrank as they rose skyward forming a pyramid, if not exactly then in suggestion.

Shen'xhin'mhen spoke with the innkeeper, words quick, and Tala'n found his true form. Me'rin did not kneel, but offered reverence to the Hierophant. The innkeeper, a spitting image of his brother, led them through a sliding screen, framed on either side by vertical rows of pictorial script. The interior was warm and clean, truths of sensation and design. The columns from outside repeated here.

Many Su'th, men and women, knelt over low stone tables, some eating, others playing games of sorts. Most of the Su'th were young, without marks of Ku'na'shi, but those with them openly displayed them. Others could not hide them even should they want to. Half-changed faces, taking on traits of their feline goddess. Furry tufts poked out from under sleeves. Triangular ears. A few had large splays of whiskers. None took the full form that Xer'tala'n did and his appearance brought silence, followed by whispering. One brave man asked what each thought, "Why does a Hierophant associate with man? Why do you bring them here into our sanctuary?"

Shen'xhin'mhen whispered to the humans, "He questions Tala'n's judgement."

Xer'tala'n at the same time answered, turning his left hand upwards at his hip. "I thought as you do, not long ago. Man has not earned our respect. But know this. Because of these, the Ta'ke'shya Ku'na'shi is found. Let that alone be your measure."

Tara smiled at the mention of the Ta'ke'sh. That much at least she understood. None questioned directly what Xer'tala'n said, but awe and confusion filled the room.

Me'rin walked through the open room to some stairs, he began speaking as he climbed them, "Is it true? Her gift is found?"

Tala'n answered, "It is. We carry the word to the Emperor."

Me'rin nodded in thought, then spoke to the humans, "It is not often that I accept man under my roof, but despite its failure the pledgestone holds some sway here. And you have acquitted yourselves, there is no doubt." He walked down the hall, turned to the left and said, "Here."

The rooms were simple, less extravagant than those on The Flying Louise. "There is a bathhouse behind the inn." Me'rin nodded politely and retreated down the hall.

Tara smiled, "Did he say bath house?"

Tala'n rumbled, "He did."

"That is a most beautiful development." Her voice filled with song. The travelers glanced at each other all thinking the same thing, then raced to the bathhouse. The hot water and steam was too inviting to pass up.

Captain Alabaster called upon the Second Eye the next morning. Shen'xhin'mhen alone took the meeting. The captain's mustache escaped its normally contained existence. His eyes were wild. "The weather has taken a rather nasty turn, Xhin'mhen."

The Su'th, wearing a single piece robe, poured tea into a cup. "How is that, captain?"

The captain leaned back. "The wind that rushed us here has subsided. The sea is still."

"How long do you believe this will last?"

"There is no way to tell."

"Discouraging."

The captain nodded, "Agreed. Pass it along to the others, I must return to my ship." Alabaster stood and walked away, nodding acknowledgment to Me'rin he said, "Your inn is beautiful."

"Thank you, captain." And with that he was gone.

Shen'xhin'mhen said to Me'rin who sat down, "We will be needing the rooms a while longer."

Me'rin nodded, "The humans as well?"

Xhin'mhen looked up, his eyes drawn tight. "Of course."

"I am sorry, but my guests questioned me about them. It is not comfortable for the aspected to be seen."

"If they question you, tell them what I told you. The Hierophant has their pledge." Xhin'mhen sipped his tea.

"We are two of a kind placing great value in the xho'ka. Others, not so much," the innkeeper said, his wife nodding agreement from across the room.

"It is sad truth."

Isaac sat behind a stone table, his legs crossed, his beard, such as it was had grown in. The bathhouse was good for the skin, but he had not shaved. A week's worth of whiskers. Not impressive when held against the aspected. Isaac drank tea from a saucer, having grown accustomed to the vessel in the week and two days that he had spent at the inn.

For the most part the wait had been calm. Captain Alabaster came every day to offer apologies. Isaac had not taken any of the visits. The others, all, had. They had gone into town, the decision had been made, they would ride for Tan'Su'th. Perhaps the wind would come tomorrow and they would regret their choice, but the choice had been made.

It was midday, the Su'th that would rise for the day had done so. Some were definitely nocturnal, Isaac had become fully aware of that fact. He still did not sleep. Not that he did not sleep, but it was not right; the brute haunted the dark side of his eyelids. He was angry at himself as he sat, that he could not put things behind him, even a bit. Xer'tala'n did his best to help, and Tara as well. He had seen all of her in the bathhouse, and it made him smile when he thought of her. But Cassandra would not let go, and he did not want her to, not yet.

As he sat in the dining room a group of Su'th, aspects of some nature all, had gathered. They made devious eyes at the man. Isaac did not know what brought on his courage but he said to them, "What do you want? Or are you going to spend the day glaring at me?"

The most blessed, as Shen'xhin'mhen would put it, spoke, her voice was a heavy purr, "So man, you have a tongue. I congratulate you on finding the heart of the Hierophant." She stood and the two men with her followed suit. One had ears shifted into triangles upon the top of his head and the other had claws. He did not show them now, but Isaac had seen them before. The three crossed the room and sat at the other side of the stone slab from the human. Me'rin's wife watched from where she sat.

The clawed one said, "I do not like your presence here, human."

"So?"

He slammed his fist on the table. "You have the grace of the Heirophant, but nothing more. Not ours."

Isaac smiled, "He's not even the reason that your brethren are here. It's the Entertainment Minister that brings them here."

The woman snarled, "The Hierophant is above all."

"Not above me." The claws came out at that. Isaac raised his left hand. "What are you going to do?" He felt a feistiness that had eluded him for some time. Isaac drank the last of his tea and stood up. "Nothing. Just what I expected from you."

The clawed Su'th leapt from his place, what Isaac had said the perfect taunt. Isaac's schooling surfaced. He stepped into his assailant and pushed him past into one of the posts. The Su'th coughed, air escaping. The other two were up. Isaac muttered, "This is stupid. Your Hierophant will not be happy."

The other man came first, using the most basic Su'th martial arts. Isaac smiled to himself. The I & A training would prove sufficient to dispatch this fool. Isaac pushed him aside and cracked him in the side of the head. Me'rin's wife stood up, worried about the debacle unfolding in her dining room.

The blessed woman hissed and burst forward. Isaac met her strike with his own. Her arm rolled over his and locked his elbow. Her thumb folded into her hand and thrust forward, clearly, from her expression she expected more. Isaac frowned. "Failed magic? The sorceress has told me as much."

Isaac grabbed her by the throat. "Now all of you. Leave me the hell alone!"

He pushed her back, she fell over the table, her slitted eyes narrowed and she held her neck. "The Hierophant will hear of this!" she exclaimed. The three hurried away from the man. He did not know where the strength had come from but was glad for it. He shook his head and thought of Cassandra. Isaac stalked from the room, turning his head to tell the wife of Me'rin, "My friends can find me in the bath. If they have the need."

She bowed in response.

Isaac spent many hours in the bath, his fingers wrinkled and still he sat. The Hierophant at last came to him, only a cloth was wrapped around his waist. It was lost to the floor. "You use my teaching against my people, human."

Isaac shrugged, "Don't let them fool you, Tala'n. They attacked me. Too bad for them that their magic had no effect. Good for me."

"Isaac."

"Tala'n, I know. I'm sorry, it just happened."

The Su'th sighed and changed the subject. "Tara and Xhin'mhen bought supplies today, camels. We leave tomorrow."

"About time. I've worn out my welcome."

The door slid open and Tara joined the two men in the small room. Isaac said, "Tala'n tells me that we leave tomorrow."

Tara sat down on a wood bench and ladled water onto the hot stones in the middle of the room. Steam hissed from the rocks. "Yes, the captain is sorry to hear it, but the debt is settled with him." She leaned back against the wall and sighed, "I'll miss this."

Isaac smiled. Glancing sideways he said, "You and me both."

Tara and Tala'n smiled.

Thirty-four

Arcane's fortress continued to grow. The walls were complete, but the animates yet toiled.

The wind howled across the dreadful landscape, making the humans shiver. A fire burned to keep them warm, lighting their soft faces. It was in moments of watching his humans that Arcane's heart would beat loudly in his chest, lusty for blood and power.

The days passed and more and more Arcane's mind turned south. A shadow would look a mountain; a swirl of dust blown from the Sinkhole would materialize into a throne room. Places he knew, but had never seen. The whispers of the Sinkhole filled his ears, his mind, his anima. The cold. The fire of her power. The Harrow heart beat strongly, each thump pushing his attention to the Harrow. The ways of magic never quite clear to him.

Arcane began to ponder the Harrow and its simple ways, attempting to augur out a future. At last he could hear the nudging no more; Arcane set in motion yet another path. His queen called for him. Arcane frowned. Not his queen, and not for him. For the Harrow he had left lifeless and burned to the heavens.

"Peter, Lie Ben, Bessemer," Arcane spoke to them from a throne of sorts, made by the animate Sirkute. The wind buffeted against the wall, forcing him to speak loudly. "I must leave you for a time, to follow, quite literally my heart." He smiled as he said it, the human phrase lost its true meaning as he muttered it. "Do not fear the separation, Bessemer knows that I will soon return. In my absence I expect you to continue my work, brother. Do not allow the animates to falter." A wave of his hand brought light to the room, ensnaring Bessemer.

Bessemer's eyes glowed brightly. It said, "As you wish it, so it shall be, brother."

"I know this to be true. As for you, my humans. Await my return. It is little consolation I know, to be freed from one pit and then left in another, but this is as I desire."

Peter sneered, shrugged and blinked three times in quick succession. The black magic of the place had defiled his mind in ways that the pit of The House of Wrath never had. Arcane did not know if it would be permanent, but his obedience was complete.

Lie Ben's blue eyes seemed to illuminate themselves. He spoke softly and the wind quieted to hear his words. "Seek the Vein Marlant, man of metal. In the Vein you will find warmth. Without the Vein, man of metal, you are lost."

Arcane stared with heavy interest. He too spoke softly now. "The Sage of Tesca speaks of things he cannot see. I will heed your words."

The Sage's head flopped sideways, heavy, his shoulders shuddered. "Of course you will. Heed the words, her voice a song..." His head snapped again, eyes closed. When they opened the Sage of Tesca was gone. Lie Ben said, "It is clearer now. As a distant forgotten dream. A memory almost remembered."

Arcane said, "It is of little consequence. I was wise in your rescue; that is all that matters. Tend your garden, and keep Peter on a tight leash." Peter shook once, humored. "Bessemer, bring me my robes."

Arcane's twin did so, and with two pops of ozone they had bonded again to his Harrow filled core. The metal rippled alive, wrapping with tenderness around Bessemer before releasing him again to the coldness of the room. The mismatched procession followed the encased animate from his workshop, out into the windy, cloudy day. Lie Ben looked up at the sun, hidden behind the clouds, a glowing diffused orb. He sneered at it, mimicking Peter's earlier expression.

The courtyard was one of brutal simplicity. The animates who had built it asked for no pleasantness and received none. If the men were less tied to Arcane they would have complained about the sparseness, but did not since they were clearly his belongings. The spider that had helped slay Finsen climbed down the tower wall and ran under the flowing robes, taking its place around Arcane's torso. Sirkute's blocky form forced a large door open, scraping a circular path across the ashy soil, and stuttered across the rock beneath. It knew that Arcane was leaving. It said, "My master, travel safely."

Arcane's head dipped under the hood, acknowledging the devotee.

"Arcane." It was Lie Ben who spoke. Arcane turned, hood pulling back.

"Lie Ben."

"Announce her coming." The man looked confused. "Tell all."

"Await my return. A new vision will return with me." Arcane turned and began south, a rolling combination of running and falling, his robes pulling him lurchingly forward, a boiling mass.

Sirkute pulled the door closed, it scraped and thudded. "Where does the master go, Bessemer?"

The metal tone was matched, "I do not know, Sirkute. I do not know." Then Bessemer shouted to all of the animates, "Gather around, my perfect workers." Peter lost interest in the proceedings as the six animates formed ranks. "Arcane is pleased with the fortress, his love is great for each of you, he tells me this. And now he requires new tasks. Accept them."

Bessemer raised both hands and the magic of Arcane, encapsulated, waiting for the moment, burst from his anima, passing along specific instructions to each of the metal slaves. All save Sirkute smiled. The violent animate frowned. It did not want to build, it did not want to create. It wanted to destroy, to tear down. But it would not disobey. The foundry would rise.

Arcane moved with frightening speed, and yet it was not enough. Pulled forward by the now consuming beat of his stolen heart, his feet rested for mere moments on the dead ground. Free of the flesh of horse and man he moved as fast as possible. And yet he wondered if Peter could not keep pace, he had seen the man move at a full sprint once and it had, despite his power, frightened his crystal core.

'Flesh should not move as Peter does.'

And that thought pleased the animate because the anomaly belonged to him. The spider shuddered as it felt the thoughts of Arcane, and the animate carried on. The Sinkhole passed in short order, days and nights, and the world became colder as Arcane flowed on.

The landscape changed from the craggy rim that circled the Sinkhole to what it once had been; a plain of immense beauty, tall grass, cut through by a lazy river. From an outcrop over-looking the plain Arcane wondered why the humans had not settled here. Save the chill it looked perfection.

He could see herds of cattle, wild, roaming. The Harrow heart beat stronger now, closer to its calling. Beyond the plain, harsh black mountains rose sharply to the sky, a foreboding wall. Arcane reconsidered his thoughts about the humans. The stone would put off all but the most brave. A storm raged against the peaks, spewing lightning. Arcane climbed from his viewpoint and began to slide his way across the grassland.

After traveling for several days he came to the river. He crossed it, moving through the outer ranges of a great herd of buffalo. The animals paid little attention to the animate, unaccustomed to such a being. A great echoing call went up, followed by a great furor, a stampede. Arcane shielded himself as best he could inside the hardened metal shell, but the beating side to side was relentless. The herd forded the river, fleeing a hunter.

Arcane felt them first while he was still being battered by the shaggy animals. His heart called to them, betraying his presence. The hunters appeared. Four Harrow armed with spears, riding two legged lizards, scales gray and blue. The Harrow wore heavy armor; Arcane perceived it to be made from obsidian soaked in magic, glinting in the reddish, almost dirty sun. The lizards circled the animate, snorting and kicking at the dirt. They stared with their mirror gray eyes set in wedge shaped skulls that bloomed into five or seven point shields, horn poked free at the tips of each.

One of the Harrow spoke; the sounds did not make sense to the animate at first. Arcane silenced his concerned anima and focused on the tongue. It became clear. Arcane smiled at the corners of his mouth, the magic stupidly simple, wanting to give away its secrets.

"What is this little thing?"

"Is it not human, hidden under the robes?"

"No, the Harrow is with it, but it is not." A female voice. Arcane focused on the Harrow and their two legged beasts, preparing what had to be done. The spider shook, not with fear, but as an alarm. The lizard behind him had swiped with its taloned hand. The robes convulsed in, avoiding the claws.

"Fraiarrch! Control your livid!" the woman snapped.

A growl answered as they continued to circle. Arcane thought of speaking but did not; it seemed that he would be addressed when they desired it. The largest of the Harrow, with ashen skin, brought his livid to a stop. He spoke, "Reveal yourself, one with the Harrow."

The others also stopped, forming a quarter circle. Arcane closed his eyes, thought of what the Sage had said, opened them revealing the golden glow, and the robes burst apart. The livids twitched, startled by the parting. The robes settled into a cape of sorts, almost wings. At first the Harrow did not react, then the large one began to laugh. Deep and loud. "Ho, ho, ho. Metal. What are you, little man of metal?"

"Do you not remember the golem, Hetralmarr?" the woman answered through a sneer. She had coal skin; save a spot of pure white in the middle of her forehead, her blood red hair was pulled into a top knot.

"It has been a long time since I was of mankind, Vein. And never in the company of mage. So golem. What are you?"

Addressed as golem he answered, metallic, "I am the Animate Arcane."

The woman closed her eyes a moment, "You carry the heart of Finsen inside of you, stealing our power."

Concern flowed through Arcane, they had not forgotten what they should not have known. "He struggled, but my need was greater than his."

Hetralmarr re-gripped his spear and said angrily, "A slayer of the Harrow, exploiter of the Harrow, but not of the Harrow. What is your business man of metal golem Animate Arcane? Quickly, before I decide to end your life and reclaim what is ours!"

The Sage of Tesca would now be tested. "I seek the Vein Marlant."

The Vein's eyes tightened and she said, "She does not seek you, golem. She gathers her strength to face the Queen. And what reason can you give to justify her interruption?"

Arcane smiled. "The Queen is reason enough. I seek Marlant, with her only shall I speak. If you are followers of the Vein take me to her. If you are not then be gone from my sight for I tire with this delay."

Hetralmarr lowered his spear, the obsidian tip pointed at Arcane's heart. "You speak as a fool, golem."

"Do I? I seek the Vein Marlant. If she is to take her place as Queen," the Harrow and the Sage of Tesca spoke through him, "She will need my power."

The nameless Vein smiled, "Power, golem? The Harrow is with you, that is true, but what power do you possess?"

"I will be a god," said his vanity.

"Be that as it may, you are not a match for any of us. Least of all the Queen and her guard. What use can your cold soul be?"

A show of power then. Arcane's anima sang to him in chorus with the heart that he now knew to be truly its own self. It would need to be subjugated. The golem drew his hands apart and the ground shuddered. The livids staggered, the smallest of the Harrow fell from his mount. Arcane's hands turned outward and his head tipped back. His arms circled forming a line pointing at the fallen knight.

The armor he wore flaked away, returning to ash. Arcane turned his left hand upward, lifting the near naked knight off the ground. His right arm made a slow cutting movement. He smiled. "I will be the death of her."

The Harrow knight twitched in the throes of magic, coughed once, and scissored in two.

Power burned the air, the river hissed, boiling the shore, baking insects hidden in the mud. The Harrow knight fell to the ground, sparkling purple blood flowing between his pieces. His livid sniffed the corpse and tore a piece of meat from the body. The Vein breathed deeply, smelling the magic, her glass breastplate raised. She said, "Intriguing, the senses are deceived."

Fraiarrch alone acted, lowering his spear. His livid exploded towards the animate, two steps. The robes whirled, stiffening, but the obsidian point pushed through the blackened metal with ease. The Harrow knight lifted the spear and Arcane high into the air. His robes sliced at the spear in two, cutting Arcane loose. He dropped in a heap and flowed away from the Harrow, back to his feet. His eyes flickered, hurt. The Harrow knight ignored a desperate spell cast by Arcane and bore down on the golem with his sword.

"Enough! Fraiarrch, let the man of metal be." Hetralmarr frowned, his ashen face segmented into stone. He was furious at the act but a cold intellect guided his thought. "Marlant would be well advised to see you, golem. Take the livid if you can. Or follow as you would. Vein, silence the fallen." The Harrow knight pulled at the reins of his livid. The lizard wheeled; curved tail snapping like a whip as it sprinted away. Fraiarrch glared at the golem, then at the Vein, then his livid also wheeled and sprinted after Hetralmarr. The riderless livid followed instinctively. Arcane's robes congealed and the animate sped after the tremendous lizards. The Vein dropped to the ground behind them and began chanting. The ceremony unheard by ears that wished it.

The livid's speed subsided slightly as they bounded across the plain, their massive legs propelling them tirelessly forward. Arcane slid in behind the single file rank that cut through the grass. The sun fell, giving way to a crystal clear night of a million stars. The livids did not tire, nor did Arcane. In the morning they slowed and then stopped, a face of pure stone greeted them, mocking them to continue.

Hetralmarr looked back at the golem, saying, "We wait for the Vein."

She joined them shortly thereafter. Her eyes were wild. She said, "His blood has been spread. His heart silenced."

Hetralmarr nodded then said, "It is not easy going, these walls." The livid under him sprung straight up, catching a cleft of rock with the dominant claw on its right foot and threw itself up the wall catching further up with its left. Arcane smiled for a moment. The other two livids and their riders followed Hetralmarr. The riderless livid looked around for a moment, distracted from the climb, cocked its head sideways to get a better look at the rock wall and followed the others. Arcane's robes bent into huge hooks, and the combination of metal and magic thrust him skyward.

Eight hundred thirty-eight feet up the sheer face gave way to a wide ledge.

Fraiarrch nodded, frowning, impressed with the animate's ability. The livids' chests rose and fell quickly, reflecting the bleak light in a thousand colors of grey and blue, shifting as they moved.

Hetralmarr said, "Do not stray, golem."

Arcane did not respond, so the Harrow knight led the way up a path, cut into a more forgiving portion of the mountain. The path led up into the low clouds, the world seemed to slow, soft and sleepy. Flakes of snow fell from above, finding no refuge as they melted upon the rocky, unforgiving ground. Half a day of the same scene passed, the livids moved slower than on the plane, the distance traveled uncertain.

Finally, out of the mist and slow clinging snow, a wall appeared, built in a great cleft in the rock, a natural fortress. Ice grew over the top of the chasm above the fort, threatening to destroy what could not be assailed. Arcane noted it and followed through the great arch into the fort.

To his right a paddock of livids, young, colored in greens, had the attention of three unarmored Harrow, each more menacing than the last. The rock walls led past stone and glass buildings and guided the hunters to one final building, a chapel. Arcane knew it as such as soon as he laid eyes upon it. Hetralmarr said, "Marlant here resides." The Harrow swung from their lizards. "We shall see if she wishes your appearance." He looked at the other Harrow. "You are dismissed."

The massive man walked up three stairs and entered the building cut cleanly into the mountain. Arcane turned to the Vein. "You obey and follow Marlant?"

The Vein answered, "I do. She is the only one that dares to rise against the Queen. I learn from her now, and in time—" She stopped herself. "What is it you seek, golem? Are you here seeking the power of the Harrow?"

Arcane looked around the colorless world ignoring the question; his appearance had begun to draw notice. "What is your name, Vein?"

"Hethfora," she answered without hesitation. Another Vein, sword of black glass in hand, joined the side of the first.

Arcane nodded coyly to her. "Hethfora. A pretty name I think." He closed his angled eyes. "In the human tongue 'Hopebleeder'. Lovely." The name hung by itself in the cold air. "I seek a means to an end. Much as I will soon be used as one."

He shrugged under his robes, a motion unseen by the Harrow. "Nothing more."

"Golem!" It was Hetralmarr; he had emerged from the chapel and stood heavy in his armor on the top step between two roughly carved columns that supported an overhang. "Marlant accepts your presence here and will summon you when she is ready."

He walked down the stairs, pulling close to Arcane as Finsen had so many nights ago. The spider throbbed as the Harrow breathed in deeply. He said, "It is confusing that one of such power scents so cold. You must allow me..." He leaned forward, taking Arcane's head in his hands, he made a slight click, barely audible. Hetralmarr turned his head listening to the sound. Arcane felt the sound in his core, rebounding and rebounding. Revealing. "Your power is hidden, man of metal, subtle." His eyes opened and he stared with fury at him. "Devious. Do not betray us. If you do...there is no hell deep enough to hide you from my anger. There is a small repository in the chapel; await her there."

The Harrow knight pulled away from the animate, took the reigns of his livid and led it away. Arcane smiled and spoke to Hethfora. "Show me to this repository."

Hethfora nodded. "Fia, tend to Core. Follow me, golem." The Vein led Arcane up the stairs through the columns and into the walls. Inside was lit by a cold, thin, blue light, ice made fire. The source always seemed around the corner but never was. The air itself was set ablaze. Arcane marveled and turned inward. Already he was learning the truths of the Harrow, of what a shadow he was. Finally, the twisting corridors came to a door, made of wood slats, ancient.

She opened the door and allowed Arcane to pass her, then said quietly, knowingly, "Prepare your heart, golem, for it will be tested."

The door closed and Arcane frowned. His robes opened and he extracted the spear tip from his side. He gave it to the spider to care for.

The repository was slightly darker than the rest of the chapel. A single padded bench sat before a stone urn that was almost as tall as the animate. A liquid, frozen, filled it. On one wall hung a scroll, a scene from a great battle. The Harrow swept over their foes as a wave.

Arcane sat on the bench, the cushion heaved as he did. Arcane tapped the center of his forehead with his left forefinger, a slow rhythmic tick. In his mind he played Hetralmarr's click again and again, from both his and the spiders recollection. Finally, he came to conclusion. 'Careless. I must at all times shield my anima from these beasts. Always they are poking, prodding, looking for weakness. That is why Fraiarrch struck at me. I showed a moment of weakness after slaying his companion. Fury drove him, but only he perceived my anima stagger from the power. If the Queen's heart is to be mine…'

The thought stopped as his heart felt the shift of power within the chapel. Marlant moved. He had not noticed before, but the entire place was filled with her presence, like a cup with wine, as she moved it swirled, pushing unevenly against the walls, buffeting him. Runes scribed down his back lit up, taking effect, shielding him from the power of the Vein. She turned her will towards him and Arcane answered by throwing his own strength into shielding his anima, at the same time he blessed Master Jannan, praying that his work could survive such trial.

The magic subsided for a moment, then the crystal in his left hand began to flake apart. She was breaking him apart from the inside. Arcane summoned more power than he believed himself to have, realizing that failure now would be his death. The Way of Health for the first time truly bent to his will and the attack was put down, his core only slightly damaged. The battle of wills raged for hours; the Vein assaulted his mind, his anima and his core. Finally the tide ebbed and Arcane slumped, tired, wary. Steam rose from his eyes, his core hot.

Marlant's power moved again. Arcane focused, waiting for another test, but it did not come, the door to the repository opened and the Vein Marlant stood in all of her power before him. Arcane did not think, but immediately bowed before her. She was tall like the other Harrow, but held a majesty to her that the others did not. Her skin, what could be seen, her hands and face, was metal silver, not reflective but alive, grabbing at the colors around her, playing with the light. Her dress, a drab gray when put against her skin, was tight on top, then spread voluptuously about her hips down onto the floor. She slid into the repository, her steps concealed by the ridiculous mass of fabric. Her coal black hair was bound on top of her head. Her lips were red, hinting at purple at the corners of her mouth. Two red dots marked the center of her chin, vertically. Her eyes alone stood from the palette, green, with flecks of gold.

Her hands were pressed palm to palm in a straight line with her arms. She looked down at the kneeling Arcane. Her voice was as one distracted by greater things, but focused on the now. "Take my hand, Arcane, and walk with me."

She offered her right hand, her left arm stayed unmoving, palm pointed towards the ceiling. Arcane rose and his metal hand slid into hers, they closed and locked together. Then he found himself again walking the halls of the chapel. "Your will is strong, animate." Arcane must have given off some sense of surprise because the Vein said, "Yes, I know you as one, we are not all as old as Hethfora or Hetralmarr. But an animate that controls the flow of magic, have the humans come so far as that?"

Given her assault against him Arcane found her demeanor to be pleasant, but still he shielded his mind. "No, they have not."

"Then how is it that you come to me?"

"I do not know why it is that I am, other than to say that I was activated prematurely, and have since that time attempted to secure my survival. The mages would see me destroyed, they have in all ways struck against me, yet I am."

Marlant nodded slowly. "Indeed, you are. I was a mage once, before becoming as I am now. Part of the Cerikanth Commission. Does Riversea yet stand? It has been years now."

"It does."

"Then my work yet does me credit. Though I imagine that my later actions purged me from all records. The Harrow were more than children's tales then. Unlike now. Save a precious few, man does not remember. I recall that bloody night with a certain fondness. Ah, never mind." They walked in silence for a time, their wills sparring lightly. She reformed the question, asking, "What is it that brings you here? Surely the heart you carry drove you, but that is not the truth of it. If it were, you would have been called to the Queen. And Hetralmarr made it clear that you searched for the Vein Marlant. And now you have found her, and this is her sanctuary."

They had wound their way back through the chapel and the halls opened into a rectangular room with a high, arching ceiling. Sunlight let in from on high through ice-filled shafts illuminated this room most brightly of all the chapel. Rows of pews faced a pulpit. The strongest shaft of light focused there. Marlant released Arcane's hand.

Arcane thought a moment, then said, "Your name came to me from a man called the Sage of Tesca."

"Tesca." She looked down at the floor. "The Divinity of Tescerot? That even in my time was long hidden. If that is what even is meant by it."

Arcane latched onto the name and then said, "If you believe the man, then our paths are tied. And so I come to you, I am to announce your endeavor."

Marlant laughed, "My endeavor? What would make you think that I am in need of your assistance? My power, my forces, my will grows with each passing day. Save this one, in which you ended one of my knights." Arcane cringed expecting reprimand. "But your offer is earnest, I have seen your motivations, though you attempted to conceal them from me."

Arcane nodded. The spider quivered with glee.

She continued, walking as she spoke, "And your power, it is grand, shown through the death of not one but two Harrow. Truly one young, and neither Veins." She turned her head and smiled. "It is still no small task to be sure. But Animate Arcane, if you are to join me in my 'endeavor' then you must be marked as mine. Given fully to my will. Without exception."

"It cannot be as trying as your earlier testing."

Marlant sat down on a bench. "Sit with me." Arcane did, he more than suspected that he had already been marked as hers. "I find you to be fascinating. I see much of myself in you, growing, yearning, unsure of the path. I would say that I cannot fathom that the mages would scorn such a thing, but scorn is a thing that they do with excellent skill."

She continued, "Fear of the Harrow King turned to scorn. Hatred for his power. So it was that when they understood that it could not be theirs they promised to forget. Our history, yours, you are of the Harrow, the heart you carry makes it so, reminds us of that dark time. The Mage Commissions while spreading the discovery of magic back to man, to your creators, also erased the Harrow from the past. It was not a hard thing to do. The tales were only in legend, and only the old wives wanted to remember and only then to frighten the children on dark nights.

"Imagine my surprise when I discovered the truth, discovered man's ability to forget important things. Already you have passed out of their thoughts."

Arcane felt his heart at ease with the Vein. Her power, which had struck against him now filled him. But his anima held the proud truths, 'I am no Harrow...it is a means...they will remember me...to an end.'

"When I was of man, an animate such as yourself in form and function could only be a dream. To see the dream made real. The world yields many promises. Some beautiful, as is yours. Some cruel, as is mine. I will throw our dwindling ranks into strife, and you, Arcane, will be at my side. The Queen sits in stillness, not attempting to re-forge even a portion of the King's work. Every day that passes could be a thousand, and the Harrow dwindles, our power dying. Release yourself to me."

It was a seductive command. One that Arcane could not ignore. He drifted a moment, and the Vein twitched with power. She sat to the other side of him, close, dangerous. "Animate, your existence is forfeit. All you are, all you have ever been and ever will be is mine. This bond is true, and it is final."

She drew back slightly, her will retreating to her distractions. Her tone changed to one of command. "Go to my followers as my herald, bring them to me. It is time."

Arcane stood, her magic working strongly on him. He dragged himself outside, where he collapsed in a heap, robes hardening around him.

It was not sleep, not in the way humans described it, but Arcane could not rouse his body, and he was not really capable of it had he wanted. Some small part of him knew of what had happened, using so much power to defend himself; in truth, as he now saw the world it seemed but a spoonful, but using all that he had. If he was human, or Harrow, he would not wake for days. He was animate. He was Arcane.

And it was that thought that finally woke him. He had not moved from the place where he dimly recalled collapsing. The spider recounted the Vein Fia prodding the hardened chrysalis, but nothing more. A day had passed, or two, the spider was poor at keeping time. Something that Arcane changed immediately. The spider did not appreciate it and Arcane did not care.

Hetralmarr stood not far away, staring at him with dangerous eyes. "At last, the man of metal awakes. I was to worry about you."

Arcane saw no reason to engage in trivial conversation. "I speak as her herald. Gather the followers of Marlant. She awaits us in her sanctuary."

A near smile climbed upon his face. "The call goes out at last. We shall rise and lift Marlant to Queen."

The host was soon assembled in the sanctuary, filling the pews with seductive power. The followers of Marlant numbered only forty-three by Arcane's count, an uneven mix of men and women. They were giddy with anticipation, at the same time joyful and brutal, a strange combination from hardened creatures.

Arcane did not know the extent of the Queen's forces, but it did not seem that they could number many if this ploy hoped to succeed, and that was a reminder that he did not know the Harrow's ways. The Vein Marlant stood before them, hidden in shadow. Hetralmarr sat near her, facing the host as well. Arcane took his place in the back of the sanctuary. Despite his status as herald, and he was unsure just what that status meant. He was still a subject of scrutiny, receiving dark stares from the Harrow that resided under Marlant's power.

Marlant appeared from the shadows like a ghost, reminding Arcane of Finsen's trick. Her power, unlike his, was overwhelming and the Harrow fell silent immediately. Her face was still, but her eyes moved from person to person, including Arcane, which she eyed longer, and he could feel her will pressing on his anima.

Unbearable.

Finally her sight passed on. Satisfied, she spoke, her voice filling the sanctuary, "You are gathered to me all as one. My knights and Veins." She pricked her wrist with her fingernail. Glimmering purple blood welled up and dripped to the floor from her outstretched arm. "We are the bloodwork of the Queen, but she is weak and tired, her vision lost. It has taken years to ascend to this peak, longer than I could have believed, but we are now ready.

"Our numbers are few when compared to the forces of the Queen. She will think us but dust." Marlant smiled, it was cold and knowing. "Do not fear, and put aside misgivings. Most of you were not born into the Harrow when the last Queen was slain. I am here to tell you that it was done by only three. I was young in the Harrow then. I will not forget the night that she died, not until I have taken the blood of her killer, my teacher.

"Yes, I was one of the three. And I say to you: what we did that night we will now do again. I will take my place as Queen." She gazed on Hethfora with a hate-filled love, "One day, perhaps, you will come for me. Such is the cycle of the Vein. Born into life and death. So my knights, take to my side. My Veins, my bloodwork, learn your lessons, you will need them all and more." She stared through the seated, entranced Harrow, to Arcane. "As the herald proclaims so shall it be. Is it time for war?"

Arcane's head turned slightly, his eyes closing. Despite the protest of the runes along his back he was well and truly under her spell, so he listened to the Harrow, to the murmur of its power. It whispered over and over itself, never quite clear. He answered. "It is."

The power of the Harrow boiled, the forty-four dark ones on the edge of blissful madness, untold years in the making. Marlant's upper lip was wetted by her tongue, her green eyes dark with power and ambition. She had to shout over the rising din, "Today we ride for Centaern!"

It was not a cheer that answered her, the sound was a chilling cry, more at home on the battlefield than in the chapel. All the same the Harrow stood and left the sanctuary. They went to prepare for the ride to Centaern, the Place of Harrow. Arcane knew it to be, as the stolen heart told him. The animate found it unsettling.

"What is it you are thinking, Arcane?" It was Marlant, she had glided across the room to his side. "Your mind is troubled."

He spoke truth, "I learn things of the Harrow, without attempting, as if the magic itself gives knowledge to me. Centaern, I do not know it, and yet I do. I see the black glass rising on the edge of a great lake. I see the hallways of glass and ice. I see the throne room. I find the ease disturbing, I have grown accustomed to the struggle."

Her eyes did not leave his; she gazed through the golden glow to his core. "The Harrow flows strong in you, your metal body takes the blessed power well. It is true though, the magic that creates us and nourishes us also guides us. The knights, only so much, they are an instrument of war, few are concerned with the machinations of ascendancy. The Queen blunts them and I shall see that they act in accordance with the King's will.

"The Vein is shown a different touch, and one that you exhibit. In opening your anima to the power it moves through you. Listen to it and it will give you the knowledge of the ancients, all that is the Harrow, you can know." She smiled, "Perhaps. Even I do not know exactly how the power will affect you. There will be time enough to examine such fine details. We will spend many days and nights in conversation. I must ready for war." The Vein slid away.

Arcane shuddered, and the spider mimicked his action. 'I can not tolerate the corruption of my anima, I must create additional protections.' His mind slowed. Marlant had exited the chapel. He whispered, "I must harness the power of the rune wards to protect myself if I am to complete this course. Failing that, I will fall fully under her control."

Arcane made his way back to the repository. It was quiet and there was little chance of being disturbed by the ever more savage Harrow. The robes separated from his shoulders and stood at attention, waiting to rejoin the life giver. Arcane closed his eyes and cast his mind back to his time in the Tan'Su'th. He had learned so many things. So many things.

The old Hierophant had guided much of his study in the runes. The panther could not create them of magic, but his knowledge of form and function was vast, passed down to each successive priest in that line. Unlike the humans, the Su'th had welcomed him, providing much instruction. Arcane had learned his lessons well, studying the stone tablets carved by the ancients and the scrolls of the Hierophants.

He opened his eyes. The spark appeared and he began to scribe the magic symbols onto the inside of his left forearm. A row of three. Already they glowed, showing that they worked to fend off the Harrow. He doubled them upon his right forearm. "The Harrow must always be fought in tandem. One alone will surely fall against such might," the panther had told him, as he shook his head. "I do not even know if the Harrow still exist."

Arcane did not tell him that he carried the heart of one in his chest.

With the set of runes in place he tested his own power. The heart continued to provided power to his will and the frozen liquid in the urn boiled. 'Had I known the events before me I would have come marked against them.'

428

Arcane took up his robes and left the chapel, satisfied with his protection against the devious effects of the Harrow. Looking out from the steps, Arcane observed the war host. Rows of livids were formed, their riders arrayed in obsidian armor and armed with spears and swords. They glimmered, reflecting and focusing the cold light. Arcane nodded, admittedly impressed with the speed and discipline with which the Harrow moved.

Marlant sat on a gnarled, massive, livid. It was a monster of fangs and scales, a frightening beast. Hetralmarr was mounted upon his livid next to her. She said something, but from where Arcane stood it was indistinct. The Harrow cheered and the Vein led her monster and the army through the empty streets, out onto the mountainside.

Arcane followed behind the rest, listening to the clatter created by the column of warriors. The glass clinked against itself and against steel, the click of claw on stone, the grunts of Harrow and livid alike. The host ascended further into the mountains, following a marked path. It led to a huge door, cut into a steep rock cliff. Marlant scoffed and waved her left hand. The door cracked and pulled, attempting to free itself from the wall, finally succeeding.

The path continued into the mountain, now descending, wide and lazy. Here a change came over the Harrow, becoming silent except for an occasional hiss from the livids. Smaller halls split from the central road and fell into darkness but the Harrow did not even look down them. Arcane moved up into the host, feeling that in this place it would be best not to stray. Hetralmarr's warning had taken root.

After a full day's travel Marlant brought her followers to a halt. A copy of the chapel was cut into the rock.

Marlant said, "We rest the night here."

On her beckoning the Harrow again burst into a flurry of activity. The livids were stabled in ancillary rooms of the maze. The dusty sanctuary was turned into a place of rest. Fires burst up here and there, with the grim faced Harrow gathered around them. Once the Harrow were all inside Marlant glided slowly to the doorway, spilling a drop of her blood onto the threshold.

The single drop of blood, spent from her wrist, spattered and then coalesced into a minute sphere. Marlant's head cocked sideways, commanding it to do her will.

The drop of blood collapsed and stretched out, drawing a line about the doorway. The line flashed white and faded, completing the spell. Marlant turned away from the open doorway and noticed Arcane out of the corner of her eye. "You are a curious creature."

Arcane betrayed no emotion, "What is it you ward out? Or is that you keep us in?"

Awe filled her answer, "There are some things even the Harrow fear."

Arcane frowned but Marlant was gone before he could question further.

Hours passed and much of the noise from the sanctuary had quieted and Arcane could hear, ever so softly, the click of something coming down the tunnel. Arcane looked out the doorway into the cavern. Three creatures, slightly taller than a man, spilled out of the tunnel.

Their upper bodies were of a woman, but their lower body was similar to the spider that nested around his torso. They moved quickly, the sound of their running was bone on rock. And that was the sound that had preceded them. Arcane could see that they wore no clothes.

Coming into the courtyard of the chapel the lead raised her hand, motioning the others to a stop. All three sniffed the air. From his vantage point Arcane could see that each was beautiful in an almost magical defiance of their form; fine features, pearlescent skin, long flowing hair and pointed ears that poked through it.

The lead creature stepped forward one step, the point of her taloned leg dug into the rock. She leaned forward and her lips pulled back revealing tiny pointed teeth. She hissed through the opening, then said with a sweet voice, "Come out, come out, I know you are there."

They could not see past Marlant's ward. Arcane did not move. The lead rotated, showing her back to Arcane and said, "Gah. It's afraid." Then all three slowly stalked from the courtyard. They walked unbalanced, almost unable to move so slowly.

They did not go far. Arcane could see them standing in the dark, eyes reflecting whatever small amount of light that they gathered.

"Marlant was wise to ward this place, man of metal." It was Hetralmarr. He had moved without sound and stood behind Arcane, looking over his shoulder.

"Are those what she fears?" asked Arcane.

"The Lillitat sisters? Perhaps." His voice rumbled quietly. "They were elves once, lustful after beauty and the power of their king. When he discovered that his own daughters plotted to destroy him he was driven into an unseeing rage, cursing them with the bodies you see now, expelling them from the company of the elves.

"The Harrow King took pity on them when we destroyed the villages of man that they ruled. He offered them their lives in trade for service, and he bound them to this place, to guard this lone path to Centaern from outsiders. They will often appear to us when we travel this path to curse and mock us, but they cannot harm us.

"Woe to the outsider, though. They will die a terrible death. Drawn like moths to flame the sisters are. Strange that they would be drawn here." Hetralmarr smiled at the corners of his mouth and stared coldly at Arcane as he said it. "Goodnight, man of metal. Do not listen to the sweetness that they speak." He returned to the sanctuary, leaving the chilled Arcane very much alone.

The sisters stood like statues; Arcane could not pull himself from watching the contradictory creatures. Another hour passed with no change, then suddenly all three sisters turned their heads looking down the passage they had come from. Each hissed, fear, and they fled down the tunnel that the Harrow had come from. Arcane smiled, if Marlant did not fear the Lillitat sisters, then this that caused fear in them must be the reason for the ward.

A great serpent spasmed and flopped into the hall, in width nearly filling the tunnel that it came from. It had no eyes to note in its soft black flesh. A great mouth with exposed teeth the length of Arcane's forearms was its only feature. It thrashed over the low wall of the courtyard, knocking stone from place with no regard to history. Arcane told his body to flee from the sticky creature, but he did not obey, hypnotized into stillness.

The worm, it was more that than snake, stopped before the warded doorway, its mouth opened, drooling a viscous fluid onto the ground. A multitude of tongues, each the greater beast in miniature lurched forward, slapping against the invisible wall of the ward. The spell that held Arcane shattered and he recoiled. As did the worm, pain rippled down its body, more slime splashed about.

Marlant stood by Arcane's side, summoned by the attack against her power.

She held out her right hand and hissed, "Back to the depths, Viholgar! You have no welcome here!"

The worm pulled back to a great height, brushing against the ceiling of the cavern as it arched up readying to strike again, but collapsed on itself and poured down a hole on the far side of the hall. Only when it fully vanished did Marlant speak. "Come to the sanctuary. The night will pass soon enough."

Arcane nodded and followed the Vein.

Peter was heaped against the wall of Arcane's workshop. His head spun, his vision blurred. He had not eaten since Arcane had left, several weeks earlier. Not that he knew that he had not. His mind was adrift, the witch mocked him. If he was not in the pit then he was in hell, and there was nothing to be done.

The collar cut into his throat, strangely tight. Peter closed his eyes. When he opened them the world tilted slightly, then righted itself. He breathed in deeply, purposely, the insanity retreating. He looked at his hand, his nails had grown long. He frowned. The thief stood up and straightened his cloak. His mind was alerted to his hunger. His forearms ached. Somewhere, Arcane had done something. Peter did not know what exactly, but it was good.

Thirty-five

Arcane did not take well to stillness knowing what lurked in the tunnels. The sanctuary had small pockets of glowing embers to light it, but nothing more. Hetralmarr guarded Marlant like a hen tending her eggs. He stood in silence, arms crossed over his armor; never did his gaze stray from Arcane. Arcane grew tired of the eye and approached the Harrow knight.

"You gaze with an evil intent," said the animate quietly, not to disturb the Vein.

"Your metal body does not hide its true intentions from me, golem. The Vein does not wish to see it. So she does not. You and I will have our reckoning."

Arcane smirked, another of Jannan's touches. "You grieve me knight. If you could see what Marlant sees, know what she, what I, know, you would hold your threats."

"I have given much to Marlant, golem. I pray that she becomes queen. I thirst for the blood of man I thirst for Su'th blood. Centuries ago I rode the dangerous road to slay the elves. They fled before the might of the King. I thirst for their blood. Do not tell me that I do not know the truth. She will unleash our majesty. We will again ride the plains, scale the mountains, burn the villages."

"It has been many years since you have seen the ways of man."

Hetralmarr smiled, his hand tightened around the hilt of his sword. "Fool. The golem did not pretend to know so much in my days as man. It would be best

433

that you did not now."

"If I so challenge you, strike me down if you dare."

"The herald of Marlant will not be harmed. You know as well as I. You yet have purpose."

Arcane nodded, though he was fully concealed. His mind probed the Harrow. "I do. And when it is finished," the corner of his robe stiffened and rose like a viper then struck forward, driving into the shoulder of the knight pinning him to the wall, "You will suffer." It was a whispered threat, not really understandable, more metal rubbing metal than words.

Hetralmarr snorted and looked at the metal speared in his shoulder. He commanded, "Leave me. It is not long before Marlant wakes, and you would not want her to see the truth of you. "

Arcane's cloak pulled from the Harrow and he walked away. Hetralmarr sneered after the animate.

The Harrow rode early. Most were oblivious to the night's distractions as they were protected by the ward. Arcane was wary, both of the tunnel and its curious inhabitants and of Hetralmarr. The rivalry was in full throat and each knew it. The path they rode carried straight through the mountain but other tunnels branched off, both left and right and above and below. The passage sloped down for a time, then leveled out. There was no softness to the carving, it was as rough as the day it had been cut. The only light came from torches carried by the Harrow. Arcane surmised that they could not see in the absolute dark; not surprising given that they were all once human.

The speed of the livids carried consistently through the day. The Harrow reached the south end of the tunnel by nightfall. Here also a large gate stood closed. Marlant, as before, opened it with a wave. Tundra stretched before them, a place of rest from the jagged peaks and treacherous valleys of the mountains that surrounded it. Wind howled down the mountainside over a massive, frozen lake and whipped at the exposed Harrow, greeting them with spite. Arcane constricted, pulling his robes close to his body. It was actually colder here than before, and he felt it, but he was glad to be out of the tunnel.

To the southwest and some odd miles away was the fortress Centaern. Awe inspiring towers of obsidian glimmered in the moonlight, standing stark against the mountains beyond them, and against the night sky as the spires peaked. They spurted sharply from the ground, a fire of black glass. Arcane was hypnotized by the place, by the power that had formed the stone and glass into such a thing.

Marlant said, "Herald. Announce my coming. We will ride behind you. Only when your work is finished will we enter Centaern."

Arcane had no choice. He rushed from the host. As he boiled through the night he moved ever closer to his foolish gambit. The Harrow rode slowly, following Arcane, who had already disappeared into the dark.

Hetralmarr pulled his livid next to Marlant. "I know that you do not believe it, but the golem is a danger to all we long for."

"Then I leave it you to keep that from happening. If he steps out of line, which he will not, correct him. It is simple."

"As you wish, Marlant," he said nodding once. It was more than he had hoped for.

Arcane flew along the frozen, hard packed shore. The fortress grew ever closer. The base that the towering spires grew from also produced many smaller towers. The tallest of the spires leaned out over the lake, supported by no natural means. The runes burned into his arms had been set ablaze. The Centaern was as much the Harrow as any of its devotees. Arcane was glad for the protection. Soon he weaved in-between man-sized growths of obsidian that blistered from the ground. He reached the smooth wall of the fortress, reached out and touched it. The click of metal on stone echoed over the perfectly frozen lake, louder than it should have been. He spun and watched the sound spread across the ice.

Arcane walked around the growths, his metal feet crushing pieces of glass into the frozen dirt. A torch light appeared ahead of him, then another and another. They moved quickly. Livids and their riders. 'This will serve well enough.'

The Harrow knights, four of them, pulled their mounts to a halt. They, as the others, wore armor made of the black glass. The knight spoke loudly, over the howl of the wind. "What is your business at the Fortress of the Queen?"

Arcane looked into the yellowed eyes set in a gaunt, light gray face. "I come as Marlant's herald. I announce her coming."

"So it is time that the Vein asserts her claim. Very well, come along, lividless. You will announce your liege to all."

The livids circled back and bolted off through the field of glass. Arcane followed, ricocheting off the monoliths as he pushed himself forward. The Harrow led him to a steel gate placed in the side of the fortress. Two Harrow stood on the inside, save for opening the gate there was no need for them. "Open the gate!" shouted the knight.

The larger of the gatekeepers smiled, baring pointed teeth at those outside and went to the crank. It was taller than the gray skinned man and he began turning it, slowly lifting the steel gate up into the wall. It screeched woefully as the chain links stressed under the weight of the gate. The livids bolted into Centaern. Here Arcane stopped, and the gate hung suspended between the heavens and earth. The darkness from outside encroached only a little way into the fortress, the cold fire light resided here as well, but unlike the chapel of Marlant braziers held burning embers that cast the light about the entrance. The knights swung from their mounts and gazed back at the herald.

"I go no further without Marlant." Arcane stretched his arms out; the runes glowed brightly under the robes, spreading little sprays of light from the sleeves. The Harrow scoffed.

"Are you afraid, little herald?"

"I am no fool, if I enter without her you will fall upon me. I await the Vein." Then he announced to the whole of Centaern, "Marlant comes, it is her power that breaks you." In response drifts of snow broke free from their frozen holdings and fell to earth, thundering down around Arcane.

The Harrow frowned. Yellow eyes squinted and pointed with a broken finger. "Do not bleed confidence, you stupid thing." He cracked his neck sideways and ugly. "Herald or no, do not imagine that Marlant can throw down the Queen."

Arcane did not respond, his robes hardened into a cocoon and he awaited the coven.

Arcane did not wait long. Marlant's massive livid roared into the clearing before the gates of Centaern. Around it swarmed the rest of her followers, their livids driven mad by the power of the place. The knights inside the fortress pulled back, less sure of their power and the power of the Queen. Marlant's feet crushed the snow, crunching under her like a creaky rocking chair as she slid, giving away her steps and she stood near her herald throbbing with power. Arcane's shell rippled and pulled back as her power washed through him. Only the runes saved him from being swept away.

She spoke softly, "I have long been from this place. And now..." She placed her hand in the center of his back. The robes writhed and wrapped around her arm, holding her touch in place, burning his skin. The metal constricted around her silver flesh, tearing it to the bone. Marlant smiled, her eyes rolling back into her head. "I return."

Arcane murmured along with her. "I return."

That was all that it took, the challenge had been delivered. The followers of Marlant streamed into the fortress. The defenders at the gate fought well, but the sheer number of attackers overwhelmed them. Yellow eyes killed three of Marlant's knights and a Vein before Hetralmarr removed his head.

Once the frenzy subsided Arcane asked, "Will not more of the Queen's forces attack?"

Hetralmarr held yellow eyes' head in his right hand. He said, "They may, but it is not likely that this will become worse." The head dropped to the ground.

Marlant said, "We will move unblocked to the throne room. I have seen it. Already the Vision of the Queen flows to me." Her voice was filled with bliss. "Reclaim the dead."

Her instructions were not necessary. The Veins already took the dead and had begun the ritual that would preserve their power. Arcane carefully watched their movement, their magic, not hearing Marlant until Hetralmarr punched him sideways. "Obey, golem!"

Arcane did not need to be told again, he knew what was to be done. He led the usurper and her clan up the long stairways. They climbed ever higher through the tower, reminding Arcane of the cliffs of Serac. Ahead of them the Queen's followers scattered, though they were armed and armored. It was clear that they were ordered to allow the Vein to climb to the throne room. If Marlant failed, Arcane feared what would happen.

Marlant knew his thoughts. She spoke from behind him, "If I die the Queen will decide your fate."

The final stairs left their defiance behind and Arcane pushed into the throne room. The room was long, stretching away from him and he knew it from his visions. The floor was smoother than the rest of the glass fortress, reflecting the room in detail. Arcane noted with curiosity that he did not appear in the reflection. The ceiling was curved and high, held up by fingers of obsidian. Between the fingers was a clear surface, perfect in every way. It was cold enough that it could have been ice or glass; Arcane did not know which. The windows filled the entire wall from floor to ceiling. Snow outside the windows reflected the muted blue light that filled the room.

The courtesans of the Queen stood from were they sat, giving a sense of insult at the intrusion. Arcane could see that each was armed, but dressed in finery instead of armor. The animate noted two oddities among them. A hairless black skinned dog man snarled at the herald as he passed. A svelte elvish woman, in beauty a match for the Lillitat sisters, watched him with disinterest. Human or not, man and woman alike were marked as Harrow.

Arcane passed all of them before two knights dressed for war moved from their place at the side of the Queen. Their full gleaming armor, including a high-ridged helm, glittered in the cold light. They crossed their obsidian swords before him and glared at the animate from under the lowered brow of their helmets. "You go no further." Arcane's steps stuttered, unsure.

"That is not your decision to make," answered Marlant, her voice echoing against the walls.

"No," the woman's voice was soft, corroded by disuse. The Queen. "It is my decision." Everyone in the throne room stopped and turned to face her.

The Queen did not move, her coal black skin blended seamlessly into cloth, and that flowed without break into her obsidian throne. It seemed that time had blurred all distinction between the parts. Upon her head was a crown of sorts, a ruby of immense fire reflected the light cast by a twisted brazier set near her. Her eyes fluttered and opened, revealing a swimming blackness. And yet her gaze was evident, falling upon Marlant.

Dust fell from her hands as she loosened her grip upon the arms of the throne, the cloth of her dress tore away from the stone, taking back much of its original texture, but it yet glimmered as glass. She stood from the throne as it pulled at her to stay. All the Harrow bowed, save Marlant and Arcane. The Queen asked, "How long has it been, Marlant?"

"Long enough, Aidenja. Long enough," the Vein answered; a drop of awe had fallen into her voice. Arcane could feel their wills already assaulting one another.

The Queen smiled, thin lipped as one knowing secrets, "You truly believe that my time has passed? I am not so old." She held out her hands, front and back to the room. "Look at me, the power flows in me as strongly now as when I first tasted it."

"You flatter yourself with such lies. Your hour grows late. Holding us back, we rot with idleness hidden in this frozen fort. Our army grows blunt and fat, losing the only thing we know. Look at your courtesans, they are not even dressed for war."

"You are wrong to say that I want the things you speak of. You will learn the truth before all is done," the Queen answered. She stretched her arm before her and the Harrow lurched from her. In this also only Marlant and Arcane seemed prepared, the rest forced back, away from her to the walls. Arcane felt the burning in his core, the runes burning on his arms. The Queen spoke again, this filled with anger, "You are wise, Marlant, I knew that long ago, but not so wise as to understand the truth of things." Another burst of magic, this focused on the Vein. "Your power will not be enough. And to come here without herald, such audacity."

Arcane's mind wondered, 'Can it be that she does not perceive me?' His mind rushed to organize the truth. He was not of the Harrow, he had been told as much, and now shielded from them by their own magic, a parasite stealing their power, leeching their strength, disguised as their own. If the Queen was the Harrow, then she could not comprehend the one that was not hers and yet was. Arcane smiled at the contradiction placed before him.

The Queen tested unused legs, moving with the same dread glide that Marlant exhibited, her steps marked by a minute ripple in the reflection of the stone. Marlant put both arms fully out, then further straightened them. The Queen smiled and raised one finger. "If that is all that you place your hope in then you have already failed."

Marlant strayed back, away from the Queen, horror in her eyes, but she did not speak it. "It is not all. Hetralmarr!"

The Queen answered as she circled the Vein. "As you wish." An order passed unspoken, and the dog man lurched forward, in between time. He was upon the knight before he could reach even Marlant. He grabbed the knight under his right arm and by the wrist, forcing him to the ground with a growl. The Queen continued, "But I do not wish that more than you bleed tonight." The knight struggled but was no match for the beast. The dog twisted, Hetralmarr's armor shattered and he growled pain.

The Queen and the Vein circled like vipers, always Marlant slid back and Aidenja forward. Arcane could clearly see which was dominant, the Harrow unimaginably strong, the air burning with power. His body grew lithe and powerful in her presence. If this prize was to be taken it would be by his action.

The animate moved, joining the slow circling of the two great snakes, a third forgettable star. Marlant, filled with fear, did not recognize his action; the Queen simply did not conceive of him, he did not exist in her reflected world. Arcane smiled and the spider thrummed. The robe split and reared back, a deadly viper in its own right. One of the guards sprang into action; not all were blind to him.

The knight was too late. Arcane struck with perfect precision, the deadly tip pierced the Queen's neck from behind, sliding between vertebrae. She coughed out a short scream and fell to her knees. Marlant spun, finding a knife from her sleeve and finished what Arcane had begun. Purple blood sprayed from the wound, splattering the Vein.

But this was not the end of the Queen, even so she rose to her feet. Blood mixed with speech, "What trick is this that brings my death?"

Marlant smiled, the fear gone from her, "No trick. My herald."

"Lies..." Her last word finished, her jaw hung open. From deep in her throat a scream formed. A direful wailing that pierced all armor, evaded all traps. Each of the nightmarish warriors shuddered, filled with dread and dropped to their knees or fell prone, helpless. The black of Aidenja's eyes evaporated away, showing their true color, a blue of deep oceans.

Marlant recoiled as the scream filled the throne room, horror again in her wide eyes, the outside edges of which throbbed with black, pushing, filling. Her lids flickered and the muscles of her throat spasmed as though something was being forced down into her belly. She coughed and staggered, screaming. "My eyesssss! Myyyraaaghhk!"

The Harrow were well and truly taken with the scene as the Vein collapsed into a thrashing mess. Arcane too was held frozen until the spider, in its new sense of time, became impatient and began poking its master's head. Arcane snapped to attention. The dead Queen lay before him face down, sparkling blood spilling over the perfect floor. She was warm; her heart, her power-filled heart, yet beat.

Beyond the throne was another stairway and Arcane dragged the corpse to it, away from the Harrow, lost in whatever magic now enacted. Up the stairs he dragged her, leaving a stream of blood. Up to a balcony, here his work would be done.

Her dress torn away, Arcane cut into the coal skin. It was far more difficult work than Finsen had been, as though some other force prevented him. But the flesh did yield to the obsidian point of the spear left in him by Fraiarrch. Skin pulled back, bone broken, tissue removed. The heart beat magnificently in her chest. Arcane plunged both hands into the gaping wound and lifted it to his smiling face. Never had anything felt so luscious, so sweet his desire. If only Master Jannan could see him.

Blood poured down his arms, warm.

Marlant stood, no it was not Marlant, she was the Queen. Marlant in part but more. Her herald, where was her herald? Blind. She questioned now out loud, "My herald? Where is the one that marked my coming?"

The part of her that was Marlant remembered the animate, but as the incarnation of the Harrow, nothing. All others that used the power of her name, she could see, she knew. But not this one. It was void. Visions swirled; faces of those not of her, faces of those of her. Churrigon. Hethfora.

"Fools! Find Marlant's herald!" she shouted, distancing herself from the Vein. She was not that one. Aidenja's body was gone, horror darker than Viholgar himself filled her mind, flooding that, her soul. The heart had not been stilled.

Hetralmarr's bile-filled yell filled the throne room as he stood. "I told you of this deception! The path leads up!"

The knight ran, leading the way, his arm hung limp at his side. Behind him followed the Quan'ma Su'th that had shattered his shoulder. Behind that he did not differentiate the clatter. Up to the balcony overlooking the lake he ran, taking the stairs four at a time. Coming to it he saw the golem holding the heart in its metal hands, his torso open exposing his deceitful core. Hetralmarr shouted, "Man of metal! Stop!"

Arcane's head turned. The magic sparked, softening the crystal of his core, the Queen's heart was plunged into it. The heart of Finsen paused a beat, then began to throb in unison with its master. Arcane's vision blurred, his torso closing. Fire burned in him, the beating louder than before. Hetralmarr moved closer, sword swinging with all of his strength. The blade struck Arcane's robe, lazily raised to block it, sparks burst forth as Arcane staggered, more from the power that filled his body than the blow. He tipped sideways, unable to right himself. The spider vomited forth warnings and Arcane plunged over the side of the balcony, a fallen star.

Drunken and disoriented, it was all he could do to pull his robes around himself as he crashed into the frozen lake. His metal body smashed through the ice, throwing pieces large and small into the air around his crater. Water bubbled up and froze. Arcane sank to the bottom and did not move of his own accord, swept by the current away from Centaern, swept away from the Place of Harrow.